Born in London and raised in Fiji, Charlie Charters spent his working life based in Hong Kong and now lives near Malton, North Yorkshire. He had an early desire to become a writer but he did very little about this until turning forty, by which time he had worked, variously, as a racing tipster, war reporter, radio DJ, award-winning TV producer and presenter. He was the youngest ever senior vice president of the legendary sports marketing company ISL. In 2004, he helped launch the British Lions-styled Pacific Islanders rugby team, featuring the best players from Fiji, Samoa and Tonga. He is married with four children and a Labrador that likes to watch the news. You can visit his website at www.charliecharters.com.

BOLT ACTION

Since 9/11, the door between the pilots and the passengers on an airliner must be locked and impossible to break down. But what if the pilots are dead? Tristie Merritt leads a renegade band of ex-soldiers. Their daring scam will take millions from a furious British government and give it to veterans' charities — if MI5 don't catch up with them first. But faced with the ultimate terrorist outrage at 36,000 feet, MI5 and the CIA find that Merritt is their one hope of preventing global disaster.

CHARLIE CHARTERS

BOLT ACTION

Complete and Unabridged

CHARNWOOD
Leicester

First published in Great Britain in 2010 by
Hodder & Stoughton
London

First Charnwood Edition
published 2012
by arrangement with
Hodder & Stoughton
An Hachette UK company
London

British Library CIP Data

Charters, Charlie.
    Bolt action.
    1. Terrorism- -Prevention- -Fiction. 2. Airplanes- -
    Fiction. 3. Suspense fiction. 4. Large type books.
    I. Title
    823.9′2–dc23

    ISBN 978–1–4448–1080–6

Published by
F. A. Thorpe (Publishing)
Anstey, Leicestershire

Set by Words & Graphics Ltd.
Anstey, Leicestershire
Printed and bound in Great Britain by
T. J. International Ltd., Padstow, Cornwall

This book is printed on acid-free paper

To my Dad, for many reasons that he would be too embarrassed for me to detail here, but a simple one has been his unwavering, unquestioned support throughout my life. And his constant exhortation to me as a writer, If You Want It To Be A Success, Make it Read Like A Dick Francis . . . Here's hoping I got it right, Dad.

And,

To Talaiasi Labalaba — my first military hero — who came from a village in Fiji only a few miles from where I grew up. He died in a place called Mirbat in a conflict that few remember, making a sacrifice that the Ministry of Defence deemed sufficient only for a Mention in Dispatches. Thankfully his former comrades in the SAS, following a higher code, knew better. And today Labalaba's valour is permanently honoured in a way that no medal could achieve — a statue of him in pride of place next to the regiment's founder at Hereford. A unique distinction.

Bolt Action is truly a work of fiction. It's make-believe. Readers may recognise certain incidents and concerns. That doesn't change the fact that I have used my imagination when it comes to the story and with details like technical aircraft specifications. Any similarity between my characters and a living person is a complete coincidence, a total fluke.

At the second tee of the Karachi Golf Club
Sindh Province
Pakistan
4.49 a.m. (6.49 p.m. in Washington)

It is not a good look for a Pakistani army general. Even a retired one. The shocking pink cardigan. Light blue plus-fours. Especially the two-tone golf shoes.

On the other side of the world someone mutters towards the video image of the general's attire, 'Talk about the dangers of shopping online . . . '

The audience watching their target by satellite phone in Langley, Virginia, has been down this road before. Many times. They understand danger and risk, but only as one-dimensional operational concepts.

A veteran Agency analyst adds, 'It's what happens when you dress in the dark because of the shitty hours you have to work,' the needle of two failed marriages in her voice.

They are diligent and attentive in their work but hardly flushed with excitement. After all, they've quarterbacked dozens and dozens of renditions and extractions, and the world hadn't even come close to ending.

1

Not until now. This time it will be different. Different because the tiniest changes can unleash the most devastating consequences. And this tiny change, this tweak that the CIA intends on making, will turn an early morning hit-up into the most perilous round of golf. Ever.

Back to the video feed, and everybody notes how the general has packed a few pounds on to his small frame since being sent into retirement a year ago (there was an uncorroborated report he wore a corset).

Each time he tops or slices or hooks his drive into the humid gloom, General Ali Mahmood Khan swears . . . *Laanat*. Damn. *Mayooskun*. Hopeless . . .

The mild swear words easily carry the dozen yards to the two wiry, dark-skinned CIA operatives lying prone under a thicket of shrubs and tall weeds. Both could easily pass for locals. The live feed of this lamentable golf is also being watched on a boat anchored offshore, to the west of Karachi, near the sandstone cliffs of French Beach. The exfiltration point.

The championship golf course lies within the sprawling Karsaz naval base, so the general's security detail this morning is light. He feels safe. Just a bodyguard and a driver for the Tiger of Baluchistan . . . his fawning local media title.

The second hole runs in a northerly direction. Par five. Good eagle chance. Two hundred yards away a huge tree stands in the centre of the fairway just before the dogleg right. It's there the bodyguard waits, holding a lightweight walkie-talkie, to report whether any of the general's

2

shots clear the tree. Nothing reported so far.

The general's chauffeur kneels over a yellow bucket of lime-green luminescent balls. Only a handful remain. Dutifully he places a fresh one on the tee. The action is illuminated by the bright lights of the general's Mercedes SUV, which is parked to the rear. Engine on, air-conditioning on. The outside temperature is already an uncomfortable twenty-four degrees.

The general waggles his rear end, wriggles his wrists. Winds up, releases and fires the ball almost sideways off the white tee marker.

The watching CIA officers duck instinctively as the shot blasts through the undergrowth above them, like the discharge from a shotgun.

The green-hued video signal tumbles.

Everybody in Langley, in the blue-lit room, watching the monitor, sucks in a collective breath.

'Are we OK, Victor Three?' The crackled female voice of concern, thousands of miles from the dangers of sliced golf shots.

Two taps on the throat mike signal, *We're OK*.

Shakily the picture re-establishes itself, focused on the features of the controversial former military strongman. The man who had once headed the ruthless Afghanistan unit of the Inter-Services Intelligence Agency, which had ushered in and then supported Taliban rule. After 9/11, the unit was wound down and General Khan had been transferred to lead the paramilitary Frontier Corps in Pakistan's so-called Tribal Areas that border eastern Afghanistan. For the next five years he excelled at not finding anybody the Americans tasked him to find. What he *could* do was dip into the almost $5 billion worth of military hardware with which the US subsidised Islamabad's side of the war on al-Qaeda.

And then there's the missing cash. Hundreds of millions of dollars. Reimbursements for losses and the wear and tear from raids and patrols within Pakistan's notorious Tribal Areas that never took place or were vastly overstated.

Which is why, irked that American national treasure might actually be keeping all these Islamic nutcases in clover, Washington wants General Khan. Reluctantly, and only under a welter of evidence and with another two billion dollars' worth of military aid hanging on the matter, Islamabad has given her tacit approval. But in a totally deniable fashion.

Five minutes later, General Khan fires off his last errant golf ball. 'Light me,' he grumps moodily to his driver, who lights a cigarette for him, and then disappears down into a long, low valley to search for two buckets of glowing golf balls.

General Khan retreats to the comfort of his Mercedes, opening the driver's side to switch off the headlights before settling into the back seat with a slam of the door. Suddenly all is dark and quiet. Mynah birds squabble in the distance.

The two CIA operatives focus on the red pinprick of cigarette burn through the tinted windows. In three weeks of observation, the general's two gofers had never taken less than nineteen minutes to return to the car. Two taps on the throat mike, followed by another two. *Good to go?*

Long pause.

In Langley, the analysts and operation officers eyeball each other, searching for the first sign of the famous CIA backslide, a real house speciality. Inevitably focus settles on one of the Agency's associate deputy directors, who is playing wallflower at the rear of the hermetically sealed cabin. The most senior officer in the room understands two things very clearly. One: it's either on or off. Right now. And two: ultimately, this whole thing will be on my neck.

Everybody knows this operation had been conceived by the wunderkinds brought in by the new president, is nothing less than a political power play, and that this particular rendition is against the expressed wishes of a number of the Agency's old hands. The bureau chief in Islamabad, for instance, who'd cabled his opposition in the clearest terms possible. 'No way. Hell no. No damned way. No freakin' chance . . . ' Fifty times in total.

But that's a minor irritant in a bigger game. The wunderkinds are trying to re-create the Agency, purging and promoting, bending Langley to a new, more inclusive purpose driven by a president who talked loftily about New Beginnings and Transformative Agendas. Code for Forget the Past. While that old warrior mentality is slowly stripped out, irony of ironies, there is still an audience that needs to know the Agency has teeth. And rendering General Khan — even against the advice of senior agents on the ground

— is part of buying some quiet.

So. The associate deputy director rubs his jaw. Lot to think about, standing here on the edge. He blinks up at the main screen and the dark outline of the Mercedes, weighing up the multitude of narrow, operational things that could still go wrong. An almost imperceptible nod of the head is followed by, 'Rock and roll. Let's do this thing.'

The now assured female voice comes through in their earpieces. 'Victor Three. You are good to go. Confirm. Good to go.'

Three and a half minutes later the dark blue Mercedes four-wheel-drive slows at the massive fort-like gates guarding the 250-acre Karsaz naval base. General Khan is unconscious but little dabs of glue have been applied to his eyelids. His tinted window is down, his hand resting on the sill, and the car eases comfortably around the sets of tank traps. There's scurrying in the guardhouse but it's quickly noted that the car details are correct. Two other bodies on board. Everything tallies with their paperwork — which is the only thing a smart soldier worries about. Later the two guards would swear the general's eyes were definitely open. Looking straight ahead. And deadly serious.

Half an hour later General Khan's driver and bodyguard are ready to expire from the novel experience of their jogtrot to the gatehouse in steam-heat conditions. There's a great deal of flapping and faffing as both men are revived. Then a fiery back-and-forth as to whether the general was in the front of the Mercedes driving *and therefore in control,* or in the rear *and in some kind of peril.* Finally, thirty-five minutes later, the alarm is raised.

As the sun's first rays edge the horizon and backlight the skyline of Karachi to the left of them, a Zodiac inflatable noses through the gentle breaking waves on French Beach. On the water, they still have the cover of dawn's shadows. Just. Navigation is by a hand-held GPS tracker. The boat scuds along at top speed due south a mile or so, to rendezvous with an eighty-two-foot Monte Fino Sky Lounge cruiser.

After forty-four minutes General Khan is carried on board like a rolled length of carpet. By flashlight, there are some basic medical checks; all personal effects, his belt and shoelaces removed. The twin diesels click out of idle and the fibreglass hull crushes its way forward as the boat powers up to twenty-three knots. The general is deposited in the VIP stateroom, the plush drapes closed. All sheets, cables, wires, glasswork and breakables have been removed. Langley gets its first detailed report by secure phone.

Only as they round Cape Monze to the west and put the loaf-shaped Churma Island between themselves and Karachi do the running lights start to flicker on. And everybody settles down, feeling well pleased. Ahead lies a comfortable seventeen-knot cruise down the eastern side of Oman and Yemen, shadowed by a US destroyer, and into the welcoming arms of America's latest foreign toehold: Camp Lemonier in the former French colony of Djibouti.

Pretty much a textbook operation. Damn it if the thing wasn't flawless, the associate deputy director was happy to report in an email to his boss.

Four days later

A telephone call to the CIA's station chief in Islamabad starts with the words all field agents hate: 'You're going to want to make sure we're on the record here, William.'

Long sigh. 'Damn it, Remmy.' The soft Louisiana accent belongs to station chief William Lamayette, who swings his feet off his desk. 'You sure about this?'

The person initiating the call from CIA headquarters in Langley, Virginia, is retired marine lieutenant colonel Remmy Gardener — the head of the Agency's Office of Terrorism Analysis, one of the twelve departmental streams of opinion and information that fold into the Directorate of Intelligence. In theory, the DI 'identifies' what the problem is and the possible solutions, then the National Clandestine Service delivers whatever is agreed as the 'fix'. Like Lamayette, Remmy Gardener is an old hand.

'Deadly serious,' says Gardener. 'The latest on your best buddy. Ali Mahmood Khan.'

Lamayette cuts in, reproachfully. 'Stop, Remmy. That's not my case.' *You should know that.* 'The White House twelve-inched Langley, so Langley turns around, spanks my ass like a two-bit whore. Ignored pretty much everything I had to

8

say on that shitbag Khan.'

The satellite phone line goes silent for a while. Just a low hum as Gardener enunciates his words carefully, 'Let's say, for argument's sake, information was passed to me that questioned the wisdom of the whole operation. Just as you outlined in your various cables. Now. Who should I share this with? The guys upstairs who okayed taking out General Khan, and are still prettying up their Ivy League blazers . . . '

' . . . More like licking each other's balls.'

Lamayette's language is famously evocative and it takes Gardener a little while to get that uncomfortable image out of his head. 'Let's just say they've confused an operational victory with a strategic success. So. Should I pass this information to them, or to the one person who advised against this in the first place?'

Lamayette almost bolts out of his chair. 'You, sir, are a man of integrity and genius.' And he gets to work setting up the software profiles, so that their conversation can be recorded, then entering the protocols of those to be copied on the file about to be generated. It takes a couple of minutes, and then Gardener recounts . . .

'The maître d' pulled me away from a dinner about, what? . . . ninety minutes ago. I was at the Marriott on Pennsylvania Avenue. The maître d' said there was a call on the house phone. Asked for me by name. Knew what I looked like, my rank. Everything.'

'And . . . ?' Nothing too remarkable so far.

In his Islamabad office, Lamayette's gaze flicks across the five flat-screen TVs showing rolling

9

news . . . the four clocks . . . Washington, London, Kabul and Islamabad . . . and the illuminated map of the world, which lights up longitude by longitude with the passage of the sun. It is 10.56 p.m. in Washington, just coming up to 9 a.m. in Pakistan.

'A South Asian voice. Pakistani probably. Well educated. Kind of nasal tone. Like his voice hadn't quite broken . . . I made sure to write down pretty much what he said . . . *'You are holding my client. General Khan. I am his representative . . .* ' '

I told them this would happen. And a spasm of cold, quailing fear drills right through Lamayette's massive frame. From head to toe. His first considered reaction is that a call to the Marriott would be untraceable after the fact. He knows the hotel. Perhaps eight hundred rooms all told. How many calls a minute in the early evening would a hotel switchboard like that handle? Too many. Then, how would someone know Gardener's movements? Somebody in his office? But Gardener was a pro, his team would be tight. Must have been surveillance of some kind. Lamayette, being a station chief, gets paid to analyse and he recognises what this adds up to. Good tradecraft, plus excellent intelligence equals . . . Take This Seriously.

'What did you say?'

Gardener continues. 'I reply, 'I don't know what you're talking about but let's say for argument's sake I understand . . . what do you want?' The guy laughs, says in his haughty voice, *'But I don't want anything. Ha. Ha. Ha.'*

10

'So I says, 'Good. So I can get back to my dinner?'

''My client instructed me that if ever he was out of contact for more than forty-eight hours I should make this call. Just to let you know that we know.'

' 'Well, thanks a bunch for doing your job. Now my dinner's getting real cold . . . '

''Lieutenant Colonel. Your table has not yet been served. You would do well to treat me with some courtesy.'

'He was right, of course. We were still on the bread rolls.' Gardener snorts, a man who doesn't enjoy being bested. 'Afterwards I walked the whole damned floor. Don't have a clue how he knew . . .

'Anyways, he carried on:

''The general was a leader to many and in his name revenge will come. By your actions, America, you have unleashed a very terrible thing. You have started the clock. Nobody . . . not even if you returned the general to us today . . . not even he can stop this thing. The forces of revenge have been unleashed. They have taken wing. And whatever happens, they cannot be recalled. For they have taken wing . . . ''

Oh, shit, thinks Lamayette. That really complicates things . . .

★ ★ ★

The object of all this intrigue, General Ali Mahmood Khan, is nothing if not a logical man.

11

With complete equanimity, he could see what was going to happen to him: obviously at some point the Americans would take him down. He had long been pulling on the tiger's tail, joyfully helping himself to hundreds of millions in Washington's military aid. But worse. Such is the soul-enveloping intensity of his hatred that he'd given over every ounce of his brilliance to help her enemies.

One day the tiger will bite back. He knew this. Inevitable, he told himself. But my money is safe. My children are young men, raised to be strong, ambitious and crafty. The new Khan dynasty will rise on my death, a martyr's glorious death, killed by the evil hand of US imperialism. There is nothing to fear in death. For every great South Asian dynasty is born in martyrdom. Nehru. Bhutto. Bandaranaike. And that wretched family in Bangladesh . . .

And so he communicates the gist of his plans to his two sons in a series of postcards . . .

The civilian leadership in Islamabad would sell him out in private, while squealing with outrage in public. Fair enough. That meant, as in a game of musical chairs, he would suddenly find himself without a seat. Therefore, when he conceived his plan he took into account two things: he should consider himself dead or as good as dead, and whatever he planned, he should make sure it was unorthodox. Because in his mind, against *this* enemy, the unorthodox would always triumph.

Macchar. The Mosquito. The message that his lawyer had delivered to the CIA man in the

Washington hotel could not have been more clear . . . *The general was a leader to many and in his name revenge will come. By your actions, America, you have unleashed a very terrible thing. You have started the clock . . .*

Khan is an avid, even greedy, student of everything to do with America. His interest more like a ghastly fascination. A pure hatred.

To a soldier like Khan, America's time has run out. The heavyweight boxer who lumbers around, punch drunk and arms flailing, a deadly mix of overconfidence and unknowingness. The watching crowd of nations complicit in one awful secret: the next challenger will put this fellow down. Just one shot, the right combination, and a new order will be born. The rest of the world watches through the ropes, willing it to happen . . .

Khan had a copy of CIA director George Tenet's *We're At War* memo, issued to all his staffers within days of September 11th. 'There can be no bureaucratic impediments to success. All the rules have changed. We do not have time to hold meetings or fix problems — fix them quickly and smartly.' Fine words, but almost ten years had passed and all of this systemic weakness has brought America to the verge of collapse. Teetering on the edge.

The US dollar was finished, drowning in trillions of debt, mostly held by foreign powers or overseas sovereign funds. A decade of stock market growth lost, *kaboof*, in months. Discredited financial and government institutions. Hundreds of billions in unfunded liabilities in

Medicare, pensions and social security about to fall due . . . and still their politicians bicker and fight and drag the country downwards.

Just what General Ali Mahmood Khan wants. To drop America to her knees. To deliver a defeat, like Port Arthur, Dien Bien Phu, or Suez. To forever change America's destiny. To leave her as the once-mighty imperial powers of Russia, France or Britain had been left. Naked, vulnerable and so very ordinary in the eyes of the rest of the world.

In his neat postcard penmanship, the general maps out his plans, the timeline his sons must follow. The narrative, he reminds himself fussily, the narrative is so important . . .

You remember my birth date? March 15th 1954. I was born on the very same day that Charles Piroth committed suicide. By then, he had only one arm and couldn't kill himself with his sidearm because he needed two hands to cock the weapon. So he mumbled his apologies to all those he had failed, retired to his bunker, clasped a grenade to his chest and pulled the pin. And as he died, on the same continent, almost three thousand miles away, your father came into this world. Perhaps the hand of Destiny. No?

Tiny, precise strokes, the nib scratching at the card and the Pashto script flowing like Arabic from right to left, his shoulders hunched over the lines, stopping every so often to rub his eyes. The

14

general's phones, his emails, everything, he knows, is being monitored. But not the mail . . . who would think to monitor the mail?

Colonel Piroth had been commander of French artillery at Dien Bien Phu. He'd bragged about the 105- and 151mm howitzers, how they would annihilate the ragtag volunteers of Ho Chi Minh, and his General Giap. But for all Piroth's boasts, his artillery never 'saw' Giap's forces, never could spot his emplacements in the jungle. Instead it was the Vietnamese, an invisible enemy, who rained hell down on to the besieged French forces. Snapped their will to fight.

Imagine. The French took mobile brothels into battle with them, prostitutes to give them courage. And Piroth's commander even issued General Giap with a written challenge, as if he were a musketeer. Understand this, my son. America right now is like France at Dien Bien Phu . . . No stomach for the fight, too fat to care.

The details of Operation Macchar covered a total of forty-eight picture postcards; ninety-six, as there were two sons. A lot of information about General Khan's extensive Pashtun connections, the almost impenetrable bonds of debt and honour that would spring into action with the correct supplication and coded words . . .

The American warlords will learn that no amount of push-button technology or military hardware will defeat a multitude of

15

people animated by a righteous cause. We will deliver that cause. We will deliver that righteous anger. We will deliver Operation Macchar . . .

He personally affixed each of the four-rupee stamps then he took the time to pack the cards carefully into a tatty chamois cloth, bound many times over with elastic band. This unremarkable package he entrusted to his senior housekeeper, who, under pain of dishonour, promised faithfully to post them if the general failed to appear any morning.

The *Why* and the *When* of Operation Macchar are detailed on the back of the postcards. Clues as to the *Who*, the *Where* and the *How* are on the picture side. There are ninety-six, but only three different images.

One card shows the faithful masses swirling around the vast, cube-shaped Holy Kaaba in Mecca, performing *tawaf*, the counter-clockwise thronging that lies at the heart of the Haj pilgrimage. This is the *Who* of the plan, a representation of Muslim innocents, those that are to be sacrificed, and whose fiery death would send up an unyielding shriek of outrage to unite the world.

The *How* is elegant, simple and totally unorthodox. A profile-shot of a twin-engine Boeing 777 in the colours of Pakistan International Airlines, on final approach, flaps and landing gear extended. The pride of the PIA fleet.

And the *Where* is a view of New York. An

aerial shot with the Statue of Liberty and Ellis Island in the foreground and in the skies above Manhattan vast plumes of red, white and blue, coloured smoke from the tailpipes of a half-dozen fighter jets. A postcard to celebrate the recent fiftieth anniversary of NORAD, the North American Aerospace Defense Command.

. . . And by his hand, we shall trap the US president into ordering the deaths of Muslim innocents. By his hand, we shall trap his country, and the world shall see the Truth.

Tristie Merritt had spent a lifetime defying the odds.

It was one of the reasons she proved so good for the British Army, and why the British Army, having taken her in as a private, fast-tracked her from junior soldier to officer. Female officers make up about one per cent of the 100,000-strong army but female officers who started in the ranks are so rare the army doesn't even keep count. There'd been none like her in Tristie's intake at Sandhurst, nor the year before, or the year before that. Singularly tough odds. Yet time and time again, she proved herself. When writing up Tristie's paperwork for the Royal Military Academy, under the section marked Other Comments, her commanding officer had borrowed a line about Katharine Hepburn: 'I have no doubt you will discover that Merritt is *the* born decider, dominator, organiser, tactician and mesmeriser'.

Sandhurst's instructors — the so-called Directing Staff — read all that Hepburn stuff and couldn't have been less impressed. *Somebody's Talking Out Their Arse Big Time*. First, there was the issue of Tristie herself. By the standards of recent female cadets, Tristie was both likeable and desirable. Uncommonly so. To the army's wise heads, that was a red flag, especially as she didn't fall in with the lesbian cadets, of whom there was always a hard core. But more than that, the DS couldn't help notice her quiet confidence. This didn't rise to the level of pride or insolence, more a subtle, certain knowledge that the army wasn't going to fault her or break her. Just wasn't going to happen. So she became a bit of a challenge, a pet project, and the DS found themselves focusing on Tristie, wanting to push her to the limit above all others.

They made her student platoon commander on perhaps the most demanding exercise, Marathon Chase, a two-day, 50-mile tactical-advance-to-battle. *Let's see how Barbie girl does with this* . . . The tab involved criss-crossing the South Downs Way, every step of the route in sleeting rain and near-zero visibility. Yet her group of thirty passed with flying colours, Tristie leading from the front or, when needed, pushing and pushing from the rear. Cajoling the weakest, swearing at the waverers, imploring her team, and then literally dragging the last two male cadets over the line. The DS platoon commander, an experienced army captain, was Old School on the subject of female officers and whether they were really up to the job of leading male soldiers. Even he noted, approvingly, in his report, *There's something in her eyes, like she's saying, I've seen it all. I will lead my soldiers and take care of my soldiers. They can trust me because there is nothing in this world that can be done to me that is worse than that which I have already faced.*

What that was, the world that Tristie had

19

emerged from, the instructors only caught in glimpses . . . she was the only cadet to have No Family listed on her forms, therefore nobody came to watch her Passing Out or accompanied her to Father's Dinner Night . . . but it didn't really matter.

Because the truth was best summed up by one of the DS, a barrel-chested warrant officer from Merthyr Tydfil whose first combat was almost twenty years before. Purposefully he'd tabbed every step of the Downs alongside Tristie, watching her, willing her to cock up.

Back in the sergeant's mess, everybody crowded around to hear the Welshman's verdict . . . *Aye, lads, You're Not Wrong There . . . She's A Pretty One, I'll Give You That* . . . He couldn't stop himself beaming with something like pride . . . *But More Than The Fact She's Damned Good Looking, Let Me Tell You, She's Fucking Brutal Too.* In the mess that was an astonishingly rare compliment towards a female, let alone a female officer.

A consequence of this was that you could walk into any guardhouse, barely take twenty paces inside an army base, and there'd be somebody who knew of Captain Tristie Merritt, or knew someone who did. Oh yes. *Her*, they would say, and there'd be a wry grin, a flash of a smile, and a story to follow.

This helps explain why Ward 13 came together so quickly. Tristie's reputation helped because it inspired confidence. But also she had no trouble convincing those she was recruiting that the Ministry of Defence had more than enough money to be doing a better job with the lives and welfare of their ex-servicemen. She knew from her own experience that all non-coms pride themselves on their radar-like ability to detect bullshit; bullshit from their officers, but especially bullshit from the MoD.

The MoD is awash with cash. But, and even the simplest squaddie knows this, the tray is tipped in the wrong direction . . . not to the serving man or woman, or the injured, bereaved or the recently demobbed. But towards people like Sir Dale Malham.

A little bit of background here, so you can understand why it was Tristie felt honour-bound to pick Malham and use *him* to bankroll Ward 13.

Tristie had five different files on Malham. A lot from newspapers and the Internet of course, but the glossies too, for as the money started flowing in, the whole arc of his life changed with it. *Hello! OK!* . . . The old Dale Malham was discarded. The new one thoroughly made over. Ginger beard trimmed back to a chin-tuft goatee. Elegant side whiskers, Richard Branson-style. Angry Socialist wardrobe junked for a range of suiting from morning coats to shooting jackets with hand-sewn edges and horn buttons . . . *Country Life. Tatler. North East Life.*

Then, a short burst of bad publicity. Long-suffering wife Maggie and their clutch of children jettisoned for a lithe former gym instructor and swimwear model. His 'life partner'.

How?

21

Malham was a seventeen-year veteran MP serving up until 1996. Aged just fifty-four, he turned in his safe seat (bagging himself a knighthood, as the exit door banged behind him). Why? He had his eye on something more rewarding. By 2000, he was a multimillionaire.

The key for Malham was his seat on the Commons Defence Select Committee. It scrutinises the military on behalf of Parliament. He had watched the MoD struggling to come to terms with the end of the Cold War. Quickly it became clear that the three services had a mass of overlapping training, catering, storage and supply, and research facilities; everything from barracks and underground bunkers, to housing, airfields, rifle ranges, victualling and ordnance yards. The combined assets made the MoD the second-largest landholder in the country. Which is well and good when readying for war but, with the collapse of the Iron Curtain, the government wanted a peace dividend: either less public money for the military or more of their spending would have to come from cashing in these overlapping or redundant assets.

In late 1994, over a long lunch, a lobbyist tugged at Malham's ear. A syndicate of German pension funds, bursting with cash, was keen to find credible and risk-free investments. Perhaps the MP might be interested in a friendly meeting? In due course he learnt that in Germany the concept of Sale and Leaseback was going great guns. What about the 44,000 homes that were owned by the MoD? If these were sold to, and then leased back from, a company fronting the pension funds' interests, the MoD would receive a huge injection of cash while retaining both possession and use of the properties.

It was a perfect bit of timing.

Malham took eighteen months to nudge and nurdle the deal through the back rooms of Westminster. It was then that he quit his seat, and things started to move quickly. Two months later, to no particular fanfare, he was announced as chairman and chief executive of a new, privately held company called Imphal Holdings. Less than a year before the 1997 election, the deal was finally announced.

On signature, Imphal paid £1.6 billion to the Treasury for the ownership of all 44,000 homes and accommodation belonging to the Ministry of Defence. The MoD leased these back for an inflation-adjusted fee of £140 million a year while also accepting sole responsibility for maintenance and refurbishment.

Note the cunning mismatch. All of the cash from the Imphal deal goes into the *Treasury*. But the maintenance and refurb costs come from the budget marked *Defence*. This being the same iron-fist-tight budget that pays for commitments in Iraq and Afghanistan. Pays pensions and compensation for death and injury. Plus a whole generation of new expensive war toys. (The MoD's twenty largest weapons projects are at a minimum £3 billion overspent and almost forty years late.) With all that stress on just one budget, guess how much of Imphal's money actually washes back from the Treasury into maintaining and refurbishing houses the MoD doesn't even own any more? Not enough.

Within ten years, Imphal had secured another dozen sale and leaseback agreements with various arms of the government. All payments recession-proofed, of course. And Malham had parlayed his success into a vast Georgian mansion set in two thousand wild acres of Northumberland woods and farms, with twenty estate cottages to lord over. And, in London, a Belgravia residence with its own internal lift and indoor swimming pool. Price tag £7 million.

While Malham was quad-biking across his green acres or tootling up and down in his London lift, Tristie Merritt was serving out her last year in the army. She had been badly injured near Lashkar Gar in Afghanistan, took a long time in rehabilitation, and by December was put out to pasture in a barracks in south Wiltshire, a place called Tidworth, while her high-ups tried to work out what to do with her.

Female, single, officer accommodation.

The gas fire Tristie shared with two other females was condemned the day after she moved in. In the next two months, nothing. No one came to sort it out. And the roof leaked. From the roof space daylight was visible between the tiles, the wind whistling constantly. She rang to report it and her complaint was routed to a call centre in Liverpool. They seemed to care less. Four weeks later an odd-job man with a ladder tried to patch it up, but complained the roofing team were 'too overworked' and 'under-resourced' to attend. The place was slick with damp. An infestation of black scum, a fungal tidemark, stained the walls at head height in all of the rooms. And, if it hadn't been the depths of winter, you could have sworn there was moss growing underfoot, lifting the carpet off the cement underfloor. The saddest smells, of damp and decay. It was like being trapped within the pages of a Dickens novel.

When are you going to stop pretending nothing's wrong? That little voice droning away in Tristie's head . . .

Ticking away in the back of Tristie Merritt's mind had been that constant tone of conscience. Maddening. She felt extreme guilt about this, hence the harping voice, but to begin with not enough guilt to do anything about it, to use the skills the army had taught her. Not yet anyway.

★ ★ ★

There are so few things left that make this country *great*, as in *Great* Britain. But the quality of her soldiers positively is one of those. The sort of excellence you could stand up against the best anywhere in the world. Now, finally, Tristie Merritt had got her act together, ready to do something. A small tip of the hat to the can-do spirit of the army that had embraced her when she edged through the door of the local recruitment office, emaciated, washed out and almost feral, aged sixteen.

When are you going to stop pretending there's nothing you should be doing to help?

So, one particularly wretched night of damp

and draughty indignation, Tristie huddled into her borrowed greatcoat, gulped down her meds and decided she couldn't wait to get out. Get that medical discharge. Get out of the whole damned show, and start up Ward 13.

The combat injury that Tristie Merritt suffered in Afghanistan had made it unlikely she would ever return to the elite Special Reconnaisance Regiment, a special forces unit still commonly known by its former pseudonym as 14 Intelligence Company, or, more simply, 'the Det'. She was posted back to the Adjutant General's Corps. Truthfully it was make-work. The army didn't know what to do with her. But it didn't matter now. All the time she was fixed on setting up Ward 13.

And her first recruit, Ferret, a sniper, would be the most important. Not least because she would want him to vouch for anybody else she might need from within the Parachute Regiment.

*　*　*

The first thing Tristie had noticed about Ferret was his hands. Exquisite long fingers. Hairless. Not a tremor or shiver. Easy to imagine those gentle fingers laid over the dark metal breech of his sniper's long-range rifle. Ferret's army docket said he was one of the few using the L115A1. He could take out a target with an 8.59mm bullet almost a mile distant. It was all in those fingers.

His fingers were about the only flesh on display as Ferret was lying in a civilian hospital bed, one leg raised and his face and head wrapped tight with bandages. About typical for what happens when you drive into a lamp-post at fifty miles an hour. The pink of his nose and little tufts of brown hair were the only contrast to the overall white of his dressings. With an IV plugged into his right arm and an ECG pulse bipping quietly on a monitor over his head, he looked a hell of a mess. There was a strong smell of alcohol sweating through his pores.

He seemed sunken against his pillow, in the middle of his own little head-spinning world of guilt.

Tristie sat down, took one of his hands. 'You're in a bit of a mess, Corporal.'

No reply. His hand was cold and still. Not a twitch.

'My name is Captain Merritt. I'm with Staff and Personnel Support. On attachment with your battalion at the moment.'

She sensed him shuffle in his bed a little on hearing the rank. He was lying a little more straight. Then he took back his hand, to work a small gap between the bandages covering his lips. Just enough to speak.

'Is that the same Merritt who was in 14 Company?'

It made her smile. The infamous Tristie Merritt. 'I don't know of any others.' 14 Company, or the Det, as it was variously known when Merritt joined, were the army's elite undercover surveillance unit, sometimes referred to as the eyes and ears of the SAS. Unusually, given that close quarters battle is a speciality, 14

Company and its successor, the SRR, actively recruits females.

'You still with the Det, Captain?'

'No. I'm in a civilian hospital with you.'

'How come . . . If you don't mind me asking?'

'Same problem as you.'

'You a pisshead, Captain?'

'No.' She chuckled at that. 'Not a pisshead. Injured.'

Ferret took his time to think on that. 'They say you can fight. Box, I mean.' Sightless as he was, his voice sounded full of wonder.

'They say you can shoot.'

'Good enough to end up in here,' and with that, and an *uuunth* sound that registered incredible pain, he turned away. Towards the light of the window.

Army paperwork showed that Ferret had had an unblemished disciplinary record until about four years before. Then the slow downward spiral had started. The investigating Military Police had even been kind enough to transcribe the incident in Basra.

One hundred and twenty degrees of heat. Battledress. Orders that required no movement. Minimal water. Plus that special jumpiness that operations in built-up areas always give you. One final factor to send a tremor through your bowels: the knowledge that in Iraq nothing is as it seems to be. Or as it should be. This was personified in the shape of the slouching Iraqi liaison officer whose real name everybody had long stopped using. He had aviator glasses, a droopy moustache and looked remarkably like

28

Saddam himself. He was known simply as Shifty.

Intelligence said the Jaish Al Mahdi would be sending through a big arms shipment made to look like a truckload of sheep, of all things. This would be their restock of the improvised explosive devices that had been decimating British convoys. The handover was to be at a crossroads.

The file said the surveillance group had been in place for about three uncomfortable, fretful hours when a short, veiled woman appeared around a corner to the rear of the carefully hidden team. The heels of her open-toe sandals raising little dust clouds as she scurried up the street. Full plastic bag weighing down one arm.

Almost as if a scent was in the air, the woman sensed something was wrong. Something that needed investigating. It had started innocuously enough: a quick burst of radio traffic, *Someone get this woman away from here.* Then the panic. A spotter from the Iraqi Army had seen her reaching under her veil; judged this to be a threatening posture, or so the inquiry afterwards had been told. There had been a surge of Arabic yammering on the radio. Back and forth. Louder and louder. Then came the translation. Shifty was now shouting in English at the top of his voice. *She's not a damned female.* More desperation and confusion . . . Shifty panicking now, *She's JAM in a veil* . . . Unsettled, the British commander made a thoughtful *errrrr* sound on the radio that seemed to take for ever to end. *On my life, she's a bomber*, promised Shifty. Silence on the comms. *Now, now, now,* he shrieked. *You must. You must.* Then one very clear order from the officer in charge, as the veiled woman took a step into the shadows at the back of the surveillance post: *Go lethal. Combatant.*

So. Ferret had taken his shot. From just over three hundred yards. Compensating for cross-wind and bullet drop, he drilled his shot through the civilian's skull. Just as he had been trained to do. Watched the faintest spray of brain fluid and blood in the tinted lens of his sight, and the whiplash jerk of the head and the tipping forward, followed by the graceless collapse. Readied himself for the next shot.

It had been a woman. Ferret had known that almost as soon as the round slugged into her, wrenching her head around and towards him. Unmistakably a woman. He had seen the dark eyelashes of a woman. Wide open. Fluttering in alarm and shock.

Moments later, racing around a corner had scooted a seven-year-old boy. Unkempt. A little toughie. Clothes covered in dust. Trying to catch up, looking for Mum.

Mum?

With his scope, like the trained professional he was, Ferret had tracked the boy as he tugged hopefully on the hem of the veil. *Mum?* He was wearing a football strip made by Umbro, the last one sponsored by Sharp: home colours for the seasons 1998–2000. White collar, black zip-up and Umbro diamonds marked out in white and black against the red of the sleeves. Manchester United. His team.

And Ferret felt his face flush with shame. That it had come to this.

The unforgiving heat notched up yet more degrees of suffering. Remorseless. He could feel the spidery touch of cramp across the inside of his thighs. And that light. That blinding light. Even when you closed your eyes it was still there. Drilling down through your skull, sawing into the vertebrae. Like the world's tightest neck brace.

Just at that point beyond all pain, there was Shifty again. Screaming in Ferret's earpiece. Babbling in Arabic, then barking in English, trying to insert himself into the chain of command: *Take down the boy*, he was bellowing. *You pussies, kill the boy*.

And that was when his life started to spin out of control . . . landing up in the here and now.

★ ★ ★

Ferret turned back to face Tristie. He put his hand in hers. Gently. Only later did she realise he was perhaps feeling to see whether she was wearing a wedding band. 'You boxed a man once in the ring.'

'A very small man. More like a boy really.'

'But you beat him.'

Small laugh. 'He was an idiot. And I was seriously pissed off. No great skill to beating idiots.'

Ferret's voice was insistent. 'But he was a male.'

Like that would have made a difference. A

31

flicker of memory stirs within Tristie; the standard army boxing ring: twenty-three foot by twenty-three in a cold, draughty gym in the middle of February. It was one of the hoops everybody had to jump through, to get into the Det. All the instructors were on one side looking up through the ropes at the recruits. The test wasn't so much to find the best boxer. That was largely about technique. No. These guys wanted to test for killer instinct. So the contests were Male vs Female: was the male tough enough to punch a female. Really put her down. Conversely could the female give as good as she got.

The test was known then, as it still is today, by the acronym GLF. Go Like Fuck.

'He wouldn't stop looking at my breasts. He was never going to win.'

She thought she saw a smile ease across Ferret's chapped lips. He reached for a water bottle and sucked on the plastic feed pipe.

'Have they breathalysed you yet?'

'They tried, Captain, but the nurse shooed them away. Said they would be back within the next half an hour.'

Tristie looked at her watch.

★   ★   ★

By the way he was holding himself, Tristie could tell that the policeman waiting to breathalyse Ferret was ex-military. A proud man, with a heavily lined face and broad shoulders. He had looked tired and tense that morning. Perhaps Ferret's case mirrored something in his own life:

32

the world biting you in the backside when you least deserve it.

The two of them exchanged a few polite words after she had left Ferret's bed. Then Tristie played her one card: Corporal, she said, my army-issue car seems to have been scratched up the side, and the tyres slashed. Who should I report this to? Her eyes had pleaded *Can I buy this kid some time?* She could say nothing more. It either happened, or it didn't.

The policeman sucked at the back of his teeth for a moment, but she sensed just the smallest glint of complicity. Thrilled to be personally putting a finger on the scales of injustice. He turned and walked away, tut-tutting as he strode down the corridor. He didn't come back to Ferret for almost five hours while he fussed in the car park, tooled about with the CCTV images, poked around some broken fences and hassled some kids on bikes who should have been at school.

That was how Ferret passed his test. But only by a tenth of a milligram. Sufficient for it not to affect the terms on which he had to leave the army.

Nobody would say anything either about the matter with Shifty, back in Basra. Because instead of taking out the kid, from almost nine hundred yards, Ferret had drilled a shot through Shifty's crotch. Bad news on so many levels.

You've got to understand the politics most of all: the hopes and dreams of the Coalition lay in the new Iraqi Army, especially their officer corps. In many eyes Shifty was the future of the country. Indeed, he was who we were fighting for. But then real soldiers are notoriously poor at playing politics. Ferret had not only emasculated him, but worse. While Shifty was kicking around in the dust holding what was left of his reproductive organs, Ferret had taken out both knees as well. 'Remarkable marksmanship,' the line officer had noted in his file. 'Sadly, not welcome back in this operational theatre.'

★ ★ ★

Two months later, when Ferret left the army, he joined Tristie Merritt. Gladly becoming the first recruit into Ward 13. Obviously she had passed some basic test of his; some gut-check sense of whether this female, former army officer was on the level or not. And through Ferret they had linked up with Piglet, who would be the linguistic expert, as well. Others would come on board once they had their hands on some of Sir Dale Malham's ill-gotten gains.

The deed was fixed for a Friday. Late afternoon. In November. There was the usual darkness, blustery rain and endless gloom.

Ferret was sat in the Concorde Lounge of British Airways Terminal 5, dressed as expensively as they could afford in a navy tuxedo suit. Playing the City gent. Tie already undone. Jacket and cufflinks off. Sleeves rolled up.

Likewise Malham, who was on the couch opposite, unwinding after a hectic week picking the pockets of the MoD. A double Scotch on the rocks rested on his stomach as he sprawled out,

34

feeding himself cashews, and watching lazy-eyed the business of Heathrow through the towering height of windows before him. Malham was booked on the six o'clock flight up to Newcastle. There, the former MP would slide into his pale green Bentley and take off to his country house. This was the fifth Friday night that Ward 13 had followed him. They knew his movements.

Tristie was in a poky hotel room almost three hundred miles away. Just a couple of hundred yards from Newcastle airport, in fact. Fretting. Thinking of all the things that could go wrong. And Piglet, recruit number two . . . he had the best gig. Waiting for a call in a distant beach bar on the north side of Grand Cayman. Probably looking out over a marina full of yachts and launches, and young, sleek women and old, grumpy men. Scrunching the warm sand through his toes, no doubt. Bastard.

Getting the money was down to Ferret and Tristie. Simple as that. There was an open mobile link between them. Ferret was in her left ear, both of them wearing hands-free phones. She checked her watch. A couple of minutes before 5.30 p.m. The flight was on time. Within the next ten minutes they'd be nudging their VVIP clients to the gate. It was now or never. The tension was tight in Tristie's chest. In fifteen minutes she was either going to look very smart or impossibly stupid, with the prospect of a lot of police forever on her tail.

She thought about Sir Dale Malham in the pages of *Horse & Hound*, at a celebrity clay pigeon shoot with his brand-new, lovely little

35

20-bore Purdey over-and-under. *How long can you pretend there's nothing wrong with this situation?* Then she thought about the appalling grot, the stench of that bathroom at Tidworth barracks. The contrast was just what Tristie needed to steel her nerves. *When exactly are you going to stop turning the other cheek?*

'Ferret. What are you looking at?'

'Biggest titties I ever saw.' This is the downside of giving expensive surveillance equipment to former soldiers. Unsupervised.

'Don't go all horn-dog on me now.'

'Hey.' Sound of indignation from Ferret. 'I'm just watching what Malham's watching. Being as one with the target.'

In the Heathrow lounge, Ferret was wearing a pair of wholly unremarkable glasses, except for the small button camera fitted into the frame just by the bridge of his nose. The image generated, the girl with big breasts, would be playing in the palm of his hand on a digital video recorder no bigger than a credit card. The same image was also being stored on a secure digital card.

'You're close enough to Malham?' There was no zoom function on the spy camera; you only achieved that effect by physically getting closer to the target. 'You've got him framed tight enough?'

'Don't worry.' Ferret's voice was reassuringly breezy. 'He looks plenty good from here. Distracted by them big bazoomers.'

'That's why God gave 'em to us. To bewitch and befuddle.'

'We're going to get this guy. Turn him upside

down and shake him for all he is worth.'

Ferret was right. Focus. Get a grip, girl. Tristie looked down at the small, boxy worktable in her three-star hotel room near Newcastle airport. The files were all tidied away. The phones were ready. She had hands-free connections in *both* ears. The paperwork was laid out. She was in control. Was never going to be more ready . . .

'OK. Sir Dale Malham. *Come on down.*'

★ ★ ★

Tristie Merritt dialled Malham's mobile number from the hotel phone. And the first response was from Ferret, watching him in the lounge. Putting down his drink, spilling a few nuts on to the couch. Fumbling through his jacket pockets. '*I hope that's you calling, 'cos he's looking for his phone.*'

'Is me. Stand by.'

'*Got the phone in his hand. Looking at the number on his screen. Confused . . .* ' Malham's screen would show the number 0191–214 . . . enough for him to know the call came from north-east Newcastle. Somewhere within a triangle of land between Ponteland, Throckley and Kingston Park that also included the airport. A lot of housing estates. Next to his former constituency in fact. Several dozen millions of pounds ago.

''Ullo?' Despite his new-found airs and graces, she knew Malham would speak Geordie to those from the city. A defence mechanism.

Tristie took a deep breath, glanced one last

time at the Internet print-off. It said that a woman called Kayleigh Brook had joined First Jet Private's Newcastle operation six weeks before. A photo off the company website showed her to be a dyed blonde and smiley. And big boned from the look of things. Size fourteen. Tristie launched into her best Geordie. 'Sir Dale Malham?' The inflection rising at the end. 'Is that you, Sir Dale?' She was as good as she was because the British Army had made her so.

'Wey aye.' Very slightly sozzled, but still with the politician's touch. 'This is he.'

Tristie continued, gushing, like a schoolgirl. 'My name is Kayleigh. You used to know my uncle. Long time back. He lived in Harydene. Perhaps you don't remember. Anyway, that was a way ago. I work in finance, at First Jet Private. You know . . . Them . . . You know . . . Those . . . ' She stumbles here, a little bit breathy. Trying to sound flustered, talking to her first ever knight of the realm. Golly gee.

'I don't know you, pet, but it's all right. I know First Jet. You're calling from Newcastle.' In her other ear Ferret whispers. *'He's smiling. He's with you.'*

'I gotta be canny here, Sir Dale. I don't want no trouble 'cos it's all very embarrassing. I'm going to get an awful rocket from your missus if she finds me out.'

'What is it, pet?' Malham sounding intrigued.

'Your birthday. This coming Tuesday . . . Happy birthday, by the way, Sir Dale . . . Well. The wifie has booked a surprise flight for ya birthday and all. Private jet, like a surprise, and a big tour round France and Venice. Three nights in some very posh places. You're not supposed to know, like.' Ferret in her left ear. *'He's nodding. Big smile. Whatever you're saying is making sense to him.'*

'We took her credit card to confirm the hotels and things. Only we didn't run all the charges, not until this afternoon 'cos you know the fuel surcharges are always last-minute, like. But her card won't work now. You know the end of the month is Sunday, so there's nothing left on her card, like. No juice.'

'Frowning now. Not a happy bunny. Going a bit red round the neck.'

'Anyways. I dunno what to do, like. It's right doing my head in, this. 'Cos I don't want to spoil your party, like, but I don't want to get a rocket from your missus if we lose all them take-off and landing slots.' Breath. Pause. Breath. 'And it's Friday night, Sir Dale. And I want to go get me dancing boots on, have a bit of a boogie. And I know this thing is going to be messing with my head, like, all weekend. So I thought I'd give you a bell and all.'

Ferret speaking softly. *'He's got a big shit-eater's grin on his face.'*

Malham sounded leery when he spoke. 'So. Miss Kayleigh. What exactly do you want me to do?'

Tristie gave a little breathless giggle. 'Well, you could just tell me ya card number. And ya PIN, of course. And trust me to be a good girl with it over the weekend.' Now a little bit saucy. 'But I've never done very well at being a good girl

39

. . . if you know what I mean . . . '

'*God's honest truth, he's playing with his balls right in front of me. Taking a drink of his whisky with one hand and playing with his fucking balls with the other.*'

Malham's voice sounds a little slurry. 'Pet. Good girl or not, as much as I want to you give you my credit card . . . I'm sure you realise that's not the wisest thing. So how's about we try another way.'

Amused resignation in Tristie's voice. 'I thought you might say that . . . so I guess I'm going to have to give you the company bank account. Do things the old-fashioned way.' She looked down at the invoice she had had faxed from the offices of First Jet Private, having spoken to the real Kayleigh Brook. It was genuine, with the correct sort code and bank address. Ferret's voice was full of excitement. '*He's getting out a pen and paper. He's going to do it.*'

'Go ahead, Kayleigh. Read me the account details. So I can pay for me own bloody birthday surprise, and keep a pretty girl like you out of trouble on a Friday night. Read it out to me. I'll check with the bank. Squirt the money through.'

'Aw. Thanks a bunch.' And so Tristie did, reading out all the information Malham would need. She had rung up First Jet Private that morning saying she wanted to put down a deposit on a package they were offering to next year's Monte Carlo Grand Prix. Asked that they fax through the invoice for payment. So it was the company's genuine details that were being read down the phone. The details would match payments Malham had made to the same company for similar trips. First Jet Private's own quarterly glossy circulars had boasted that Malham travelled with them to Moscow and Rome for the final of the Champions League, to Milan for some opera and a whole range of trips to Germany. To see happy pension fund managers.

The First Law of the Great Con: if your mark can't see your point of profit, all defences will be down and you can get him for anything. '*He's writing it all down.*' And he did, even reading it back to make sure.

Tristie's final words. 'Please, pretty please, can you make sure they start the payment thing rolling tonight. Please.' And that was the last time she heard Sir Dale Malham's voice.

Five minutes later Tristie was out of the hotel room and in her rental car when the email from Ferret arrived. It was a high-resolution video clip lasting just over three minutes, taken from the secure digital card recording off his camera lens. Malham calling his Jersey bank.

One of the things Tristie had had to learn when she was in the various care homes of her childhood was lip-reading. It was a survival thing. The need to communicate about their 'carers', to mock or ridicule, or warn others, but always fearing their wrath if they were caught speaking. Silence indeed golden.

Watching him on screen, it didn't take Tristie long to read off Malham's sort code and account number. He was making no effort to be discreet.

He explained on his mobile that the account he wanted to tap was his call deposit account. Instant access. Funds in excess of £50,000 required. She scribbled all of this down, her heart beating a little too fast. They were still a long way from victory. Fewer than forty per cent of word sounds are distinguishable by sight alone.

He spoke the amount he wished to transfer to First Jet Private, and confirmed it once again. The numbers were easy because the visemes, or visual units of speech, were simple to pick. Answered a random but fairly obvious-to-anticipate security question. Then Malham gave the first line of his address, and postcode. Next, his authorisation code, or password. That was when the fun started.

It took Tristie a couple of minutes of playing it back and forth before she could even take a guess. No, she told herself. *Can't be.* She went back over it again and again and again, and the pinprick of emotion that started as anxiety somewhere in her stomach had spread. Becoming anger. Then her whole body tightened with fury. *Money For Old Rope.* His password was *Money For Old Rope.* She could have been wrong, of course. *Money* and *Many* lip-read the same. It helped that so many of even the Jersey call centres were using East European staff, so Malham had had to enunciate it carefully. It kept coming back to the same thing. *Money For Old Rope.* Perhaps she was being unfair. Perhaps this was a book title or obscure Dire Straits album he could have been referring to? Or was this really what he thought of his armed forces connections, and the millions he had accrued? *Money For Old Rope*.

Quickly Tristie checked the airport website. The flight to Newcastle was showing Closed. Pushed back from the gate. He'd be out of contact for the next seventy-five minutes at least. So she dialled up Ferret, told him carefully what she knew, and asked him to get to work. He would be the male voice that rang the bank, no point her trying. Only he could be Sir Dale Malham: transferring out chunks of £50,000. They'd agreed, keep ringing back until you exhaust the daily, weekly or monthly limit, or he simply runs out of cash. Allow two minutes between each call and you would be assured of a different person answering each time. All transfers to the Ward 13 account in the bank's sister branch in Grand Cayman.

Good luck, Ferret, she said, feeling guilty, hoping he understood that she had done everything possible to minimise the risk, short of making the calls herself. The pre-pay mobile he used was brand new. No history. Possibly, they could back-triangulate the calls to within fifty yards of where he was in Terminal 5, which gave them a pool of about five thousand suspects. There was much more of a trail leading to Tristie, but that didn't stop her worrying that Ferret was carrying too much of the risk.

She waited in the hotel car park. Laptop fired up, and the website set to www.openatc.com so she could watch the slow progress of Malham's BA flight to Newcastle as it pushed north

43

through England's congested skies. The assumption would be that he'd make a call or get a message on his mobile as soon as the flight landed. Perhaps he would harangue his partner about her spending, discover in fact there was no birthday trip planned, maybe get a call from a supervisor at the bank, worried that an account had been flushed clean of cash. Seventy-five minutes was their time frame.

The only thing to do was sit back. Look through her rain-spattered windscreen. Try and remain calm. The longer she waited, the more her mind grew accustomed to the idea of getting caught. At least they had a good shot at some publicity: the British love the idea of a noble failure. The girl with no parents, attractive, single, exciting but deeply classified army career, tilting at windmills. Maybe she could make some sort of celebrity D-list, surviving as a rent-a-quote security expert on TV and radio. She felt her nails dig into her palms at the thought . . . an awful reality.

'Captain?'

Huh? She jumped. It felt like only seconds later but Ferret was back in Tristie's ear. Panicky, she glanced down at the laptop and gulped. Steady. Openatc.com showed Malham's flight over the North Sea making its turn towards Newcastle airport. Take it easy. Deep breath.

'Yes?' She cleared her throat. 'Things OK?'

Ferret sounded way down. 'He's run out of money already.'

'Oh dear.' Instantly, Tristie was thinking about Plan B, how to keep Ward 13 alive, how much

44

would she have to borrow. And where from. 'How much?'

Ferret sighed. And in her cold, boxy little rental car, she could feel his gloom wrap around her. How small was the amount they'd managed to scavenge? she wondered. Tell me it's not too embarrassingly small . . .

'A one and four zeros.' Ten thousand pounds.

Ferret's disappointment was obvious. Yet a tiny, sneaky part of her was relieved. Look on the bright side, she felt herself wanting to say. It was a small amount, not what they needed as seed money, but at the same time not enough to set off an international manhunt. Perhaps, she had the words ready to say, she'd over-egged the opportunity. 'I'm sorry, Ferret. I really am.'

Quiet followed. And in that silence she searched for conversation, a female instinct, some meaningless words to soothe the sharp edge of male disappointment . . .

Which was when Ferret erupted in a gale of laughter. Almost maniacal. Then the quietest whisper. 'One point two five million.' He gurgled with delight, saying it again, softly. 'A one, a two, a five and four frigging zeros.'

Tristie's first panicked reaction had been, Put the Money Back.

'*Put it back??!* Tristie, excuse my English, but are you fucking crazy? This guy calls us Money For Old Rope, and you want to give it back?!'

And, of course, Ferret was right. They didn't. And in the Caymans, Piglet picked up the banker's cheque ninety minutes later: £1.25 million. An hour after that, he was off, on a

45

scheduled flight to the Bahamas. (Army humour . . . the guy is Piglet because he is the scion of a wealthy family of Jewish traders. Reubens. His father allowed him to use one of the family's long-dormant and untraceable Cayman Island accounts, have it renamed Ward 13 Operating Funds.) Piglet then banked the cheque in a brand-new Bahamas account, and suddenly the whole thing was in business. Ward 13. This half-crazy, half-stupid idea had become reality.

Operation Macchar,
minus eighteen days

US Embassy
Diplomatic Enclave
Islamabad, Pakistan

First impressions: the CIA station chief in Islamabad is bald, shiny bald. And even with a nose-guard's broad frame, he looks seriously overweight. And when William Lamayette frowns somehow the whole of his scalp and fleshy neckline frowns with him, folding into ridges and gulleys that speak of anxiety and tension. There is something about his intensity, the way he sucks up the pressure of the job, that reminds people of Colonel Kurtz, the Brando character in *Apocalypse Now*. Then there is the unusual get-up. For tonight's cross-examination with Washington he's wearing a specially tailored black cotton salwar kameez. Not typical Agency office-wear, but damned comfortable nonetheless.

Some whisper that, like Colonel Kurtz, he is already insane. Only forty-eight years old, they tut, as if *real* CIA people couldn't be losing their marbles until they were at least fifty-five. As to Lamayette himself, it's soul destroying to feel that he is the only person taking all this seriously.

'Jeez. You'd think these screwy bastards might

have a handle on what their frigging generals were up to.' Lamayette blows a thick stream of cigarette smoke to the ceiling. Frazzled. His hefty back and shoulders carrying his bulk distort his body to an upright turtle shape. 'Bit of command and control wouldn't go amiss in a country with a goddam nuke bomb. I've flushed away turds . . . small pebbly turds, and each one with more smarts than some of their staff officers . . . '

On the US end of this tirade, the Agency's director of the National Clandestine Service, the spook arm of the CIA, interjects. Sensing this discussion needs to be brought back in hand.

'Listen, Bill . . . ' The NCS director's name is Krandall Meyers. He speaks smoothly. 'You haven't given us enough to put this Khan thing top of anybody's list, let alone the president's. No way is he picking up the phone to the Pakistani president or prime minister on this. So what, General Khan's people might have made some silly threats. We don't even know what he's threatening to do. So. I'll say it again: have you got anything on Khan? What he might be up to?' Long pause. 'Anything?'

Lamayette looks aghast at the fascia of the telephone, its fancy screen, electronics, flashing lights, and riles at the smooth but very pointed, slippery-simple question from Washington. 'What the bloody hell do you think, Krandall?'

It would take just under three seconds for his words to process through the encryption software, bounce about through outer space and then be reassembled on Meyers's desk.

Let's see what you make of that . . .

Lamayette knows he looks a wreck of a man. Pushed to the edge by the sheer excesses of the job. And the tragedy is that after almost three years, he's only now beginning to understand how things work here. Not that this hard-won sense of wisdom is providing any particular insight right now: General Khan was willing himself to death someplace. Like some heart-broken animal. Refusing food and water. The shrinks even had an expression for it, Passive Learned Helplessness. After ten days, Washington's verdict was clear: not impressed. This guy's a peon. A bag-carrier. How smart is starving yourself to death, not dealing your way out of trouble? Highly strung perhaps, but no way is he some kind of tactical genius. End of story.

Having your judgement questioned was like . . . like losing the whole game. Lamayette understands this better than most. His stock within the top circle at the CIA was sinking fast. Too many new faces and too few who would speak for him. *He's lost the plot, Old Bill.* He could almost script the chat at the water-cooler. *Did some good things, like, last millennium, but a freaking headcase now.*

Lamayette fingers the outline of a long, thick slab of granite given to him by an old friend. Many lifetimes ago he had attended the frogman training centre at Aspretto on Corsica run by the French Secret Service, the Direction Générale de la Sécurité Extérieure. He became fast friends with the deputy head. Both kept in contact as their careers progressed; his buddy now chief of the private office to the minister of defence. Therefore, behind the president and defence minister, he was Number Three Cheese-Eating Surrender Monkey. Lamayette had sent off the appropriate Simpsons T-shirt with his own grinning face screen-printed over that of the character of Groundskeeper Willie, who'd uttered those immortal words.

When Lamayette was posted to Islamabad, one of the first things he received, under diplomatic escort from the French embassy, was the plank of granite. Engraved into the stone and gilded were de Gaulle's famous words: 'You may be sure that the Americans will commit all the stupidities they can think of, plus some that are beyond imagination.' As irritatingly humorous as his friend's gift had been, there had been moments, many moments, in the conduct of this War on Terror when he could imagine the imperious, beak-nosed de Gaulle chortling with delight.

Back to now. And Meyers sounds like he's about to go dyspeptic. 'Bill. I have to say . . . I don't think . . . I don't think your anger is called for. Is it unprofessional for us just to want to know what's going on? To ask a little more of your work-product than for all this anxiety you're generating to be nothing more than random and unverifiable guesses?'

Lamayette laces his fingers together, cracking his knuckles. 'I just don't have anything, Krandall . . . What do you want me to do? I could make something up. Yeah. I saw his tactical plan in my Cheerios this morning. All the little hoops came together like magic. Showed me what he was planning: Khan was going to take a stick, not any kind of stick but a conductor's baton, and shove it up the president's ass. At the White House correspondents' dinner. Watch out for him, Krandall, in the woodwind section. He'll be the guy pretending to play bassoon. Can't play for toffee. That'll be your clue.'

Too late, of course, he realises he's crossed the line. Yet again. He's vented his feelings but his words, his overall attitude, are tantamount to professional suicide. Sure, the CIA is civilian, all casual clothing and comfy shoes, but at its core the structure and thinking are military. No matter how much free expression they encourage, do not confuse that with criticism of those higher up the pole than you. You do not mock your seniors within what used to be the fabled Directorate of Operations. Not if you're serious about your career.

He's pretty certain Meyers is doing some breathing exercises on the other side of the world. When he finally speaks the oily confidence in his voice is a little off. Just a tick or two. 'Well then, Bill, how about you just cool off with these crazy messages you keep sending. You're screaming the house down but proof, Bill. Proof. That's what runs the engines here.'

'That's my miserable bloody point, Krandall.' He crushes out his cigarette. Holds another between his fingers. 'Every bone in my body, every drop of blood, every single grey cell, tells me we're in trouble. But you want proof . . . I don't have proof . . . ' He pauses, frowns as he waits for the sound and reverb to settle from the speakerphone.

The excruciating high-pitch tone tells Bill Lamayette he's lost his audience. Krandall Meyers. Langley. And Washington. All hung up on him.

And in the bleakness of General Khan's cell in Camp Lemonier, Djibouti, there is only the perpetual whine of the mosquitoes. Droning.

On and on.

Despite himself, the general can't stop smiling.

Operation Macchar, minus thirteen days

In the cab of a hijacked refuse collection lorry
Waiting by Kew Pier
London Borough of Richmond

Tristie Merritt is sitting just an arm's length from Whiffler and he can't stop thinking about her. Not straight-out lusting, but not very pure thoughts either.

You're not supposed to have contemplations about a female like this, Tristie being his boss, a former army captain and all. It's making Whiffler's blood run cold. He bites his lip. Someone's going to have my pecker off if I'm not careful. Shit. Probably she'd have my pecker off, probably with the serrated edge of that two-inch Ladybug folding knife she keeps hidden in her boot.

The captain's hair is ash blonde; she has a short, no-pissing-around haircut. No dingle-dangle bits for a combatant to wrap around his hand. No way she is ever going to embarrass herself, or us, by having some frou-frou hairstyle. Five foot seven inches, 139 pounds. Two-time army welterweight boxing champion, and not a scratch or bump on her after twenty-seven bouts. A drop-dead smile that sucks the blood from your brain and a gorgeous, dirty belly laugh that tingles the skin, makes you feel the most important man in the world.

Don't get the wrong idea. Whiffler is not one of those who thinks females are only good for shagging. He never had a problem with females in uniform, which makes him something of a gay-boy radical. Females as officers, or NCOs. Not a problem for him.

But Captain Merritt is different. She's solid, proved herself again and again. And that's why Whiffler knows he shouldn't be thinking like this. Especially not about someone who served five years with the Det. Northern Ireland, Kosovo, then Iraq and Afghanistan. The physical she passed to reach the Det, or 14 Intelligence Coy., is the equivalent of the P Coy. test all Paras have to pass. Roughly the same failure rate as well: of each batch of one hundred people who take it, only six make it through. That, and everything she's done for Whiffler and the boys, that's why she has Respect.

Once Whiffler had reckoned it would help if he visualised her as an Angel. Their collective Angel. But Weasel had put it better: Captain Tristie Merritt is Our Moral Centre. Weasel's a bastard like that. Too good with words. 'Face facts, boys.' Weasel had glazed eyes, holding a half-drunk pint of Snakebite as he spoke. 'We'd be screwed without her,' and he took a whacking great drag on his king-size Senior Service lung-shredder. In a singular moment of clarity, all of them, Shoe, Piglet, Ferret, Button and he, had nodded. Long and hard. Weasel spoke the truth.

54

She is their Moral Centre.

(Of course, Button wouldn't know what he was agreeing to, but Whiffler had watched him bob his ginormous, straw-filled head along with the rest of them. Probably thought a moral centre was one of those crap Milk Tray chocolates, like the Praline or Truffleicious that everybody leaves for some other mug.)

You can't understand how important she is without knowing the rootlessness of what they'd all become since leaving the army. That they'd been yearning for someone to come from somewhere, as officers are supposed to, lead them away from the slow death of their sad-sack existences. Top marks in the desperation stakes went to Shoe, who'd gone from three stripes in an elite anti-tank platoon to sexing day-old chicks when Captain Merritt found him: squeezing the poop out of their little butts so he could see whether they were male or female. He reckoned he could do almost ten thousand a day. You never saw a man smile like Shoe when she fished him out of that job.

That was why they need Captain Merritt. She made them whole again. She gave them back a sense of honour and pride. And comradeship. It's not the same as belonging to the best regiment in the army, but close as. And an honourable cause to fight for. Just like, back in the day, when the Paras were the whole of their lives.

One thing they all understand is this: lift a finger against her . . .

The last time her hair colour came up in

conversation had been at the end of a long night drinking in Aldershot — 'blonde up top, but sure as hell, black box down below'. Well. The whole place went quiet. Shoe, Piglet, Ferret, Button, Weasel and Whiffler looking at each other. Trying to control their anger. Thank Christ she wasn't there. You've got to hate people who disrespect. You expect it of civilians. But the guy mouthing off was a toerag corporal from Signals . . . bastard crap-hats. Even the empty bottles and pots of beer on their table seemed to shimmy with the tension of a big problem about to break. Someone talking about Captain Merritt's pubic hair? Death wish, or what?

It was left to Shoe and Whiffler. Closing time they all ambled outside. Palling around as they lurched to the chippy and found somewhere good and dark. Whiffler got the corporal in a hammerlock. Then Shoe whacked the crap out of him. His face red with anger. Each kick thumping out a very clear message. You. Watch. Your. Tongue. About. Our. Captain.

Back to the now. Captain Merritt is right in front of Whiffler in the driver's seat of this light green, ten-wheel monster. A Volvo FL6 refuse collection vehicle. The captain's head is just inches from Whiffler. If he could tear his eyes off her high, almost gaunt cheekbones he would be able to see the boathouse of Kew Pier through the windscreen in the distance. Her dark blue balaclava still rolled up, sitting on top of her head. He could reach out and run his fingers over the fuzzy ridges of her scalp.

There was a serious smell in here of engine oil

and garbage. So Tristie has a white-spotted red handkerchief over her mouth and nose, tied off like a Wild West bandit's, scented with Opium, which takes the edge of the stink.

Sandalwood and jasmine hang in the air. The scent of a woman . . .

Whiffler is in the back, in a little cab with its own set of side doors. Button and Shoe sitting beside him. Weasel in the front seat with Tristie. All of them silent, apprehensive, togged up like they're about to go and empty dustbins. Gloves. Beanies and fleece neck gaiters, or full-on balaclavas. High-visibility jackets with the orange plastic strip. Thick anonymous coats. Cuffs and trouser legs discreetly taped up so that not a shred of evidence gets left behind.

Shoe already has his balaclava rolled down. Eyes blinking nervously as he looks forward and back. Scanning. Nervously pressing his thumb along the thick, purple scar that runs the length of his cheekbone and right down his neck to his collar-bone. They all have their reasons, but that scar is Shoe's. The reason he was turfed out of the army at age thirty-one.

Button takes out his dental plate and pockets it. Grins at Whiffler, showing his four missing front teeth. A sign that he too is ready . . . He fits his thick cap over his great ox head.

All are waiting for Ferret, on a motorbike following the target on the other side of London . . . waiting on his Go signal. Their hearts drumming quietly. Feeling good about them-selves. Adrenalin dancing through their veins once again. Back in that groove. Waiting for that

57

surge. That signal: Green On — Go . . .

Button catches Whiffler's eye, and taps his nose. The perfume. Shakes his head in amusement. This is the first time any of them have been led by *a woman*. Females don't pass the P Coy test. They just don't make it as Paras. You need a combination of speed and strength. Nothing against women, it's just that those who tried and were beefy enough weren't fast, and those who had speed didn't have the basic brawn.

But Tristie Merritt had earned her command of these ex-Paras, and won their loyalty. So Whiffler shrugs his shoulders at Button, the perfume. *Women, eh . . . what can you do?*

★   ★   ★

There's a *beep-beep* on the captain's mobile. She looks at it carefully, lowers the handkerchief. As she turns, everybody sees the smile spread across her face, the light playing off her powder-blue eyes.

'They're coming,' and she rolls down her balaclava, guns the huge diesel engine. 'Let's give it another minute . . . they've just passed the first marker.' About two miles away.

The Volvo refuse truck edges out into the tiny feeder road and the former Paras are gripped by the sweetest sensation. Not just about going into battle. This is about dishing out some payback. The Ministry of Defence is going to get a serious slapping . . . thanks to the team that Tristie Merritt has gathered around her. Ward 13.

Nobody had turned her down . . . but very few that were recommended got an invitation to join. She had looked closely at all the candidates knowing she needed not just something like the best, but the best of the best. Near enough was not going to be good enough. With the benefit of their army paperwork she tried to get inside their heads and work them out; finally Tristie surveilled them in their communities.

Dicking them, the old IRA style of watching, took her around the country, to the various towns and cities that her potential recruits had shrunk back to since leaving. It gave her a good idea of what sort of a man had once filled out that uniform.

She was recruiting to fill six positions. The basic SAS unit structure is four people, likewise the Pathfinders from the Parachute Regiment. Ward 13 needed a specialist in communications, a linguist, an explosives expert and a medic, plus two more skill sets beside. A mobility expert — covering everything from getting up and down mountains to fast cars and how to fix them. And a sniper, because in this game you never say never. Tristie had already learnt that to her cost.

She started with forty names.

There would be some basic, simple rules. No matter what, she wouldn't put up with any thieving, no drunks, bullies or mercenaries. She didn't want the sort of soldier whose default setting is violence and anger. She was looking for brains. Calm operators, who could think on their feet, work through the unpredictability of a live situation. Restraint on the trigger has not always been a Parachute Regiment strength, but Tristie considered this especially important for her unit, the one she'd already taken to calling Ward 13, because they were all civilians now. They might still live to a military code but no matter what they held in their hearts — about battle honours and courage under fire — Civvy Street would give them no special breaks. As much as possible the violence would have to be non-lethal and with an absolute minimum of firepower. Also, because she would be the sole officer type, Tristie wanted nobody whose record showed an obvious problem with females.

Which brought her to an age-old problem. The boy-girl thing.

By this stage she was down to less than twenty names. To each of them, she offered the same cautionary advice. 'Don't think for one second that I'll ever send you a signal that in any way could be interpreted as an offer even to hold hands. Do you understand?'

Some had nodded, understood straight away, and straight away she had seen the acknowledgement in their eyes. Most had kept their thoughts to themselves, except in their eyes, of course, where she could read their minds. The self-satisfied smile, the cocksure desire and hope. A clear sign they couldn't be trusted to take her seriously. Down to only ten names now . . .

To only one of them, a ginger-haired lad called

Whiffler, had she found it necessary to explain herself.

'Your file says you're an explosives expert . . . correct?'

He'd nodded with boyish enthusiasm. She'd already made up her mind to recruit Whiffler, sensed he was right for Ward 13, so it was just a case of testing him with her Nothing Personal But I'm Just Not Interested policy.

'If you fire a thousand rounds of eighty-one-mil mortar shell, how many duds would you expect?'

Whiffler had rolled his eyes, started moving his lips fast, doing the maths. 'Depends . . . ' The 81mm was the British Army standard light mortar. Somebody as good as Whiffler could drive his crew to a rate of fire of as many as twenty rounds a minute.

'I guess anything worse than one in a thousand would be a real shitter.'

'Mostly those duds are fuse problems, right?'

'Running through the jungle or wherever, that'll get moisture in the fuses, yeah. Screws them up good and proper.'

'So when you try to make sense of what I'm saying to you . . . the fact I *will* not be interested in you in that way . . . think of me as one of those defective fuses. A one-in-a-thousand. I'm the faulty wire, the damp firewood, call it what you will. But you try and put it on with me, and it will end badly. For all of us. Understand?'

Whiffler had rocked forward, a question already formed in his mind. *What happened to you?* But immediately thought better of it.

Caught the crystal-clear expression on the woman's face, and in her suddenly bleak eyes the warning, *Don't Go There*. Gulp. And he nodded his understanding. Tristie Merritt is off limits.

Finally, in her selections Tristie had had to be mindful of that famous battle cry you sometimes hear, the sign you're really in deep trouble: married men with family hold firm, single men . . . with me. No point beating about the bush on this. Dependants would be fine so long as they were well out of the way, and being cared for, but her very strong preference was for the unrelationshipped. After that Tristie was looking for those who still held to the basic discipline of elite soldiering: you have your fun, enjoy your downtime, but you arc always prepared.

From a starting-off point of forty names, Tristie recruited a colour sergeant and a sergeant, two corporals, a lance corporal and the oldest private (thirty-four) in the Parachute Regiment. Six in total, plus her. All had quit or been booted in the previous six months.

And so it was that a woman became the leader of six hard, brutal men shaped by training and battle. Smallest by height, and lightest in the group. The only female. She knew she wasn't going to outmuscle any of them in a straight-up competition but there were opportunities that would fall to the right female that no Para comes close to achieving.

★   ★   ★

Right now Ferret and Piglet are tailing the mark. The other four are in the cab with Tristie as they wait by Kew Pier. She looks at them in the rear-view mirror, and brief snatches of conversations come to mind from some of those first face-to-face meetings. Always interview-style in a room in the nearest motorway hotel to where they lived.

Button. Private, A Coy., 3 Para: Button's conduct in the field was always exemplary, cool-headed and brave ('the very best of the very best', as one officer commanding noted), but he was something of a recurring feature in the guardhouse when off duty.

'Says here you were once busted down from corporal to private. That's a hell of a tumble. What happened?' The copy of the file said only, *Unspecified-conduct incident, US Ambassador's Residence, Winfield House. December 2008. Refer Foreign and Commonwealth Office*.

He has a big wide face, boyish, simple looking in a way. 'Are you sure you want to know?' Trace of red rising up his neck.

'No secrets.'

'I was company medical technician. Helped save some American's life in Helmand. That got me invited to a function at Winfield House, to meet a senator. Frankly some of their soldiers were pretty lightweight, all dicky sunglasses and chewing gum. Anyway, all the chat, the politeness, the pain of being on best behaviour, add a dozen or so sherbets on an empty stomach, and I sort of lost it a bit. Found myself in some crapper needing an up-chuck. Didn't quite get my head in the bowl. Sort of coughed everything up into a nice fluffy towel . . . '

'Why was that a problem?'

'Well, I don't know what I was thinking, but I didn't put it in the laundry basket. Wanted to cover my tracks, sort of.'

'Where did you put it, Button?'

'I sort of folded the towel back up again. Made it look like nothing had happened. I thought I was being dead clever.'

'And then you put it back in the cupboard?'

Button's neck had flushed with embarrassment. But there had been a wry look of humour in his eyes too . . . he'd have worn no end of grief for this from his officers. Even more unforgiving would have been his mates.

'And I'm presuming they had close-circuit television.'

'Well, there was that. Also it turned out I was in the private crapper of the senator, and the wife took a shower that night and . . . well, she sort of . . . got the towel . . . and it wasn't what she was expecting. Not the sort of freshness and fragrance she was used to. And so she got a bit fucking stressy. Don't quite remember . . . ' He shakes his head, as though still a bit mystified. 'Hell of a kerfuffle that was.'

'Yes, Button. I can just imagine how delighted everybody was.'

'There going to be any nobby social engagements in this line of work, ma'am?'

'I'll keep them to a minimum for you . . . '

Shoe. Colour Sergeant, C Coy., 3 Para: 'You

64

don't like my tattoo?' He looks at her, genuinely shocked.

'I think you need to let your hair grow through . . .'

Shoe's scalp was shaved bald. Above his neck, like some Hells Angel gang member, he'd had the words *Utrinque Paratus* freshly tattooed in Gothic lettering. Ready for Anything, the Para motto.

'You're finding it hard to let go, aren't you?'

There's a brief flash of light in Shoe's eyes, a fleeting thought that he could hold the lie. Then his body droops, and his eyes follow the patterns on the carpet around the hotel room until he feels strong enough to look up at her again.

'I was part of a team. Best damned team in the world. We had élan. *Esprit de corps.* We trained. We fought. We held up our end . . . ' His voice breaks with emotion, and it's a tiny child's voice that whispers, 'and now it's all gone and I feel so dead inside . . . terrible.'

He told her how he'd got a job at McDonald's. He'd read something about the team ethos they had, which sounded vaguely Para-esque. 'I started as a batch cooker then they put me on HBOS.'

'HBOS?'

'The guy in the window of the drive-through: Hang Bag Out and Smile. I must have looked into a thousand faces, dipped my head, said my *Thank you, sir* or *Sorry about the mix-up, sir.* And all the time I'm asking them, Do you know, do you even care, how many people are risking their lives for you right now?'

'You didn't get the answer you wanted . . . '

'Not even close: between the bastard youth of today and the politicians who've never served, don't know what the armed services is about, what it *means* . . . it was doing my bloody nut in.'

'Shoe. Listen to me. I'm serious about the hair. You have to let it go. You're a civilian now; that *Utrinque Paratus* stuff, it's over. It's like school: nice to remember back, but when you're done, you've got to walk out those gates. Walk away, with your honour and your memories. What I'm here to discuss is not rejoining the army on the sly. But it's also not flipping burgers and sexing baby chickens either. It's a decent cause, using what you know and what you've been trained to achieve, so that your mates and my mates and hundreds of people we've never met can get the deal they deserve . . . OK?'

Piglet. Corporal, D Coy., 2 Para: Tristie had looked up from the file, a little bewildered. 'So your father sued the MoD . . . '

'Well, it was my sister actually. She's the lawyer. My family is quite tight like that. But Dad was determined to hammer them. Said that was the only way to teach a big organisation to change, though it pretty much brought the curtain down on my time with the Paras.'

Piglet's file showed that a couple of months after getting his wings in 2000 he'd been part of a contingent scrambled to Sierra Leone to protect a United Nations contingent. Operation Palliser. As the Hercules droned across the steaming West African jungle, they'd passed out the anti-malaria tablets. But there were not enough. And the MoD had supplied a less effective brand instead of Mefloquine. Over a hundred Paras would catch malaria, cursing them with recurring bouts of fever, vomiting, joint pain and worse.

'My father, you see, comes from a very wealthy family. Serious Jewish money. He was always uncomfortable that I joined up, had his own plans for me. In the end he took a bit of quiet pride in what I was doing, until, that is, I got the malaria. He got really ugly about that. Just found it outrageous that a set-up like the Ministry of Defence would do such a thing. Putting us in harm's way is what we get paid for. But without basic medicines? I mean, who would do something like that? In the event it turned out to be nothing more than a dry run for everything that happened in Iraq and Afghanistan . . . '

Chiswick roundabout
Junction of M4/A4 and Chiswick High Road

It's all about the timing. Always the timing.

Piglet powers the Honda sports cruiser bike in and out of traffic on the old Great West Road, trying to make sure they keep close to the black cab. The road ahead seems awash with black cabs all nose to tail, heading into London with the long-distance, early morning Heathrow arrivals. Ferret cinches his thighs together. Clutching tight on to the rear seat using desperate muscles he's never put into service before. He needs both hands to thumb a text message.

On the left, about twenty yards ahead, is the off-ramp that leads down to the Chiswick roundabout. When the cab leaves this round-about, Tristie Merritt on the other side of the river gets her second text message. Only two markers after that . . . the Kew Bridge railway station on the right and a thousand yards later, when they come off the bridge itself on to the south bank of the Thames, by the top of the Green.

Ahead the lights are red and traffic is backed up from the roundabout. Piglet nudges the bike up to the rear of the stationary cab. Discreetly. Dougal MacIntyre is the poor guy's name. Ferret feels the slightest wince of pity for what is about to happen. The trouble they are about to cause. Then easily dismisses it.

The senior official from the Ministry of Defence has his head laid out on the back headrest, his thick grey hair dishevelled and clearly visible through the rear window. Zonked out. Just to his right is the redhead. Dalia. One of Tristie Merritt's mysterious friends summoned up from her shuttered past. The redhead is curled in towards MacIntyre. Not quite à deux but with a slender inch of air between them. A promise of good things to come.

Beyond the name Dalia, Ferret has no idea who the redhead is. Never saw her paperwork. Tristie's assignment for him was simply to contact, shadow and facilitate. So. They had met at Washington's Dulles International the previous evening, in a Starbucks on the other side of the airport to the Virgin Atlantic check-in. He'd been reading a copy of *Exchange & Mart* and she swept up to his table, dousing him in Chanel No. 5. He could feel the stares from males and females alike. She was strikingly beautiful in a lush, accessible sort of way.

An easy, transatlantic sort of accent. 'You must be Ferret.'

He nodded mutely. The woman had him off balance already.

'My friend, the lady captain, tells me Ferret is short for Womb Ferret.' Her hair was auburn, mid-length, and her dark eyes heavy with mascara and bronze eyeshadow. 'Fancy yourself as the Womb Ferret, do you?' Just like the captain, Dalia was absolutely no pissing around.

'W-why don't you sit down?' Ferret stuttered. Then, 'Can I get you something?'

'Doesn't the Womb Ferret even stand up for a lady?'

Ferret clambered quickly to his feet. Couldn't help but stare at the shape of her body busting through her creamy silk blouse. 'Thank you,' she breathed, crossing her legs so provocatively half of Starbucks had fallen sideways out of their chairs. 'Now tell me what makes the Womb Ferret such an expert on women . . . '

That was how she was. All business. Ferret didn't even have a chance to muss up his hair and get his puppy eyes working. Dalia was full on. Just as Tristie had said she would be: 'Think of her as a fire-and-forget missile. Don't walk her to the target. Just give her all this information . . . and let her get on with it.' And the captain passed over the surveillance photos and the dozen pages of background she'd been able to trick up from her contacts in the Adjutant General's Corp. The subject? A Scot. MacIntyre. Forty-seven. Two divorces. A weakness foretold in his habit of trying to expense-claim on hotel bills unnamed pay-per-view purchases and massage treatments.

Ferret had then watched from a distance after they had boarded the flight. MacIntyre had made a solemn, rather pompous introduction while Dalia was at the bar at the back of Virgin's upper class. He came on like a real prig. For a second Ferret had wondered whether this whole scene would work, but then Dalia took over, playing the man the whole nine hours they were airborne. Not more than a kiss passed between them — as far as he could tell — but she had him all the same.

Ferret had trained on both the Starburst and Starstreak surface-to-air missiles and the fire-and-forget analogy was a good one. That was just how Dalia operated. Tiny adjustments to her onboard gyroscope, tweaks to her accelerometer: little bit faster, then easing off. First in complimenting this rather lugubrious character by choosing him over the other men at the bar. Then laughing easily, throwing her head back, running her fingers through her luxuriant hair, a quiet whisper in his ear followed by a throaty laugh, running her hand softly over his cuff. All the time tuning that gyroscope and accelerometer, all the time squeezing off the space between them. Eventually — as the flight map showed the 747 crossing the west coast of Ireland — moving to sit at his feet on the little ottoman, all the better to stoke the slow sizzle of seduction.

Men. Such idiots. The guy looked absolutely toast this morning as he stumbled off the plane, Ferret trailing some distance behind. Just like a guy who'd been fed single malt whisky for nine hours; a hard-on for this out-of-the-world woman giving him no hope of sleep. At the luggage carousel, for just a moment, Dalia had eased off MacIntyre's arm and with a barely perceptible flick of the wrist pointed out the object of the exercise; the case Captain Merritt

71

was after. Ferret had texted an appropriate description.

As Piglet powers the Honda down the off-ramp, Ferret wonders. Perhaps there's a factory somewhere that churns out women like this Dalia and Tristie Merritt . . . and his mind trips to the hybrid human-alien *SIL*. The Natasha Henstridge character in *Species*: a big shag-fantasy in 3 Para during his time. A babe fashioned by splicing human DNA with that of an extraterrestrial. As one of the scientists reflects wistfully, after *SIL*'s murderous sexual rampage across Los Angeles, 'We decided to make it female so it would be more docile and controllable.'

Yeah, right, Ferret thinks, the widest smile under his helmet. His cheeks dimpling as he laughs. Like this female was ever going to be docile and controllable.

Certainly the man from the ministry, Dougal MacIntyre, has no idea what is about to happen . . .

★ ★ ★

The redhead eases herself closer to MacIntyre as the cab runs along Forest Road. To her immediate right is the overground District line and beyond that the modern-brick and glass wingspans of the new National Archives, the Public Record Office.

'Dougal. Wake up.' She nudges him. 'I think this is your place.' The cabbie eyes them knowingly in his rear-view mirror, before

72

swinging left into Bushwood Road, a long line of three-storey, red-brick Victorian houses on either side. Halfway down to the left is the rear end of a refuse collection vehicle — the front end poking through into Priory Road, which runs parallel with Bushwood. Workmen are across the street tugging green wheelie bins backwards and forwards.

The cab slows, the driver craning left and right to find number 79. MacIntyre makes a long, low groaning sound. His eyes blink, close, and then open sharply as he inhales the redhead's presence. 'Hello, again.' He straightens himself up. Leers intently.

Seventy-nine is on the left-hand side, just beyond the rump of the rubbish van. A half-dozen yellow warning lights are rotating at the back end and there's a constant and awful screech of garbage being compacted by huge hydraulic crushers. The taxi eases up, double-parking next to two family saloons.

The redhead plays with the lapels of his grey herringbone suit with her gloved hands. 'You must call me tonight, won't you?' She looks him in the eyes. 'Just like you promised.'

To the untrained observer, what happens next would appear fast, furious and apparently unconnected.

The cabby steps out, moves to the front passenger door. Offloads on to the kerb two extra-large Italian leather wheeled holdalls, MacIntyre's checked luggage . . . The rubbish-bin men weave in and around the taxi, whistling, joshing loudly . . . Inside the cab the man from the MoD holds the white calfskin glove of one of the redhead's hands, all lecherous intent . . . The cabby stands by the open rear door. Clears his throat noisily. Wanting this lovebird stuff to be over with . . . behind him, one of the wheelie-bin men guffaws loudly. About Spurs. *Bunch of tossers!* . . . MacIntyre twinkles his eyes into Dalia's. 'I am going to give you such a seeing-to tonight.' The redhead smiles; a long, sexy, try-your-best sort of a smile. 'Of course you will,' she exhales . . . And MacIntyre turns, humps on to the roadside the two aluminium briefcases, his hand-carry luggage, one slightly smaller than the other . . . then crouches his way out of the taxi. Stands with his feet astride his two briefcases . . . More loud japing from a different wheelie-bin man about Arsenal. *All of them, bloody poofs, need a good kicking* . . . MacIntyre passes two twenties and a ten, asks for a receipt from the driver, who returns to his seat, starts scribbling . . . Dalia turns it on one last time. 'Aren't you going to give a girl one last kiss?' and beckons him back inside . . . he reaches out blindly for the receipt with his left hand, half-fits himself back into the cab . . . and gets a long awkward embrace, which ends with a lingering kiss and a breathy promise that would give Elton John the shivers. 'Tonight, my darling . . . be ready.' There's a discreet *phhisshh* of airbrakes being released, as the refuse collection vehicle eases away, job done . . . MacIntyre blows a kiss on the end of a finger, before reversing his way back on to the road. He shuts the door carefully, watches the London cab move off and quickly accelerate to the end of the street. Dalia looks back, beaming at him. He waves. Amazement and gratitude written on his face. Brake lights, pause, then the cab turns left, disappears from view.

Quiet and calm returns. All is as it should be on pretty Bushwood Road.

And then a long, loud howl pierces the dignified quiet of this London suburb. As if a too-thick needle was being pushed through the tip of someone's nose. The MoD's Deputy Chief of Defence Material (directly controlling an operating budget of £16 billion per year and assets of £76 billion) bends down to gather up his luggage. Notices he has three bags instead of four. And the one that's missing . . .

★   ★   ★

It is just after midday when an exasperated MacIntyre finally tracks down Professor Sir Roddy Kerr, the MoD's chief scientific adviser. As would be expected, the old man has a particularly dusty and vacant voice, bordering on contemptuous. Recently Sir Roddy had been char-grilled by the defence select committee, wanting to know why five hundred computers and laptops had gone missing from the MoD over a five-year period. His only defence had been an embarrassed ramble about the difference between missing-misplaced and missing-stolen. The MoD comprises more than four thousand sites, almost fifty thousand separate buildings on a quarter-million hectares of land.

With an estate that large we must be allowed to lose a few things every so often.

Kerr's voice sounds suitably irked. 'So long as your computer is encrypted, I don't think you'll have much of a problem.'

MacIntyre grips the phone so hard he thinks he might end up crushing it. 'But *is* my laptop encrypted?'

In the background, he hears the tap-tapping of a keyboard. Pause. Then a *hmmmm* sort of sound as a list is slowly reviewed. MacIntyre is halfway up the wall with worry . . . 'The serial number I have for your laptop . . . yes, it has the usual encryption features on it.' The scientist explains the technicalities: the MoD uses a tailored version of an open-source encryption program to make-safe the dynamic random access memory, or DRAM chip. 'I hope you didn't leave it in sleep mode . . . ' But MacIntyre isn't even listening now.

Knowing his laptop is encrypted means losing it represents only the slightest stain on his administrative record. A trifling matter. Which is just as well. MacIntyre knows better than most the MoD are not frightened of making an arbitrary example of someone. The tethered-goat principle. He'd seen it before . . . he'd even happily set people up himself. Watched from a distance as the media pecked away till not even bones were left. As far as he is concerned, it was the easiest way to teach a sharp lesson to a large organisation. Memories of a wooded glade in Oxfordshire . . . a bloodstained penknife . . . and the ignominious end to the storied career of an

76

MoD analyst called David Kelly.

Thank Christ for encryption, he thinks, sinking back into his couch. His pulse returning to something like normal.

Nine hours on the single malt has papered his mouth with what feels like cheap wall-to-wall carpet. So he rumbles off into his kitchen to find a glass, pours a generous measure of Laphroaig. Hair of the dog. Fishes out the boarding pass from his shirt pocket. Oh, happy day. Dalia's mobile number is written in red. With a big love heart, and a cartoonish drawing of a kiss. The number looks . . . familiar. Vaguely. Perhaps she'd read it out to him on the plane . . . last night, this morning, it's all a bit of a blur. MacIntyre can't wait to mess up her pretty little face.

He looks at the dialled number one more time, comparing it to the boarding pass, and presses the green button. A sequence of letters springs on to the Nokia's screen. FSLCNS. A sign he's calling a number already in his memory.

Strange.

He rubs his eyes, looks again . . . FSLCNS. That doesn't make sense but his brain is so bloody gummed up. Working awfully slow. He checks the boarding pass again.

'Hello? . . . Hello? . . . ' A tinny voice intrudes on his confusion. 'Dougal, is that you?'

In a heartbeat, a shaft of memory opens in his mind, shimmering through the fog of whisky. Himself, opening up his computer while they were snuggling on that Virgin flight. Himself, taking a picture of the two of them together with his little in-computer lens. She had nibbled his ear, tugged on his ear, nuzzled against his ear. The two of them giggling as the rest of the cabin slept . . . her body pressing into his . . . and then her fingers lightly rising up his thigh. So delicate, yet so totally suggestive.

So distracting too . . . which is why Professor Sir Roddy Kerr's one simple query, '*I hope you didn't leave it in sleep mode . . .*', he can't truthfully answer. That particular memory is sealed in the foggy mess of last night's lust.

'Hello? Dougal?'

And MacIntyre's whole body groans as he puts the mobile phone to his ear. And prepares to explain himself to FSLCNS. The First Sea Lord and Chief of Naval Staff. How the hell did Dalia get *that* number? Who is she? More importantly, who is she working for?

He must hold nothing back. Dalia. The computer. The schematics of the software that the Pentagon had finally coughed up.

He knows he has to own up to every last thing. Purge every last piece of information from his memory. Then throw himself on their mercy. With just the thinnest thread of hope that the magic of encryption might still save him . . .

★ ★ ★

That morning, by the time Dougal MacIntyre had snivelled the first lines of his *mea culpa*, three other things had already taken place.

First. A brief, anonymous call from a brand

78

new pre-pay mobile phone alerts emergency services to a break-in at one of the depots handling refuse collection within the Borough of Richmond (this was Weasel putting on his best Essex-boy accent). A police car attends, finds five men in arm and leg restraints, lying on the main garage floor but in no great state of distress. Quite comfortable, all things considered. Their heads are resting on little airline pillows. And each man has a 250ml Ribena carton in front of him with the little straw already punched through. Nice touch. None of the men offers any significant clues. Their masked attackers seemed well drilled and professional. Two of them were carrying handguns, which, from descriptions, sound like a pair of 9mm Browning Hi-powers. Common enough. Aside from the guns, the threat of violence was implied but definitely not used. All communication was through a series of flip charts on which their orders were pre-written. *Who Has The Truck Keys?* No sense of panic or tension. *You Won't Be Tied Up For More Than Two Hours.* Disciplined.

Of course, the use of handguns kicks the whole thing up a level, and, as a scene of crime is formally set up, the first-responding police officers are tasked to secure CCTV coverage. Neither of them is surprised — given how meticulous things had been so far — to discover the depot's five static and two dome cameras have been disabled. As had, late last night, the two borough cameras that covered the approach roads to the depot. These guys are good, the older policemen had acknowledged, almost approvingly.

The rubbish truck itself would be discovered almost a day later. Parked on the ground floor of a deserted factory in the Dagenham dockside, on the other side of London. Because the site is to be demolished within the next twenty-four hours — the explosive charges are being fitted as the police arrive — all local CCTV cameras had been removed.

Second. A large brown envelope is dropped into a postbox on London's Oxford Street. First-class stamp. Untraceable, and completely shorn of any forensics. Marked for the attention of the First Sea Lord and Chief of the Naval Staff at the Ministry of Defence offices in Whitehall. *Re: Dougal MacIntyre's Laptop* is stencilled in small letters on the top left corner of the envelope. The letter inside spells out a demand for the payment of £315 million over three years (equivalent to less than one per cent of the annual defence materiel budget, it points out). In return, the laptop.

The content and layout of the letter are striking. Those who first read it at the MoD are chilled by the intercutting of the demands with passages from something called (rather blandly) *Army Doctrine Publication Volume Five*. Basically the armed forces' bible. They quickly realise they have a problem on their hands . . .

Military Covenant: Soldiers will be called upon to make personal sacrifices — includ- ing the ultimate sacrifice — in the service of

80

the Nation. In return, British soldiers must always be able to expect fair treatment, to be valued and respected as individuals, and that they (and their families) will be sustained and rewarded by commensurate terms and conditions of service . . .

Then the letter goes on to say . . .
'£157,500,000, being half of the money required, to be divided as follows: 50 per cent to Help For Heroes, the balance equally between three organisations. The Soldiers Sailors and Air Force Families Forces Help, the Army Families Federation and Women's Royal Volunteers Services.

' . . . Of all the forces that influence the battle spirit of the soldier, his morale is the most important. Morale is a state of mind. It is that intangible force which moves men to endurance and courage in the face of hardship, fatigue and danger. It makes each individual in a group, without counting the cost to himself, give his last ounce to achieve the common purpose.

'The remaining half, £157,500,000, to be divided equally between the following eleven organisations: The Royal British Legion, Seafarers UK, the Army Benevolent Fund, the Royal Air Force Benevolent Fund, the Royal Naval Association, British Limbless Ex-Service Men's Association, Ex-Services Mental Welfare Society, Royal Air Forces Association, Forces' Pension

Society, War Widows' Association of Great Britain and Veterans Scotland.

' . . . Soldiers accept an open-ended commitment to serve whenever and wherever they are needed, whatever the difficulties or dangers may be. Ultimately it may require soldiers to lay down their lives. Implicitly it requires those in positions of authority to discharge in full their responsibilities and their duty of care to subordinates . . .

'Each organisation's fixed sum shall be split into three equal payments: the first to be paid on the first working day of next month, and then two remaining payments in twelve and twenty-four months' time. Payments shall not be recouped by deductions against any other existing commitments to soldier welfare programmes, and cannot be set off against extant financial or material support for any of these groups.

' . . . 'Courage, you know, is like having money in the bank. We start with a certain capital of courage, some large, some small, and we proceed to draw on our balance, for don't forget courage is an expendable quality. We can use it up. If there are heavy, if there are continuous calls on our courage, we begin to overdraw. If we go on overdrawing we go bankrupt we break down' — Field Marshall Sir William Slim . . .

'This financial arrangement, this new-found support for these organisations and charities, shall be announced to the House of Commons by the Secretary of State for Defence no later than a fortnight from today. It can be dressed up in whatever manner is most expedient. But it must be an irrevocable commitment to provide new funding to the amount of £315 million from the Treasury's Urgent Spending Budget.

' . . . Soldiers universally concede the general truth of Napoleon's much-quoted dictum that in war 'the morale is to the physical as three is to one'. The actual arithmetical proportion may be worthless, for morale is apt to decline if the weapons are inadequate, and the strongest will is of little use if it is inside a dead body. But although the morale and physical factors are inseparable and indivisible, the saying gains its enduring value because it expresses the idea of the predominance of morale factors in all military decisions . . .

'Three days from now you will receive proof that the TrueCrypt encryption has been broken. Be ready.
'Signed. Ward 13.'

* * *

A woman steps out of a black London taxi and enters a hair salon just off the Euston Road. She enters with long auburn hair and leaves just

83

under ninety minutes later with it very sleek, a wet look, short and black. On leaving, Dalia first walks to nearby Russell Square. Stops to cross herself in front of the small memorial to the victims of the bus bomb on 7 July. Then she turns back on herself, sets off, secure in her new disguise, strides getting longer and longer, to St Pancras and the next train to Brussels. And onwards.

Dalia settles back in her first-class seat and watches absent-mindedly as the urban sprawl of north London silently whizzes by. The champagne helps unwind the tension within. She closes her eyes and, not for the first time, contemplates the magnitude of the debt she is trying to repay.

As the sunlight ripples across her closed eyes, filling her mind with bursts of reds and yellows, her thoughts ease back to a different time. Full of darkness and fear. Before she was Dalia, when her young, scared life had been saved by Tristie Merritt . . .

★   ★   ★

'Wake up.' She hears the words. But the tone and voice miss her altogether. Her mind is screwed. The previous night she'd stolen three Valium and four Co-codamols, Hoping it might be enough to ease her away. Take her out of this place for good.

So in her drugged-up fugue, she assumes what she hears is the sound of Enoch Potts come to take his revenge. Come to sit on her bed. His cold hands and fetid breath. Come to dig the sharp end of one of his keys into the small of her neck until she relaxes, takes her hands off her chest, opens her legs and receives him as if he were her lover. The sweaty, matted hair on his back and shoulders . . . There is a reason she is alone in this special observation dormitory. No one can hear her. Slowly she opens her eyes.

'Wake up.'

Screw you, she decides. I won't wake up.

She turns over and buries her face into the pillow. Do what you want. Hurt me. Kill me. Just make it finish. Let it be over. At least the drugs mean she is close to oblivious to what is about to happen. Among the girls, there's been talk of chair legs and crowbars. Of bleeding that just won't stop.

'It's Tristie . . . will you please bloody wake up. And get dressed.'

She is someone flat out of hope. She can't bring herself to look towards the voice. Too frightened that she'll be let down again. Tristie is three years older, which is like for ever in this demented world. She's also on the outside now. They all know her story . . . from the Holyhead train station, into care in Gwynedd, a succession of foster homes, then back into care. The ugliest stories.

'I heard what happened,' she whispers, moving close to her face so she can see her by the pale moonlight in the bleak, wood-panelled room. She sees her smile at her. Her honest open face. Brilliant smile. Offering comfort.

She takes Tristie's hand and she leads her

noiselessly through the long passageways. She is sure part of her knows where they are going . . . but she is conscious only of her body being just a jumble of bones, tugged along. Following Tristie.

Enoch Potts looks shocked to see them. His mouth forms a perfect O shape, the size of an apple. The light beaming off his shiny head and crimson cheeks. He throws at them a huge pot of Vaseline that he'd been holding as they burst in. That seems to really irritate Tristie. She stalks across the room and backhands him so hard he tumbles over a futon. Goes down in a splay of dressing gown and pyjamas.

Ten minutes later and Potts has finished writing his confession. On several sheets of A4. Handwriting a little jerky, but clear enough. What he can remember of the dozens of faceless little souls he had interfered with. The Freemasons. The police. The whole sickness.

She remembers the long and broad, blue industrial flame from Tristie's butane torch, how she would let it play over what hair remained on Potts's head. So he could feel the heat and smell the crisping of his scalp. And boy, did it help him write . . .

Now all they have to do is end it. They're both wearing surgical gloves and it had taken for ever for her to focus enough on the ends of her fingers. 'Your choice,' Tristie had said to her. 'But my advice, we have to finish this. We tried doing the right thing . . . but the right thing obviously wasn't right enough.'

Her head is still feeling all messed up. She sees

Enoch Potts in front of her. Hanging upside down. His eyes pleading with her, his mouth firmly taped up. Little dark scorch marks up the side of his head, the neck and shoulders sagging on the floor, hands tied off behind his back. His face turning nicely purple as the blood flows downwards. Potts is hanging upside down underneath a long gym bench that they've placed over a desk in his head-of-care, deputy warden study. His feet wiggling furiously, but the duct tape still holding tight.

She takes the long hunting knife from Tristie and suddenly it's very clear what she has to do. And it gives her a thrill to know just how long Potts will be in pain; gravity and the flow of blood will see to that. Even more of a thrill to know that when the police come the next day, no doubt they'll want to drug-test her. Then they'll realise she would never have the wit to do what she's doing now . . .

The day after the heist
— Operation Macchar,
minus twelve days

Outside the village of Elton
Derbyshire Peak District

Whiffler, Button and Tristie are in the low-ceilinged kitchen of a little seventeenth-century gritstone farmhouse that was rented with the first slab of cash they 'earned'. Ward 13's first income. A white Rayburn keeps the place snug. Twenty-three acres of grassland and larch wood separate the house from the nearest minor road to the south; immediately to the north, east and west, is the uninviting craggy upthrust of Cratcliffe Tor. Feels very cut off, therefore secure. 'Decent OPSEC,' Shoe had grunted after walking the perimeter.

Ferret, Piglet, Shoe and the Weasel had left this morning for RAF Lyneham to meet an incoming plane carrying the body of a sergeant major with 3 Para. A legend among legends, apparently. A random mortar dropping out of the sky into a mess tent in one of the rear camps in Afghanistan. Another almost unnoticed death; yet another huge hole opening up in a handful of lives.

There had been an unreal tension in the air

this morning as the boys thought this through. Readying their medals, shining up their shoes, ironing the creases from their lumpy Civvy Street suits. This was a sort of displacement activity as the thought rumbled through their collective consciousness: was it better to die than live some kind of twilight, caged existence?

Yes. Better to be out of everybody's hair in one clean hit, better than pulling down your loved ones with injuries and anger, and that eternal sense that the best of your life was behind you. Out of the army, there would be little to show but a nothing deal from the MoD. And if that didn't permanently screw you up, then reading the newspapers certainly would, being full of £120,000-a-week-Wayne-Rooney this, and £135,000-a-week-Frank-Lampard that.

Tristie never had the benefit of much loyalty in her childhood. Who was her father? Where was Mother? She could never have imagined in a thousand years finding happiness in a structure as regimented as the British Army. So, not surprisingly, she had wanted to add to the MoD letter a coda from the army regulations that specifically addressed the importance of loyalty. She had felt this intensely when, for the first time as an officer and (most unusually) as a woman, she had been asked to lead men trained in the use of lethal force, and she saw them placing their faith in her, looking to her for answers:

Loyalty ties the leader and the led with mutual respect and trust. It goes both up and down. It transforms individuals into teams. It creates and nourishes the formations, units and sub-units of which the Army is composed . . . Those who are placed in positions of authority must be loyal to their subordinates, representing their interests faithfully, dealing with complaints thoroughly, and developing their abilities through progressive training.

It reminds Tristie of the first time, lump in throat, she had seen the Remembrance Day march-past at the Cenotaph. The second Sunday of November, and suddenly sliding down her cheeks were tears of pride and sadness. How emotional it was to see such collective pride, the belonging, created and nourished by loyalty flowing up and down the ranks, yet at the same time to realise such incredible loss and sacrifice. People willing to give their lives to protect her. *Her?* She wanted that belonging. And a small seed was sown . . .

That's why she gets on with these people. Button, Piglet et al. Her sort of people. All with problems and dramas of one degree or another in their lives. Yet, for all that, for all of their shortcomings, following a simple and predictable code. These are people who run *towards* danger. Not away from it.

Sure. You make adjustments to your expectations. Army conversation about the wider world can be limited. Reading matter is more pictures than words, and in terms of cuisine British Army Meals-Ready-To-Eat beat any other store-bought food combination.

But these are people who won't let you down.

The question Whiffler had for Tristie was this: 'Imagine you're a female Jack Bauer. You've got sixty seconds, and you have to pick one man to screw, or the world's going to explode. Who would you pick?'

'Am I giving or receiving of this joyous gift?'

Typical. In her experience, Paras in particular, but non-coms in general, have three lines of conversation: shagging, drinking and fighting. And then shagging again. Working in the Det — where their primary mission was deep, covert surveillance — Tristie had lost track of the number of times she was buttoned down in watch posts, stake-outs and hides, unable to move. Trapped in earnest, whispered discussions. Celebrities You Fancy But Shouldn't. Ugliest Munters Slept With. Worst Accidents Involving Own Testicles.

Whiffler's freckled face frowns and he quickly runs a hand through his spiked gingery hair. 'Receiving . . . ' He leans on the other side of the marble-top eating area, holding on to one of the heavy beams, like an orang-utan.

'And how long am I staring up at the ceiling for?'

Whiffler grins. 'That's all in the choice. If you choose me, for instance . . . ' And Button hoots with laughter at this. 'Just for argument's sake, of course. I'd be hammering away for hours and hours.'

'Would you now?' Tristie sounds a bit distracted, because she is. Multitasking. 'All of this hammering away, sounds to me more like a

91

punishment.' While she's having this conversation she's actually trying to concentrate (her hair under a surgeon's cap and a gauze face mask on). The man from the ministry's laptop is open, with all but one of the screws holding the keyboard together now undone. The laptop is plugged in, still in sleep mode, and the hardware buried within still feels warm to the touch.

'So . . . who is it going to be? To save the world?'

She looks into Whiffler's eyes and gets a very strong sense he'd like nothing more than to hear his own name. As if. Button is watching too, munching slowly on an unbuttered slice of white bread. Intrigued. 'First, can I say officers do not normally enter into discussions like this . . . '

'Yeah . . . that's right, Whiffler.' Button's voice from by the kitchen window carries an irrepressible giggle in it. 'They're too busy thinking about their fish knives, and whether it goes to the left or right of the butter knife . . . '

'Thank you, Button,' she says, getting rid of the last screw and lifting off the fascia of the laptop. 'An officer's life is full of responsibilities. Cutlery settings being just one.'

'So . . . ?'

Tristie looks inside the laptop, comparing what she sees with a manual to one side. Looking for the DRAM chip. 'Stephen Hawking would be my answer. If I had to save the world, that is.'

Button and Whiffler's response chimes in stereo. 'Who?'

'That physicist guy. The bloke in the

wheelchair, with the voice synthesiser.'

Button grasps the obvious detail first. 'But he's bloody well paralysed. His pecker probably doesn't work. Can't get out of his chair.'

Tristie taps her nose. 'And that's why I'm the officer, Button . . . and don't even think for a second I want to know who you chose. I can feel my butt cheeks puckering up just thinking about the horror of it.'

A paratrooper's way of fixing things is simple. If you can't hammer it back into service then it's seriously screwed. Broken beyond repair. Not the best way to get into Dougal MacIntyre's laptop. Instead Tristie is trying a solution courtesy of some wacky graduate students at Princeton, who made a startling low-tech discovery about a high-tech design flaw.

With Whiffler and Button clustered near her, she looks through a magnifying lens that makes her iris the size of a grapefruit. Needless to say that's what fascinates Whiffler and Button. 'Pass me that can of furniture spray.'

A couple of long squirts of Pledge on to the underside of the DRAM chip and its temperature has dropped to about minus fifty degrees Celsius.

The chip is where the software architecture dumps all of the computer's most recently used data. This would include any keystrokes used to unlock an encryption program. Like the MoD's system. The DRAM chip holds that data fresh in its system until power is switched off. Then the chip is programmed to close down, in the process purging itself of any sensitive data. That purge takes a couple of seconds to complete.

Only, MacIntyre's laptop was not switched off. So no purge.

'We use the Pledge to freeze the chip. Freezing the chip means it saves everything on its system, while we . . . ' and here she takes a deep breath ' . . . remove said chip from this laptop and place it . . . in another.' There's a reassuring click as the DRAM chip fits into place. No sirens or flashing lights and she can start screwing the rest of the fascia back into place.

'As easy as that,' mumbles Whiffler.

The DRAM chip is now in a near-identical, already booted-up laptop. A USB plugged into its side gives her the capability of copying what's on the chip, through a simple memory-imaging tool. She starts the program running.

It takes another twenty minutes. A lot of fine-tuning to correct obvious errors in the recovered memory, lines of obvious garbage text, for instance. Whiffler and Button watch with rapt fascination. Finally Tristie is ready to reconstruct the keys the MoD had used for encrypting the plans that the Pentagon had entrusted to them.

High-fives all around.

Not wanting to gloat — not too much anyway — they decide to print off only three pages. Randomly selected from the supposedly secure files within MacIntyre's hard drive. Some nice stuff laying out the technicalities of how the Trident's Mark 4A arming, fusing and firing software can be reprogrammed while the nuclear missile is in flight. The sort of knowledge that would make the whole programme redundant, and — as Whiffler observed approvingly — 'blow a hundredweight of conkers out the arse of the MoD'.

'This really is *it*,' says Button, grasping the significance of the moment, as he carefully places the pages inside the envelope. 'We're going past the point of no return.'

And he speaks the truth. By posting it off, with proof they've hacked into the country's only active nuclear weapons programme, Ward 13 is entering a whole new world of trouble. Not like anything any of them have ever faced before . . .

Three days after the heist
— Operation Macchar,
minus ten days

The Pepys Suite
Fifth floor, Ministry of Defence HQ

Whitehall
The threatening grey sky hanging over
London perfectly matches the mood of this
opulent room. Seven men are seated around a
long mahogany table. In varying degrees of
distress. And one robust, middle-aged woman
with a tight silver perm stands at the window,
listening to the angry exchanges behind her:
Outrage! Treason! She's quite enjoying herself
actually, in a prickly sort of way, as she looks
down at the River Thames from the Embankment side of this impressive Portland stone
edifice.

After long study, she is sure she prefers the
view from her own corner office of M15's
Thames House building farther upstream, by
Lambeth Bridge.

Her name is Sheila Davane (known to one and
all, behind her back, as Noppy — as in *No Oil
Painting*). She looks like a comfortable granny:
sensible country tweed suit, large bifocals on a

long gold chain, and an elaborate brooch. In truth, she is anything but.

Among her peculiarities is everything that an unbendingly Protestant upbringing in the County Antrim farming community of Carrick-fergus could give her. For instance, she must be one of the very few who thinks *papacy* when she hears the word *Whitehall*. It's a simple reflex action bred of severe, suspicious parents and a watchful childhood. It was, after all, from Cardinal Wolsey's extravagant new palace, built in its white ashlar stone, that Whitehall got its name.

She places her thick hands on the cold of the window. Then turns to face the room. Five of the seven men are senior soldiers of one description or another but none is in uniform. The Chief and Vice-Chief of the Defence Staff, who look glum, heavy jowelled but, in this matter, basically impotent. The First Sea Lord, called Craddock, who is handing out most of the outrage and reminds Davane of a boiling kettle screaming for attention. The chief scientific adviser, Sir Roddy Kerr, very bored. The chief of Defence Materiel, deeply embarrassed, and his number two, the hapless and about-to-be sacrificed Dougal MacIntyre.

The seventh man in the room is Bill Grainger. The deputy director-general of MI5. Nominally her boss — but in practice, and especially when there's a scare on, more of an equal. He is bookish and cerebral by inclination, a fine frontman for parliamentary committees and collegiate dinners. If he is the shine and polish, then she is the steely, cutting edge of the M15 blade. A person of instinct and action. Yet unobtrusive. Someone best suited to the shadows.

Davane puts her hand up and, strangely enough, within seconds the room is quietened. The meeting grateful for somebody to show leadership.

She moves stiffly towards the table, grips the back of one of the chairs. 'Forgive me . . . but what will it mean if these three pages are in the public domain?'

'Bloody disaster, that's what; what?' says the throaty, cigarette voice of the Vice-Chief of the Defence Staff. An air chief marshal.

Her urbane colleague from MI5, Grainger, steals the moment. He speaks mechanically, like a lawyer, from a sheaf of notes. 'Sheila, I think we can summarise the information as follows:

'Each new prime minister writes a personal letter to the commanders of the four Vanguard submarines that carry Trident. The letter is basically advice from the PM to each commander about what to do in the event of a nuclear incident that takes out the command-and-control functions of the UK government . . . ' Grainger clears his throat for an irksome detail. ' . . . which would have to be a massive, end-of-the-world sort of attack.

'Only the PM, and verifiable authorisation from the PM, can launch a Trident missile. Except, of course, in an end-of-the-world scenario. If this happened, the submarine commander could elect to put himself under the command of another force, the Americans, for instance, or he could attack on his own initiative. Either way the commander and his senior weapons officer would select a pre-designated target and, on his sole authority, the missile could be independently fired . . . '

'I've got all of that, thank you.' Davane sways against the back of the chair. Slightly irritated. 'What I need to understand is the significance of *these* three pages.'

Craddock, the First Sea Lord, taps an impatient finger on the lustrous mahogany surface. 'These three pages explain the fail-safe system that would allow us, or anyone with the knowledge, to neutralise an independently fired Trident . . . '

'So anybody with this knowledge could . . . could bring the Trident down?'

Craddock again. 'Not exactly bring it down.' His finger beating faster and faster. 'The fail-safe is designed for a scenario where we've been bombed to hell. Therefore all of our high-price technical communication stuff is finished. Anything with a chip in it. Burnt. Exploded. Irradiated. Whatever. The same would apply to navigation, which is normally by Global Positioning System, or variants thereof. All gone.' And, to underline the point, he swishes his hands vigorously. 'In that scenario, on board a Trident is a software system that maps out the stars. The sun, the Pole Star, Spica, for instance. Just like sailors, using the stars to navigate.'

'I get all of this . . . I do . . . '

'These three pages tell you how to activate the

fail-safe. How to override the submarine commander's instructions. How to talk to Trident after it's been launched. It's very low-tech because we're assuming that a massive nuclear attack will not leave us much to communicate with. So, it's a simple radio signal basically. But the consequence is just as final . . . '

These people could *really* beat about the bush. 'And what is that consequence?'

'The fail-safe tells the missile to select the brightest of the stars it can see — and the dear old Trident will just keep progress towards it . . . no atmospheric re-entry. No target acquisition.'

'You mean, keep on going . . . ?'

'Keep on going until it runs out of fuel. Somewhere up there. In outer space. The point is it won't come down. Not here, anyway. Which is what the fail-safe is all about.'

Davane nods carefully. Drums her fingers on the back of the chair. 'The Royal Navy have only got four subs in the Vanguard class, a dozen missiles on each boat, and only one of those is on patrol at any given time. So why not just reprogramme the software? Tweak the system a bit?'

The gloom is so thick and heavy she can almost feel it weighing on her shoulders. Heads and shoulders sink. Eyes look down. The disgraced MacIntyre, so abject his forehead is almost touching the table.

It's Grainger who speaks up. 'We don't actually own the Trident missiles. We have a lease agreement on a certain number of Tridents belonging to the US Navy. Fifty-eight all told, out of a US cache of more than five hundred. But the rocket, the propellant, fuses, the motor sets, guidance system, the overall technology solution, it's all owned by Uncle Sam.' Grainger makes very sarcastic inverted commas with his fingers. ''Our missiles' are actually their missiles, stored for us at a submarine base in Georgia. We can't tweak the software . . . without . . . '

' . . . without telling the Americans,' Davane finishes the sentence. 'And if we tell the Americans, they might just, *what*? Kick us out of the programme.'

Craddock looks around the table, before nodding gravely. 'The principle of deterrence is that your enemy never knows the disposition of the forces he is facing. The what, when, where and how.

'Some of it he can work out, or guess, or war-game. But it's the value of your last card, that continuous at-sea deterrence, that submarine making quiet on the floor of the Atlantic, which makes this whole thing a guessing game. That's why it was termed mutually assured destruction. If you do it to me, then I'll give it back to you, with interest. That's how deterrence has kept the world safe for almost seventy years, and why this government is wagering a billion and a half pounds a year that it will keep us safe for another seventy . . . '

Had Davane really been in a black mood, it would have been at this point that she would have observed that the principle of deterrence

101

had done exactly nothing during the Troubles . . . there were plenty of citizens in Northern Ireland who hadn't felt the least bit protected by Trident.

' . . . but if the enemy knows your last card — even more than that, knows how to neutralise it . . . Then. Really. It's game over. We're just so many little pigs hiding out in our straw house.'

A long, dismal silence fills the elegant conference suite.

Davane is suddenly aware of ghosts. For the men at this table had not just failed themselves. They'd failed all the military leaders who'd preceded them, who'd championed nuclear deterrence in this very room during much more hostile times and who, when finishing their terms, must have felt they were passing the baton on. Entrusting it to the next generation, with stern words. *This is the iron rock on which Britain depends. The very Last Line of Defence.* Not just the weapon itself, but the relationship with the United States, through which is defined Britain's role at the top table. That *special* relationship. Agreed to by no less a president than John F. Kennedy in 1963, for the Polaris programme, and restated by Ronald Reagan in 1982 for Trident II.

The room wore its history well, as if to underline that this was *the* conference suite. Proud traditions shouted from each panel of darkened oak. The Pepys Suite. Named after the diarist, who served Charles II and James II as their Admiralty Clerk. And in one corner of the room, a very serious display cabinet. Locked inside, the Letters Patent: the vellum manuscript with the Queen's Great Seal of the Realm attached, from which derive all the powers and responsibilities of the armed forces. The right to wage war, to be answerable to Parliament and so on. Hand-enscribed parchment like a living page of history.

The ghosts in the room are not happy.

Craddock nervously rattles his teacup. And Davane straightens her back, works her shoulders from side to side. Feels a big smile coming over her face. Gentle chuckle under her breath. It's quite simple really.

'I'm sorry to say, gentlemen . . . ' She sniffs rather regally. 'On this one, I think you're screwed. Good and proper.'

Which is when the shouting starts up again, with cries of *Outrage! Damnable woman!* Nothing she hasn't heard before.

*   *   *

The next turn of events is something of a surprise. Less than half an hour later, emerging from the ladies' on the fifth floor, Davane is accosted by Dougal MacIntyre. Panicked, he takes her by the wrist and leads her along the polished floor of the long corridor to a vacant office. Closes the door behind him, leans back against it. Gasping slightly.

When he turns to her the man's eyes are wired with anxiety. 'They won't tell you the truth.'

'Who won't?'

'Them . . . inside there,' and MacIntyre

103

nudges his shoulder towards the Pepys Suite.

'And you will?'

'Look. I know this doesn't look good for me.' And he turns away, then swings around decisively. 'This Ward 13 . . . it isn't the first time.'

'Why should I believe you?'

'How much *worse* could it be for me? Why would I be lying to you right now? For what earthly reason: a little grease on my noose perhaps?'

Fair point. MacIntyre had already been measured for his MoD coffin. You could almost hear the thing being hammered together. A leak to a friendly journalist on a Sunday paper would do the trick, start the stampede.

So Davane moves in close. Well within MacIntryre's personal space. She looks up at him, and the heavy layers of her neck dangle as she speaks. 'You screw me up here, and I will personally make you suffer pain. Vast pain. Understand?'

Understood, MacIntyre nods gratefully. And he proceeds to tell his tale . . .

★   ★   ★

Earlier that morning Davane's black Jaguar had nosed out of the MI5 basement car park for this meeting at the MoD, and as the first splats of rain hit the windscreen and the powerful wipers started *whup-whupping*, her colleague Bill Grainger had asked a straightforward question.

'I sense you don't have much time for the

104

people we're going to meet.'

She had smiled at him. A grim look, because her teeth, like much else about her, she didn't waste time over. 'You sense correctly.'

'So, is this going to be a problem today?'

'We'll just have to see where the discussions take us.' There was a sparkle in her eyes, and it seemed it was all Grainger could do to stop himself from laughing at the prospect of a roomful of stiff military types coming up against Sheila 'Noppy' Davane.

'I don't suppose you'd care to enlighten me as to the reasons for this . . . animus?'

Which is why they had spent the relatively short drive in discussion. Not something she was planning to do, but Grainger had asked, and he deserved to know. And that brief dialogue had brought those dark, angry shapes into sharper focus in her mind, given clarity to what it is that so claws at her . . .

. . . those typecast men who would be around the table (excepting Grainger, of course). Each one red faced and blustering, and *but-butting* his disapproval.

What steels Davane's backbone is a profound disrespect for what becomes of officers once they're sufficiently senior to come into contact with the Sirens of the Ministry of Defence.

They start out so promisingly. Revved up and full of action. *We'll fix this, change that, think outside the box.* But as inevitable as the slow creep towards autumn and the dark of winter, the civil servants win out, deaden that reforming

105

spirit with the shrewdness of their indecision: overwhelm them with committees, White Papers, consultations, policy reviews and five-year personnel strategies. And before the reforming zealot knows what's hit him, he's been sucked into the system. Suddenly he's not seeing an issue in black and white, but in all those bureaucratic, indecisive shades of grey.

In all of this, Davane's affection for the British soldier is real and visceral. This from someone who has given every last atom of her life to MI5, to the service's motto, *Regnum Defende*. This after being kneecapped in 1975 and tied up to a lamp-post in Catholic West Belfast. For her, the young men of the British Army were the only force strong enough to hold the line. To keep the United Kingdom whole. And good men — 763 in total — had died delivering something like peace . . .

Traffic was always so slow around Parliament Square. Davane had glanced at a newspaper kiosk, a poster with the first edition from the *Evening Standard* boiled down into six easy-to-understand words. *New Govt Shame Over Injured Troops.*

Looking at the queues of people huddling around the kiosk, Davane had spoken quietly. 'If word of this Ward 13 thing gets out, gets into the media, this government will fall.'

Grainger had sounded shocked. 'How do you work that out?'

'Take from the rich, give to the poor, and we're working the wrong side of the street.'

106

Davane drew her initials, SAD, Sheila Anne-Marie Davane, in the condensation.

'I don't see the connection.'

'It's Robin Hood . . . ' In the tiniest corner of the remaining condensation, a fleeting tribute to a distant memory of dreams and wishes as a young girl, Davane marks out the letters MM with her fingernail. ' . . . the greatest story ever told.'

★ ★ ★

The arrival of a working lunch has mellowed conversation in the Pepys Suite. Trays of sandwiches, quiches, vol-au-vents are wheeled in. Flasks of tea and coffee. Gassy or still water.

Craddock, the First Sea Lord, is giving a rather toneless briefing on the Ward 13 investigation to date. The next step is involving the police, in some form or other. That sends shivers through the room. The downside, the admiral murmurs, is the inevitable leak to the media — either from the police themselves or through the process of interviewing suspects. To date, Ward 13 is being handled in-house. Specialists from 34 Section of the Royal Military Police's Special Investigation Branch, based in Hounslow, working alongside a team from the MoD's defence fraud analysis unit . . . Davane isn't really listening. She's intrigued by the Vice-Chief of the General Staff loading up with mini pork pies. He must be an addict. Building a low encircling wall of them around one side of his plate.

'This name, Ward 13 . . . ' Davane clears her throat. 'Am I the only person who doesn't know what it means?'

The vice-chief blinks his bushy eyebrows at her, looking startled, a pork pie between his thumb and forefinger, and glides easily into a smile, realising the oversight.

'Why, in the military it's shorthand for the funny farm.' He takes a napkin and lays it over his plate. 'We used to have a military hospital in Woolwich. The Queen Elizabeth. Something like two hundred and seventy-odd beds. Closed in 1996. Let's see if I can remember this right: Ward One was a children's ward . . . umm . . . Three and Four were general medicine . . . Ten was oncology. Anyway, Ward 13 was where the drunks were sent,' and he snorts an all-purpose signal of contempt, 'and those who were getting messages from outer space.'

Davane closes her eyes. Lets out a long breath. So typical of the higher echelons of the army to have allowed *that* ward to be called Ward 13. 'That knowledge would be fairly specific, to people who served in the armed forces?'

'That's where we are focusing our investigations,' says Craddock. 'Military and ex-military types.'

'Exactly what sort of a pool of suspects does this give us?'

The senior officers look at each other. Carefully, knives and forks are placed on the side of plates. Chewing stops. Concerned looks back and forth. Then mouthfuls are quickly swallowed. A mixture of embarrassment and unease, as if somebody's honour had been grievously affronted.

The Chief of the Defence Staff brushes away a speck from the lapel of his dark suit before looking up from his seat at the head of the table. His eyes narrow and his deeply lined cheeks suddenly flush. 'I was *assured* your presence here, Ms Davane, was going to be helpful.'

As at a tennis match, all eyes roll to the other end of the table. To Davane, standing by the back of a chair. 'Well. In that, you were flat out wrong . . . '

Grainger neatly inserts himself into the rally. 'I think what my colleague is trying to get at is that we can be most helpful if we understand the true extent of the problem.'

Davane leans forward, steeples her fingers, as if in prayer. 'Just so you're clear, General, I'm not in the business of being helpful. You're the one with the problem . . . we might just be able to find you a solution. But that certainly is not going to involve me saying, *What jolly good chaps you are . . .* This Ward 13 . . . it strikes me, we might as well consider any and everybody who leaves the armed forces to be a potential recruit. And that would be — *what?* — upwards of five, ten thousand people a year. Am I wrong?'

She looks carefully at each of the MoD officers in front of her. There is no immediate reply, but hostility lights up their eyes. Their body language frigid. Knuckles whitening on the mahogany tabletop. *How dare you?*

Davane understands this unspoken message for what it is: these are men who get obeyed in an instant; who, with a twitch, can dispatch aircraft carriers and planes and divisions of fighting men. And then along comes Ward 13. A crisis you can't be trained for. No battle space or salients or bridgeheads to dominate. No flanking manoeuvres or reverse-slope defence.

Once you see these defence chiefs for what they are — scared but clinging on to whatever levers of power they have left — well, there's no reason to cut them any slack whatsoever. The gauntlet is about to be thrown down.

The Ulsterwoman crosses her arms and glares down the table. Her eyes hot little lamps of pure brilliance. 'And while you're sitting on your hands, getting all red faced with me . . . ' Davane stalks around the long table, limping heavily, seeming to take an age as she pegs the length of the room, finally reaching the side of the Chief of the Defence Staff, professional head of the UK armed forces and principal military adviser to the Secretary of State for Defence and the government. ' . . . can you tell me *exactly* when the hell you were planning to tell me about Ward 13 ripping off Sir Dale Malham and his multimillions?'

Davane looks around the room, watches her audience quailing. 'I mean Dale *focking* Malham. What a bunch of *idjits* you people are.'

Well. You could have heard a pin drop. For several minutes afterwards.

Operation Macchar,
minus five days

US Embassy
Diplomatic Enclave
Islamabad

US ambassador Nancy Zoh is giving Bill Lamayette a severe dressing down, an indignant, by-the-numbers special, flashing anger in her eyes, and colour rising up the white of her neck. All eighteen stone of him can think about is what fun it would be to rip off her ambassadorial clothes and run amok amid those long, willowy legs. Try as hard as he can to prevent it, he feels a grin edging across his face. There are three ex-wives and any number of former girlfriends who wouldn't be at all surprised at the simplicity of Lamayette's thought process.

This Come-to-Jesus meeting had actually progressed in two parts. Just as Zoh was working up through the gears the first time, the alarms had started to blare. '*You are advised to evacuate . . . secure all windows . . . secure all classified material.*' The stentorian tone over the loudspeaker system was from the on-duty Marine guard, but the drill was being run by the State Department's Bureau of Diplomatic Security.

So. They had duly scampered, following a

111

much-practised evacuation plan. Lamayette hustled quickly, despite his bulk, in his fawn-coloured salwa kameez. Zoh was almost lifted off her feet by a pair of escorting Marines in their desert-styled combat-utility uniforms. Down the long corridors. Funnelled into their respective armoured cars. Squeezing in tight. Go. Go. Go.

Nine minutes and forty-five seconds it had taken to empty the whole campus-like compound.

Uniquely among all of America's embassies Islamabad has a softball field, a restaurant, tennis courts, even a fifty-metre swimming pool. As the address indicates, it is an enclave, in the truest sense of the word because the world beyond the high fences is too dangerous. Nine minutes forty-five is not good enough. Lamayette knows. They had been hitting under six minutes when he first arrived. Five thirty-seven remains the record. True. In those days, as President Musharraf's government took on all comers in the final stages of its death-grip strategy, you could sometimes *hear* gunfire in the distance. Gunfire was wonderful for focusing the minds of scampering diplomats. The smell of burning tyres even better.

Now they are back in the ambassador's office and Zoh is midway through the second iteration of her telling off.

Through the reinforced glass of her windows, behind Zoh's bobbing, chattering head, Lamayette can see the first security lights flick on. Dusk is approaching. And soon the whole panoply of security measures designed to separate Pakistan from the embassy is brilliantly lit. The concrete ramparts, the reinforced crash barriers and the many miles of slick razor wire.

I could really go with a smoke right about now, thinks Lamayette, dropping from one thought to another. In fact, breaking open a fresh pack of Luckies feels like an imperative; certainly it counts for a hell of a lot more than listening to Nancy Zoh. Long legs or no long legs. He crash-bangs into her monologue. 'Look. Madam Ambassador . . . '

Lamayette feels the nicotine twitch getting stronger, moves his weight from one foot to another. ' . . . I'm here because you asked me. We're all busy, you're whacking off on this and that, so I've gotta ask, what does any of this have to do with me?'

Zoh looks a little stunned. Her lips part just a bit in shock. She moistens them with a slow touch of the tongue.

The ambassador rises slowly from behind her massive desk. Fifty-two years old. Sharp nose and hungry eyes. Dark blonde hair tied back tightly in a bun. In fact tied back, or tied down, seems to say a lot about her. She'd spent a lifetime playing at something she wasn't. That was Lamayette's pop-psychology view of things. Passed her realtor's licence in '89, married a geriatric husband in '91, buried him two years later and was worth fifty million by '95. Fifteen years fund-raising on the West Coast and here she was, serving at President Hannah's pleasure in Islamabad.

It was the first time anybody could remember Pakistan being a non-career appointment. But that was the point, President Hannah had his surrogates intimate to the relevant Senate committees. If a patronage appointment is good enough for Canada, Brazil or the United Kingdom, it's good enough for our new friends in Islamabad. It sends a signal. It's how the great democracies respect one another.

She stabs a button under a telephone set and starts again with the deep eye contact. Lamayette, standing on the other side of the desk, feels a charge in the air, like they're about to go seriously off-manual. 'When I started selling houses, we had a term for people like you. The butt-rubber. The worst kind of vendor. Like a dog with a sore ass, he glides over the carpet in front of everybody else, itching himself, expressing his anal glands, thinking only about himself. Nobody else matters. Big smile on his dumb face even while everybody else in the room is flat-out horrified. Shocked. Revolted. Maybe even laughing at him behind his back. I used to hate clients like that. No matter what you do . . . no matter how fast you move to discount . . . nothing, nothing is going to close that deal now.'

Lamayette makes a mental note to check whether it was only male dogs that did this sort of thing. There was a lot of 'he', 'his' and 'him'.

'Now, you can try to get awfully upset with a dog. But he's got no social code. No sense of what is politic or not. You on the other hand, Mr Lamayette, should know better. Your fascination

114

with this General Ali Mahmood Khan . . . ' she shakes her head gravely ' . . . You see how it is: We're trying to close the deal on Pakistan. Help them rebuild the social fabric of their country. Empower free media, celebrate the independence of their judiciary, energise a responsible civic society . . . and there you are rubbing yourself all over this General Khan business.'

Lamayette likes the analogy enough to stay silent, and in his place. Butt-rubber. He'd been called many things in his life but never that. He could see her point. How terrible it must be to have constructed such a wonderful fiction about democratic renewal and then have him lumbering through it. Telling inconvenient truths.

The ambassador moves around the table, past the framed picture of her embracing President Hannah at his inauguration ball, and the one with her paw in that of the late Benazir Bhutto's. She leans comfortably against the edge of the desk. She's wearing a pair of cream-coloured ballet flats. Off-duty shoes. 'You're gonna need to learn that lesson.'

Naughty talk. That Van Halen song, 'Hot For Teacher', screeches in Lamayette's mind. Visions of schoolboys and long-legged tutors dancing in their gymslips. He knows he should be more respectful, but, really, this is getting way too preposterous. He's only here because she is good to look at. But now she's *lecturing* him. She. Nancy Zoh. The woman who uses people with real work to do, embassy staffers, to wrap her personal presents, get her pictures framed, to go shopping on her behalf. Talk about an Innocent

Abroad. 'You're going to be teaching me . . . what exactly . . . home staging skills for the successful realtor?'

'Very good. Smart come-back.' Then the dismissive little sneer of a smile. 'Won't be me. I don't care for you, Mr Lamayette, and I certainly won't be wasting a second more of my precious time on you.'

Lamayette rubs his thick neck. The nicotine is calling. 'In the circumstances I'm going to say, Shit. That's a pity. Now open your claws and let me go.'

'Not so fast,' and Zoh puts up a hand, and a bracelet of thick gold charms chinkles in the quiet of the room. 'Just so you know how much muscle this side of the table has got. Before we started our little chat, I got a call. From a very important man.' She mouths the word slowly, v-e-e-h-r-r-e-e, like she's reading to a child. By the cat-got-the-cream look on her face, she could only be talking about President Hannah. Big jug-faced idiot.

'Sad news. Very sad. General Stangel. Your boss. Well. I don't want to spoil the surprise. You'll be advised in due course, the usual TOP SECRET cable. He resigned . . . ' She pauses, looks over at a clock face that shows Washington time, nine hours behind — it was eight in the morning there, past five in Islamabad — she corrects herself. 'Sorry. I didn't mean resigned, past tense, I meant *will be* resigning, future progressive tense. In about eight hours' time.'

Now. That *was* a good punch and Lamayette is embarrassed to feel himself stunned. His turn to blush, to feel the heat of anguish scorch his cheeks. The hits come at him quickly. Stangel gone. The CIA again without a real meat-and-potatoes boss.

Jerry Stangel was a holdover from the previous administration and, by common consent, on the president's termination list, waiting for the necessary political cover. Different folks for different strokes is the simple rationale. Hannah had pushed and chivvied his own people into a range of the most senior CIA positions, all clustered around the general, like a bear-trap, hoping the old-timer might do the decent thing.

Stangel had been about the last guy willing to hold up a candle for Lamayette. The certainty in the CIA is that you rise and fall with your most senior friend. Now he would have nobody in that building. As in all big organisations, the faceless monkeys at the heart of the CIA have an instinct for political power, for whose mojo is rising or falling. With Stangel finally gone, the new wunderkinds would already be chopping out the pit props from under Lamayette.

Zoh looks down at the little pale bow on each of her shoes. 'Bad health. Poor man only has six to nine months left.' Then to herself, an aside. 'Testicles. I always said nothing good could come from them.

'Anyway.' She throws her head back, breathes out. 'General Stangel leaves with the grateful thanks of the president no doubt ringing in his ears.' Grateful never sounded so hollow.

Lamayette, stumbling around in his personal mental nightmare, misses that the side door to the ambassador's office is opening. Somebody summoned up by Nancy Zoh.

'Come,' Zoh says softly, beckoning this mystery person forward. She turns back to Lamayette. 'Now. I can't force my people on to your team. But in this time for you of . . . ' and she makes quote marks with her fingers '"imminent transition', it would be smart of you to understand that within this embassy, where we all work together and live in each other's pockets, having a shadow who I can trust and who is working alongside you would be the responsible thing to agree to. Very smart. Especially when you know I just need to make one call . . . '

Cue the person at the door. The staging is pure Hitchcock.

Lamayette doesn't notice the woman's grey, two-button business suit, hand-tailored to hug the curves of her body. Nor the tanned face, hands and calves, evidence of serious outdoor endeavour. It's the white silky headscarf which clings in his mind. Big time. Because fringing underneath the headscarf, just a hint, is her hair. Pure Rita Hayworth, when she was a flame-coloured redhead. The most beautiful woman in the world. Circa 1944 in *Cover Girl*, '45 *Tonight and Every Night* and '47 *Gilda*. Even when she was filmed in black and white, Rita could do the most marvellous things with that lush red hair.

Also, that hair spells Danger. Peril. For the first time, Lamayette can understand those kookie Arabs; why it is they celebrate by firing off

118

AK47s, wild with delight, until the clip runs out. For that smallest second, a charge of the sharpest lust ever runs through his body. And, if he had an AK to hand, he might be firing it off into the air too. Just thinking of Rita Hayworth, and looking at the woman standing in front of him now.

She walks forward. Young and confident. And sassy, as they used to say. Leaving the CIA chief at a loss. By rights he should be hating this woman. How could anything but trouble come from this . . . ?

Nancy Zoh studies Lamayette from across the room, one of her eyebrows slightly raised. 'This is Ms Kirsten Ackerman. Think of her as my personal envoy. Treat her with respect, and you and I will get along fine until we don't have to get along any more, Mr Bill *Lah* — *May* — *Eight*.' And she bites off the final 'T'.

Crunching down on the sound like a goddamn shark.

Operation Macchar,
minus three days

Outside the village of Elton
Derbyshire Peak District

Poor Button. Tristie Merritt's heart goes out to the guy. One of the biggest men the Paras ever recruited . . . and look at him now. Washing up a day's worth of plates, pots and pans . . . six foot six and 250 pounds . . . in an outlandish two-piece red Santa miniskirt with a plush fur trim. His thick, tree-trunk legs squeezed into the striped stockings. His huge shoulders and long bare back dwarfing this sexy little number, and his baggy, greying underpants hanging down, prolapsed out of the bottom of the skirt. It's a vision from a cross-dressing lingerie nightmare.

But the rest of Ward 13 love it.

Amidst all the cackling and teasing in the small farmhouse kitchen, Button sees Tristie's concern and his eyes twinkle. 'Don't worry, Captain. I'll jam 'em up next time.'

'It's not a good look, Button.' And he nods. Yeah. Not good.

This is humour British Army-style. You mess up, you pay the penalty. And the best penalty is some kind of slur on their manhood (females, technically, can earn a Para beret, but cannot actually serve with them in combat). *After all, who would want to be a girl? Different frigging species.*

Button's sin had been coming last in the morning PT drill. Run a mile. One hundred push-ups, then a hundred crunches. Run another mile. Seventy-five push-ups and seventy-five crunches. Run a third mile. Fifty push-ups and a final fifty crunches. The end.

Each losing member of Ward 13 gets to set the next day's PT but first has to go through the ritual humiliation: all the house-work and domestic chores to be performed either in the Santa dress, or a supposedly sexy green milk-maiden dress. Purchased online from an American website called Love My Plus Size. A full-length black fishnet body stocking with a halter top had had to be retired injured several days ago. Weasel, who runs proceedings as adjutant, expressed concerns that the bodysuit was becoming too popular. He thought Whiffler might even be deliberately losing just to wear it. Whiffler furiously denied this, but it was a denial not much believed . . . his freckled face blushes too deep for it to be wholly untrue.

Time to roll up the sleeves. 'Button. When you're ready.'

'Give me a couple of minutes . . . I'll be right with you. Just put this pansy dress back in Whiffler's locker. Like he asked.' More laughter, and young Whiffler's head ducks under his newspaper as an avalanche of tea towels and laundry rains down on him.

When Button's back in his civilian clothes they

121

gather around the marble-topped kitchen table with its cups of coffee, tea and ashtrays full of smoking cigarettes.

Tristie kicks off the discussion. 'It's Day Eleven since we delivered our demands. Three more days until the MoD make their decision.' She looks at each of them closely and they scrutinise her. Eyes eager. Knowing today is one of the mini-deadlines that had been set.

So she pulls out a copy of this morning's *Times*. Turns to the classifieds section. Spreads it out slowly on the top of the table so everybody can see, and takes out a lime-green highlighter pen. There's a nervy silence in the kitchen. Everybody knows what this is about . . .

Ward 13 had made one demand, and sent off two letters. The first — a warning that they had MacIntyre's laptop, and the second — proof that the encryption had been cracked and the Trident plans were theirs. That was the sum total of the communication.

In that second letter, Tristie had added a series of short texts. Three classifieds that they, the MoD, had to place in the personals column of *The Times* to prove their good faith. On Day 6, Day 9 and the last one, Day 11. Today.

Last week, when Day 6 came around, Tristie had snuck down to the village shop in Elton. Alone. She could hardly bring herself to look at the news-stand. Even then, when she had the paper in hand, she made reading it last for ever. Thumbing through the comment pages, digesting the City Diary. She was a jumpy bag of nerves by the time she got to the Register section. Her eyes traced slowly across the Court Circular. Births, Marriages and Deaths . . . bridge and chess news. Finally personals. *Was it there?* Her chest so tight at this point from holding her breath for minutes . . . Legal Notices . . . For Sale.

Then. There it was . . .

'*Gollum. f.* Woman obsessed by desire to get a ring on her finger to the point of self-debasement and self-loathing.'

Yes, yes, yes, Tristie roared. She'd curled right over, almost hugging her knees as she pumped the air with her fist. And the little old lady behind the counter enquired, 'Did you get lucky with the lottery, dearie?'

Day 9 the classified was there as well. Only this time she sort of knew it would be.

'*Gollum. mf.* Sexual partner intent on slipping their finger into your precious ring.'

And today, Day 11, the final classified. Hence the sense of expectation. Delight even. Everybody in the room understands how the army works and the MoD would be no different. A mass of paperwork and sign-offs. The big thrill is that somebody at the MoD would have had to submit a requisition note for the expenditure, get it approved and countersigned. Perhaps, in some darkened room, they have a posse of code breakers sifting through these gags to work out who they were dealing with. Their psychological profiles. The whole thing appealed to the team's strong collective sense of the absurd.

So. Tristie leans forward and with great confidence circles the final classified. Turns the pages around so they can all see.

'*Gollum.* 'That bird I had last night was a right Gollum. Blimey. Must be medically trained, checking my prostrate out like that.' From William Shakespeare's *Two Gentlemen of Verona.*'

A cheer goes up and there are high-fives around the table. Then Button wants to know whether Shakespeare actually wrote like that. ''Cos at school it were shit boring.'

'No, Button.' Tristie shakes her head. 'We got these off the Internet. They're jokes.'

'Oh.'

Shoe adds, 'We're trying to mess them up, Button. This would have gone up to the Chief of the General Staff. He would have seen these, and he'd be the guy who'd press the button, to get them published. All this stuff about sticking fingers up arses.' He repeats this with emphasis. 'The Chief of the General Staff. Do you see?'

'Oh,' says Button. 'I get it now,' and he smiles, wolfishly. 'Screwed 'em up here, haven't we?'

And his Para colleagues chime in. 'Yes, Button.'

Tristie watches her men goofing around, and allows herself a long, contented sigh of relief. This is *really* happening. They might actually make a difference. Now the only thing left to do is wait. Wait a few more days, and get out of the country in time for the trade.

Operation Macchar,
minus two days

Marghazar Zoo
Margalla Hills
Islamabad
Pakistan

The zoo is remote, at the head of a finger-like ravine pointing northwards from the city into the earliest foothills of the Himalayas. Except for the occasional random sounds of caged animals from the far side of the thick surrounding walls, it's dark and silent, coming up to eight in the evening.

By one of the rear entranceways, two hunched figures hide in the shadows. Trying to lift something.

'When they warned me about you . . . ' Kirsten Ackerman bends down to grasp the two handles on her side of the white plastic body bag (' . . . *a body bag?*' she says to herself, hardly believing what she's about to do) ' . . . I didn't imagine we'd be doing this on our first date. You. Me. And a dead gorilla.'

He guffaws. 'Any time you wanna go back to sticking coloured pins into maps so that some deputy assistant desk jockey can watch your ass wiggling . . . '

Facing her, no farther away than the width of

the body bag, Lamayette counts off, ' . . . two, three, UP . . . ' and easily lifts his side of the bag. The body weighs in at nearly four hundred pounds. She had seen the paperwork. A little startled sound escapes from Ackerman as she hauls her side up. *Nnmmghh*. Crap, this is heavy . . .

The CIA station chief whispers, 'Let's go . . . ' Their Ford SUV is parked under the dark of a sprawling fig tree and Lamayette's local driver appears from its gloom, shaking his head in disbelief, as so often before. Moments later, with the body bag hefted into the back, the car is barrelling down the winding Margalla Hill road, headed towards the Chaklala Military Airbase. Hangar 14.

Exactly why, Ackerman has no damned idea. She clasps her hands together rather primly on her lap. 'The deceased. Mind if I ask, what was his name?'

Lamayette turns, a look of shock on his face. 'He had a name?' Mocking her.

'All zoo animals have a name. Especially gorillas.'

Suddenly serious, the CIA chief's eyes are everywhere, scanning nervously through the darkened windows for signs of danger. They have no outriders or support vehicles. A big risk for a diplomatically plated car at night, even one rocketing at speed. Finally he relents and looks across at her, and with a simple flick of some internal switch he fixes his eyes on her in such a way that she knows he's speaking the truth. It's a powerful effect. 'His name was Tickle.'

'Tickle?'

Lamayette gets a handkerchief and wipes down his bald head and neck. 'Tickle. They were going to put him down. Sick boy, he was. Then I arranged for his treatment and had him shipped here.'

'And where did this gorilla come from, this big lump of frozen meat we've been carting around the place?'

Lamayette's look changes. As if he's expended his quotient of seriousness for the moment. 'Some jungle a couple of miles from here.'

Ackerman crosses her arms. Irritated. 'They don't have gorillas in Pakistan.'

'They don't? Hafiz, is this true . . . ?' and the local driver cranes his head around, baffled. And with sarcasm hanging heavy in the air, Lamayette slips back into silence. Scanning. Nervous. Alert.

Ackerman takes the hint.

She stares out of the window, watches mutely as the white-on-green road signs flash past, counting down the miles to the international airport with which the military airbase shares a runway. There is only the uneven, raspy breathing of the driver and the rhythm of Lamayette smoking. Cigarette pack. Lighter. Sharp, stiff inhale. Long, slow exhale. Pause. Again . . . Finally, the *sshhhfff* of the stub crushed into the ashtray. Then again. Cigarette pack. Lighter . . . It would appear he has no need of conversation.

Lamayette's not a bad guy . . . truth be told. He had yelped with alarm on hearing she'd followed the exact same college pathway as Hillary Clinton. Slapped his big shiny head. *Oh! Crap. Wellesley and Yale.* But she had detected a lot more teasing than the wariness that men commonly transmitted. That's not to say she feels in any way charmed by Lamayette. It's just that he is so different. Free-wheeling. Hey. First date, and she's sharing a car with a frozen, dead gorilla. Go figure.

The clincher had been her knowledge of languages. Sure, Ambassador Zoh had railroaded the two of them together. Hardly a promising start. But the dynamic of the relationship changed the moment Lamayette learnt about her languages. In his eyes, she was no longer some supercilious broad, come to gum up his works.

Like Lamayette, Ackerman is fluent in Urdu and Dari, the main languages respectively of Pakistan and Iran and parts of Afghanistan. And both could speak Arabic as well, not surprising given the number of loanwords spread through the Koran.

Her ace is Pashto. The language of forty-odd million Pashtuns living either side of the two-thousand-mile mountainous border that separates Pakistan and Afghanistan. Given the roaming nature of the Pashtun, they often had Dari or Urdu as second languages. But the nitty-gritty of their lives and culture, the uncompromising Pashtunwali honour code and the interplay between the more than a thousand tribes and sub-tribes is always transmitted in Pashto.

It's only as the driver turns off the main road,

128

bumping down on to some rutted tarmac and slowing up for the complicated process of security clearance, that Ackerman decides she's had enough of the silence. 'I'm sorry,' she murmurs, ruefully.

Cigarette in mouth, Lamayette grips the headrest in front of him tightly, steadying himself. 'Sorry for what?' he finally replies.

The car edges inside the Chaklala compound, past a guard-house on one side, and on the other a row of vintage Pakistan Air Force planes, all well lit and arranged on plinths. 'I know what they're doing to you.'

'And what is that?'

It feels like she's trespassed on a private grief. Now that she's raised the subject, Ackerman is almost too embarrassed to continue. 'The Inspector General's investigation . . . the visit next week.' Whoever said the CIA eat their own had been dead on the money.

Lamayette shrugs his massive shoulders, grumbles, 'Bunch of do-nothing back-stabbers,' as the SUV swings out from the shadows of the hangar wall and drives on to a floodlit apron. The car heads straight for an ungainly-looking helicopter sitting up on its back wheels. The unmistakably ugly lines of a Soviet design. Five drooping rotor blades hang limply from the main turboshaft.

The Caucasian crewmen in green flying suits clamber out of the CIA-run, Russian-built Mil-17 as the car draws alongside, stopping within inches of the drop-down doorway. Lamayette rubs his hands with glee as he steps out. 'Look and learn, toots!' A big toothy grin. 'Little bit of history here. This beauty of a flying crate took the then Islamabad station chief into Afghanistan. Twenty-seventh of September 2001. The very first American boots on the ground. They landed just north of Kabul. Come to take names and kick ass. Hence the codename. Jawbreaker.'

He pauses for a moment, listening to the stillness, sniffs the dry, hot night air, takes another Lucky Strike. As the cigarette dangles from the side of his mouth, he switches on his sincerity eyes. 'Should have been me . . . Jawbreaker. The guy who rode this chopper instead was running down his final ninety days before retirement. Nine-eleven was supposed to be my moment. *Where are you, Bill?* my bosses cried. We need you in Tajikistan. Jawbreaker is yours. *Where the hell are you?*'

He looks thoroughly embarrassed. 'And do you know where I was?', this huge beast of a man standing at the foot of the helicopter door.

Ackerman wonders whether a wisecrack would be appropriate. Getting your oversupply of testosterone treated. She decides not. 'No idea.'

He glances away. Crewmen pre-flight the helicopter. Kick the wheels. Poke a torch up into the landing gear. Tickle's body bag is being stowed. A thought plays through Ackerman's mind. *Am I going somewhere?*

Lamayette puts his weight on the foot of the three-step, fold-down door. Can't bring himself to look at her. 'I was in Hilo, Hawaii. Of all the damned stupid places to be. My country's hour of greatest need, and I'm in a locked room under judicial supervision. Negotiating with three sets of divorce lawyers representing my beloved ex-wives. No children, mind, and each of them remarried at least once. But the judge ruled I'd failed to appear at the alimony proceedings in one lawsuit, hadn't turned over the financial records demanded by another. Said I was a flight risk, said I couldn't leave the state until I'd squared things away. And do you know how that feels? You can't imagine . . . having nothing but talk to cover your shame; not being ready when your country called.' He offers his hand up the stairs. 'Remember that tonight.'

Listening to this *mea culpa*, Ackerman had had her face set to Sympathy. Too late. She suddenly realises she's been co-opted into something she doesn't understand. *Remember that tonight.* Remember . . . remember what?

What the hell *am* I supposed to be doing tonight?

Against all her instincts, she finds herself putting her hand into his. Climbing aboard. As they buckle in, and the rotors start to spin and the turbos whine, she nudges his shoulder. Shouts into his ear. 'No chance you're going to tell me what it is we're doing?'

Lamayette is preoccupied, looking forward, through the open cockpit door to the two pilots and the flight engineer. He gives them a thumbs-up and moments later a sideways lurch takes the Mil-17 into the air.

Operation Macchar, thirty-six hours to go

Pearl Continental Hotel
Khyber Road
Peshawar

Just past three in the morning and the few lights of the five-storey Pearl Continental twinkle in the near-distance. It's not a fancy hotel. A sixties-designed box with plenty of concrete cornices. But then Peshawar is hardly tourist friendly: less than forty miles to the Afghan border and that same distance again puts you in Tora Bora, which is where US and British special forces lost Osama Bin Laden. It's also a lawless, modern-day Saigon full of no-go areas: encircled by anti-government Taliban, and deeply penetrated by radical Muslim preachers fronting sympathetic political parties. Proof of this is the shroud of tarpaulin and scaffolding that hangs over part of the hotel's front, after a suicide bomb that killed almost twenty people.

In the quiet of the hotel car park Bill Lamayette is fine-tuning things, with the help of the most trusted driver he has. 'Is she the one, Mr Bill?' the tall Pakistani asks in his courtly manner.

'The one what, Jahanghir?' The two of them

are trying to dress the dead gorilla. Tickle is sitting upright in the front passenger seat of yet another black Ford SUV. A 2009 model Expedition. This one registered to the US consulate in the city, and used exclusively by the CIA. So far they've managed to get a 5XL Louisiana State sweatshirt over the corpse's head. Getting the stiff, leathery fingers through the sleeves is not easy.

'The one,' and the moustachioed driver emphasises, '*the* one.'

Lamayette fumbles to get a Tickle thumb out through the cuff. 'In this critical moment for our two peace-loving countries, Jahanghir, and all you can think about is the jiggy-jiggy.'

'Most important thing, you told me once, Mr Bill. Sex with monkeys.'

'Monkey sex, I said,' he corrects, fitting his college football ring on to the third finger of Tickle's left hand. Just as he wears it himself.

There's a moment of studied reflection from Jahanghir as they continue their struggle. 'Mr Bill. Is that legal in your country? Sex with monkeys?'

Lamayette speaks through clenched teeth, bent over to fit a pair of shoes on Tickle's feet. 'Sex with monkeys . . . good question. I am sure it is legal. Somewhere. Probably in those godless liberal states, like where Ms Ackerman comes from. Vermont. And New Hampshire. Massachusetts. Definitely California.'

Happy with the information, Jahanghir pulls the sweatshirt over the ape's gut. Tucks it down. The body had been frozen for more than a

133

month now, and as it thaws it radiates a desperate chill. Jahanghir had been a direct hire by Lamayette himself, not somebody inherited. The station chief made a point of keeping his Peshawar driver off the agency's books and so had no cause to ask how old he is. He can only go by what he sees. Flashing eyes and a hard, worn face of studied integrity, which could as easily be twenty as sixty years old. Not a pinch of fat on him. Time and time again, the Pakistani had proved himself. Like right now. Thinks nothing of being asked to clothe a dead four-hundred-pound gorilla. *Right you are, Mr Bill*, and gets on with it. The sort of hire who quickly becomes more family member than arms-length employee. Hence the line of questioning: Jahanghir remains constantly anxious about his boss. Mortified that three women, *three*, had divorced him.

'Very becoming hips. And she speaks excellent Pashto, Mr Bill.' His voice cautioning, don't let this one go. 'She will follow the path of honour and virtue.' As he talks, Jahanghir Khan, kneeling on the driver's seat, concentrates on folding the vast lengths of Tickle's arms across the gorilla's lap. 'She will make a very obedient wife. I see many children.'

'Obedient? The modern American woman? I don't think you read her quite right, old friend.' Tickle's thick, dark head lolls towards the passenger door, where the American stands, an unlit cigarette in his mouth. Lamayette's medical alert bracelet is already on the simian's right wrist. (Jahanghir had enquired, 'What is your

134

sickness, Mr Bill?' 'Unforgivable weakness around women.' 'Oh.' Pause. 'I think I have that too, Mr Bill.')

Lamayette knows the best he can hope for is a twenty-four-hour start . . . the Pakistani police would be first on the scene, and would recover fragments of a 'corpse' from the burnt-out wreckage. The Federal Investigation Agency and Inter-Services Intelligence will sniff around too, trying to get a fix on the bomb and who they can blame. But this being a CIA matter, a death involving a senior diplomat, the cadaver will be locked down by the local consulate at the Khyber Medical College, until a US specialist team arrives. They'd come to this protocol recently after a Homeland Security official stationed in Islamabad died by gunshot in his bathroom; the details of the autopsy were widely leaked by the Pakistan Institute of Medical Sciences to an already overheated local media. To avoid that happening again Lamayette's corpse would be flown to Germany for a full post-mortem, and that's when his ruse will be up. A twenty-four-hour window. The obvious skeletal difference, the braincase and teeth arrangement, will have been missed by the boys from *CSI: Peshawar*, scooping clods of burnt flesh and bone into a dustpan. But not by a serious pathologist.

So in that window, those twenty-four hours, the ID will be called on what Peshawar police find at the scene. The car. Bracelet. Mobile phone and pager. His college football ring. And now for the final touch. Something which, with

135

great bitterness, he knows will definitely survive a blast ... but will be lost to him probably forever.

It's a pair of dog tags, one bent in half almost at ninety degrees. They belonged to his US Marine sergeant brother, killed early one morning in October 1983 in Beirut along with 240 other countrymen by a suicide bomb that destroyed the Marine's Battalion Landing Team HQ. The blast, equivalent to 12,000 pounds of explosive, was so strong the entire four-storey building was jumped into the air, then, freed of foundations and support columns, the structure crashed down on itself. Those inside had had no chance. Lamayette's brother was found finally, five days later, crushed to death, in the boxer shorts he slept in.

He looks at the beaded chain and bent stainless-steel tag. Closes the palm of his hand. Feels a prickle of tears, a memory of that singular moment. The pair of naval officers approaching his parents' porch. A Friday morning after the Sunday blast. His father falling to his knees, hands clasped together. The door creaking open. Everyone begging, begging that they'd got it wrong. 'The Secretary of the Navy has asked that I inform you ... '

Lamayette kisses the metal. Feels the cold rub of the raised lettering against his cheek one last time. Jahanghir is watching from a distance, like an honour guard, proud and erect.

LAMAYETTE
JOHN J

136

743-99-8179
USMC L
NO PREFERENCE

'Bro. This being Memorial Day weekend and all, I hope I'm doing the right thing by you. But I don't know.' Tears film his eyes. 'That's why I always said I needed you around. Forgive me, please, if I'm not.' He glances away, rubbing his eyes. Pinches the bridge of his nose hard. Slowly collects himself. '*Semper Fi*. Love you, bro.' Finally, he places the chain around Tickle's neck. Straightening it slightly so that it hangs just right. 'Always faithful.'

★ ★ ★

The set-up is simplicity itself.

First, the Ford Expedition is lifted up using an inflatable car jack, a big, reinforced yellow canvas bag, like a life raft, attached to the exhaust pipe and wedged under the SUV. As the engine idles, one side of the car eases up into the air.

Next, Jahanghir rolls several canisters of oxygen under the Ford. To create a devastating thermobaric effect. Packing them in tight. Then Lamayette deploys the power-step running board (naturally, the CIA car has all the extra options). The electric motor drive quietly extends the high-strength aluminium bar to a convenient stepping height.

The hand grenade is a Soviet-style RGD-5, which you could buy in a Peshawar bazaar for a couple of bucks. Lamayette pulls out the hooped pin, then slides it into a long, tall Collins cocktail glass. The sides of the glass trap the lever in place, ensuring the four-second fuse is not triggered. He places the glass carefully on the ground, lining it up so that it's immediately underneath the extended running board on the side of the SUV that's raised up into the air.

The car park is still quiet. Deserted. The two of them retreat behind the trunk of a date palm bordering the hotel wall. A dozen yards from the Ford. 'Right, my friend. Let's screw with some government property.' And faithful Jahanghir hands him the loaded Kalashnikov, with a devilish grin of the whitest white teeth.

* * *

Ackerman is sitting on her own in an old red 4WD Mitsubishi Pajero parked on the Khyber Road almost opposite the Grand Continental. Civilian plates. Feeling pretty vulnerable.

Suddenly she's aware of movement between her and the hotel. Two people stalking through the car park, their bodies silhouetted against hotel lights.

Cries go up. Long adulatory cries, ringing clear into the night. '*Allllllaaaaahh Akkhbaaaar*.'

'*Allah Akhbar*', God is Great. Again and again.

The gunfire starts, she ducks instinctively. Bursts of four or five shots. Little streaks of tracer, spraying up into the sky and around the car park directly in front of her. Metallic *ting* and *twang* noises.

The two figures sprint from the shadows. They

138

dash across the empty road. Round the far side of the Pajero, pressing themselves against the car. Crouching. She picks out Lamayette's unmistakable buffalo shape.

Through the window, she hears his muffled voice. 'You'd better get down.'

'What's going on?'

'Get down!'

Several bursts of 7.62mm rounds have been fired directly into the canvas gut of the inflatable car jack. It's slowly giving up its air. Hissing to the ground. As it does so, the extended running board sinks, crushes down on the tall Collins glass. Releasing the lever of the hand grenade, starting the fuse.

Ackerman insistent now. 'I said, what's going . . . '

The first explosion cracks loudly but not devastatingly. Enough for Ackerman to turn around, face towards the hotel, *What's going on?* written across her face. Then the oxygen canisters erupt, *whuummmpp*, one after another. Bucking the 2009-model SUV twenty feet into the air, riding a bright ball of flame. In total there are four thick, concussive blasts smothering the night sky in plumes of light. Finally the SUV crunches to the ground on its back and the gas tank ruptures. Consumed by fires of the most perfect intensity.

Breathless, Lamayette opens the door. 'Now this is what I need you — '

'Stop. Stop.' She's waving her hands, disbelievingly. 'Have you just blown up that embassy car?'

Ackerman sees the whites and yellows of the

fire reflecting in the shiny glaze of Lamayette's forehead. 'Yeah,' like, of course I have. Sundry small explosions leap from the burning wreck. Little pockets of gas.

'Jesus, Bill. That's the end of your career. You do know that?'

'Look, maybe it is. Then you get to blab to Ambassador Zoh how you were there, you saw it all, what a monster I was. That makes you today's paper-shuffling, do-nothing hero of the hour . . . '

Commotion streams from the hotel. People stumbling towards the fiery wreckage. From a long way away, there's the faint sound of sirens.

' . . . But maybe I'm right, in which case you can still be the hero. Maybe tonight we can flush out the truth about General Ali Mahmood Khan and what he's up to. If I am right, there's one thing I need you to do. Please. *Now*. Just one thing. Either way, you're in the money on this thing.' Jahanghir fusses around behind Lamayette, peering this way and that. Unnerved and agitating to get away.

She closes her eyes. *Aaaaarggh*. 'What?'

He passes a handwritten note. A mobile telephone number. 'Get inside the hotel. Tell them in your best bazaar Pashto you need to call your brother. That you've been visiting your sick husband. Drama, drama: big explosion. Now brother must pick you up. Ring this number. It's one of General Khan's sons. A big fat-headed gasbag called Shafiq. Tell him . . . ' and here Lamayette looks a bit self-conscious, trying to

140

bend his limited Pashto into shape ' . . . *Amri-kaayi CIA saaqhib tshaawd.*' American CIA chief dead.

'Shit, your language is off, Bill. They use verbs as well, you know.'

'You get the drift. The CIA boss man is dead. You saw it. Big bomb. Lots of gunfire. Shafiq's a big cheerleader for this sort of terrorist drama, a tittle-tattling lounge lizard. He'll check with the police, then the news will roll. Text. Emails. Websites. He'll tell the world I'm dead, so he can play the man who shot Liberty Valance. My bet is, that'll flush them into action, things in the Khan household will start to move.'

As the sirens near, Ackerman pulls down the Afghan-style veil. She stands by the car, readying to cross the road, and her eyes find him one last time through the little lace window. 'Give this up. I'll vouch for you. I promise.'

He gives her a wink and a confident thumbs-up. 'Get going, Red.'

Operation Macchar,
twenty-six hours to go

*In the Swat River valley
Malakand District
Two and a half hours by truck north of
Peshawar*

Eight hours later. They're known as jingly-jangly trucks. Or just jinglies for short. The forty-year-old Bedford truck, labouring under a huge gaudily decorated wooden super-structure of painted gold and silver motifs, has broken down. The rear axle deliberately but artfully sheared in two, requiring the vehicle to be beached by the side of the narrow road that heads down to the river crossing. It's conspicuously busted and out of action.

The driver and his assistant, close family to Jahanghir, have begun the slog towards the city of Malakand twenty-five miles away. Making sure not to go too fast. The only person remaining is a guard, fierce looking with an up-to-date Kalashnikov, dust-streaked dish-dasha, angry eyes and a beard as long as a shovel. He stands watch. Instructed to be firm and rude in refusing all offers of help. Another Jahanghir cousin.

Inside the vehicle's wooden cabin, hidden

142

within the superstructure by tight-packed sacks of molasses and fertiliser, are Bill Lamayette, Kirsten Ackerman and Jahanghir, together with an icebox, a lot of expensive optical and audio equipment and two dangling drop-lights wired to a car battery. Plus another pair of assault rifles and a dozen or so clips of ammunition. A reminder they are in seriously lawless territory.

The only thing in the cabin that even vaguely resembles high-tech is the surveillance gadgetry. Positioned against a series of peepholes, they are watching a madrasa some four hundred yards away. A two-level whitewashed adobe building configured around a tiled compound the size of a football pitch. The school has carefully tended plots of land on three sides and on the other the bubbling snowmelt waters of the River Swat. Thrusting up through the rich, loamy soil, and shadowing the whole structure, are thick stands of evergreens. Pine and olive trees.

It's an idyllic setting. Remote. Secure. And, surrounded by open space, easy to protect from interlopers. The school has invested a serious amount in barbed- and razor-wire fencing. The only access is through a single cinderblock guardhouse. It was from there that a posse of mean-looking goons, with Kalashnikovs and bandoliers, had sauntered, to check on the Bedford and make sure their stop was genuine. Evidently the lie had worked, because on a second visit there was none of the menace and they came offering Jahanghir's guard oranges and mint leaves.

To get here, they'd driven through the night,

weaving and creaking up one of the most dangerous roads in the world. Gearbox whining, sliding into each other as the venerable truck hugged its side of the winding pass.

At first there'd been good news. Exactly as Lamayette had predicted. Jahanghir has a briefcase holding a dozen mobile phones, their numbers known to various radical cells. Within twenty minutes of Ackerman calling General Khan's son Shafiq, the phones erupted. One after the other. Different correspondents. Wave after wave of text messages. Like gossiping honey bees abuzz, in equal measure jubilant and vengeful. All knowing. The CIA chief is dead. A mighty blow has been struck . . .

Ackerman was stunned by it all — SMS software can handle only 160 characters, yet, as Jahanghir read off each screen, the Pashto messages seemed to cram into so little so much precise detail. These were mass mail-outs moving at breakneck speed. And in the dead of night too; imagine the volume if this were daytime.

What's that Mark Twain line? A lie can travel halfway around the world while the truth is putting on its shoes . . .

Central to the surveillance is a holy man called Pir Durbar. He lives in a small outlying house at the madrasa, giving holy-man consultations to the rich and the bewildered in these suitably ascetic surroundings.

On the journey up, Lamayette had explained his theory to Ackerman: the Pashtun don't think about today and tomorrow, their plots span across an almost glacial time frame, to win prestige for their clan's people, across the generations, for ever . . . that's the measure of Pashtun success.

Lamayette continued: General Khan knows it will be left to his children and their children to roll out the dynasty, using the hundreds of millions of US dollars he's embezzled from the Defense Department's Coalition Support Funds . . . he will have sacrificed everything, including his life if necessary, to give his descendants the chance to deliver.

'OK. I get the theory.'

'Only trouble is . . . Khan's children are fucking nitwits. Like Laurel and Hardy, but without the laughs. You spoke with Shafiq. He's number-two boy; a fat, indolent prick. Low, greedy cunning but no damn balls. Just sits on his ass, watching movies, planning his first cabinet, talking big. Never walking the streets, or agitating a crowd. You don't know Hamza yet. Son number one. Unlike his brother he probably knows he's hopeless. Everything's on his shoulders yet he's so lacking in confidence it's painful. No charisma: tall. Skinny. Nervy jitters. Biting his nails. Classic daddy-whipping-boy screw-up.'

'And . . . ?'

'Well . . . ' and in the darkness of the truck bumping along, Lamayette had lit one cigarette from the butt of another ' . . . Hamza has taken to visiting this guy Pir Durbar. At the madrasa. The old holy man, after much crossing of the palm with silver, has convinced Hamza he just needs to lie back and be wafted into power by these benign celestial forces that only this holy-man witch doctor can summon. My bet, when he hears I'm dead, Hamza will scoot up here. If you're that inadequate you'll want to hear from your own holy man, have him regurgitate one more time why the universe continues to smile on you, how come you keep beating the odds, drawing royal flushes every hand.

'It's a chance, a small chance, that we might be able to get a fix on what the fuck they're up to.'

That was the plan. Outlined almost eight hours ago it had sounded reasonable. Intriguing even. But that was then.

It's now midday. A crow caws overhead. Bored out of its mind, like the rest of us, thinks the young woman.

A whole third of a day has passed with them on this mindless vigil. Staring through the shimmering fields at the school. The only thing moving is the sun, mature in its slow daily track. Whatever adrenalin they'd been running on has long since flagged. Those in the madrasa are taking their two-hour lunch-slash-siesta.

Just so you're completely in the picture . . . Team America has *bupkis* to show for eight hours of cramp-inducing hanging around. Worse still, the window on Lamayette's spectacular deception is closing . . .

There's not a breath of air in the back of the truck. The sun beats down on it with furious intensity. Turning the insides into a kiln.

The CIA station chief has flagged too. Hell,

146

he's not even smoking. Just hunched morosely in a director-style fold-up chair with his head in his hands. Asleep? His bald head prickles with sweat. Faithful Jahanghir continues to peer through a periscope arrangement. Waiting for who knows what.

Ackerman leans back. 'Bill. It's not that I'm not enjoying myself. It's been a blast, really has . . . but what happens now?'

His voice grumbles through his clenched fists. 'Leave a guy to die in frigging peace.'

She can't think of a retort. Too flaked out.

The CIA file on General Ali Mahmood Khan lies within reach, so Ackerman crosses her legs to sit down on the floor. A bottle of water on her lap.

She flicks through the pages. There's a sequence of CIA cables stamped TOP SECRET. She skim-reads each of Lamayette's reports back to Langley and realises she's reading the case against General Khan.

It boils down to straightforward embezzlement. The Defense Department had run a programme with the Pakistan military called the Coalition Support Funds. Worth just over a billion US dollars annually since late 2001, CSF is designed to put some backbone into the Pakistan armed forces. Pay them to take on the al-Qaeda and Taliban-style radicals that are hopscotching back and forth across the lawless mountains that separate eastern Afghanistan and western Pakistan.

By working his contacts within the Islamabad embassy and the Pakistan military, Lamayette had uncovered a funding hole of staggering proportions. (An *alleged* hole, Langley kept pointing out in reply cables.) In the tribal areas of Pakistan there had been almost no military activity for several years now after former president Musharraf signed what would prove to be an unworkable peace treaty with tribal elders. Ackerman remembers hearing President Hannah encouraging a new version of that same plan, saying, *We must be brave enough to give peace a chance.*

However . . . Lamayette's analysis showed that even though the Pakistan military had been stood down, the invoices kept coming. Reimbursements for supplies, wear and tear on equipment, transport, fuel and logistical costs, per diems for soldiers from the lowliest private all the way up to theatre commanders. In a separate tranche of funding, the US was also paying for the construction of new garrisons and army posts in the tribal areas, complete with barbed wire and bunker material.

Yet. According to Lamayette's cables, none of this was happening: no army manoeuvres, no garrison-building. Nothing. ('*Allegedly* none of this has happened,' a CIA finance officer had corrected. No. Not Allegedly, You Incompetent Halfwit, Lamayette had reply-cabled, breaking a thousand rules on government communications and mutual respect for fellow officers.)

To prove his point, Lamayette's reply included coordinates for a dozen garrisons in and around the tribal areas that Islamabad had invoiced Washington for, and which just did not exist. On

148

the from-above satellite shots there was some activity on the ground, but from-the-ground photos and video referencing the exact same GPS coordinates showed nothing more than some land cleared, brush cut back and a lot of camouflage netting. A modern-day Potemkin village.

And the person in charge of the Pakistan Army in the tribal areas through this whole period? . . . General Ali Mahmood Khan. The total amount invoiced over thirty months of make-work: $247 million.

So that's what this is all about. A quarter of a billion dollars. In Pakistan. In General Khan's hands. Wow.

It pains her to think further. The only thing skipping through her mind is that age-old warning she'd learnt on her first deployment: 'You'll never buy the loyalty of a Pashtun. But they're pretty straightforward to rent.'

A quarter of a billion dollars bought a lot of leasehold . . .

Her brain too frazzled to unravel any more of this ghastly tack, she flicks on through the file. Looking at the black-and-white pictures of Khan's family.

Eldest son Hamza does indeed look like a tortured wretch. Rake thin and an arrogantly sneering gaze. Someone happy to pay for soothing advice. Shafiq too is everything Bill described, plump and furtive. Wholly unattractive in a grubby, porcine fashion. She could see him as an elaborately bejewelled eunuch in the court of Caesar, a paid motor-mouth.

She closes her eyes. Concentrates on the little bursts of red at the edges of her vision. Breathes out . . .

Dammit.

Why is Hamza not here?

Dammit! Where are you, Hamza?

Startled, she glances around nervously. Not certain if she'd spoken those words out loud, or just thought them. How embarrassing. By the light of the cabin's two bulbs she sees Lamayette still immobile, and Jahanghir still craning with his shiny tubular eyepiece.

But something *has* changed. And she's too rational and self-aware to walk away. For the first time, this State Department officer has crossed the line. She *believes*. That's right: *Believes* Lamayette. Wants him more than anything else in the world to be right.

Good Lord, Kirsten, she chides herself, is this Stockholm Syndrome? Too much time with your captors; Patty Hearst and the Symbionese Liberation Army . . .

No. It's not. Just plain old-fashioned fear, she realises. And the knowledge of what these ancient people are capable of. Washington had paid out the money, but the money was never spent. Yet the money must have gone somewhere. And it was Lamayette's assertion that until they knew where the money was, how to sequester it somehow, it was too risky to take out General Khan. To do that was to invite major retribution . . .

It makes so much sense. Pashtun, like the general, live for their vengeance, in whatever

150

shape or form they can take it.

She has her hands clasped together. Imploring. Praying for the first time since the night of her seventeenth birthday: Oh God. Please deliver Hamza to us.

Please.

Operation Macchar,
twenty hours to go

By the Swat River
Malakand District
Two and a half hours by truck north of
Peshawar

A hiss of airbrakes, whooping and shouting, and the tow truck has reversed into place. It's past nine in the evening. It's eighteen hours since Tickle and the Ford Expedition were exploded, and fifteen hours since they started surveillance on the madrasa, hoping for sight of General Khan's son Hamza.

A posse of scruffy foot soldiers from the madrasa have come for another nose around, this time with flashlights. Getting in a steam over some detail of tow-truck etiquette, flapping their arms, clutching their Kalashnikovs.

Already, thick, looped chains are fastened under the Bedford's sheared-off axle. The venerable truck, hiding Bill Lamayette, Kirsten Ackerman and Jahanghir, is nearly ready to be winched up high.

And in their secret cabin inside, the feelings range through stir crazy, exhausted, washed out, bereft. Still no sign of Hamza . . .

Jahanghir's tinny little radio makes clear that

152

the Lamayette death story continues to lead all the Pakistan radio bulletins. The BBC and Voice of America had led with 'uncorroborated' reports of the CIA bureau chief's violent demise. Vengeful versions of his assassination pulse regularly over the SMS text network with gleeful elaborations, how his severed head went bouncing off like a golf ball down the Khyber Road . . . all well and good, except that by Lamayette's calculations his 'corpse' should be almost in Germany by now. Once there, it would take no more than half an hour to work out this was no human body. Surely Washington would deliberately leak that information, if only to try to spike the guns of those claiming to have got one over on the CIA. That would be the moment Lamayette's ruse would be blown. Postscript: he'd probably be heading for jail, certainly out of a job. This would be a first even in the Agency's long history of employing complicated head-strong individuals.

So. Time is close to run-out on this caper and the next words are a big surprise, cutting through his anguish. 'I want to stay with you, Bill.'

Jahanghir's eyes, still glued to his surveillance eyepiece, widen with pleasure. *As I said it would be, so it is* . . . Gently bobbing his head in appreciation of her tender feelings for his boss.

'Listen, sweets . . . ' Lamayette doesn't even look at her, he's putting handfuls of detachable box magazines for his AK74 into a double gymbag slung around his neck. 'The best thing you can do is sit your tush in the embassy in

Islamabad. If we get a hit, I need someone there
. . . I need someone to get in front of
Ambassador Zoh. Someone batting for our side.
It's the only way to get Zoh on the big phone to
the president . . . '

'But Bill . . . what are you going to do?'

Outside, there's a sudden definite jump in the
intensity of chatter. An ululation. Someone
coming. Ackerman strains to hear the Pashto
cries. Sounds of excitement, not danger.
Jahanghir is bent over his periscope, swivelling to
the left and right, tracking. The tension spikes
through his long, muscled back. Like an electric
charge.

He pulls back from the lens piece. Wipes his
hand across his eyes. Looks again.

When he turns to face them, there is a
beaming smile across his mouth. Unrestrained
joy . . . 'Hamza's car. Range Rover.' He mops a
line of sweat from his top lip. 'Very definitely, Mr
Bill.'

Like Bambi, Lamayette bounces excitedly to
the wall space by his trusted driver, grabs up the
lens. Jahanghir gives Ackerman a discreet wink
and thumbs-up.

The CIA chief snatches a cigarette from
behind his ear. It's in his mouth by the time he
pulls back from the periscope.

'We need to buy some time here. Jahanghir.
Get one of your cousins to let down a tyre. Front
axle. Slow leak sort of a thing. Quick smart, old
friend.'

Jahanghir's smile reaches its apex. 'Very good,
Mr Bill.'

154

The Bedford and its tow truck are sitting to one side of the unpaved road that leads past the madrasa guardhouse down to a ford across a Swat river tributary. Hamza Khan's super-charged V8 Range Rover Vogue just manages to squeeze past.

It's a damned tight fit. Concern that the 4x4's expensive grey bodywork may get scraped prompts Hamza to power down his darkened window, and poke his beakish nose into the light spilling from the back of the tow truck.

'That's the bastard,' yips Lamayette, back at the lens, watching proceedings. Also noted, Hamza is travelling with a driver and five other bodyguards. All heavily armed.

The Range Rover slowly eases past the Bedford, the run-flat wheels crunching on the gravel. Ahead of them, a group of bandolier-wearing guards are making a big performance of escorting the car along the road and towards the madrasa. Big Man come to pay a visit.

Various cameras hidden within the superstructure of the CIA truck give a night-vision feed of Hamza's procession grinding its way from the guardhouse towards the two-storey religious school. Easing uncomfortably along the approach road.

As Lamayette watches, the truck's trapdoor opens and one of Jahanghir's cousins fires off a quick update. The coast is clear. Let's get to work . . .

155

Lamayette breaks open the aluminium carry-box of his CIA listening device, passing six curved panels to the cousin outside the trapdoor to click together into its parabola shape, like a vast wok. Jahanghir arranges the rest of the electronics. The listening device works up to five hundred yards. By their reckoning they would just be inside that envelope: the school being four hundred yards away and Pir Durbar's small house a further fifty beyond that. Still within line of sight from the Bedford, but to the left of the madrasa, nearer the river and the glades of pine and olive trees. Inside Pir Durbar's house, the walls and floors had been plastered with cow dung. No pictures, no ornaments. Just a homespun carpet, two lumpy cushions for visitors to sit on, and a low writing table.

Before resuming watch through the lens piece Lamayette pins up mugshots of the two people they want: Hamza, his angular features and disdainful far-away eyes, and Pir Durbar, the holy man.

It's the first time Ackerman has a picture with which to make real her thoughts about the holy man. In the close-up he is standing in front of an old taxi, a marketplace somewhere, wearing a typical kurta top and dhoti, tied off like a lungi. Gandhi-style. He looks perhaps fifty and slightly built. His hair is short, almost crew-cut, but what staggers Ackerman is the flowing beard, a thick semicircle of white thatching extending from ear to ear like a primitive headdress. Also distinctive, the widest-frame glasses she's ever seen. With a wood-effect fascia, as if to suggest that in this splendid isolation he had hand-crafted them himself. Their ultra-thick lenses give his pupils a demonic out-of-this-world size.

Ackerman glances at the night-vision feed that's now playing on the rigged-up monitor. Lamayette, working the lens, squeezes into close-up on Hamza and Pir Durbar embracing in the driveway of the school. A couple of assistants wait near by holding kerosene lamps. And behind them is an embankment of heavily watered lawn studded with a thousand small rocks that spell out in Arabic a Koranic verse: *God admits those who believe and lead a righteous life into gardens with flowing streams. As for those who disbelieve, they live and eat like the animals eat, and end in the hellfire.*

* * *

Lamayette sits cross-legged in the cabin watching the TV monitor; a locked-off wide shot of the school compound. Annoyed with himself yet again that he'd not mastered the Pashto language. Smoking. Flicking irritably at the ash-stains on his salwar kameez trousers. Thirty-two minutes of surveillance now. Into the red zone.

On top of the Bedford the curves of the parabolic dish continue to suck in the tiniest sound waves from the dimly lit hut, drawing them into the hypersensitive microphone.

Outside, Jahanghir has a pair of headphones and a notepad, scribbling down a rough translation of the chitchat between Pir Durbar and Hamza. Kirsten Ackerman stays within the cabin, but does the same thing. Different pair of headphones, different recording device. Both of them scrolling back and forth in case they miss something or need to double-check.

Two separate audio feeds. That's the key.

The CIA station chief's fear is that, in their enthusiasm, Jahanghir and Ackerman would contaminate one another if they worked in the same room, listened off the same source recording: confirmation bias, selective intelligence, the Noble Lie, call it what you will.

The trapdoor tilts up behind Lamayette. Jahanghir. Frowning and a little ragged. 'Time to go, Mr Bill. The guards come from house. This tyre has been changed almost twenty minutes. Trouble if we stay.'

Lamayette's vast shoulders and stomach sink. He's right, of course: this was no place for an armed engagement. They'd be hopelessly out-gunned and even if they prevailed, so what? It would simply alert Hamza, and they'd be stuck out in this vast Yankee-hating wildness, certainly with no friends for hundreds of miles.

So. Reluctantly he nods his assent. 'Wait . . . tell me . . . ' and he screws up his face like he's sucking a lemon, desperate not to hear bad news. 'Anything?'

Jahanghir swallows hard on his Adam's apple, distraught. 'Bits and pieces, Mr Bill. I think, only little pieces. No smoky gun.'

Crap. He drums his head against the wall. 'No smoking gun,' he corrects, under his breath.

He turns to Ackerman, whose eyes are closed

in tight concentration, one hand pressing the headphones tightly against her ear. She scribbles furiously, turning over a page, and as she does so, he catches her eye. Makes the universal finger-waggling signal that they're packing up.

She shrugs unhappily. A look that says she too only has some inconsequential bits and pieces. It's still . . . no smoking gun. And yes, she understands, they must leave.

Quick breakdown of the listening-device parabola, while Lamayette reminds himself to put on hold those heroic welcome-back plans. The ticker-tape parade through the Canyon of Heroes in Manhattan's Financial District. He'd been working out a few delicious details in his head: President Hannah trotting behind his open-top limo wearing nothing but a dog collar, and Ambassador Zoh pole-dancing on the hood. Crap.

That would've been a hell of a show.

★ ★ ★

Fifteen minutes later and all three of them are leaning against the back wall of their cramped cabin, Lamayette in the middle. The day's third, or was it fourth, great spike of adrenalin has eked away, leaving a terrible hangover, a hollow numbness in which their minds moon around listlessly. To make things gloomier, they can feel the Bedford being towed with its rear axle aloft, tilting the cabin almost forty-five degrees. Out of kilter with the floor, bumping into every pothole, it feels like the inside of a doomed spacecraft.

Jahanghir's notes are in Pashto so mean nothing to Lamayette. Instead he's holding Ackerman's pad, deciphering the frantic scribbles by the glow of two precariously swinging droplights.

Lamayette heaves a great, shaking sigh from the depths of his stomach. Almost hoarse by now, his voice pleads, *Let's go over this one more time*: 'Fruits and frigging nuts. Hand-pounded rice . . . that's like half of what they talk about.'

Silence. As the truck judders particularly badly, the icebox loosens, slides intermittently down the tilted floor towards them.

Ackerman has her head in her hands. Frustrated. 'This holy man has a really big thing about roughage, bowel movements in general. I don't know what more to say, Bill. Perhaps it's just a straightforward health consultation . . . '

Jahanghir chips in. 'Ms Kirsten is right: Hamza complaining very much about gas, sharp pains in stomach.'

'I must be going mad, I can't believe this . . . ' Lamayette feels as if a shiny metal band is being tightened around his skull. 'Maybe this poopie-pants, Special K-stuff is code for something else.'

Like all CIA field operatives, Lamayette has taken basic coursework on matters alimentary: how to use a Bristol Stool Chart to get a chambermaid to help give the literal low-down on the health of some prime minister or president. He knows, for example, that a stool sample tested for a pathogen like *Candida* is a quick way to prove that somebody's receiving treatment for cancer.

But this? Two crackpots, crazy as moonbeams, prognosticating about their turds. Number of. Quality. Duration of toilet. Density of material. Sphincter, tightness of.

There's long contemplation on this point. The Bedford grinds through its gears as they head uphill.

Exhaustion finally pushes Ackerman over the top. 'They've got those supercomputers at Fort Meade. You could call up the National Security Agency: Hi . . . ' she feels the giggles welling up from deep inside her ' . . . Bill Lamayette here. You thought I was dead, but I'm not actually. Anyhow, over here in Pakistan we've got some dudes talking about their O-rings and their axe-length wallylogs. Care to crunch that for us, tell me whether this is cipher for some kind of terrorist attack . . . '

Lamayette is ready for some silliness. The whole thing now too ridiculous for words, that he'd risked his career, his whole life, for *this* . . . 'Hey, Ackerman. What are you yuking about? You're the one who's got to take this to the ambassador, or have you forgotten?' The CIA officer gets into his stride, noting she's doubled over, crying with laughter, dabbing her eyes with the long sleeve of her traditional embroidered kaftan. Panting. He puts on a falsetto voice: 'Ambassador, we worked out the code: one pint of prune juice and a two-flush turd that steamed like a bowl of Chocolate Malt-O-Meal . . . '

It's at this moment, that look of hysterical desperation on her face, that Lamayette knows

161

he could have her. Her chest heaving, tears leaking down her face. All he needs is to wind up his boyish charm, keep pressing those buttons, and he would bend her to his way. For sure. Even if it amounts to nothing more than sympathy sex, so what? A guy going down in flames deserves one last roll of the dice, one last rummage around on government property. Almost in anticipation, he can't help but admire those breasts, filling out that kaftan so nicely. There's nothing quite like the full, heavy breasts of a woman laughing out of control. And that Rita Hayworth hair . . .

God bless.

It's only Jahanghir's blank, wearied face that keeps him from riffing on into the night. His look of anticipation, of hungry expectation: *Mr Bill, what do we do now?* How about you disappear in a puff of smoke . . . *Darkest hour is the hour before up comes sunshine, Mr Bill* . . . Go away, Jahanghir, and he forces his thoughts back on to those laughing titties. Random imaginings about hefting them in his hands, gently blowing across the nipples and waiting for the response. Like a schoolboy stretching out each last moment of the holidays, he's feverishly blocking off the looming horror: the board of inquiry, yammering lawyers, depositions, explaining the gorilla, the exploded car. *This* sackable offence . . . and *that* one . . . all the goodies waiting for him. Still Jahanghir waits for instruction . . . *Never give up, you say that, Mr Bill.*

In that moment, whatever chemistry there is

with Ackerman, an alignment of planets perhaps, fizzles out under the earnest gaze of an upright, loyal Pashtun. *I'm going to damned well dock him some pay for that look of disapproval.*

Lamayette shakes his head wistfully, takes the wrapper off another packet of Lucky Strikes, rolls the cellophane into a tight ball and flicks it away. 'We really have got stuff-all here, haven't we?'

Ackerman sniffs, wipes her eyes then the dripping tip of her nose. Does the breathing-exercise thing. Inhale. Hold. Exhale. Again. It's such a performance that the two men are in rapt attention, waiting for her to ready herself.

'I did have two other things. First. This line of chat about the Qissa Khawani Bazaar. It was a bit unclear. Sort of muffled.' She flicks a look at Jahanghir, seeking confirmation, and he nods sideways. Go ahead, and she takes her notes from Lamayette . . .

'It starts with a fragment of a question from Hamza: . . . *always gives me inspiration. How do you remember the Massacre?*

'Pir Durbar: *Qissa Khawani was the unravelling of British rule. Full stop. Not just in North West Frontier Province. But in whole of India. We heard our fathers and uncles talking, we closed our eyes and could see the hundreds of young men and women coming forward to take the place of those killed. Innocents. Every one of them. Pashtun baring their chest to bullets. How wonderful. Offering no resistance, embracing promise of martyrdom. The Badshah Khan told his followers: I am going to give you such a*

163

weapon that the police and the army will not be able to stand against it. It is the weapon of the Prophet, but you are not aware of it. That weapon is patience and righteousness. No power on earth can stand against it. *Which is why after Qissa Khawani the British would say, only thing more dangerous than a Pashtun with a gun, is a Pashtun with no gun.*

'Hamza: *And it is true each of the martyrs reached for the Koran?*

'Pir Durbar: *Very many did. Those that fell in the bazaar were clutching the Koran, and those that followed stooped to pick up holy book and with Allah's strength walked with grace into battle. The true mujahid. The power of that sacrifice was what doomed British rule. Be damned to Gandhi and his salt marches. A triviality. A nothing, simply for the news cameras and his Western friends. It was the martyrs of Qissa Khawani that crushed imperialists.*

'Hamza: *And so it shall be again. Tomorrow we shall make Qissa Khawani famous again. Operation Macchar. Patience and righteousness shall once more be the weapon of the Prophet.*'

'Operation *Macchar* . . . he's talking about a mosquito?' Lamayette shakes his head at the Urdu word. The name means nothing. Dammit nothing. No operational detail. 'What else?'

Ackerman explains there had been general cooing of agreement on the Macchar Qissa Khawani, that it would be a political game-changer in Pakistan, but the discussion had quickly moved on to more consultations: Hamza had passed a stool earlier in the week which, in

164

the right light, looked like the spectacled hood of the cobra so beloved by the Hindu deity Shiva.

Ackerman, with her scribbled translation, asks, 'Do you want to know the significance?'

'Enough about bowels already,' Lamayette mutters, shuffling uncomfortably. 'I think I need a history lesson on Qissa Khawani. I feel like the only one who doesn't know what's being talked about.'

Jahanghir, to his left, starts. 'You know Qissa Khawani Bazaar, in Peshawar?'

'Sort of.' Lamayette shrugs. In truth, Peshawar had doubled in size in the four years following the Soviet invasion of Afghanistan. Where there might once have been a charming boulevard or a clutch of shady mango trees, there is now concrete. Most of the architecturally pleasing things in the city had been gobbled up in the rush to accommodate this new diaspora. To Lamayette, Qissa Khawani is typical. He knew it only as yet another of the city's nondescript, overbuilt roads. Jammed up with a mix of noisy one-man commercial operations: teashops, dry-fruit sellers, barbers, tyre retreaders, DVD stores, leather goods, hi-fi emporiums. He's aware of its Kiplingesque name — the Storytellers' Bazaar — and how it had been the pre-eminent place for travellers to stop and gossip by the now demolished Kabuli Gate. Above street level loom impenetrable, low shabby blocks of offices, darkened unfriendly windows, dripping air-conditioners and thickets of telephone and electricity lines. You assume all manner of illegal activities are countenanced. Not the sort of place

165

a CIA station chief chooses to tarry long.

Jahanghir rolls his moustache between his fingers. 'In 1930, the local Pashtun allies of Gandhi were arrested by the British. These people were called Redshirts. The people of Badshah Khan. Our King of Chiefs. Very famous people; Badshah Khan taught Pashtun how *not* to fight. Can you imagine-that? Us? Pashtun? Anyway . . . ' and the Pakistani whispers ' . . . All held in Kabuli prison. This very much angered local people,' and Jahanghir puffs his chest out, 'we local people protest next day, marching to prison, marching along Qissa Khawani Bazaar. There, in the bazaar, that is where they are being shot. Two hundred dead certainly, maybe even as many as four hundred.'

Lamayette is startled. 'Four *hundred*?'

'You are sounding surprised, Mr Bill?'

'Four hundred dead, and I never heard of this before . . . ?'

Jahanghir rolls his head. 'Very great tragedy of my people. These were Pashtun who die. Even worse, they were Pashtun who worked with Gandhi, and therefore not friends with Jinnah.' He looks dolefully back and forth between his audience of two. 'After Partition, it is Jinnah's people not Pashtun who write the history books of this country. And for the friends of Gandhi, we are too Muslim, not Hindu enough for the history writers of India. All Indians want to write about is the salt satyagraha. It makes them feel very good about themselves. Very brave about such a . . . ' and Jahanghir squeezes his thumb

166

and two fingers together ' . . . such a small thing.'

Ackerman segues into the discussion. 'The satyagraha happened early in April 1930, the breaking of the salt tax. The Qissa Khawani Massacre was on the twenty-third, almost three weeks later. The worst that happened to Gandhi and his followers were beatings and jail, but it was enough to spread his fame throughout the world.

'But in Peshawar, it wasn't just sticks and stones. This crowd of Redshirts walked willingly down that narrow bazaar into a fusillade of gunfire that lasted almost six hours. Wave after wave, they kept coming. By any definition the danger and intimidation that Badshah Khan's followers faced was many orders of magnitude greater than Gandhi's. Walking to their deaths, into a blaze of machine-gun and rifle fire without a thought of retribution or violence. They were called the Servants of God. It turns out to be one of the most important occasions of Muslim non-violent resistance.'

Lamayette examines his big meaty hands as if in the folds of his palms he's written the answer to some perplexing question. 'Important maybe to some fucking dusty academic. But nobody knows about it. So how much use is that?'

'OK. Not a lot, I grant you. But it's a powerful thing that people in *these* parts remember. The Indians remember overthrowing the salt tax, we celebrate defying the British tax on tea, and the Pashtun have the Qissa Khawani Massacre.'

Frustrated, Lamayette slams a fist into his

167

palm. 'That doesn't give me a *when* or a *how*, a *who* or a *where*.' So close . . . so close he can almost sense the shape of this thing. Almost.

'What the hell is this Operation Macchar?'

Operation Macchar, less than fifteen hours to go

MI5 Headquarters
Thames House
London

It's early evening on a Sunday, the Sunday of a long weekend, and Sheila 'Noppy' Davane is standing at the window of her MI5 office. Just light enough for her to be gazing down on the slow, brown, rippling surface of the River Thames.

Just to her left is Lambeth Bridge and beyond that, down-river, is Westminster Bridge. The London Eye beyond that. She watches in the far distance the tiny, bobbing heads of another surge of visitors crossing Westminster Bridge towards the South Bank facing her. No doubt heading towards Waterloo Station, and onwards to homes in places like Raynes Park, Virginia Water and Eastleigh. Places most people couldn't point to on a map, but which are the very essence of this country's being. From her lofty vantage point, she thinks of them all as her people. The famous unseen, silent majority on whose behalf she is striving. These are the people who, if they were to know the dangers Davane has to face on their behalf, the rules

169

she has to shade, would no doubt quietly nod. Get on with it, they'd say. *Stick it to them*.

Noppy Davane has what management consultants like to call 'institutional memory'. She had started with MI5 back in 1975 at the height of the IRA's first bombing campaign on the mainland. More than thirty years of total and unyielding sacrifice.

She had started in a pool of headphone-wearing typists, copy-taking messages from agents and informers who were ringing in from public phones to a free-of-charge number that MI5 used to run. She'd been brought to London to make sure callers from both sides of the Irish border would find a kindred spirit who could understand the accent. They weren't likely, either, to hang around spelling out place names, or explaining the geography of a place. Often, they needed to speak quickly and quietly because what they were doing would get them killed. Simple as that.

Murdering Mick bastards. She sighs as she thinks of what the other secretaries used to mutter, as they transferred to her the informers who were risking their lives to help MI5.

The Thames flows slowly under the bridge. From her window, she watches almost in a trance, through the outline of a stand of lime trees between her and the river's edge. Her office space is very twenty-first-century — modern, functional and grey. The only colour comes from her niece's oil paintings of favourite County Antrim seascapes.

There's a *phhsssh* sound. Davane's sound-proofed door is pushed open and a young secretary who she had bossed into working today, to help make sense of Davane's computer, and her backlog of emails, pokes her head around the corner. Glasses up on her head. 'There's a call you might want to take, Ms Davane.'

'Who is it?' She gently nudges her forehead into the triple-glazed glass sheet in front of her. Feels the blessed cool on her skin.

No answer. She turns, and sees the door already closed. Staff these days . . . she curses under her breath as she labours towards the desk. Her leg paining more than usual.

The voice at the other end of the line she recognises instantly.

'Mr Bill Lamayette. Well. This is an honour. The BBC are reporting you have reached the Other Side. Got your seventy-two virgins yet?'

On speakerphone, the drawling Louisiana accent comes through crystal clear. 'They're virgins, all right, but only because they're ugly and old. Wouldn't touch 'em with my dead dog's dick.' Slight pause, and crackle from the satellite relay. 'No disrespect meant.'

'None taken,' and Noppy's face creases into a smile. 'You must be in a whole world of trouble calling me. Your employers have been putting out the hard word about your *quote* unreliability *unquote*. Erratic behaviour. Pending internal investigations. And so on.'

'Straight from the Langley playbook.'

'Both of our playbooks, I fear.'

'Yeah. Well. Whatever.' Lamayette sounds embarrassed, disappointed to discover what he feared was true all along: in time of crisis, there is no shame in blame. 'Listen. I've gone a little bit off reservation on this one. I'm about a hundred and fifty miles north of Peshawar. Been surveilling a madrasa. Some full-of-shit holy man got a visit from a guy who's wired in with the wrong side of Pakistan intelligence and has money to burn. Hamza Khan is his name, son of General Ali Mahmood Khan.' Davane nods slowly. She saw her fair share of MI6 and CIA work-product. General Khan rings distant bells, so her eyes squint, trying to work out where this is going.

'Anyway. In watching Hamza we might have turned up something . . . Operation Macchar. Mean anything?' He spells out the word and the possible ways it could be Romanised.

She thinks for a while, tapping the top of her desk with an HB pencil. 'No, can't say that it does, Bill.'

A hint of desperation in his voice. 'How about an Operation Mosquito?'

'I'm going to put you on hold for a minute.' And with that she calls through to MI5's archives, asks them to cross-reference their databanks and all intercept traffic for any Operation Mosquito, or Macchar.

When she comes back, the news is not good. She smiles as she reads a handwritten note. 'There was an Operation Mosquito in 1944. Near Caen. The Germans had purposely made stagnant some marshes and a couple of canals,

172

so the whole place was overrun with mosquitoes and wasps. Hence Operation Mosquito. The 26 Field Hygiene Section sprayed oil and cut down some hedges.'

For a long time, there's not a word said. Just static on the line.

'Doesn't sound promising,' admits Lamayette, finally.

'No, Bill.' Davane puts down her pad, sharing in his disappointment. Part of her notes, rather clinically, that she is experiencing an unusual sensation: empathy.

'Promise me this . . . '

'Sure.'

'Plug Qissa Khawani and Operation Macchar into Dictionary. Let that be my last loving gift to the world.' Dictionary is the vast software program that sifts and analyses keywords and phrases sucked out of the electronic ether by the Echelon listening posts scattered across the world, but centred on the National Security Agency at Fort Meade and GCHQ in Cheltenham. MI5 is one of the biggest beneficiaries of the processed surveillance data.

'You're a rogue, William Lamayette . . . I hope whatever it is you are doing this for, it pays you back in spades.' She makes a note. Qissa Khawani and Macchar, *check spellings*.

So. When Sheila 'Noppy' Davane hangs up the phone, there's a look of consolation, anguish even, on the thick flesh of her face. It's a call she was glad to have taken. Somebody right at the bottom of a big hole, trying to get himself out. From the Old School, like herself. Looking for

173

help. Hoping to do the right thing.

Good for you, boy.

★ ★ ★

Minutes later and Lamayette is striding back towards the cab of the tow truck, his distinctive features obscured by a grey turban and shawl arrangement. Jahanghir struggles to keep up. To make the call to London, the tow truck, with the stricken Bedford, had parked off the verge off the busy Malakand road. He'd made the call from inside the cabin, leaving it to the driver to find the highest point on the pass to get the best signal. It's barely a two-lane road. Buses and lorries roar past in gales of exhaust fumes, headlights and horns blaring. Noise. Dust.

The American has to raise his voice to Jahanghir. 'Look, old friend. Travel with your cousins in the front. Me and the lady, we're just going to chill out in the Bedford. Don't worry about us.'

And Jahanghir smiles wolfishly, his teeth flashing in the light of an approaching truck.

'Just tell me this, old friend. How long have I got? Where's Peshawar from here?'

The Pakistani looks left and right. Either way the curved mountain road hugs the side of the valley, snarled with traffic, pinpricked with the coming and going of truck lights off into the distance. 'Maybe we have made ten miles from the madrasa, so another . . . ' shrug of the shoulders ' . . . fifteen to Malakand and

174

one hundred and fifty to Peshawar. Long night.'

'Gotya.' And he stands by the tow-truck front door, scoots Jahanghir up and inside: 'You got that big pickle jar. My beautiful little cornichons. Get me that, and one of those kerosene lamps in there. And that coat. I'll give you a call on the mobile when I'm in the cabin and I've got the trapdoor closed. OK?'

Jahanghir gives a thumbs-up. His right thumb missing from the first knuckle owing to an unspecified altercation with a rival. 'Mr Bill. Monkey sex.' Big grin.

'Monkey sex,' Lamayette confirms, returning the thumbs-up. And he holds up the big fat bottle of cornichon pickles. Seventy-five-ounce jar. One of the many uses Lamayette has made of the diplomatic pouch.

Good man, Jahanghir. A lot better than I deserve . . . and Lamayette slides away to the rear. Shoulders sloped, more than a little ashamed of what he's about to do.

The Bedford, once so proud in her boastful ornamentation, looks bereft, rear axle in the air, as though her modesty is being violated. He crabs underneath the chassis, squeezes himself towards the trapdoor, and pops his head up into the wood cabin.

A couple of minutes later he ends the quick call to Jahanghir and closes down the mobile for the last time that night.

The diesel engine growls and he waits for the clank of chains and towbar and the snap of the Bedford as she lurches forward. Whichever cousin is driving tonight revs hard. No finesse. A shriek of horns, even a few sirens sound, as the two conjoined trucks cut across the road and pick up the flow of vehicles towards Peshawar. The tow truck with Jahanghir and his cousins, transporting the Bedford with Kirsten Ackerman stowed inside, is soon lost in the procession. It disappears around a bend . . .

. . . none of them any the wiser that Bill Lamayette is crouching by the side of the road, on a scree slope, watching them chug fitfully into the night.

'You take this lamp, and the coat,' he had said, trying not to look at Ackerman. The auburn hair, the contours of that kaftan, the laughing breasts. He couldn't look because he was fearful she'd be making come-to-bed eyes at him like that naughty lioness in *The Lion King*, and he was pretty certain he wouldn't be strong enough to resist. So he'd put on his best, tight, business face. 'You wrap up in this coat. It'll be two or three hours till we get to Peshawar. I'll travel this leg with Jahanghir, I need to break the news easy to him, about me and the CIA. That I'm giving myself up.' Two whopping great lies, dished out to two people who had done Lamayette no harm.

He shrugs. Turns towards the madrasa. Squints into the lights of the oncoming traffic, folds the *shemag* and shawl right across his features and starts the two-hour trudge. He's still not certain he's done the right thing: an American, in perhaps the most lawless place on

176

earth. No Pashto skills, no gun. How stupid is that?

All he has is a phone, a throwing knife and his big jar of Ragin' Cajun cornichons. Plus an over-abundance of fury.

Threshold of Runway 12
Benazir Bhutto International Airport
Islamabad, Pakistan
On board PK412 to Manchester, England,
and thence to JFK, New York
0219 Pakistan time — Monday;
2119 UK time — Sunday evening

The particular kind of mosquito that General Ali Mahmood Khan had in mind when he conceived Operation Macchar is an awesome sight. Especially at dead of night. A wingspan of more than two hundred feet, a tail reaching sixty feet into the air, and two-thirds of the length of a football pitch. For the company building the plane, it was a huge leap into the twenty-first century. The first time Boeing had produced a fully glass cockpit: the contractors had to build aviation's largest ever central computer to manage the fly-by-wire system that controls the jetliner. Five hundred software developers wrote more than 600,000 new lines of code to handle the flight and navigation functions. One such behemoth now stands with its two massive General Electric turbofan engines idling, on the threshold of Runway 12. Waiting for final take-off clearance from Islamabad tower.

Call sign Victor Sierra, *City of Risalpur* is the last of the nine Boeing 777s purchased by Pakistan International Airways in what was the country's largest ever capital goods order.

In command of tonight's 412 flight to Manchester is Captain Saaed Salahuddin, known to one and all as Harry, a nickname bestowed in the early 1980s by the grizzled United Airlines instructor who trained him up as a Boeing 747 first officer.

The old, seat-of-the-pants instructor was dazzled by Salahuddin's ability to escape all manner of simulated emergencies, multiple-engine failures and thirty-knot crosswinds. 'Salahuddin, you're no ordinary pilot, more like a goddamn Harry Houdini.' Later, while demolishing an excellent bottle of twelve-year-old single malt whisky, they agreed Saaed *Salahouddini* didn't quite work, but *Harry* Salahuddin . . . that sounded right.

With his van Dyke beard, waxed moustache and slightly faded movie-star looks, Salahuddin has the absolute authority of a man with more hours' flying time (21,000 hours and rising) than anyone else in the airline. But no additional airline baubles hang around his neck: no Chief Pilot Technical, no Chief Pilot Fleet 1 (Boeing 777s). Not even Chief Pilot Lahore Base (where Salahuddin lives). No. His reputation as an ornery, argumentative and uncompromising stickler has put him in the wilderness of airline politics.

That's OK with him. It gives him a certain freedom. Like the time he wrote an open letter to the Civil Aviation Authority, copied to his employers and all his fellow captains. Beware: the centrelines of a freshly painted taxiway leading in and out of a maintenance hangar at Karachi have been incorrectly measured. Even though taxiways and aprons weren't the airline's responsibility, he knew if he didn't warn nobody else would. So he paced it himself with a measuring wheel. Three times. He sketched out the problem and warned that the dimensions guaranteed an on-ground collision sometime in the future. There was simply not enough separation.

Harry on his hobby horse again, his brother pilots had no doubt mocked, *Captain Doom* . . . but sure enough it happened — a wingtip from one 777 ripping off the tail cone of another, early one morning when both were being tugged into position.

Salahuddin went on to ruin a perfectly good cocktail party by raising his voice to, . . . *That was your people's responsibility, and so this is your fault* . . . and finger-poking at some of the country's most senior CAA board members. His lack of deference was striking: *You are all too interested in politics to do your jobs properly.*

When he spoke to the clutch of TV reporters who had staked out the family farm after his letter came to light, Salahuddin was slightly more diplomatic (on instruction from a furious wife). The incident would have been comical, a Mr Bean sketch perhaps, he said, except that $300 million of inventory almost got destroyed.

Salahuddin keys the radio, irritation in his

voice. 'Islamabad Tower. This is Pakistan 412. On threshold, Runway 12 . . . awaiting your instructions.'

After a lengthy delay a thin voice stutters out a reply, embarrassed, as if this is the first time he's ever spoken into a microphone. '*Four one two. Please hold . . . traffic in vicinity.*' Salahuddin frowns, a pair of half-glasses balanced on the end of his nose. The pilot's eyes sweep left and right. Nothing. Moreover, he knows from checking the approach frequencies nobody is inbound.

He turns to his first officer, Mirza, a painfully anxious and washed-out-looking man with bony knees that almost touch the glass screens of the cockpit instrumentation. 'Must be a lady working in the tower tonight. All the randy old goats off preening themselves in the washroom.'

First Officer Mirza looks blankly at his captain. Understanding the words but not the joke. Somewhere deep inside Salahuddin his soul weeps a little, for the blandness of these young pilots, for their lack of vitality. Mirza's 'position and hold' approach to the threshold of the runway had been . . . nervy.

What worries him is that this new generation of pilots had never actually wrestled with a stick or control column. Or, as he had done on too many occasions, coaxed the engines of an overloaded craft, fluttering her off the runway at Chitral high in the Kush and nursing her home, with the mountains soaring above on either side and the wind clawing from four different directions.

His father had taught him to watch both the

trees, the way they move, folding and bending to the pressure of the wind, and the birds, how their feathers splay open on landing like fingers reaching for safety. Learn about flying from those that actually fly, he would always say. Even a kite, playing the currents, taught you more about bare-bones airmanship than some of these FOs would know, spending all their downtime in darkened rooms playing the latest Microsoft Flight Simulator package.

His wife, having moved to Dubai more than five years ago to be with their son and grandchildren, pecked at him consistently about flying for Emirates, or Etihad or what was left of Gulf Air.

'Why do you stay, Harry?' would be her constant refrain as she knitted away, and he detailed his battles within the company when they were together. 'It's not as if they even like you.'

True enough, but how could he explain what keeps him in Pakistan?

Firstly, there is the job. When Pakistan was created in 1947 it was the national flag carrier that kept the country whole, shuttling back and forth between east and west Pakistan and servicing the remotest, most dangerous of airstrips — creating a visible, secure bond between a fledgling government and her disparate peoples. That strong sense of nation-building, that the airline's destiny was wrapped up in his country's, would never leave him. I am working for the national flag-carrier, he would tell his wife, *I carry the flag*, and she would cluck noisily at her teeth.

It worked both ways, of course. Salahuddin's employer was only as competent as the government, more specifically the management, that it put in place. So as the country lurched into its first bout of madness under General Zia, slowly at first, then at a gathering pace over the years that followed, the airline found itself towed backwards by its political masters and the turbulence of poor decision-making that they churned up. Many did walk away, took jobs in the Gulf or with the low-cost start-up airlines. But, to Salahuddin, that was not what you did when your country was in crisis. You stayed. You gave your all. And when you saw something you didn't like, a compromise, a fudge, you raised your voice. Loud, and louder still, and hoped somebody listened.

Perhaps also, he stayed in Pakistan for selfish reasons too. Because it is only somewhere like Pakistan that a pilot can indulge himself in something truly wickedly mischievous. The sort of real flying that first world airline pilots dream of, as they gaze glass-eyed at the computers flying them hither and thither. Sneaking to the Walton airfield in Lahore, being paid to fly the club's Cherokee or Cessna 152 around the city. Doors taken off. Wind whistling through the cabin. No ashen-faced first officers, no paperwork. Breathing freely at last as he bombs the citizens from five hundred feet with leaflets about some new Coke promotion, or a must-see movie. Or angling the plane on its side so he can tip sacks and sacks of flower petals, blessing the opening of a factory, or the nuptials of a newlywed couple.

That is freedom. And only in Pakistan . . . a crazy-eccentric sort of place, where you still have the freedom to do crazy-eccentric things.

First Officer Mirza clears his throat. A gentle reminder. Mirza is handling the take-off, so Salahuddin works the radio. 'Islamabad Tower. This is *still* Pakistan 412. *Still* holding on threshold, Runway 12 . . . '

And the reply comes back quickly, a little too strong, as if to say, *Why the delay, Salahuddin?*

'*Pakistan 412. Permission to take off. Runway 12. Surface wind 110 degrees. Four knots . . .* ' A different voice from earlier.

Salahuddin thinks about a smart reply, *Sorry to keep you from your beauty sleep*, but decides against it. His professional instincts tell him it's not worth the distraction. Instead he confirms the controller's information: 'Wind four knots, at 110. Four one two.'

He looks over his half-glasses, gives a little flick of the head. 'Pre-take-off checklist . . . ' And Mirza, in command, calls off the few remaining items on the console between them.

'Parking brake . . . '

'SET,' replies Salahuddin.

'Throttle . . . '

'IDLE.'

'Flap position lever . . . '

'FLAPS FIVE DEGREES.'

'Spoilers . . . '

'RETRACTED.'

Another twenty seconds and the list is

completed. Salahuddin, leaning on his armrest, says in his most encouraging voice, 'First Officer Mirza, take us over the oceans and far away.'

And within a handful of seconds the Boeing 777 is bounding down Islamabad's long east-west asphalt runway. Then rotation, and a slow right-handed turn through almost 180 degrees until the plane levels, still climbing, on a westward track. Towards Europe. Crossing into Afghanistan just north of Peshawar to pick up the international air corridor that will take them all the way through to Manchester in the United Kingdom. Then onwards to New York.

Three hundred and nineteen souls on board.

Just an average, everyday flight travelling through the average, everyday night.

★　★　★

By the time PK412 takes off, in both Britain and the United States more than sixty separate data fields in each individual's Passenger Name Record or PNR had already been crunched by high-powered computer programs looking for red flags, payment in cash, one-way tickets, names on a particular watch-list. Tonight's flight offers nothing that shouts, *Alarm*: a large delegation from Gujranwala (City of Wrestlers) — twenty-nine athletes and another thirty close family members in support, travelling to the east coast of the United States for various collegiate wrestling competitions. All okayed by the US embassy in Islamabad, which always has an eye to winning hearts and minds in Pakistan.

Forty-four moderate Islamic scholars, women lawyers and government officials travelling together to attend a conference on sexual politics and Islamic ideology in Denver. Excellent. To be commended. And the US consular section almost couldn't issue the visas fast enough.

But the largest contingent on the flight, almost fifty, are former members of the Peace Corps who had served in Pakistan during the 1960s, returning home after spending more than a fortnight touring the various places they'd served over forty years before. People who gave some of the best years of their lives to what was then a young country, to improving public and rural health, and starting off farming schemes in faraway places like Sialkot and Dera Ismail Khan.

For General Ali Mahmood Khan and his Operation Macchar to have such a cross-section of good, decent folk on board, especially those Peace Corps volunteers — all grey-hairs, in their sixties and seventies, pillars of their communities in Tiny Town, Idaho or Missouri — is an astonishing bonus.

More than he could possibly have hoped for . . .

★ ★ ★

As the mosquito that gave its name to Operation Macchar starts its long journey from Pakistan, droning onwards into the cloudless night sky, Bill Lamayette trudges back to the madrasa. His

186

mouth parched, his eyes becoming heavy with sleep, operating only on some kind of primitive autopilot. The one thing in his mind, helping him slap one foot down in front of another, the banging rhythms of Twisted Sister. Mumbling. How he wasn't going to take it. No, dammit, I'm just not going to take it.

★ ★ ★

High above Lamayette, at almost thirty thousand feet now and twinkling with strobe and anti-collision lights, Captain Salahuddin and First Officer Mirza note from their glass-cockpit navigation display that they are directly abeam of Peshawar. Salahuddin slips into a little routine about how it was from Peshawar airport that the American Gary Powers departed in 1960 in his doomed U2 spy plane . . . how Powers ended his days as a helicopter traffic reporter in California, how he died when his Jet Ranger ran out of fuel. 'Of all the mistakes for this great pilot to make . . . '

. . . and in a factory space just north of Peshawar airport, faithful Jahanghir hops down from the tow truck. Smiles up at the jingly-jangly Bedford truck and the lack of any sign of his boss, Mr Bill.

He decides it would be a good thing to let Mr Bill and the nice lady with the red hair, the flashing green eyes and very becoming hips spend as much time together as they need.

He mimes to his four cousins that they should exit quietly. Leave the garage door ajar . . . have some food, relax, and wait for Mr Bill to unwind himself from the arms of a giving woman.

Very good.

Monday morning — the day of Operation Macchar Memorial Day in the US; May bank holiday in the UK

In a farmhouse
Outside the village of Elton
Derbyshire Peak District
0601 UK time, 1101 Islamabad time

While they wait, Ferret is retelling a legendary story, a little light entertainment before the parting of the ways. Everybody in the farmhouse kitchen looks on, steaming coffee or tea in hand, faces already smiling: how an American Ranger had unzipped himself on to a bar stool and whacked one of his testicles with the heel of his shoe (Button, Whiffler and Piglet wince instinctively). According to Ferret, this one-upmanship happens in a pub in deepest Wales after a joint Para-Ranger exercise. It was nothing less than a challenge. Ferret continues: so, the Para sergeant major calls this private over and tells him, for the honour of the Regiment, get your balls out now, lad, and here, use my boot . . .

The air is quietly sucked out of the room as Tristie Merritt walks out of the shadows of the hallway, wearing a stunning ivory twill skirt suit with pinstripes and a lace hem. A dark smoky look. Deep blue eyeshadow heightening the aquamarine of her eyes.

In her hand a series of thick brown envelopes, £5,000 in used notes and another £5,000 in stored-value credit cards. Both untraceable. She deals them across the table to each of the men in Ward 13.

For a moment the envelopes lie untouched. Shoe looks to Whiffler, a reassurance, who turns to Ferret, an acknowledgement, who glances across to Button, and he nods. Quick meaningful exchanges, everything transmitted in the eyes or a tip of the head. The looks are not about what they feel in their loins, but in their hearts first, and their brains following. They understand once again why it is they will follow this woman to the ends of the earth. Part organiser, part tactician and part mesmeriser.

Tristie's gaze takes in all of her men, one by one. Then, with a wry smile, 'You all understand this is goodbye, for a while?'

Shoe, Weasel, Ferret and Piglet nod their understanding. Pocket their envelopes. They are staying behind in London, to play a waiting game. The Ministry of Defence's deadline runs out within twenty-four hours and Tristie needs at least part of the team on the ground for whatever eventuates.

By contrast, Button and Whiffler, the medic and explosives experts respectively, are flying to New York with Tristie later today. Many Paras have valid multiple-entry US visas because they do more and more of their jump training in America, especially Fort Dix in New Jersey. This allows them to train with US chutes and rigging, and learn their signals and terminology. Button and Whiffler's visas are the most recently issued, have the longest to run. Hence their selection.

From another envelope she deals out new SIM cards, which the team begin to fit into their mobiles, crushing or snapping the old ones. Everybody knows the protocols. The mobile numbers are re-entered but this time slightly altered with a simple code that renders the digits meaningless to anyone not in the know. Shoe had spent much of last night going through everybody's belongings, taking away notebooks, diaries, pads, BlackBerrys, anything on which names, numbers and addresses of the Ward 13 team may have been stored. What wasn't burnt is zipped up in a duffel and will be stored away.

Tristie ladles three teaspoons of instant coffee into a mug, plenty of milk. 'We're going to communicate with the MoD from a bolthole in America because if this craps out, that is the one place the British government won't dare to touch us. To extradite us from there, they'd have to completely show their hand — that the Trident software has been compromised.'

She brings the hot coffee to her lips and sips gingerly. 'Their weakness is going to be our strength.'

Ramada Piccadilly
Portland Street
Manchester
0615 UK time, 1115 Islamabad time

Hotel room 703 — the man remembers being told that waking up is the nearest thing to knowing what it feels like to be born. Delivered into the world, truly a child, your eyes opening to a blank canvas. Then the brain powers up, senses activate and memory drops into place. Those shapeless fragments of the past fold into the present, into coherence.

His reaction to the start of the day runs as follows: he senses the comfortable plumpness of the hotel pillow and the cool starch of the sheets against his thighs and calves. He blinks at the whiteness of the walls (the notepad by the phone bragging *Best three-star hotel in the North-West*). A little green light winks at him from the smoke detector in the ceiling . . . but none of this tells him where he is . . .

His eye is drawn by the bright colour of the jacket hanging over the trouser press. Tailored. Powder blue. The single gold band around each of the sleeves. His uniform . . . he knows that in the past, in the decadent Western years, the

192

airline had used designers like Pierre Cardin and Sir Hardy Amies. Now Pakistan International Airways uses a local and that makes him happy. He is crewing for the *national* airline, after all.

Then it comes to him. Of course ... *today* ... it is happening today ... and the man in Room 703 finds himself overcome by a burst of happiness so intense and fulfilling that, as when facing the sun's purest rays, he knows he must close his eyes if he is to make sense of it all. The shattering truth of his grandfather's words which have rung through him like the muezzin's cry, unanswered for all these years ... *Standing for an hour in the ranks of battle is better than standing in prayer for sixty years.*

Finally. Grandfather will be proud of me. Today. *Praise be to Allah, Lord of the Worlds.* Finally I will avenge my grandfather. Killed in that bomb blast on Gulshan Iqbal Road. *The Hereafter is for the pious, and there is no enmity save towards the unjust.* Killed in an explosion so huge that in the mind of the man in Room 703 he is always eight years old, and Mother still holds him tight, as the ground thunders beneath them and the air is sucked from the room ... twenty-one years ago it was, masonry and plasterboard clacking to the floor. *I bear witness that there is none worthy of worship save Allah alone, and I bear witness that Muhammad is His Slave and Messenger* ... Dust snows gently on to their backs as she cries for you, her father, my grandfather, the one she feared they would take. *May Allah bless him, his pure Household, his noble Companions, and all those who follow them in goodness upto the day of Judgement.*

You will be my Sleeper.

That was what the General had promised, coming to Mother and him only a few months after Grandfather's death. General Ali Mahmood Khan's early smile had masked a searching stare as he scoured the eight-year-old's eyes. Probing for a weakness, for a tic or flinch that spoke of doubt. Finally, satisfied, he had cupped the boy's jawline with leathery palms and moved closer still. Eyes blazing like hot coals. Be my Sleeper, but never let go of the Anger you feel now.

The General had given them a new life. And to seal the pact was a flawless set of documents: suitably aged birth certificates and Ministry of Interior-issued passports, even a back-dated school registration that connected both of them with a completely different family tree. All properly worn-in with careless stamps and random grease-stains, so that when the time came for the young men to join the airline there was no trace of his family's radical past. Not a red flag in sight.

One day your Grandfather will need your Anger.

★　★　★

Beside his hotel bed is a small, sealed package. Covered in Chinese characters and the picture of an enraged, red-eyed cat swatting at a pesky rodent. Dushuqiang is the name of the formulation. Chinese for Extra-Strength Rat

194

Poison. 'Odourless, tasteless and water soluble'. The man in Room 703 says the words to himself. Odourless. Tasteless . . . miraculous.

The poison is so potent it was formally banned in the 1990s, the government even setting up an anti-Dushuqiang task force. But, China being China, the farmers in the faraway provinces keep using Dushuqiang and couldn't care less what the World Health Organisation has to say. On the tried and tested principle that what Beijing can't see isn't going to hurt them, illicit factories churn out the soluble white crystals, all using the same active ingredient, tetramethylenedisulfotetramine (TETS). But quality is haphazard: a shop owner from Nanjing was executed after sprinkling a light dusting — no more than five milligrams — over the snacks sold in a rival store and killing thirty-eight people. A year later that same dusting, on the food served at a funeral in Hubei province, and this time only ten died.

The sample in Room 703 is an eye-popping thirty-two per cent concentration weight for weight. Devastatingly lethal. At least a hundred times as powerful as potassium cyanide. And there is no proven antidote to TETS. Once ingested, the poison attacks the membranes of the neurone cells, causing death by convulsion in seconds.

It was last night that the small, sealed package had been handed to the man in Room 703.

At the time, he had been pecking away on the Internet in the small crew room set aside for airline staff at the hotel. Blogging. Writing a

195

commentary about 'gay' Manchester. The Ramada Piccadilly stood on the edge of this tide of sin. The epicentre is Canal Street (or Anal Street, the nickname, which is enough to send shooting needles of pain through his temples). Having overnighted in Manchester many times before, he was still capable of being outraged, almost rhapsodically revolted, by what he saw. Saunas. Sex shops. Louche bars where same-sex couples rubbed against each other like animals. To him, the historic canals that cut through the area, giving it some charm and a leafy, bohemian feel, were nothing more than open sewers, carrying the dark polluted water of this bestial world to all corners of the city. Five times — *five times* — he watched men having sex in the shadows of various alleyways. The man from Room 703 had looked on, open mouthed. Shocked.

Tapping away at his blog, he had just typed in two well-known *hadithas* on homosexuality from the Prophet Muhammad (Peace Be Upon Him) — *When a man mounts another man, the throne of God shakes* and *Kill the one that is doing it and also kill the one that it is being done to.* Working fast, two fingers, angry words poured out like a wellspring.

'Sir. The electronics store delivered your CD player.' The accent was from Manchester. A native English speaker. The man from Room 703 had continued to type. Lost in his whirl of thoughts.

'Sir. Your CD player.' *Tappity-tappity-tappity . . . tap, tap . . . tap.* Slowly he had turned from the screen, surprised. *What CD player?* The eyes of the blond-haired porter beseeched him to look at the package he was holding. He looked to be mid-twenties. Freckled and fair faced, the gold buttons of his uniform straining to keep his tubbiness together.

The box said Sony Sports ATRAC portable CD player, but it was the slight wiggle of the man's thumb that did it. It revealed the slenderest scrap of paper, no bigger than a salt sachet. Tightly wadded, it opened to disclose the words *Operation Macchar.*

He had blinked with surprise, *What?!*, then looked up for reassurance from the porter's eyes. This plump, pale-skinned porter would be an ideal messenger. A convert maybe, perhaps a believer, maybe just someone in the pay of one of General Khan's Pashtun allies. Who would think to tail a white man?

'Your CD player,' the porter had repeated for the second time. Somewhat loudly.

'The instructions are all inside.' A smile playing behind his brown eyes. Then a whisper, his lips barely moving.

'May Allah bless your martyrdom with an abundance of casualties.'

And with that fine thought pulsing in the front of his mind — Allah . . . casualties . . . and glorious martyrdom — the man from Room 703 bounds out of bed. Getting ready for work with a real spring in his step.

Crew call for today's flight is in less than an hour.

In the outskirts of Peshawar, Kirsten Ackerman wobbles her way unsteadily from beneath the jingly-jangly Bedford truck. Then pauses. Checking this isn't some bizarre dream looping through her mind. *Where the hell am I?*

It takes her a while, standing in the silence, to work out that she's in a long, darkened garage with pulleys and hoists hanging from the roof, ramps and workbenches. The place is empty. Soundless. There's a sharp smell of oil and petrol, and through a small crack in a door in the distance beams enough light to show up dust motes floating lazily. She can just make out somebody outside . . . speaking in Pashto.

She checks her watch . . . shit. Asleep almost ten hours. She feels a tweak of anger. Where the hell are you, Bill?

Slowly Ackerman inches her way around the tyres and spanners and bits of tubing towards the door. The closer she gets the more she is sure that the voice is Jahanghir's, telling a story about the unmanliness of Tajik men. She edges carefully to the doorway, the slit of sunlight almost blinding. Jahanghir's voice quietens, very conspiratorial with his audience . . .

198

Ackerman finds herself smiling as she listens: a Tajik man is standing in a window at the top of a burning building. Screaming to be rescued. On the other side of the street a Pashtun warrior is becoming irritated. All the noise is disrupting his quiet cup of tea. *Help. Help me*, the Tajik squeals. Reluctantly, and only because the Pashtun knows there'll be no peace until this is resolved, he moves across the road towards the inferno, still holding his tea. 'Call yourself a man . . . why don't you stop crying like a girl? [*Guffaws of approval*] Here. If you want to save yourself, jump into this cup of tea. [*Laughter*]' Flames licking around him, the Tajik thinks about this carefully. Weighing up the pros and cons. And makes up his mind. 'No . . . no way I can trust a Pashtun.' He shakes his head. 'When I jump, you'll just move the cup . . . '

Creak.

As the American woman pushes against the door frame, her eyes squinting, there's a tumble of chairs tipping over. Kalashnikovs being readied.

Jahanghir wades into the scene. 'Stop. Stop. Stop . . . ', his arms windmilling. The little group stands easy. 'How nice to see you, miss.'

Ackerman shields her eyes from the sun. 'Nice to see you, Jahanghir.'

As she gets used to the light, she notices he appears to be particularly delighted about something. A beaming smile on his face. Pristine white teeth flash.

'And Mr Bill?'

'Yes. Where is Mr Bill? I need to get back to

Islamabad.' Her mouth feels parched.

His eyes smile even more widely, and he looks over her shoulder towards the garage behind. 'You and Mr Bill. Both of you were . . .' Then his composure deserts him for a moment, a worry line snagging his brow. ' . . . Mr Bill is still there . . . Perhaps he recovering?'

'Recovering? Mr Bill was with *you*, Jahanghir. He told me he was travelling *with you*. In the tow truck. Back to Peshawar.'

More worry lines fracture across his broad forehead, and Jahanghir's black eyes hold a blank look of genuine incomprehension.

'I've been in the back of that cabin. Asleep. *On my own.*'

'No Mr Bill?' he pleads.

Ackerman draws a sharp breath, not wanting to lose it with Jahanghir in front of these other men. 'For the love of God . . . *No Mr Bill*,' she says quietly.

Another whirl of arms and Jahanghir barks out a series of sharp commands. Two men in identical grey dishdashas rush into the darkness of the garage. AK74s braced against their chests. Ackerman watches a series of overhead lights flick on, eventually illuminating the whole length of the garage.

'He must have told the same lie to you that he told me.'

'Then . . . if he's not here . . .' A look of complete darkness and uncertainty settles over Jahanghir as the logic of the situation unravels in his mind. He mutters under his breath, tugging forcefully on his whiskers. ' . . . Mr Bill's gone back there. To the madrasa.'

'Probably, yes.' The two dishdashas return, shaking their heads, very solemn.

'But why not take me, take my cousins? Without us, surely he will be killed. In the daylight. An American. On his own, no speaking Pashto . . . ' Jahanghir's face falls as he works through the multiple dangers. ' . . . In *that* valley. That is very, very not good for Mr Bill.'

The look on the man's face is almost too much for Ackerman. A proud warrior crushed by the rejection of a man who, when the chips were down, did not want his help.

She takes a step closer, beseeching him with those sea-green eyes, turning her lamps on full beam. 'Is there *anything* we can do?'

1347 Islamabad time, 0847 UK time

Bill Lamayette is colder than he's ever been in his life. So cold, even, he has no idea where his cock is, let alone his balls. They packed up and left town a while back. Cold enough that he doesn't have the brainpower to care any more.

He'd tried thinking about various honeymoons with various ex-wives. Girlfriends. One-night stands. Ambassador Zoh on the Great Seal rug in her office, long legs all akimbo like the outstretched wings of the Bald Eagle. Even that State Department chickadee Kirsten Ackerman and her laughing breasts. But, try as hard as he can to think positive, to think happy, smiley, that bastard Pir Durbar keeps intruding. *Wrap my fucking hands round his scrawny neck . . .*

Half an hour ago Lamayette had eased into the river, leaving the relative warmth and safety of the embankment and the latticework of exposed tree roots that had been hiding him. The CIA didn't run courses on trees of the world, but Lamayette thinks he'd been balled up under some kind of flame tree. A dramatic overhanging thing, whose proud position on a dogleg of this Swat river tributary had almost, but not quite, been undercut by the fast-moving churn that

202

flowed past the madrasa. From behind the cover of its thicket of support, he had slid into the frozen waters, anchored himself in position with his arm looped over a root that was as blanched and smooth as highly polished bone.

He had done this because Pir Durbar, at last, had made another appearance on the facing bank, overlooking the river. His second of the day as far as Lamayette could tell. The holy man had started with a little prayer-job in the direction of Mecca, then moved on to callisthenics, shaded by the stand of olive and pine trees that separated him from the school farther back. He was giving himself the full Indian-rubber-man workout. The whole she-bang.

Thirty long and exceedingly cold minutes later he is finally finished . . . while Lamayette's brain and body have become deep-chilled by the water bubbling around his mostly submerged body. This is ice-melt straight off the Himalayas.

Pir Durbar is finished, though looking a little wrung out as he heads for a bracing dip. All alone. No security this time. Lamayette watches as the old man lollops from one smooth rock to another. Heading towards him, heading towards the water's edge on the far side.

Only the top half of Lamayette's bald skull is poking out over the water as he watches. Breathing through his nose.

On the far side of the river, and fifty yards downstream from him, Pir Durbar starts unwrapping his Gandhi togs. Last item are his wood-frame glasses. Once naked, he steps gingerly, wincingly, over the smaller, sharper rocks and into the shallows. Bath time. He is tiny, rake thin, his limbs looking like twigs of cinnamon. He crouches to splash water over his body and through his thick white half-moon beard. Then looks down into the frozen water. Willing himself to jump in.

Upstream Lamayette hears a little hoot of shock as his target emerges from his first full immersion.

Cue Lamayette, who pushes off from the bank and lets the river take him in her grasp. The dimensions are straightforward. High-school trig with Mr Hindle. The triangle is thirty yards across, and fifty downstream. *The square of the hypotenuse equals the sum of the square of the other two sides.* He'd had the best part of six hours to work this out: there are fifty-eight yards to the target if he manages to drift in a straight line.

With his arms by his sides and his hands fanning the water, he gently pilots himself across the flow of current.

Thirty yards now, and closing. He can feel the water tugging at him, pulling on his salwar kameez. His fingers almost senseless. He remembers to keep his mouth shut . . .

Just after seven o'clock this morning, Pir Durbar had made his first appearance. With four guards, each one modelling that timeless classic Pashtun look. Semi-automatic assault rifle and bandolier. Angry eyes. Wild hair and dirty dishdasha. Lamayette knew, even with the element of surprise, he couldn't handle four

204

guards, every one triggerhappy.

The old man had hurried them all the way to the river's edge with an unexplained urgency. (This was the point at which Lamayette had slid into the water for the first time; the water was even colder then, and the shock was so great he found himself panting like a puppy.) The reason for the guards' scowling was soon apparent. Pir Durbar unwrapped himself, reversed, and took hold of a pair of supporting arms to squat over a little rock pool, for a serious bowel movement.

Hence the closed mouth as Lamayette paddles onward again. There had to be other holy men upstream, doing their bit for the nitrogen cycle, giving the River Swat the Good Word.

But now, at this moment of impending drama, the holy man is resting, fully immersed, lying on his back. Head and toes exposed. Shaggy silvery hair with a jet-black topknot. His body just below the water surface. Only twenty yards paddling to go. And a big grin spreads over Lamayette's face . . .

★   ★   ★

When you join the CIA you seem to spend the first year doing little but filling out forms so that the Agency can get at your darkest and most mundane secrets. At least that's the way it was in 1987 when Bill Lamayette enrolled. Behind closed doors, his answers would have been pored over, cross-referenced with an assortment of psych profiles on a clunky old IBM with disco lights and a golfball printer. Working out whether

205

they wanted a man who still ate Cap'n Crunch for breakfast and never slept with a pillow.

One of the questions had been Favourite Film. In his uncomplicated way, Lamayette had answered *Rambo: First Blood Part II*. He even put in brackets the year of release: 1985. He wouldn't do so now, of course, that would be putting too much on the table, besides which profiling had become so monolithic he had long since learned how to fake the answers to beat the system. But, hell, it was 1987 and he was a newbie. Reagan was still in office, and at the time there still wasn't a day he didn't wake up and think about his brother dying at the hands of that amped-up Islamic suicide bomber. Dear God. How meekly the US had pulled out of Beirut, with nobody brought to book for all those dead Marines.

That's why, as he porpoises towards Pir Durbar, Lamayette finds himself transported into a parallel, celluloid world. Perhaps it's the cold, perhaps nicotine-induced dementia, but repeatedly playing through his mind is his all-time favourite scene from that screenplay. The CIA chief as Sylvester Stallone, on the run in the jungle from Soviet and Vietnamese forces but expertly picking off his pursuers one by one.

Shot of featureless matted vines and wall of mud. Suddenly A PAIR OF EYES **SNAP OPEN**

SHOT OF THE GUARD, kneeling over dead Vietnamese soldier in the foreground.

Behind him there is silent movement among the gnarled roots and vines in a muddy embankment. Blending flawlessly with the mudbank, Rambo's mud-encrusted figure has been in PLAIN VIEW, YET CONCEALED, until he opened his eyes and moved. He emerges noiselessly and moves up behind the guard, looming above him . . .

Lamayette fills his lungs one last time. Takes his bearings and eases underwater. The sun shines brightly as he slides through those final yards. The current tugs on long strands of green weed and the river is awash with colour, like stained glass on a bright day. The holy man is blissfully unaware. Through the blur of water, Lamayette can make out the bony ridges of his shoulders.

Then . . .

Blending flawlessly with the river, Lamayette's figure, which has been IN PLAIN VIEW, YET CONCEALED, emerges noiselessly and moves up behind Pir Durbar. Looming over him.

A hand, as big as a ham, clasps over the old man's mouth. And pushes underwater. Deep. With barely a splash. The holy man wriggles and claws but Lamayette is motionless. Holding him down. Waterboarding without the board. He casts around quickly. His eyes taking in every part of the facing bank, the whitewashed tops of the madrasa just beyond the treeline. The ramshackle guardhouse to the right. No movement. Not a peep of sound.

He tightens his grip, twists the old man's neck hard to the left. Bubbles break to the surface, big mushroom bubbles of air. That and the swishing of legs the only sound of disturbance. Life and fight slowly eke out of the old man's body.

Welcome to *my* world, holy man . . .

Manchester Airport
Monday — 0911 UK time,
1411 Islamabad time

At Gate 206 the pilots who will fly this morning's PIA Boeing 777 service to New York are at work. Setting up and primping the computer systems that will manage the flight across the Atlantic. Systems so competent and sophisticated as to make their jobs almost irrelevant. In fact there are two captains today, Iqbal Hussain and Imtiyaz Jamal. The latter, sitting in the left-hand seat, will actually command the flight. By complete chance the crew roster has thrown up two veterans who could not be more alike. Tweedledum and Tweedledee. Both are heavy and round shouldered and for each their first order of business had been to crank out the maximum seat adjustment so they could see over the instrument glare-shield and down the line of the nose. Hussain and Jamal are ex-Pakistan Air Force officers, having served with 12 Squadron and flown VIP transport in Boeing 707s and 737s before joining the national airline. Both are also proud, very proud, of their facial hair: Captain Jamal has a dark, spade-shaped beard which

209

almost reaches to his chest, while Hussain has a broad, thick silvery moustache that curls over his top lip and almost, but not quite, tickles at his gums.

Behind them, in one of two sheepskinned jump seats, is Captain Saeed Harry Salahuddin. Very much not hard at work. He's relaxing with a copy of the *Daily Telegraph*, the tabloid-sized sports section, digesting county cricket batting and bowling averages. Salahuddin should have been under a hot shower by now but is, instead, dead-legging to New York, replacing a sick pilot who was due to command Wednesday's return flight to London. Of course, there'd be a seat for him up in the first-class section. In the meantime all he needs, while the passengers are boarding, is a cup of tea, the *Telegraph* and a chance to grumble quietly to himself.

There's a smooth, relaxed air of informality in the cockpit. The three captains are on friendly speaking terms, a pleasure not always guaranteed. These are good people, Salahuddin notes to himself, and good airmen too. No tension from nervy first and second officers, over-prepared or under-confident.

The two pilots, Jamal and Hussain, process through their prep work, reading off a computerised list displayed between them on a console screen just fore of the two engine throttles. Jamal calls out the task, Hussain responds, and as the on-board computer recognises each action, the item turns from white — *to do* — into green — *accomplished*, and it scrolls on to the next task.

Most important is setting up the inertial navigation system (INS), the primary navigation tool, which drives all of the inputs into the various automatic pilot, fuel and engine control systems. The plane's flight management system will constantly cross-reference with other on-board positioning data, everything from the modern satellite-based Global Positioning System to old-school VHF Omnidirectional Range (VOR), which relies on intersecting radio beams. But INS is the mother ship system. Once the pilots tell the plane's computers where she is in the world, the exact location down to the nearest degree, minute, second and decimalised fraction of a second, the INS uses on-board gyroscopes to measure turn and accelerometers to gauge speed and calculates the plane's position accordingly. Simple . . .

Next up to input are the four mid-Atlantic waypoints, the simple longitude and latitude markers that the automatic pilot will direct the flight towards on the journey across the Big Pond.

Normally there are five North Atlantic Tracks offered to pilots. Alpha, the most northern pathway, through to Echo, the most southerly. The specific path of the corridor is computed twice daily by the Gander/Shanwick Oceanic Flight Region, which controls all airspace from one side of the Atlantic to another and between forty-five and sixty degrees North.

Captains Jamal and Hussein have opted — as most westbound flights do — for track Charlie, the middle of the five choices, which generally has the least unfavourable winds.

The entry point for today's transatlantic corridor, the one designated Charlie, starts at way station SUNOT and exits at way station SCROD. But what the system really wants to know is what happens in between. From SUNOT, where does the plane fly to, out *there*, when she's long gone over the horizon, where, for thousands of miles, there are only the unforgiving, slate-hard waters of the Atlantic?

Hussain reads out the coordinates of the four oceanic waypoints for Jamal to enter into his system. When the plane reaches these waypoints, the crew call up the Shanwick or Gander controllers. Or alternatively, if the headwinds make things particularly slow, they report in every forty-five minutes, whichever is the shorter. Position reporting is key to the system working. The flying is way beyond the range of land-based navigation aids and communication relays . . . you can build a mini-robot the size of a pinhead but not a radar that works in the middle of the Atlantic.

So. If the pilots don't call in on time, the alarm is quickly raised. At that point the working assumption has to be simple: that a plane full of passengers is in distress somewhere over the mid-Atlantic. In a world of trouble, and far beyond reach.

The short-stay car park
Manchester Airport
Four minutes later

Tristie checks herself in the flip-down mirror of the front passenger seat. Nothing astray. The dark wig is an effect nobody in the rented Volvo estate has seen before. Piglet, the driver, and Button and Whiffler in the back, can't help but stare. It's as if there's a stranger sitting with them.

'We've got plenty of time,' she reassures them. 'Relax.'

Next job, the mascara, and Tristie gets to work, her mouth widening and pouting, as she starts at the base of her lashes and works out to the tips. The heavy-lid look.

Button bites at his bottom lip, an irritation snagging his thoughts. 'Why can't we go BA, Virgin or even United, for Chrissakes. Something that's not *this* airline?'

Tristie stops for a moment, to consider her work so far. 'Because I think that's too great a risk.'

Whiffler readjusts himself in the back seat, a tremor of alarm in his voice. 'You mean they might be looking for us?'

213

'Of course they're not, otherwise we wouldn't have made it out of the farmhouse.'

Whiffler looks nervously towards the terminal. 'I thought this airline check-in will be crawling with MI5 and Special Branch surveillance.'

'That's true, but they're not looking for us. For the three of us, you understand? They're looking for people on their watch-lists.' And Tristie resumes with the mascara wand, working at the inner corners. 'It's about playing the odds. On a Pakistan International Airlines flight to New York, a through flight from Islamabad, we're less likely to see somebody who knows us, a friend or an old enemy perhaps . . . somebody you served with, maybe an officer, maybe one of those hooligans from Hereford, someone who might, however haphazardly, think to put two and two together and come up with Ward 13.

'I know we're talking tiny odds here . . . ' Tristie is dabbing at the outer corners now, her voice hushed ' . . . but we've got more than three hundred million riding on us getting safely and anonymously to America. There's no point taking chances we don't have to.'

Monday — 1427 Islamabad time,
0927 UK time

The landscape of the Swat Valley has an exciting geologic history. Across it, primeval batholiths and basalts sprouted in abundance, all with different and hard-to-explain isotopic compositions.

One such geological burp is the massive fist of granite that in its distant liquid-magma past bubbled its way up through the surrounding landscape. It formed a steep-sided island mountain, slightly smaller but just as incongruous as Ayer's Rock. It's up this that CIA station chief Bill Lamayette is pounding. Short, jolting steps, water sploshing off his clothes. Over his back is the naked body of holy man Pir Durbar. Almost drowned, but not quite, Lamayette being something of an expert on dancing that particular fine line. The Pakistani whines quietly, venting a stringy vomit of river water down the soaked back of the American.

Lamayette had first noted this place when they'd surveilled Hamza, scum-bucket son of General Khan. From high ground, Lamayette and Jahanghir had watched through top-of-the-range binoculars as the younger Khan's plush

Range Rover nosed its way around the myriad of dusty tracks, before the turn into the madrasa. As Lamayette had looked down the valley, this singular rock, a piece of timeless solidity, rose almost above them, off to his left. Four miles downstream from the madrasa.

'Help,' Pir Durbar gurgles in Urdu. 'Help me. In the name of Allah the Merciful . . . '

Lamayette feels the strain in his thighs, and the moisture in his eyes is no longer river water but sweat. Not a good time to ask for help. 'I've got two words for you, Fuckface: *Qissa Khawani*.' Speaking over his shoulder, Lamayette takes a fresh grip on the wet of the man's bony ankles, looks up the track. Hundred yards to go, straight up . . . he powers on, the body swinging from side to side.

For the first time, the American senses the holy man coming fully to life. Trying to straighten up, to regain some semblance of control, as if he's only just realised this is *serious* now. Pir Durbar machine-guns his next words, panicky. 'You must not torture me. I forbid it. It is absolutely forbidden. I have rights. I am citizen of a sovereign country. With rights. Do you understand?'

'You can kiss my ass with your rights.'

Lamayette leans into his stride, feeding off the stinging burn in his muscles, the quick-fire bounce of his shoulders making it impossible for Pir Durbar to speak further. Counting off the paces in his head. Five . . . Six . . . Seven . . . Lamayette allows himself a little burst of breath as he says each number.

The reward for reaching the top is the most insanely cooling breeze.

He drops Pir Durbar off his shoulder, making sure the old man's head impacts with a particularly nobbly cushion of granite; his cry of pain thins into nothingness like a talking doll running out of battery. *EEEEEEEeeeeeeeeeeeeee.* A dazed Pakistani whose slick-wet hair and beard might make him look like Father Christmas, but whose brain, the CIA chief is betting his life, is filled with the worst kind of secrets . . . no doubt triple-locked and burglar-proofed against all usual forms of coercion.

But this is going to be different. So different.

Lamayette tests the strength of a triangular rack he'd created before capturing the old man. He had come across the thinned-out spinney of *Chir* pines as he crabbed across the fields near the madrasa after the early morning light had broken. The meatiest lengths of pine had already been chainsawed into firewood by the locals, but Lamayette was after the offcuts and had gathered what he needed, poking around the matted debris of sawdust. Two lengths about eight foot and another of about five. The wood is a warm yellow, the colour of ripe bananas.

He had humped his three branches to the top of the hill and was lashing them together, just as the sun rose above the quiet of the sleeping valley. Binding it all together, he'd had to use strips from his *shemagh* headdress.

He felt like Grizzly Adams. A frontiersman. Not a freakin' CIA station chief. *Correction:* ex-chief. Thinking this reminds him of how consumed by doubt he really is, not least because he had not one piece of technical equipment with him. Except the mobile phone. He kept the battery and phone separated so nothing could give away his position. But even the mobile offers no consolation.

Last time he checked, it blinked back at him the same miserable answer: only one bar of battery charge left.

★ ★ ★

Two minutes later . . . There are six madrasa guards. Each as confused as the next. Each in turn using the snout of their semi-automatic rifles to nose through the holy man's clothes at the water's edge. Six proddings of the same spot still reveal nothing more than various short lengths of cotton, Pir Durbar's dusty, worn-out sandals and his expensive spectacles. Not a stitch of evidence to show where he is, or what has happened.

A big problem: no Pir Durbar, no madrasa. The terribleness of this begins to dawn. Despite the guns and the fierce demeanours, there is not an ounce of natural leadership or courage to be had between them.

Blame and the avoidance of blame become the next obvious tasks. They shuffle uneasily from foot to foot, each taking his turn to make clear in convoluted and dramatic language where they were and what they were doing when the holy man disappeared. Whitewashing the walls, tilling the fields, collecting firewood . . .

Now, with each of their stories secure, the eldest of them tugs on his beard apprehensively, speaking in Pashto to the five others circled around. 'It's like he disappeared into thin air.' Good for a couple more minutes of wild exclamation.

Eventually some kind of plan falls into shape. Five of them will head downstream, the obvious direction in which an ailing old man might have floated. The sixth, lame-footed and slightly deaf, will head upstream, in the unlikely event something has taken their holy man in that direction.

'Agree?' the eldest offers as their six pairs of dark, suspicious eyes cast around at the others. Nobody breaks rank. And so, they part ways. Happy to be doing something, anything.

Five, loping easily like wildcats, follow down the course of the fast-flowing water. One stumbles upstream. Each of them trying to make sense of this ominous disappearance.

Terminal 2
Manchester Airport
Monday — 0933 UK time,
1433 Islamabad time

Three minutes later . . . With the palm of one hand clasping his temple to silence the headache, the normally unflappable PIA airport manager Majid Ali Khan leans his other hand against the overhanging check-in sign. PK412 to New York JFK. It's a public holiday, Khan is short handed and more than a little pissed off. All of the computers but his are logged out. Officially 412 is closed and 342 passengers are now in the process of boarding or reboarding.

But in front of him are three first-class passengers looking to check in late. All blaming road works on the M60. To Khan, that sounds plausible. The M60 is a horror of a road. So, the PIA airport manager is sympathetic, in spite of the circumstances. He's thinking this through, doing some speedy sums in his head.

Two men and a woman, white and British. All have confirmed seats, valid Passenger Name Records, and have paid full fare for their tickets. That means the tickets will be easily transferred to another carrier and it will be PIA that will lose out if he doesn't take them. He either uploads all of them, or none.

Majid Ali Khan is the sort of nervous worker who is kept awake at night by his revenue yields, trapped in a nightmare of rising costs and falling margins. We're talking here about three full-fare first-class tickets . . .

More mental maths in his head. Less than thirty minutes to scheduled departure . . . the May bank holiday. *Could these three make it?*

He looks at the e-tickets in front of him, then flicks quickly through the pages of the passports, searching for a reason not to upload them. All are valid. Visas good. With the travel documents in his hand, he looks at the anxious faces in front of him. The rest of the check-in area is deserted. 'Merritt . . . where is Merritt?'

From behind the huge frame of one of the men, a woman peers out. Slowly edges forward. Khan swallows hard. Long dark hair, and sea-blue eyes that suddenly twinkle as she smiles shyly, showing a full set of flawless teeth. 'Is there a problem?' she asks in a Tweetie Pie voice, her head slightly cocked to one side.

'In this photo,' he waves her British passport, 'your hair is different.'

'Yes. A blonde . . . ' She casts her eyes downward for a moment, crestfallen, 'but it wasn't really . . . the colour came out of a bottle.' Her distress seems almost palpable and Khan feels himself tilting forward, ready to comfort, *So sorry, I didn't mean to pry.* She looks up and wows him again with those flashing eyes. Puts a finger to her lips. 'I hope you can keep a secret.'

Mischievous. A touch of Marilyn about her.

A tingle of electricity had run several times up and down Khan's trouser legs before he realised what it was about this woman. We're talking Christy Turlington. Circa 1994 . . .

When he was growing up, Khan's Pakistan-born parents had insisted he and his brothers and sisters attend a youth study circle in the local mosque. Khan was one of many teenagers who didn't care for the endless *khutbahs* and *salats*, some old goat haranguing the Muslim girls about the dangers of dressing promiscuously. Khan had sat at the back, making money, quietly trading pictures of Elle, Cindy, Linda, Naomi . . . and of course Christy Turlington. Nothing too risky. But the supermodels, the way their eyes came at you right off the page, well, that gave everything a hormonal young buck needed.

This woman, this Tristie Merritt, could be a dead ringer. He thinks this wistfully, looking from her picture to her face.

Only afterwards would Khan recall something strange about this female: the way she shielded herself from view. He would find it hard to explain this. She was certainly the most attractive white woman he had seen on a recent PIA flight. Yet she held back, kept herself inconsequential, almost reticent. Incredible to say this, but it was as if she knew the sightlines of the pinhole cameras, the ones that Special Branch and MI5 installed in the light fittings above the airline's check-in booths. *But how could that be?* How would she know about those little black nodules?

They were designed to be totally inconspicuous behind the bright lights, as they fed video and audio data into the computers and hard drives on which churned the latest face-recognition software. PIA services into and out of Britain, Manchester in particular, are the most heavily surveilled flights in the world. Bar none.

He hands back the passports and tickets. Smiles. 'OK, this is what we're going to do.' He grabs a marker pen, and starts dialling through to the departure gate. 'I'm going to have you bring all of your luggage on board.' Between printing off their boarding passes and shouting down his colleague on the other end of the phone, Khan lays out the deal: 'I'll try but I can't guarantee that you'll all get your first-class meals . . . I'll do my best. I promise.'

The giant male grins, rubs his chin. Looks quickly to the man and woman behind him. 'That's tops, man. Not a problem. Not a problem at all.'

'Good.' And Khan bounces over the weigh-in and leads them on a dash towards immigration, security and the Boeing 777. *City of Risalpur*, callsign Victor Sierra.

Operation Macchar is twenty-two minutes from take-off.

Swat Valley
Pakistan
Monday — 0938 UK time,
1438 Islamabad time

Five time zones to the east of Manchester
Airport is the holy man.

Pir Durbar moans slightly as Bill Lamayette
picks him up around his thin waist and humps
the naked body towards the triangle of pine
branches.

He had spent time — heaps of time this
morning, nothing but time — making sure the
lengths of fabric were just right. Longer strips
would be needed to bind the wrists than would
for the feet. So he doubled the length. With all of
this crystal clear in his mind, and enjoying the
peace and solitude of a craftsman getting on,
doing his thing, the CIA man tugs a bony wrist
over one set of interlocking branches. Feels the
dark leathery skin as he makes the first tie-off.
He quickly whips up a pair of constrictor knots,
over and under, and over again, and under, then
threaded through into a son-of-a-bitch tight
knot. One tying the strip to the angle of the
branches, the other using what was left of the
shemagh to bind up Pir Durbar's wrist. There is

224

almost no undoing a constrictor knot once significant tension has been applied . . . that would be some other schmuck's problem to solve.

He repeats the process quickly, hopping pixie-like to the remaining two corners of the triangle until the holy man is firmly and inescapably bound to this crucifix of pinewood. Then he lifts up the shorter side of the three, by Pir Durbar's head, and manhandles his creation, dragging it across the top of the deserted hillock until it's in just the right place.

He eases it down, not out of any respect for the holy man, but out of fear of ripping the *shemagh* knots, or severing the old guy's spindly wrists and wasting a morning's work.

The three boughs of pinewood now rest on the ground, their considerable weight dragging downwards on the arms of Pir Durbar, tugging at him like a medieval rack. But his body is actually being held up, resting on a table of solid granite as big and well defined as an office desk. He can't move. Not a muscle, not even to turn his silver-thatched head from one side to another.

'What are you doing to me, American man? . . . You heathen . . . Faithless man of violence . . . Apostate . . . CIA man.'

Lamayette moves around so he can get a good look at Pir Durbar's set-solid face, the cold eyes, as lifeless as a shard of beer-bottle glass. 'You see. I know who you are, CIA man . . . '

'That's good, holy man. Wouldn't want you to be at a disadvantage. Not with you lashed down and powerless. And me not having had a fucking smoke for twelve hours.'

Pir Durbar's eyes swivel around in his skull, as if he is entering a trance. His voice hits a strange, remorseless monotone. Pre-programmed. 'If you reject my guidance you will suffer even during your lifetime here on earth. You will endure life here on earth as if it is hell. I am here to tell you that God will condemn a man to hell who rejects my guidance. And I am your guidance, Mr CIA Man. We are together now because I am your proof of His mercy.'

Lamayette props a knee up on the table of granite. Wipes the sweat from his brow. 'Long time ago, I got a good piece of advice. Kind of handed down over generations from some reverend guy in England.' He shakes his big bald head with a real sense of wonderment. 'You just don't get it. Your God, my God, anybody and everybody's God. Why would he be some jealous, childish, merciless tyrant, like you're making out. He's just a guy asking us for a regular diet of good actions — not your fucking ill-composed threats, zinging people with eternal apprehensions. Who wants a God like that?'

A strange, eerie silence falls over the top of the hillock.

Just the whisper of a breeze. Two men looking at each other, examining. So close, yet so far away. It's the Pakistani who speaks first. Again with the bug eyes, the same words, and that grating, monotonous drone: 'If you reject my guidance you will suffer even during your lifetime here on earth . . . ' The holy man

226

wriggles his arms, trying to get free. Tightening the knots. 'I'm not going to tell you anything. Nothing. You understand.' His thin voice carries a desperate resolve.

'That would be a pity. You see ... I'm someone who's got nothing after this. Nowhere to go, no more rope to hold me up. So. It's not just that I hate the way you talk. Or that I haven't eaten for almost a day. And haven't had a smoke. It's that you're playing now against a man with no options. No fallback. It's either you or me, bud. I need to know what all this talk is about, you and that idiot toad Hamza Khan ... *Tomorrow we shall make Qissa Khawani famous again. Operation Macchar. Patience and righteousness shall once more be the weapon of the Prophet* ... ' Lamayette squats down so that he can examine his prey closely. Eye to eye. 'What is Operation Macchar? What little shit-storm have you guys got planned for today? You tell me now and we both walk off this hill ... '

There's a complete lack of sound.

The sun beats down on Lamayette's still-sodden clothes. Nothing moves but their breath as the two of them stare intently at one another. Pir Durbar tries again to shake himself free of the bindings. But gives up, exhausted. They both watch as a trickle of sweat gathers into a little dewdrop at the end of the American's nose. Their eyes following it as the drop bulges bigger and bigger, then falls on to the hard, hot black surface of the granite table. It seems to sizzle.

Lamayette rises slowly. 'Your choice.' And

227

begins to move clockwise around the pinewood rack. Measuring out each pace to give rhythm to his story: 'Long time ago, Mr Holy Man, when I was seven and growing up in Louisiana, my pappy gave me a pet.' The Pakistani tries but fails to turn his head. 'Lovely little thing, about ten pounds heavy, and so big,' Lamayette measures out a span of two feet with his hands.

'I got Billy Bob on account of the McIlhenny family. You understand who I'm talking about? The Tabasco people. You know Tabasco? . . . ' Lamayette chuckles. *The clock is ticking on some terrorist outrage and I'm banging on about Tabasco.* 'Billy Bob was what they call a nutria. Halfway between a small beaver and a giant rat, if you will. Anyway, the McIlhennys were a big deal in my part of Louisiana and they decided to breed nutria, for their fur. So the patriarch of the McIlhenny clan released a dozen of these fellows in about 1940. They sure knew how to root because next thing, about fifteen years later, there was more than twenty million of the little critters. Destroying the bayou, they were, with their big teeth. You've never seen teeth till you've seen a nutria. Boy. I tell you, Billy Bob bit a friend of mine once, snipped the end of the finger clean off. Right through the bone . . . ' Lamayette draws near Pir Durbar. Puts his hand down on the man's bony shoulder and pushes all of his weight through the palm of his hand. Feels the bones shifting.

The holy man is blinking hard. Something is coming. His eyelids flutter, he's steeling himself. Perhaps trying to think himself outside of his body, perhaps just disoriented by the strange arc of Lamayette's story. Still trying to wriggle free. The start of something like panic.

Lamayette rises. 'Now this is the point when I'm supposed to jump up and down on you. Bang your head on the rock. Break your fingers one by one . . . ' His voice slows and Lamayette shields his eyes. 'Heck. You know it is a mighty fine view from up here.' Gazing out over the wide, lush valley from this unusual geologic eyrie. 'Such a nice day as well,' he laments. 'You see, Mr Holy Man, I know you're up to something bad today. This Qissa Khawani thing. And I am going to break you . . . ' he pronounces with great certainty.

'First, though, I want you to understand why it is I've been telling you my beautiful Huckleberry Finn life story. You know about Huck Finn and his best buddy Tom Sawyer?' Lamayette leaves the question hanging in the still air, walks over to the torn remains of his headdress, a discarded tangle of cloth half overhanging the edge of this vast rock, like a weathered prayer flag. Hundreds of feet below rush the teeming Swat river tributaries. The American talks over his shoulder as he squats down and carefully, tenderly picks something up. Cradling it against his massive chest. 'You see, growing up with Billy Bob gave me a certain, how shall I put it . . . a certain affinity for these little furry fellows. I came to understand how they think and work.'

Lamayette turns, smiles with delight at the old man's startled, terrified reaction to what he is carrying. Uselessly, the holy man shrinks back. The saggy skin over his naked buttocks clenching tight, and he rattles his wrists against the pinewood frame, trying to kick out with his feet. And slowly the thin, old, purple lips of his mouth form into a perfect circle of horror.

Earlier that morning, when Lamayette had set off by himself for the madrasa, he'd taken precious little with him. His only sustenance a seventy-five-ounce bottle full of jalapeno-spiced cornichons. Chewing on these and holding the sliced jalapenos under his tongue until the roof of his mouth was ready to lift off had been about his only way of staying awake and putting one foot in front of the other. That, and some mindless singing.

Cartons of this delicacy are delivered twice monthly to the CIA's headquarters at Langley, to a former secretary of almost overpowering maternal instincts towards Lamayette. Thence packed into the various CIA pouches shuttling to Islamabad. No doubt there'd be some taxpayer coalition against government waste that would be duly outraged if this, or any of Lamayette's other epicurean smuggling rackets, came to light. But that's a worry for another day.

One small taxpayer comfort: Lamayette is a master of interrogation.

Throughout his early years at the CIA, he had brought a childlike enthusiasm to this ugly, thankless task. He was marked out as the Hitchcock of his generation. No waterboarding or expensive chemicals. Just an old-fashioned understanding that the most powerful weapon in

230

separating a person from their secrets is to screw with their imagination.

So it is that Lamayette brings the tall glass bottle up to his face. Reaches inside and runs a finger lovingly down the thick brown pelt. Scratching at its shoulders. 'Me, and these creatures, you see, we're like buddies. These fellows like to move at night and they're a bit obvious when they're hungry. When I'd worked out where their run was, trapping one was a cinch.' There's a skittling sound of minute toenails scratching on glass and strikingly shrill squeals. Pir Durbar is breathing fast and flinching, to make himself as small as possible.

'We're supposed to call this guy *Rattus norvegicus*. But that's such a lame handle for a dude to have, so let's name this fellow . . . not Billy Bob, but Billy Ray. Like Billy Ray Cyrus. Same nice, shiny teeth. Lovely thick brown hair . . . See how Billy Ray's standing up on his back legs. Can't wait to meet his first holy man. First ever terrorist ringleader . . . ' and Lamayette puts the bottle right up against Pir Durbar's leathery cheek. The twelve-inch-long rat paws wildly at the glass, and as the Pakistani squirms, the CIA chief presses the jar harder. 'He *really* likes you. See how he's trying to touch you with his cute pink paws, his little fingers.' The rat is frenzied with hunger. 'And, while you're so close, take a look at those teeth. Especially those two incisors. You know he has to eat about a third of his body weight each day to survive. That's what he was trying to do last night when I caught him. Kind of tough to do when you've been in a jar for twelve hours. So this fellow will be down a good five or six ounces of chow. Boy, will he be hungry.'

Lamayette nods his head incredulously, then, remembering something, makes an *aw-shucks* noise. 'I clean forgot that he'll be so *thirsty* in there too. A rat that big needs about six fluid ounces of water a day. But what with this heat and being in that jar . . . boy, Billy Ray'll have anything that's moist. Just lap it up.'

Billy Ray's squeaks get louder, as if he understands the words.

The American puts his hand across his mouth, speaking confidentially. 'You know round about now Billy Ray will be going a little bit crazy. Loopy-loo.' And he twirls his index finger around and around near his temple. Nutcase. 'Just your average Darwinian psych-out. Such a tiny, primitive brain, and it's telling him he might never eat or drink again. How terrible must that be? Gee, will he be ready to use those teeth.'

A long slick of saliva eases out of Pir Durbar's mouth. The terror is palpable. Against the glass, the old man's body is palpitating with fear. As if he has a feverish chill.

Lamayette gives a low whistle, which makes the rat pause. It looks around, blinking fast, rubbing its nose anxiously with a forepaw. Lamayette whispers, like one of those nature presenters on TV trying to keep quiet in the jungle. 'I don't suppose your madrasa has a sort of Sierra Club section?' Pause. The Pakistani's eyes are transfixed by the rat. Those two long, yellowing curved incisors. Only inches away. 'I guess not. Then perhaps you don't know this: Billy Ray, our out-of-his-mind-with-hunger-and-thirst rodent, well, he's actually an omnivore. Yep. Billy Ray, he's partial to a little bit of anything. He'll eat meat. Crustaceans. Shellfish. Heck, I saw a clip on Discovery Channel of a brown rat catching a goddamn fish once.'

Lamayette tugs hard on Pir Durbar's one exposed earlobe. Pinching the delicate skin between his fingernails. The Pakistani protests. *AAAAaayyyyeeee . . . AAAAAhhhhhhhhhh.*

The American's voice rasps with deadly menace and a thousand years of cigarette smoke. 'If I put a bit of spit in your ear . . . then hold this glass jar over it . . . what do you think my poor starving friend would do?' Pir Durbar wails, high pitched, through almost clenched teeth. 'His brain's running real hot right now. There's a wild, wild hunger in charge of those sharp little teeth. All he sees in you right now is a long row of Big Macs. End to end. Nothing but soft, yummy tissue right the way through to your brain.'

Sweat streams down the holy man's face, twisted and tensed into ghastly apprehension.

Lamayette slowly works up a mouthful of saliva. Leans over the ear and, like a lover, lets his lips run softly over the sensitive skin. He clamps his hand tightly over the skull, like a vice, making it impossible for Pir Durbar to move. Then carefully spits into the ear canal. Fills it up nice and tidy. Not a drop wasted, nor a dribble in sight.

Billy Ray's twitchy little nose picks up the

scent. He starts hopping up and down inside the shiny jar, twittering madly. He knows what's coming . . . and the Pakistani knows too.

'So Operation Macchar. The clock's running.' And Billy Ray is lifted from the jar, held just over the holy man's head such that the tiny pink forepaws can claw at his skin. 'What's it going to be . . . ?'

Gate 206
Terminal 2, Manchester Airport
0946 UK Time, 1446 Islamabad time

At last the three of them are on board. Just passing through the front passenger door and stepping inside the plane, Tristie feels the tension ease out of her shoulders. The same sweet, sweet relief as when you make it back from a particularly hairy mission.

'You all right, boss?' Whiffler looks at her anxiously.

'Why?'

'You just seem to be acting a bit . . . strange.' Whiffler turns away to pack his carry-on in the overhead locker. 'Never seen you smiling so much.'

'I'll remember to be more of a hard-arse.' But he is right. An inane grin has been on Tristie's face for the last ten minutes. Something of a record. In fact she's getting cramp in her cheek-bones. Her smile muscles are complaining. As Tristie has long since learnt to do, she's tightly wrapped and packed away all the emotions, drawn down all her feelings into a little tight pellet and pinged it out into space.

There are two rows of first-class seats. Big and

comfortable. Sixty-plus inches of pitch. Button has 1B, but there is nobody sitting in the 1A window seat. Whiffler and Tristie are next to each other in the central bloc of aisle seats, 1C and D. He's already kicked off his shoes and is happily poking around with the in-flight entertainment panel. Apart from a uniformed pilot in 2F, snoozing against a window to their right, the rest of the front cabin is empty.

Looking down the two aisles that stretch almost two hundred feet to the rear, she sees that the economy-class section of the flight is full. A mix of the red-eyed and weary who've been on the flight since Islamabad, plus the fresh-faced and eager, who joined in Manchester.

The rest of the passengers are looking at the three members of Ward 13 as if they're the reason the flight isn't already dancing down the runway. Tristie's mind logs their tired, strangely hostile glances. Mostly from the women. Though a number of the men flash a glancing grin. It tweaks a powerful memory that suddenly has hold of Tristie by the throat. That remembrance, that singular vision, of looking up the aisle. Hostile glances and leery grins. It always chills. Returns her to a past time . . . a train to North Wales . . . Holyhead . . . Tristie, aged six and Mother. The recurring nightmare . . .

★ ★ ★

Mother is wearing white knee socks and a brown cotton, striped dress with satin buttons, cap sleeves and a silk tie belt. The dress reaches

236

down to her calves. She looks dazzling. Radiant. *One day this dress will be yours*, she had promised, holding it against herself as she swished from side to side in front of the mirror. A world of hope swimming in her eyes.

It is a lovely summery dress, and her blonde hair falls to her shoulders. Tristie imagines Mother wearing it and running through a meadow filled with flowers. She promises that, at last, she will find happiness in that dress. The only trouble . . . it's the middle of winter. And everything feels cold. Frigid. Surely she must feel that cold too. The little tremor in the middle finger of Mother's right hand somehow connects with the tremor in the pinkie finger of her left. Like an invisible current dancing across the long dark table that separates them in the railway carriage.

Tristie clutches her crayons. A tight, sweaty grip. A few pages are left in her colouring book.

Focus on the little farmyard scene, she tells herself. Just three crayons left. Purple, black and orange. She holds her tongue between her lips and teeth and works to get that apple tree just the right shade of black. It takes a lot of imagination to see what she sees. Purple for the sun, which leaves orange for the chickens and pigs. Concentrate on colouring inside the lines. She bites the tip of her tongue. Still, the worry coils tight within her.

Let's go to Dublin, Mother had announced that morning with a fresh, ear-to-ear smile. *We'll have fun. A train ride and your very first trip on a ferryboat. It will be exciting.*

237

Yes, Mother.

New beginnings, my sweet, and she curled her hand around the side of Tristie's head. *Life is all about do-overs, Tristie. New beginnings. Let's have a new beginning.*

Yes, Mother.

But what kind of a new beginning, she asks herself. She is something of an expert on new beginnings. They always seem to involve some uncharted fear. A realisation that each fresh terror is not the end-point in the journey of fears. Merely a way-stop. By that logic, there are many floors still to visit.

Anxiety never leaves her. Seems as reliable a feature of her existence as the sound of her voice, or the rise and fall of her chest. That sense of slow suffocation.

Would you like a Coke, Tristie?

Thank you, Mother. Across the table Mother smiles, and Tristie offers to share her crayons. Something like uncertainty passes quickly across Mother's brow and those pale blue eyes. She glances quickly at her watch. *Let me go and get you a drink, Tristie.* She speaks over burbled announcements from the tannoy. *Then, I'd love to help with your colouring.*

Tristie leans out and watches her move down the aisle, swaying as the train shudders across points. It seems that the gaze of several people is also following her as she walks. Men. Looking at her in a hungry way . . . but why would they be interested in her mother?

Tristie does not leave her seat because Mother is coming back. It might take a while but, eventually, she will return. And her heart will lift, and that cold blade of fear that ices the bones in her body will be banished for a little time longer.

The train reaches Holyhead, in North Wales. It is almost midnight by the time they find her. She hasn't moved. Not once. Because she knows Mother is coming for her. Like she has in the past. That is what mothers do.

The chubby, red-faced man shakes his head. *But no one's left on the train, little one.* Baffled. *Everybody's got off. And you'll have to get off too, my pet.*

She never sees Mother again. It is a month and three days before her seventh birthday. Twice she had wet herself. Simply too fearful to move.

★   ★   ★

The airline's airport manager, Majid Ali Khan, is flapping in the galley in front of first class, the other side of the bulkhead, explaining himself to one of the cabin crew. He is arguing the case for accepting the late first-class passengers even though there are no meals on board. *How dare you?* The conversation switches from English to Urdu, and starts to get shrill.

Somebody else's problem, Tristie thinks to herself. Settles against the soft pillow, trying to shake free of the last memory fragments of that wretched train journey . . .

There's a *too-wwoi-ing, too-wwoi-ing* of sitar background music drifting through the cabin. For a second she's overcome with hunger and

239

her stomach knots tight. Pavlov and his dog would be proud: Sitar music equals curry house, equals *panch rangia* and *murgh jalpuri*.

Button comes over, crouches and smirks impishly. 'You're going to think I've gone all Village People here, but I think we deserve a group hug. Good bloody work everybody. Especially you, boss.'

'Seconded.' This from Whiffler. And before Tristie can say a thing, such as that their cover story is that they don't actually know each other, she's smothered by the thick, strong arms of her colleagues.

It's enough to put her on the edge of tearful. Something she really tries not ever to be . . . and she is saved from her errant moment of high emotion when Button complains that Whiffler is perving. Sniffing his hair.

★ ★ ★

Forward of Tristie Merritt and the three other members of Ward 13, the heated exchange between Majid Ali Khan and the purser in charge of first class runs its course. An explosion of anger that fizzles. The two of them have removed their argument into the recessed area of the forward galley for greater privacy.

'Get over yourself!' Khan had hissed in Urdu. 'I'm sorry you thought you'd have no work to do today. But the last time I checked, this airline was in the business of taking money from people who want to fly. Understand?'

'Arsehole British monkey boy.' And the purser

turns away. Conversation over.

The large galley work area takes up the centre and right side of the forward section, so that the cockpit door, unusually, is set to the left of the plane's centreline. The galley is surrounded on three sides by all the stowed equipment: airline carts at floor level, and above this, what are called galley inserts, aluminium boxes that hold soft drinks, bottles of water, games for kiddies and so on. One wall of the galley has heat elements. Rows of steam and convection ovens for food preparation, and taps for hot and cold potable water.

Inside the galley the purser is trying to calm himself down. *La illah ha illallah.* Muttering quietly under his breath. *La illah ha illallah.* Prissily wiping down the work surface as if he hadn't already wiped it down a hundred times before. *La illah ha illallah.* No God but God.

It's OK, he says to himself. It *must* be OK. He breathes deeply. These extra passengers must surely be in God's plan. *La illah ha illallah.*

He runs his hand nervously down the side of his trousers, his heart throbbing with anxiety, until he touches a small round vial. He fingers it eagerly. Dushuqiang. Extra-strength rat poison. Odourless, tasteless and water soluble, the purser reminds himself again and again.

Just as he had earlier that morning, when he woke up in Room 703 of Manchester's Ramada Piccadilly Hotel.

Swat Valley
Pakistan
Monday — 0952 UK time, 1452 Islamabad
time

Just as a Boeing 777-340, *City of Risalpur*, is being pushed back from parking stand 206 at Manchester Airport, on the other side of the world, a man called Ahmad is having a long, splashy piss. He holds his dishdasha high on his chest, waggling himself at the thorny bush in front. Hands-free.

One of the madrasa's security guards.

Fifty yards beyond the bushes is what is known locally as Satan's Gourd, Lamayette's immense, dark rocky outcrop. Sterile of soil and plant life, and the subject of much local superstition. If Ahmad leans back he can just make out the crown of Satan's Gourd but it means looking directly into the afternoon sun. And that dazzles him, making little red spangles dance in front of his eyes.

Immediately behind him, the ledge of soil he's standing on drops down sharply to the riverbank, and waiting at the water's edge are the other four members of the downstream search party. They are perhaps a hundred yards away,

242

squatting on their haunches, also avoiding the sun's glare.

Ahmad's ablutions are interrupted by the most awful scream — of apocalyptic proportions — coming from the heavens. Surely not . . .

'*Audhu billahi min ash shaytan ar rajim.*' Ahmad mumbles the supplication quickly, hoping to wrap himself in Allah's protection.

Shading his eyes, he looks up towards the top of Satan's Gourd. Sees nothing.

Someone shouts. Words he could understand if he spoke English, but he can't: *Tell me what fucking flight. You MOTHER-FUCKING piece of shit.* Bellowed so loudly his first instinct is to look around him. Who said that?

Then, again. One pure note of agony, *AAAAhhhhhhhhh.* Floating on the wind. Longer and even more desperate. Surely a man in the jaws of death . . . perhaps a virgin giving birth to a large ox . . .

A thought flashes through Ahmad's mind . . . *Pir Durbar?*

He drops his dishdasha and spins around. 'Did you hear that?' he bellows in Pashto. But there's no movement from the water's edge. They've heard nothing. Looking in the other direction. 'Hey . . . ' Still no reaction.

He grabs up his Kalashnikov. To loose off a burst of five rounds. Just to startle them awake.

But it doesn't quite happen that way. A little channel of his urine had zigzagged sideways and soaked around the wooden butt of his semi-automatic rifle.

With a volley of swear words, Ahmad fumbles

243

to wipe it off with the hem of his clothing, and fires off the shots . . .

★ ★ ★

The gunfire registers in Bill Lamayette's mind, but barely. Acoustics up on this craggy rock are made haphazard by the wind and the wide-open space of the valley below.

Anyway, Lamayette is too deep into the urgency of his situation to notice. Trying to break down this shit of a man. Watching Billy Ray going to town. Blood streams out of the ear, splashing down, flecking the solid black rock with fat shiny globules as the holy man listens to his very own audio canal being gourmandised.

When all you've got is a hungry rat and an oversized jam jar, it doesn't work out like the shows on TV. No time for big productions, good cops and bad cops. Making them sweat, leaving the room, fiddling with the thermostat. Lamayette hasn't once broken eye contact or loosened the grip he's got on the back knot of the holy man's greasy hair. He's got just the one go at this. And Pir Durbar needs to know that Lamayette has nothing to fear. Will happily follow him over the edge of the cliff if that's what it takes.

'You're making this too hard on yourself . . . it doesn't have to be this way.'

The Pakistani's eyes bulge as though a great boot is pushing through from the back of his skull. A hideous sight, not totally unexpected. Slowly the mouth opens but the tongue doesn't

244

move. Stays perfectly still.

'What are you seeing? Can you see Billy Ray, his little sharp teeth? Gnashing his way inside your head. Can you . . . *can you see?*'

No change. Pir Durbar's expression is locked in place, frozen. Lamayette feels a professional sense of disappointment about what is happening, running almost to shame. The guy is shutting down. And *you* weren't able to finish the job . . .

Billy Ray snouts about in his glass cage, his busy little feet and fur slicked with dark red, puzzled by all this blood, trying to clear a way through. Still obsessed with that taste of meat.

Screw 'im. Lamayette throws down the old man's head and it thuds against the rock like a rolled-up wet towel. That awkward look of mortal terror is stitched on to his features. Eyes open, mouth agape. Dead from the neck up.

Lamayette backs away. Lowers the glass jar so that Billy Ray can make his escape. The rat looks up, blinks a couple of times, and shimmers away over the pitted rock surface.

There's only one person that Lamayette thinks to call and he retreats to his *shemagh* headdress, where the two parts of his mobile are hidden. Still time to stop this thing. His big, thick fingers are trembling as he clicks the battery into place. It's hard to hit the keys. Must hurry. He starts to punch in the numbers. In the United Kingdom. For Pir Durbar had given up some things before collapsing on him, but would it be enough? The information related to a flight. Today . . .

We can still stop this thing . . .

Lamayette's just about to put the phone to his ear when . . . *Shit*. His chest tightens, a freezing shiver runs through his veins. Only twenty yards away . . . the crown of someone's head.

A traditional headdress, a *shemagh*, bobbing its way uphill. Towards him. Then another. Three, four in fact. Heads still down, watching their feet as they clamber up the steep incline. He sees rifles and bandoliers, and all manner of stuff he hasn't got.

Shit.

Lamayette turns. Runs. And the last thing on his mind is making the call.

On board PK412

The man from Room 703 of the Ramada Piccadilly Hotel in Manchester is strapped into his seat and facing the passengers in first class. But he doesn't see them. His mind is in turmoil. *Why have we stopped again?* His right foot is tapping and he can't help himself fretting over the creases on his trousers.

There's not even a window for him to look out of.

A long time ago, when General Ali Mahmood Khan first briefed him on Operation Macchar, the general made it clear that the point of greatest vulnerability was while the plane was still on the ground.

'Zaafir,' General Khan had said, clasping the young man's shoulders, and looking deep into his soul. 'Zaafir, once the plane is airborne then the whole world opens up for us.'

And the Boeing 777 is still taxiing. Damn it.

Zaafir feels like he's drowning in sweat. He is flapping his steward's jacket, trying to get some air, some ventilation to his skin, when the intercom crackles. First in Urdu, then English.

'Ladies and gentlemen. Captain Iqbal Hussain from the cockpit. Sorry for the delay. We've been assigned runway Twenty-four Left for this morning's departure but to get there we have to cross another active runway. The good news is there's just one plane to land and one to take off, then we should be in position.

'We'll be taking off in a south-westerly direction this morning, heading . . . ' And in Zaafir's fevered mind, the captain's voice drains away to nothing, background chatter. He puts his hands up to his head, presses his sweaty palms tight against the pain in his temples.

Allah, I pray to You on this our journey for goodness and piety, and for works that are pleasing to You. Allah, lighten this journey and make its distance easy for me . . .

O Allah . . . O . . . And Zaafir shakes his head, almost on the verge of tears. *O Allah. Will you please get this plane off the ground.*

★ ★ ★

Bill Lamayette is also closing his eyes and saying a prayer. To a different god. He'd called Sheila 'Noppy' Davane yesterday but that had been the number for the MI5 switchboard, and he'd only got that by ringing up the hotel he stays at in London, Brown's on Albermarle Street, and begging the concierge to go through the local directory. The perils of being on the run from the long arm of the CIA . . .

He pushes redial for the same MI5 general number. Cautiously he puts the phone up to his ear. Just the one bar of battery life. Public holiday, of course, in the UK and Stateside.

Please God, let there be an operator . . . He doesn't like what he hears. Mutters 'You son of a bitch . . . ' in answer to that pert voicemail delivery. Julie Andrews as Mary Poppins: '*This is MI5. If you have information you wish to give to the Security Services please hold. Your information is valuable to us and an operator will speak to you shortly . . .* '

Shit. Shit. Shit. He turns to look up the giant rock to the summit. Bends back a couple of branch leaves and sees the madrasa guards scrabbling in confused agitation around Pir Durbar.

' *. . . You can also provide your information by contacting MI5 through our website, www.mi5.gov.uk. That's www.mi5.gov.uk . . .* '

Hell's bells . . . he can't bring himself to look at the battery charge.

' *. . . If you're interested in a career with MI5, you can find more information at our website, www.mi5careers.info. Our recruitment agency . . .* '

Lamayette punches a number, any number, to jump out of the Julie Andrews talkfest. Moments later he hears the familiar double-pulse ring of a British phone.

The voice on the other end of the line sounds startled. '*Hello? Can I help you?*'

Lamayette covers the mouthpiece, whispers. 'This is urgent. I am calling from Pakistan. I am a senior CIA officer. I need to get hold of Sheila Davane. Noppy . . . '

'*It's a public holiday here, friend.*' From the earpiece comes a sound of someone blowing across a steaming cup of tea. '*I'm just a security guard, answering the phones and whatnot.*'

'Can you see if she's there?'

'*If who's where?*'

Exasperation. 'Sheila Davane. She's like the number four or five in seniority in the whole organisation.' Lamayette can feel his blood pressure drilling up through the top of his head. A couple of the madrasa banditos are looking down towards the valley floor below, scanning, casting their eyes in his direction. Urgent whispers of encouragement. 'Noppy. Everybody knows her as Noppy.'

'*Is that right?*' Sound of a biscuit crunching in his overfull mouth. '*Noppy . . .* ' Like it's the craziest thing he's ever heard.

'Do you know who I'm talking about?'

More slow, deliberate biscuit-chewing followed by a swallow. '*Not the faintest idea, pal.*' Lamayette grips the phone so hard his knuckles show white. Above him, he's alarmed to see that the body language of one of the guards is tensing up. Something interests him, hands shading his eyes. Looking now straight in Lamayette's direction. The CIA veteran feels the skin on his face tighten.

'*I don't suppose you have an extension for this Noppy?*'

Seventy-two hours he's been tamping down his rage at the betrayals, humiliation and crass stupidity that he's endured, and that's without factoring in the last twelve hours' total absence of nicotine. And this . . . this tea-drinking, biscuit-chewing jobsworth is the ultimate. Suddenly the purest anger he's ever known screams through his body. 'OF COURSE I FUCKING WELL DON'T HAVE AN EXTENSION . . . '

Too late to undo what he's done.

Within seconds his hiding place is peppered by gunfire. Spits of dust flying all around him. *Twu-twu-twu-twu-twunnngg.* Five semi-automatic rifles laying down six hundred rounds per minute. Wildly inaccurate but scary as all hell.

Especially when you don't have a gun yourself.

A chilling cry echoes from the top of the slope. And Lamayette can't help but gape. Without thinking of the holy man, the five guards career down towards him. Dishdashas flapping. Some holding daggers above their heads, shining blades glistening in the sun. Rudyard Kipling would have recognised that timeless bloodlust.

'Hello? Hello? . . . ' From the handset, the very faintest voice from London. *'What's going on there?'*

But Bill Lamayette is running for his life. Barefoot. Winding this way and that. A huge beast of a man sprinting across ploughed fields and open ground. Desperate. But clueless as to what to do now.

Best guess, he has about a thousand-yard advantage . . . but safety, if you could loosely describe Peshawar and Islamabad as safety, is hundreds of miles away. Everything in between crawls with danger and menace. A thousand yards' head start is as nothing.

One of the disadvantages of working a bank holiday is that it increases your chances of bumping into Sheila 'Noppy' Davane, who, famously, doesn't do holidays. Long weekends serve only one purpose for her, the chance to poke around this massive structure and descend on some junior staffer, get them to show her some new piece of technology or walk her through a particular surveillance operation. Again and again. Until she's satisfied.

Today's victim is a floppy-haired, pale-faced 'watcher' whose official job description is CCTV surveillance monitor, as in someone hidden away in an audio-visual booth in the deep bowels of the massive Thames-side fortress. Nothing more to do than monitor CCTV cameras. Today's watcher had been ploughing through hours of footage — perhaps scrolling a little faster than he should — logging major incidents, skimming through the others. Taking calls on his mobile, sending off a text or two, as he worked. Plugged into his iPod, of course. Singing tunelessly to

252

himself in a comfortable little bubble of existence.

Then the unmistakable shape of stout, grey-haired Davane shouldered into the sound-proofed room, her inquisitive mind itching for company. And a 'watching' task that would have taken a couple of hours . . . well, it won't get finished today. Not at this rate.

'Why isn't it possible to teach a computer to watch this footage, do all the real-time analysis for us?' The Ulsterwoman leans across the young technician, dabs a thick finger at a stationary black object on one of the quartered screens. They're looking at surveillance of an Internet café on York Way, one of the roads bordering King's Cross train station. 'That bag, for instance . . . it's been there for at least five minutes.'

'You mean like an algorithm?' *Someone please take Granny away . . .*

'I don't know what these things are called,' she says fussily. 'But it can't be beyond the wit of man to tell a computer that leaving a bag unattended is worthy of our interest.'

Shrug of the shoulders. 'I guess.' The mumbled answer speaks to the fact that this is the second hour of Davane's inquisitional riffs. *Why can't we do this? Has anybody thought to do that?* All well above the young man's pay grade and not helping him process through this York Way footage.

'It would save us a lot of time . . . ' The shrill *bleep-bleep* of the phone stops the conversation. The watcher leans back in his chair and lazily collects up the handset. *Please let this be for Noppy . . .*

Big smile on the watcher's face, 'That's the front desk, Ms Davane,' his white-as-paper hand covering the mouthpiece. 'They need you down there. Some kind of weird call for you from Pakistan. Some CIA guy said it was urgent.'

'Put it through . . . put it through here right away.'

'The signal must have dropped off.' Another shrug of the shoulders. 'Or the guy hung up. They're dead keen for you to go down.'

'Tell them to trace the call. Get a number . . .' Davane's already tugging at the massive door covered with heavy soundproof cladding. 'And help me get this ridiculous door open.'

Swat Valley
Six minutes later

This barefoot business is not the way to run through the hills. Especially hills studded with sharp-edged chips of granite. Bill Lamayette is gasping for air. His feet are shredded.

He wipes down his face with a sleeve. But still ... still he's ahead of his pursuers. Don't give up. They're gobbling up the distance but he's ... he's not dead yet. Climb. Keep on climbing, Bill. Above the valley.

The landscape has become alpine and Lamayette's one plan is to reach the top of the valley wall. Maybe some pro-American yeti will intervene.

Wherever he looks are rocks, creeping plants, low, scrubby thickets. Absolutely no cover whatsoever. Two hundred yards back, his pursuers, hooting and hollering, are scrambling behind him. Firing indiscriminately.

It suddenly strikes Lamayette that this landscape is familiar; videos of Osama Bin Laden in his pre-9/11 phase had been shot in places like this. Dressed like a typical tribal hayseed. Skipping from rock to rock along remote pathways. Padding through mountain

255

passes. Looking like he belonged, and was not in fact the pampered son of a Saudi billionaire. It had amused Lamayette there always appeared to be a goat somewhere in the background, quietly chewing its cud, looking up as Bin Laden mooched past. Thinking, *Who the fuck is this idiot?*

What a thing it would be if I bumped into Osama right now . . .

Then indeed, two extraordinary things happen. Totally unrelated.

The phone in his hand, which he's long since forgotten about. It starts to ring. He pants. 'Ha . . . low?'

No sooner does his brain register the voice on the other end of the line than there's a terrible cacophony of gunfire. Violent and rapid, and a strangely different timbre to what he's heard before. Deeper. *Tdug-tdug-tdug-tdug-tdug.*

Enough already.

He dives to one side, downhill, into a spongy mattress of scrub. In mid-tumble he registers two quick facts: that new, sonorous drilling of gunfire means he's either dead and doesn't know it yet. Or he will be soon, because he's stopped running. And Pir Durbar's guards will be upon him.

Lying on his back now, winded and dazed, Lamayette looks up to the heavens. Chest thumping. Big bass drum pulsing in his ears. Dazed and in a staggering amount of pain, he puts the phone back to his ear . . . fully expecting these to be the last words he ever says.

MI5 Headquarters
Thames House

Sheila 'Noppy' Davane is getting impatient. *What is going on?* 'Lamayette. Bill Lamayette. Is that you there?' The security guard and two network engineers look on. Pensive. The audio room is dark, lit only by a small anglepoise lamp and the backlit features of the various recording devices.

'*Oohh . . . mmmtmmhgh ffffukkkkk . . . iiiing bbbaahhllllll tsssseeeekkk.*'

She turns to face the three men, who have their arms crossed in front of them. No more clue what it is going on than Davane. 'What did he just say?' They shake their heads. No idea. One of the engineers fiddles with the gain settings on the audio equipment.

'*I rrrrppppppd meeee ffffukkkkk . . . iiiing bbbaahhllllll tsssseeeekkk.*'

One of the engineers uncrosses his arms and pushes away from the wall. 'I think he said . . . something rude.' A baffled thought plays across his face. '*I ripped my fucking ball-sac.*'

'Ball-sac?' flares Davane. 'Lamayette . . . Lamayette, what's going on?'

Silence from the other end.

257

'Lamayette . . . Bill?' Davane angles herself closer to the small microphone. Speaks very slowly, as if to a child. 'Bill. What. Do. You. Want. To. Speak. About?'

This time the response is crystal clear. The first disorienting flush of pain and nausea has passed. '*Sheila. I think I lost my testicles about two hundred yards ago.*'

The security guard and one of the engineers stifle a laugh. Davane wags an angry finger at both of them. Her eyes fierce behind her big framed glasses. 'You rang me up to tell me that . . . '

'*No, Sheila . . .* ' And Lamayette breaks off for a second. A huge clearing out of the lungs and a gigantic spit follow, sounding like someone ripping up bedsheets. He's still breathing heavily. '*Today. Sheila. Pakistan flight . . .* ' Wheezing noisily. '*Stop PIA. To New York . . .* '

Pause.

Davane stabs a button on the internal communication system, direct through to one of the always-staffed operations rooms. She speaks clearly. 'This is Davane. Top priority: get me a status on all local PIA flights today to New York. Stand-by Special Branch, stand-by all our airport officers. We might be grounding some planes . . . '

In the meantime one of the engineers has been playing with switches and a dial. Out of the background ether he pulls Lamayette's voice, very distinct: '*Hey. Lookee here. The damned cavalry have arrived. Whoopdi-doo for the Special Forces.*'

Davane raises her voice. 'Focus on me, Bill.' Gently pounding her fists on the wooden work surface. 'Bill? Bill?'

'*Sorry, Sheila.*' Lamayette's breathing is steadier but he still can't squeeze out more than a handful of words at a time. '*Big hijack planned . . . Nothing like we've . . . ever seen before . . . They're going . . . to . . .*'

'Bill . . . which flight? Who's involved? How many?'

'*Owwwww. Shiitttt. What did you guys do that for?*'

'What is it, Bill? Bill?'

'*Some Green Beret bastard . . . just . . . shot . . . me . . . with . . . a . . . trank . . . daaaa-rrrrrr . . .*'

'A tranquilliser dart?' Davane frowns. Tugs on the thick chain of her glasses. Fretting. Trying to make sense of all this . . . weirdness. 'Bill. Bill. Bill . . . What are the hijackers going to do?'

'*Shit . . . shot . . . Again . . . 'ucking swine . . .*'

There's a lion-like roar from Lamayette as he struggles mightily to hold back the dark curtain passing his way. Enough energy for just one last thing . . .

'*Qissaaa . . . Khawani . . .*'

And then there's a sound the like of which those in the tiny cramped audio suite have not heard before. Relying only on their sense of hearing and the power of imagination . . . it sounds very much like the death-roar of a bull elephant followed by its sudden and final collapse earthwards.

Nearer than Lamayette could have imagined, less than a mile away, someone else is also relying on wits and a fevered imagination to work out what the hell is going on.

The State Department's Kirsten Ackerman sits on a bench facing towards the scowling form of Jahanghir. They've just landed in the rear of a MH47E Chinook helicopter. Unable to move, because, standing fore and aft of them, are a pair of Green Berets from 3rd Special Forces Group. Each with an ever-ready trigger finger cocked to the side of a machine gun and looking underwhelmed to be babysitting 'friendlies', while overmatched and underpowered 'combatants' engage their colleagues in a firefight outside.

The rotors of the Chinook spin on an idle power setting and through the open rear ramp Ackerman can see shadows of the three blades swooping by. She lets out a long, draining sigh.

Who knows who was to blame? She had worked the phones on realising that Bill Lamayette had doubled back to the religious school. Perhaps she'd been indiscreet. Not thought things through. In the absence of an actual dead body . . . Washington's assumption is that Lamayette has gone rogue. She knows that now. To whom he had defected and why, well, that's how come they want him captured so badly. One thing is certain, nobody had been in the slightest bit interested in her tale of holy men plotting evil deeds. The people in the helicopter are not thinkers — they're doers, and as far as they're concerned Lamayette is a nutcase, gone way off reservation.

It must have been that one of her calls had been pinged by the CIA or even the Pakistani spooks. As she and Jahanghir had been preparing to leave the Peshawar garage and head back to the madrasa, the real military had arrived. Pakistani soldiers. Effectively kidnapping them, disbursing Jahanghir's rent-a-mob, and keeping the two of them blindfolded, under guard and out of circulation until the Green Beret Chinook came to pick them up at an undisclosed location. By that time, the mission to get Lamayette was prepped and the helicopter left as quickly as it had arrived.

Lamayette could at least rest easy knowing he had made himself a king-sized pain in the ass.

The hardware needed to capture him was impressive: from the USS *Ronald Reagan* in the Persian Gulf, an E2 Hawkeye early-warning-style twin-engine turboprop had triangulated Lamayette's mobile phone signals to within a dozen yards. Two drones had flown figures of eight in the skies over the Swat Valley, waiting for that mobile to be powered up. And when it was finally switched on — for long enough to get a meaningful fix — the drones fed live imagery of Lamayette and his phone up to, among others, the Special Forces team inside the Chinook.

But the best indication of Washington's ardour is that somebody had actually okayed inserting US troops and hardware into the situation. Into Pakistan. A wild and woolly place at the best of times. Only somebody at cabinet level could push that button.

Which explains why the helicopter had spent three hours standing off, circling the same spot at 9,000 feet, out of earshot of the ground.

The team sergeant had used those hours to brief and rebrief his troops with the aid of a twelve-inch portable monitor, pointing and shouting over the full-force racket of the Chinook's twin rotors. Ackerman had caught a glimpse of the drones' live feed filmed from tens of thousands of feet in the air, and, realising that the pink cue ball dead centre was Lamayette himself, found herself smiling. Happy in the knowledge he was safe. Temporarily, at least, and still throwing monkey wrenches into everybody's lives.

Then the signal came: Mission Go. And the helicopter started its rapid descent, bumping to the ground so heavily that Ackerman almost bit her cheek. She remembers counting sixteen soldiers sprinting down the ramp in pursuit of the five guards, who were themselves still running after Lamayette. Almost an episode of *Tom and Jerry*, with the dog hunting the cat, who is chasing the mouse.

The theory of tranquillising humans Ackerman understands. To have effective stopping power, you must know the weight of the victim, to create the right dose. Too much could be fatal, too little would have no effect. That's why tranquillising is not recommended for law enforcement or basic home protection. Too many imponderables.

But in the case of Lamayette, they knew his weight. Three hundred and thirty-eight pounds, according to his last medical. She'd watched the two guys prepping their darts. Each needle looked about an inch long, attached to a coloured test tube with a feathery-looking flight stabiliser at the rear. They'd drawn the doses from what looked like a drip-bag stored in a grey-coloured icebox.

'Is this stuff safe?' she had asked of her sergeant from Iowa. Nodding in the direction of the airguns.

He'd smiled his reply. *For what this guy's done*, his eyes said, *I really could care less.*

Shouting from outside draws Ackerman back to the present.

With two American soldiers per cadaver, the first of the five body bags is carried on board, starkly framed by the interior of the ramp. It's hard for Ackerman's eyes to adjust from the brightness outside to the twilight in the rear of the Chinook. The dead body is lumped to the ground. The rest follow with cold military precision, quick-time, stacked three on the bottom and two on top. Right in front of her. The bags are unmarked, silver with black web carry-handles in the four corners, and two sets of strong zippers.

Jahanghir takes this public display of killing power the worst way possible. He seems crushed.

Ackerman tries to catch Jahanghir's eye with a soothing look. 'He's going to be OK,' she comforts. But he glances at her quickly, then back to the bags as if they are some manifestation of evil. There's moisture in his eyes, a look of complete breakdown.

'They haven't come to kill him, Jahanghir . . .'

He waggles his hand at the dead bodies.

'Do any of these bodies look big enough for Mr Bill? Where's the big tummy?' The cadavers might have been tall or short but to a man they must have had the same trim, wiry frame. Perfect for neat stacking.

She turns, noticing a change in the beat and urgency of the Chinook's rotors. *Thump-thump-thump*. Faster and faster. And the helicopter hesitates, imperceptibly above the ground, dancing on the edge of flight. Commands that would have been shouted become hand signals, conveyed from the crew on board to those Green Berets manning the perimeter of the landing zone. Fists bump chests, then their heads. Fingers splay-against shoulders.

Most, but not all, of the Green Berets reverse towards the ramp. Their M240s still menacing an unseen enemy. They fan out either side of the rear.

Against the shrieking roar of the turboshaft engines Bill Lamayette finally appears. Carried litter-style with a soldier at each corner, he is laid out on top of an unopened body bag looking blissfully happy as they hump up the ramp. His dish-dasha riding up to his knees, his strong legs hanging either side.

A metal stent of some kind has been plugged into his mouth, to stop him choking or swallowing his tongue. But it looks like a bong that he's sucking on . . . A fabulously wasted

Roman senator being shuttled to yet another orgy.

The helicopter pitches nose forward and speeds off, the rear ramp slowly drawing shut. In the confusion of soldiers milling around, Ackerman moves carefully towards Lamayette. Kneeling beside him, she touches the side of his face, feeling for a pulse, before realising that, with the juddering of the airframe, it would mean nothing.

She looks up at the team sergeant, a Hispanic, with eyes as dark as night. His combat boots rest on Lamayette's thick shoulder and he looks at her suspiciously.

She cups her hands. Shouts. 'What happened to his phone?'

He mimes his reply. *What. Phone?*

Dipshit. 'You traced him using the signal from his phone . . . '

More mime. Each word enunciated very clearly. With maximum sarcasm. '*Oh. You. Mean. This. Phone* . . . ' He reaches into his pocket, draws out two Ziploc evidence bags, and grins, like he just might be the cleverest man in the world.

One with a snapped-in-half SIM card, the other containing a very crushed and out-of-action mobile phone.

MI5 Headquarters
Thames House

Nothing more from Bill Lamayette. They chased the trail as far as GCHQ, the massive listening post outside Cheltenham. Spoke to the senior watch officer. 'No signal, Ms Davane,' the Somerset accent pronounced. 'If there was a signal before, it's very much gone now.'

Then, to compound Davane's anxiety, the officer wants to talk some more. 'Did you read this morning's digest?' The digest of electronic intelligence gleaned from the Echelon listening posts throughout the world.

Davane shakes her head. 'Can this wait?' *What does this guy want to talk about now?* 'We're a little bit busy at this end.'

'Thought you'd want to know . . . those keywords your office asked us to insert into Dictionary . . . '

'What keywords, what about them?' Davane's mind is completely elsewhere. Her office is always submitting fresh phrases for the Dictionary software program.

'Operation Macchar . . . Qissa Khawani . . . just in the last five or six hours, from almost nothing to suddenly off the graph. A huge spike in traffic . . . '

266

Davane covers her mouth with her hand. The keywords had been Lamayette's request from yesterday. His final gift, he had said. Her mind blanks. 'Oh God . . . what the hell is happening here?'

★   ★   ★

It's fifty-nine minutes since PK412 departed Manchester Airport for New York. The operations room knows this, plus the flight's altitude and heading. On a full-sized screen everybody's watching the radar track of the plane's progress towards the vastness of the Atlantic. Watching, and waiting for the Boeing's next radio transmission, for any hint of trouble. PK412 is using a SECAL cockpit radio system, meaning that any transmissions not relating to their flight are filtered out. That's why M15 is listening to dead air at the moment . . .

In a separate room, another team is handling arrangements for this afternoon's scheduled PIA flight from Heathrow to New York, but still inbound from Karachi. A suitable somebody from the Department for Transport will tell their manager in London that this afternoon's flight had best stay on the ground. Davane knows PIA has good people, who knew the drill and were keen to cooperate.

Working the phones between MI5 officers already dispatched to Heathrow and the Metropolitan Police's Counter Terrorism Command is not something Sheila 'Noppy' Davane wants to be doing. Not now. A third team is handling that. Trouble is, it's a public holiday. Britain's security posture, which can't help but relax every weekend, seems to be terminally asleep on public holidays. Government has never thought to give MI5 (a mere intelligence-gathering operation) the authority to do anything useful like scramble RAF interceptors. That can only come from a higher realm. In truth, though, at the moment, she has precious little hard evidence to offer. Everything hinges on Bill Lamayette, a man whose reputation is being trashed with great gusto by his own side. Hardly a compelling witness . . .

So, she had given that third team very specific instructions: be as sharp as you need, rude even, just get the alarm raised. Get people by the phone so I can speak to them. Her gut is screaming that PK412 is *the* flight. *The* one.

The pulsing red square moves steadily north-west, slowly skimming across the top of Northern Ireland. The rest of the screen is a jumble of yellow dots and indices representing other transatlantic flights.

There are a dozen or so in the room with her, getting busy, thumbing through files, working the phones. In her own quiet pocket of contemplation Davane notes that the track puts the plane directly over Rathlin Island, a boot-shaped crag six miles off the Antrim coast, some fifteen miles from the southern tip of Scotland's Mull peninsula. The local tourist board would have one believe that it was in a cave on Rathlin that Robert the Bruce was taught a valuable lesson by a plucky spider building his web. If at first you don't succeed, try, try and try again.

Her cheeks and neck go cold at the thought. Coincidence or fate? Robert the Bruce . . . what was it that Lamayette had asked about? Operation Mosquito, or Macchar in Urdu, as he had explained. Robert the Bruce and spiders. General Ali Mahmood Khan and mosquitoes?

Two secretaries huff their way into the room, flapping files of paperwork. Obviously dress-down day — one of them wears a pair of boot-cut jeans and a pink striped shirt that looks like pyjamas. Pyjama-girl lays out whatever she had been able to find on the subject of *Qissa Khawani*.

The other, in a pair of hiking boots and outdoorsy waterproof trousers, puts in front of Davane three separate bundles of information. First, the technical information relating to the actual flight, including fuel load sheets and cargo manifests. With this is a print-out of 412's flight plan, starting with the waypoint known as SUNOT at which they enter Shanwick airspace, the eastern half of the North Atlantic Flight Information Region. There too are the five plots of the proposed track across the Atlantic up to their exit point at way station SCROD, a couple of hundred miles off the Canadian coast. Finally, there's the route on to New York. Crossing the Canadian coastline near the Inuit settlement of Nain in Newfoundland, cutting down through north-eastern Canada, into New York State at a place called Hogansburg and on to John F. Kennedy International Airport.

A second stack of papers relates to the crew

and passenger list. All relevant Passenger Name Records, including each person's complete name, date of birth, citizenship, sex, passport number and country of issuance, residence, Green Card or alien registration, address while in the USA, religious and ethnic information (derived from choice of meal), affiliation to a particular group, data relating to place of residence or means of contacting an individual (email address, details of a friend, place of work) plus any relevant medical history. And perhaps most importantly, how their tickets were routed and purchased.

A last stack of information is plunked down by Davane's side by Hiker-girl. Information relating to those passengers with US and/or UK visas, including all their biometric data with a wealth of financial information as icing.

A lot of paper to be sifted, with even more to come. And the exact same review has to be done for the second PIA flight due to leave Heathrow for New York later in the day.

Davane unclips her brooch, a design of amethysts studded with pearls, laid out in the shape of a salamander. She has a particular way of reading through documents. It's the hasp she wants . . . using the point of the needle to work her way down the list of names.

Slow work. Steady work. Pricking the page once next to a name that intrigues, twice for something that alarms. Still no sign from her number-three operations team of any higher-ups being ready to talk to her.

Better to be doing something now than

nothing. Slow work, she tells herself. Steady work.

Davane is halfway through her list:

LORRIMAN/BERYLMRS
LORRIMAN/RODNEYMR
MCANDREW/DAVIDMR
MCATEER/LUCYMS
MANSOOR/FAHIMDR
MANSOOR/SEETAMRS
MERRITT/TRISTESSEMS
MUHAMMAD/SAEEDDR
MUKHERJEE/ROHITMR

She has the tip of her brooch fastener raised by the name MERRITT/TRISTESSEMS, some distant connection swimming in the dark of her mind, picking irritatingly.

'*Shanwick Radio, Pakistan 412 position.*'

The audio link bursts into life, connecting MI5 through to the flight controllers in Prestwick and their radio transmissions, which are relayed to transatlantic flights from transmitters near Shannon in Ireland (hence the portmanteau Shanwick).

Davane looks at the two photos in front of her. Captains Iqbal Hussain and Imtiyaz Jamal. Identical round-faced twins. Impossible to tell whose voice this is.

'*Pakistan 412, this is Shanwick Radio, pass your message.*' A dour, efficient Scottish reply.

'*Pakistan 412, passed SUNOT 1017 Zulu, FL360, Mach 0.84, estimate 58N 20W 1109 Zulu, 59N 30W next.*'

Davane watches somebody translate the key information on to a whiteboard. The plane entered the Shanwick Flight Information Region at waypoint SUNOT four minutes ago. At 1017 Zulu or GMT, or 1117 British Summer Time. They're flying at 36,000 feet at a speed of Mach 0.84 or 560 miles per hour. Next is waypoint longitude 58N 20W, which the pilots estimate they will hit at 1109 GMT. In fifty-two minutes. After that 59N 30W, right in the middle of the Atlantic, where PK412 will be handed over to controllers based at Gander in Newfoundland.

Shanwick confirms all the information by reading it back to the flight crew: 'Pakistan 412, passed SUNOT 1017 Zulu, FL360, Mach 0.84, estimate 58N 20W 1109z, 59N 30W next.'

'Correct read-back. Thank you.'

'Shanwick Radio . . . '

Barring any disaster, this should be the last time they hear from the flight for almost an hour.

Davane reaches across her piles of papers for the phone. Taps a three-digit extension number. Answering is one of the engineers who'd been with her when they last spoke with Lamayette . . . in an audio suite facing a desk of expensive gadgetry.

The silver-haired MI5 veteran gently kneads the underside of her droopy chin. 'You pick up anything unusual, any stress in the voice?'

The operations room hushes . . . everybody waiting on the answer. Davane nods her head. Listening.

The phone is put down and everybody in the room leans forward. Tense.

'No stress.' Davane looks around the knot of anxious faces. 'If it's happening on that plane, it hasn't happened yet.'

On board PK412
At 36,000 feet
1124 UK time, 1624 Islamabad time,
0624 Washington time

Credit card swiped. Number punched in. Heartbeat raised . . . Zaafir, the man from Room 703, waits nervously in an empty first-class seat for the technical stuff to happen. For the phone signal to blip from the underbelly of the Boeing 777 to the nearest satellite, for his call to be channelled onwards.

He's alone. Two passengers and Captain Harry Salahuddin are asleep. The woman, the one with the dark hair and serious cheekbones, is in the forward left toilet. Zaafir's taken the precaution of drawing the blinds so he can work in relative obscurity. He'd instructed his stewardess colleague, a plump, moon-faced woman, that they would be delaying the drinks and meal service. She'd made a cow-like grunt of agreement, folded out one of the rear-facing seats, and is pushing at her cuticles with a cocktail stick.

It takes fourteen seconds but feels like hours. Then the ring tone . . . and Zaafir really feels his pulse race.

'Hello . . . '

Zaafir whispers in Pashto. 'It is me.'

'*Praise be to Allah.*'

Almost inaudible. 'Five minutes and it shall be done . . . '

'*Tell me, Zaafir, are there many infidels on the flight?*'

'Many infidels, yes,' then Zaafir's voice quavers, as he remembers row after row of eager, excited Pakistani faces to the rear of the plane. 'Many believers too.'

The words that come back to him are a soothing balm. Delivered in Arabic with a hypnotic beat: '*Only Allah holds the knowledge of the unseen and does not reveal these mysteries to anyone, except those He selects as His messengers. He watches over them through guardians that advance before and shield them from behind that He may observe the proper delivery of His message. He is aware of all that they do and maintains a strict record of all things that exist.*'

Not much one can say to that, and the airline steward knows it. God works in mysterious ways. Zaafir feels duly admonished, his skin hot with embarrassment. The best he can do is repeat: 'Five minutes . . . and it shall be done.'

'*You are a blessed man, Zaafir . . . *' and the man on the other end of the phone sounds as if he wants to hang up, wants to be doing something else. Urgently. So his final words of counsel seem a little rushed. '*Remember. Those admitted to Paradise shall experience true bliss.*'

Never shall they know want, nor will they suffer old age.' A rote.

Zaafir is about to ask a question, when he realises the phone link is already dead, and he has been sent on his way. *Five minutes.* Yes. I can do this. *Five minutes.* And the spirit flows through him, tingling his senses, strengthening every muscle and sinew in his body.

He is watching me, through guardians that advance before and will shield me from behind that He may observe the proper delivery of His message . . .

Of course Zaafir is an idiot, but he's a faithful idiot, and where would we be without faithful idiots?

Four thousand five hundred miles away, in a dusty warehouse off M.A. Jinnah Road, Karachi, Hamza Khan, son of the general, closes his mobile phone. An anonymous pre-paid Motorola handset. He turns to eyeball the rows of young, expectant faces lined up on either side of the three long tables, lit by a rackety collection of chipped and downright dangerous light fittings, hanging cobwebbed from the ceiling. The walls hum with energy, with the footfall of shoppers on the move, for the warehouse is on the ground floor and packed all around them, and three floors above, is a shopping plaza.

These young militants, unthinking in the totality of their hatred, are drawn from the scurrying mass of the poor and half educated. Forty in total, packed tight by the warehouse's towering boxes of crockery and children's clothing and footwear. Each had ten Motorola handsets and three plastic drinking cups. In each cup fifteen different SIM cards. One thousand eight hundred SIM cards in total, each one programmed with 250 mobile phone numbers spanning the big networks of Ufone, Mobilink, Paktel, Waridtel, Telenor and Insta Phone. The subscribers' phone numbers have been harvested from various content providers. Not from people who download the latest jokes, funny wallpapers or cricket scores, too secular. No, the 1,800 SIM cards are prepped with the contact details of believers, both fanatics and those teetering on the edge of fanaticism. Those who can't be without the sound of their muezzin and download MP3 files of the *Azaan*, or call to prayer. Or the Islamic devotionals of singers like Muhammad Rashid Azam. Or those who subscribe to the many SMS services fanning the latest radical rage against Coca-Cola, Danish cartoonists or British oppressors in Afghanistan.

So. Forty sets of fingers to send text messages. Four hundred handsets, 1,800 SIM cards, each with its pre-programmed field of 250 mobile numbers. Almost half a million text messages a minute. Tens of millions of people to be touched by this fantastic evil with the speed of gods.

And the first message will read: '*Beware. 300 Muslim Innocents To Be Slaughtered By Infidel Warplanes. Pakistan Aircraft. Developing story. Please forward urgent.*'

Followed five minutes later by: '*Do You Know Anyone On PIA Boeing 777 To New York? To Be Shot Down Off Coast Four Hours From Now. Developing story. Please forward.*'

Next message: '*Confirmed. PIA Boeing 777. Flight No. PK412. 300 Muslims To Be Killed. 90 Females. 44 Children. Please forward.*'

This to be tagged five minutes later by a well-known Koranic verse at the heart of the Islamic law of jihad:

'*Murder of 300 Muslim Innocents. Koran 22: verses 39–40: Permission to take up arms is hereby given to those who are attacked because they have been oppressed — Allah indeed has power to grant them victory — those who have been unjustly driven from their homes, only because they said: 'Our Lord is Allah'.*'

It's all so intoxicating.

Like caged animals, the bright, shiny faces looking at Hamza Khan share a burning desire to get to work on this. To stoke the fire's flames as big and as hot as they can. To bring Pakistan, the Middle East, the whole axis of Western imperialist power to their knees.

All they need is the signal. From their leader . . .

Hamza closes his eyes, rolls his bony shoulders again and again. *Here it comes, here it comes,* pulling up from the deep, a fiery religious frenzy. A species of mania.

He sweeps forward towards the nearest of the tables, his audience already rapt in their own delirium, and slowly raises his scrawny arms, his fingers trembling like talons, feeling for his father's spirit, entreating it to enter him. And he thunders: 'O you who believe! Fight those of the disbelievers who are close to you, and let them find harshness in you.'

278

And on the word *harshness*, the first mobiles are lifted. The first text messages formed . . . and the first terrible sting of Operation Macchar is released.

Outside the cockpit
On board PK412
Three minutes later

The sole female passenger in first class is exiting the aircraft toilet. It's a tight squeeze so she waits with the door half open. Zaafir, in the gangway leading to the cockpit, motions her forward. You go first. There's a half-length mirror to the left of the passage and it's his observation that all women stop to look at themselves. This one doesn't.

Strange.

Zaafir is carrying a tray with drinks for the cockpit crew. In addition to the business with the mirror, there's something about this woman that strikes him as odd. Out of place. They each move to one side so the other can pass. He nods to her, still trying to work out what it is about her. She smiles. Blue eyes. Lovely white teeth. And slides past.

The passenger, Zaafir's list says her name is Ms Tristesse Merritt, moves to the left and out of sight. Presumably back to her seat in the front of the first-class section. No matter. More important things to worry about.

Two glasses.

Zaafir grips the edge of the tray to make sure there's no chance of spillage. He has to laugh, gallows humour. If he spills the drinks now, there will be no Operation Macchar. Simple as that. His every last grain of Dushuqiang has been used.

Zaafir runs his spare hand over the cockpit door fascia. It hides its secrets so well. He doesn't understand the intricacies but this much he knows: accessing a plane's cockpit has never been harder. Nobody knew for sure — not even he — how the heroic martyrs got into the cockpits of those four famous 9/11 flights, American 11 and 77 and United 93 and 175. The story kept mutating. One whispered version of mosque gossip was that they threatened the flight attendants to get hold of the key. Another, that they'd cut up one of the hostesses to draw the captain out of the cockpit. Who knows? Whatever the truth, the events of 9/11 changed cockpit doors for ever.

First step for Zaafir is keying the correct four-digit code. Facing him is a thin blackened LED screen about the size of a cigarette lighter, and below that the number pad, with numbers zero to nine in green, and a red Enter pad. Eleven keys in total, arranged two across and six down.

Matching the correct code is not enough, for the cockpit crew check who is at the door. Above his eye level, to his left and right and behind him, are a series of bug-eye cameras that give the pilots a field of vision of the area beyond the door as well as the passageway and galley areas.

Only the cockpit crew can disengage the four hardened steel locks that hold the door firm. The latch body itself is machined from treated aluminium and features a dummy knob on the cabin side. Only on the cockpit side is the knob actually fitted to the latch bolt.

Zaafir knows the door will withstand repeated blows from an axe, stop a clip of 9mm bullets, and barely be scorched by a standard M26 fragmentation grenade placed right up against it.

A 'smart door', they call it, because it also has to be light. As little metal as possible to save on overall plane weight.

Four-one-two-nine is this month's code, set by ground engineers in Karachi. He moves his fingers from button to button, noticing a slight tremble as he presses each key.

The steward looks in the camera to the right . . . the one focused on him. Remembers to smile. Look friendly. Unthreatening. He runs a hand across his hair. Tidy too. It's as he hears the bolt-action metal locks *thwunk* into the open position, and the door rise fractionally out of its frame towards him, that he realises. Damn it. The female passenger had dark hair when she boarded and he settled her into her seat. Curled over her shoulder. But now, coming from the toilet, she was blonde. Cropped, ash-blonde hair.

Super-fast, this tiny inconsistency churns through his mind. His synapses firing off an exchange of questions about the woman in seat 1D. Hair colour. Significance? *Important. Or not important?* Then he draws the cockpit door open and suddenly this concern seems like nothing.

From the gloom of the gangway, Zaafir is startled by the flash of light. The sun pouring through the expanse of windscreen and bouncing piercingly off all the glass surfaces. In the background, the deep blue of never-ending sky. It's an apparition, surely. The young steward's mind, so febrile and overwrought, takes this sudden burst of radiance as an omen. Paradise. And all thoughts of Ms Merritt in 1D vanish in a puff of fevered revelation . . .

It is sparkling light, aromatic plants, a lofty palace, a flowing river, ripe fruit, a beautiful wife and abundant clothing, in an eternal abode of radiant joy, in beautiful, soundly constructed high houses . . .

Already he senses Paradise.

He steps forward past the thick, reinforced door. Doesn't even register that it seals shut behind him. Bolt-action locks click back into place. Secure. With him inside.

And on the Internet, the information superhighway where you never need let the truth get in the way of a good story, three — no, five, suddenly twelve, jumping to nineteen — extremist Pakistan-based websites report that PK412 has been hijacked.

* * *

The truth is that neither of the two captains, Iqbal Hussain and Imtiyaz Jamal, have much time for Zaafir. Once they see his aquiline nose and the sharp features of his face on their internal TV monitor, they want him in and out.

283

As quickly as possible.

'Come. Come . . . ' Hussain motions Zaafir forward. The steward looks a little stunned. His eyes squinting against the sunlight. The flight deck is silent. No radio transmissions. 'What have you got for us there?'

Hussain and Jamal had traded stories about the steward with fellow captain Harry Salahuddin while the Boeing 777 was still on the ground. Both a bit crestfallen that he would be the one serving them, for the man carried an uncomfortable air about him in keeping with a hair-trigger sense of injustice. The three pilots had agreed that he bristled with wrong-headed woes and warped anxieties.

Salahuddin had crossed swords with Zaafir before: a cat had somehow got on board a PIA flight out of Manchester that he was due to command. There had been a small window of resolution at the start of the drama when the animal appeared trapped, though docile. But Zaafir had seen some unimaginably small breach of health and safety regulations: neither he nor the cabin crew could possibly participate in the animal's capture. Regulations. Hard to believe, Salahuddin had said, but by the time professional handlers had been called in the cockpit crew were out of hours. Not allowed to fly. The plane took off twenty-six hours late.

And here he is now, Zaafir: clearing his throat as he looks down at the clear plastic cups he's offering in the cockpit. 'A Malawi shandy?'

'Malawi shandy?' The two pilots look at each other, puzzled. 'Never heard of it,' says Captain

284

Jamal in the left-hand seat, craning round to look at the tray of fizzing drinks. He pushes back his seat to the limit of its runners. 'No alcohol?'

Zaafir shakes his head fiercely. 'It's a tonic. Kind of a pick-me-up.' The steward more at ease now. 'I made a jug. Dash of orange cordial. Splash of bitters. The rest is half ginger beer. Half lemonade. And lots of ice, of course.'

Jamal takes his glass. The bubbles are still jumping and popping, and prickle his nose as he sniffs. He looks concerned . . . then happy, his face resolving into a broad smile. 'Sort of like a Chapman's.'

Zaafir chews his bottom lip. 'I suppose . . . but unlike Chapman's this is very important to serve quickly.'

Iqbal Hussain, in the co-pilot's seat, reaches across to take his. His chair also as far back as he can push it. 'Why so important?'

'If you lose the bubbles, you lose the layers of flavour. It goes flat. Like tap water.' Then with a look of petulance, 'All that hard work . . . might as well throw the jug away . . . ' and his words trail off.

In the calm of the cockpit there's the unwanted threat of an emotional outburst. Drama.

The pilots look at each other. An unspoken thought passes between them. If they drink this quickly, Zaafir will leave. If they don't, he's sure to see the hand of some conspiracy at work.

Captain Jamal tips his head imperceptibly towards his co-pilot. Raises his eyebrows. *Let's get this over with.* And the two of them neck their drink. One go. Down the hatch.

Not too shabby. Both of them are pleasantly surprised. It is a very refreshing drink. Uplifting almost.

And fifteen seconds later both pilots are dead.

★ ★ ★

The smell is awful. Sharp and toxic. Sprays of bloody vomit slide down the windscreen, glare-shield and electronic fascia of the cockpit. It changes the light. The sun now dapples through what looks like a froth of marmalade. Beneath this strange tincture the six liquid crystal display screens keep on blinking their information. Engine performance. Heading. Air speed. Weather radar. The two captains are clutched in the painful rictus of death. Fingers clawing against straps. Eyes open and bulging.

Zaafir is thrilled. Absolutely pumped. Superquick, he gets to work. He doubles back to the cockpit door. Tugs on it to make sure it is absolutely secure. Good.

Takes out his biro and, using the point, stabs it at the soft reset button to the side of the door's combination-lock mechanism. Blanking the previous code from its memory. He pads in a random four-digit code, his fingers moving too fast for him even to register what it was. When the LED screen shows the numbers, he holds down both the reset and entry buttons for five seconds. The new code flashes. Flashes. Flashes. Then blank. Zaafir's combination is locked in. Good work. The door is secure.

Next. Look up . . .

Above the pilots are a series of overhead panels. Those in closest reach relate to important features of the aircraft in use during every flight. Punch-button switches that control a range of things from cross-feeding fuel from one wing to another, to the plane's air-conditioning system, the ignition switches for the two engines, and the famous *ding-dong* seat-belt signs. Farther back is a panel devoted solely to the circuit-breakers that back-stop this complex array of electronics. The overhead maintenance panel. That's what Zaafir is interested in.

His head tilted backwards, his eyes straining, Zaafir walks his fingers down the array of circuit-breakers. Little, round, black buttons with an ampage printed in white. Everything from the tiny half-amp circuit-breaker for the motor of the alternate landing-gear extension system, to the meaty twenty-five-amp breakers needed for the big display screens that show basic flight information to the pilots.

Two and a half amps . . . two and a half, Zaafir mumbles to himself. Two and a half . . .

He stops. In a line of two-and-a-half-amp breakers, and between something labelled GLOBAL POS and another CAPT CLOCK, is one marked simply DOOR. Delicately he pulls the little head, no thicker than the cross-section of a pencil, towards him.

It falls into his hand. And in an instant rush of power to his ego he pointlessly crushes it under his heel. Pointless because whether the circuit-breaker is in one piece or a thousand makes no

287

difference. So long as it's not lodged in the correct slot in the overhead maintenance panel, the door is immobilised. No circuit-breaker means no power to operate the bolt-action locking mechanism . . .

. . . assuming, of course, that somebody could first work out Zaafir's new, random four-digit combination. 'A four-digit code has ten thousand possible combinations. Ten thousand to one.' And, in his briefing with Zaafir, General Ali Mahmood Khan had started a list on a whiteboard to prove that point: 0001. 0002. 0003. 0004. By the time the general got to 0051, Zaafir had understood.

Last job. From his pocket he brings a small MP3 player with a curious array of wires that lead to something like a suction cup. It takes a moment to untangle. To do it, Zaafir sits in the jump seat immediately to the rear of the central instrument pedestal between the two pilots. Captains Hussain and Jamal face one another. Mouths open. Aghast. Their faces forever frozen.

Zaafir reaches behind Captain Jamal for his headset. It's hooked just below the left windscreen panel. He fastens the suction cup against the mouthpiece and runs his fingers down the length of red audio cable to the MP3 player, making sure there are no kinks or snags.

This bit will be tricky. With the MP3 player and headset in one hand, he loosens the over-shoulder straps in the captain's seat and rolls Jamal's corpse forward and to the side. Pushing the fleshy figure down towards his left. If he stretches, really stretches, Zaafir can now

288

reach over and key the plane's radio, using the talk button on the left-hand grip of the captain's control column.

But first he takes out a white handkerchief and wipes down the mess of guts, phlegm-spray and blood that is congealing on the W-shaped flight column.

'*Allahu Alam* . . . ' Allah Knows Best, he mumbles to himself, and clicks down. To transmit . . .

And the story jumps from the extremist fringes of the Internet to the mainstream as someone on Twitter sets up an outraged tweet under the inflammatory heading *#PakistanHijackCrisis*.

Shanwick Oceanic Area Control Centre
Prestwick, Ayrshire

The chocolate-coated Hob Nob biscuit is halfway to the controller's open mouth. Has been for almost thirty seconds now.

' . . . *you must read the Koran, it is the word of truth. To enjoy the blessings of our Lord, Allah requires us to die and kill in his name. Read the Koran and you will find this truth, this absolute truth and never again can you deny this because the Koran says so, and the messenger of Allah, prayers and peace upon him, who told his believers this, and so we cannot allow your laws to push us from this path until you leave our lands, until you hurt like we are hurting . . .* '

'Can you believe this?' the controller hisses to the handful of colleagues who've wheeled their chairs across the bright blue carpet from their various grey blinking consoles. 'One of my planes. Bloody hijacked.'

'Any change to the transponder?' asks one of the junior officers. He's querying the secondary radar pulse which pilots normally set up to transmit the plane's altitude to flight controllers. At the first opportunity pilots will surrepetitiously dial their transponders across to the code

290

7500, the international signal for unlawful interference, otherwise known as a hijacking.

'Not a thing, and no way of knowing what's going on out there, except what we've just heard,' mutters Hob Nob, in a mournful Scottish brogue. 'Two hundred and fifty miles is as far out as our wee radar can reach.'

Major Operations Room
MI5 Headquarters
Thames House

VHF radio doesn't work out there, in the wild reaches of the mid-Atlantic. So the live audio feed is spotted with crackles and hisses typical of any long-distance high-frequency transmission. Like an old wireless set. Even though the words are burning up and bouncing about in the ionosphere, the intent is very clear. You could hear a pin drop . . .

' . . . *You want to know why? Because in the Muslim lands there is killing and raping and mutilation. So I am only avenging the actions of the Americans and their fellow traitors such as the British and the Jews. Non-believers should not be in the land of the believers. If you do not leave our lands your lives will forever be filled with pain. There are so many more like us, thirsting to strike until the law of Allah rules this earth . . .* '

Davane's assistant, Pyjama-girl, in her striped pink top, feels her stomach drop to the floor as the angry words snarl at her through the ether. She bustles out quickly to get her boss. Noppy's going to go bloody ape-shit, she thinks to herself, as she brushes past her gawping, statue-like colleagues. And starts to jogtrot, then run down the corridor.

In Davane's office, the Ulsterwoman is midway through reciting this morning's events into a speakerphone. Trying to impress upon her polished and urbane colleague Bill Grainger, deputy director-general of the service, that too many random pieces were coming together for this to be sheer chance. Bill Lamayette. General Ali Mahmood Khan. Qissa Khawani. Macchar. The GCHQ monitoring reports . . . She has nothing yet by way of a smoking gun, but a lot in the way of gut instinct.

It had taken a dozen calls and a lot of badgering before someone had gleaned the mobile number of the golf caddy Grainger is using. He is playing the Ganton course, near Pickering in North Yorkshire. He must have had his pager switched off, and Davane knew he didn't like carrying a phone while on the course. 'Finest inland course in the whole country,' Grainger had groused, as if he were a surgeon being interrupted during a life-saving operation, instead of on the tee-box on the par-five thirteenth.

Pyjama-girl pushes through the heavy door. Her breathing ragged. Her face set in stone. Interrupted, Davane looks up, frowning. How forward . . .

. . . but the young woman makes straight for the handset, pecks at it furiously to give a live audio link with the operations room, and within seconds that same angry voice can be heard both on speakerphone and at Grainger's end. Garbled a little but deadly clear all the same.

'... *learn to like the taste of hellfire because it is what I will bring to you, while in Heaven, in Paradise will live the Muslims who died due to your attacks. Like waves crashing on the beach, one martyrdom operation will follow upon another. Crashing on your heads like rain, on these Kuffar until there are no more non-believers in our lands* ... '

'Are you getting this, Bill?' It doesn't matter now whether they talk over it or not. Davane's point has been proved ... Martyrdom broadcasts always have an awful lot of what Davane calls 'self-serving bog-shite' in them. Rarely anything useful operationally. But just in case, intelligence analysts would be poring over it already ...

'... *Don't try to put me in one of your boxes, your psychiatric trick boxes. You may call me a terrorist; but we are more like avengers. And we will keep on avenging until there is no more need to teach you a lesson* ... '

With his dreams of golfing greatness postponed, Grainger's response is hushed, resigned. ''Fraid so, Sheila. 'Fraid so.'

'We need Downing Street up to speed. And this thing's headed to New York. The modelling I've seen shows — what with the winds and weight on board — about seven hours runway to runway. The flight took off two and a half hours ago ... '

'Can you follow it on a screen?'

'Not the actual track. But the Shanwick

controllers use computer models to calculate speed and reported winds . . . ' On a pad of paper, when she had first watched the flight's position being plotted, she had sketched a basic schematic of the Oceanic Flight Region to help her get a grip on the geography of what was going on. Small blob for Iceland. Bigger one for Greenland. Then the Canadian coast. And the curving lines of latitude and longitude that marked out the vast space of ocean. The drawing is very basic, year five standard, but it allows her to speak with confidence. ' . . . according to those projections the flight should be about to pass through longitude Twenty West. They're supposed to call in when that happens. And perhaps they will.' But don't bet on it, Davane mouths to herself in silence before continuing.

'Fifty-plus minutes from now and they'll cross Thirty West. That's halfway. And then they're on the other side of the Atlantic, under the jurisdiction of the Canadians.'

'I'll get to the car. Make the calls.' An acknowledgement of sorts that they're in a handing-over process. From MI5, with their intelligence gatherers toiling in the background, this has to be passed on now to the higher echelons of Whitehall. The political superstructure needs to take over, and command the whole of the British security apparatus. From here on, it would be government to government, one set of politicians at the highest level dealing with another; even the airline itself would have to take a back seat.

'Just make sure you tell the Americans about

Lamayette. He knows more than he was able to tell me. Of that I'm positive . . . '

Grainger sounds drained already. Defeated. 'I'll pass that on.' For him this would count as a failure . . . a successful hijacking originating from a British airport.

There's a moment of silence, and through the speakerphone the two women in the office can hear the wind whistling off the moorlands of Yorkshire. To Davane's ear it sounds like Grainger's got himself stuck in bloody *Wuthering Heights*. She hears him take a deep breath. 'How many on board?'

Davane runs a crooked arthritic finger over the numbers. She knows what he wants. 'Including crew, three hundred and sixty-two.' She repeats for clarity's sake. 'Three. Six. Two. Sixty-one British. Twenty-nine of those Brits are female and fourteen children.'

'Not that it matters . . . '

'No, of course.' Davane glances up at Pyjama-girl, who looks like she's about to be sick. Sixty-one. More than were killed in the 7/7 bombing or any single IRA atrocity. 'Not that it matters . . . '

Tenth floor
Headquarters of the Federal Aviation Adminis-
tration
Independence Avenue
Washington, DC
0711 Washington time, 1211 UK time,
1711 Islamabad time

There'd been a heap of cock-ups on September
11th 2001. Some big and some small. But one of
the worst, one of the few yet to be satisfactorily
explained, had been the apparent communication failure, which meant that the Pentagon's
National Military Command Center didn't know
what the FAA knew in real time. Forty minutes
was the delay, between the FAA finding out
about the four hijackings, and that same news
passing to the all-important NMCC. In particularly unhelpful testimony to the subsequent
presidential commission, somebody from the
Pentagon had said they'd actually war-gamed the
9/11 scenarios assuming no delay, and were
certain that they could have shot down all four
planes before they got to their targets.

It was anguishing on so many different levels
for anybody who worked in the rather drab
seventies-style, glass-fronted FAA building

because most of them were driven by a passion for aviation safety. And it didn't help that it was this cock-up more than any of the others, involving as it did two arms of government, which gave most credence to all those wacky conspiracy theories.

Today's FAA duty hijack coordinator is Todd Packway, a lean, intense man with rimless eyeglasses, and a love of long, involved policy reviews. Every inch of his desk is stacked with thick, bound documents, which, up until a couple of moments ago, he had fully intended using his morning shift to dissect with his precise lawyerly skills.

He's been informed of the hijack by the duty officer at the Civil Aviation Authority offices in London, who is curt and to the point, and forwards all the relevant information and a compressed audio data file of the rambling radio transmission about Allah and *Kuffars*. The CAA man seems quite glad to be shot of the whole thing.

In his office, fiddling with files, check-listing all of the post-9/11 protocols, Todd Packway is seriously delighted to access the now permanent communication web with the NMCC and hear that they've already been alerted. The Pentagon is on the case. Moments earlier, Shanwick control had contacted their opposite number in Gander, and Gander had red-flagged PK412 within the vast US — Canadian surveillance programme, the North American Aerospace Defense Command, known as NORAD.

For Packway it's a surreal feeling: an actual

hijacking, actually in progress. There'd been so many drills. So much training, role-playing and make-believe had been done in the name of Operation Noble Eagle. Now. At last. It's happening. A real hijacking. Let's do it . . . AND THIS TIME, LET'S GET IT RIGHT.

Down below his windows traffic is light on Independence Avenue. Joggers pounding their knees to death. Wind kicking up a bit. People's newspapers turning inside out. Everybody blissfully unaware of what's about to break.

A TV studio
Lahore, Pakistan
1714 Islamabad time,
1214 UK time, 0714 Washington time

Text messages driven by Hamza Khan's hothouse operation continue to fizz around the country, outraging all those who are ever quick to outrage. PK412 in trouble. Three hundred Muslims to be killed.

Then, once the story crosses over into the mainstream media, everything changes again. National anger.

Chef Bindar is a TV chef with a difference. The cheeks of his continually sweating face, as wide as his head is long, are permanently creased in a leery grin. His particular talent is not cooking, but sharing bawdy and indiscreet gossip about politics, cricket and film stars, while he prods his various guests into showing him how to prepare *adrak* or use *amchoor*. His sixty minutes on air are never short of drama or spice. A vaudeville experience delivered in a machine-gun mix of Urdu and English, always ready with a wink-wink to camera. His audience loves him. And his audience share of a regular twenty-five per cent means his homely studio set is

300

festooned with advertiser products, oversized mobile phones and giant cartons of laundry powder.

Live on air, Chef Bindar is heading to his second commercial break of the show. 'We'll be back in a couple of minutes . . . ' His hands are sticky with ground black pepper and, with a comedian's sure touch, he wipes his face with them, squinting at the Urdu text of his autocue. ' . . . when I'll be trying to work out why this whole country is going mad about a Pakistan Airlines flight. My producer . . . he has a girlfriend who is a stewardess, one of our country's flying angels . . . lucky man, lucky man . . . our producer is saying . . . people are sending text messages . . . '

And he starts building towards a sneeze. ''It's . . . it's going to be shot down. Our flight to New York!' ' Chef Bindar shakes his sweat-drenched head. 'Crazy stuff. Crazy. Crazy. Crazy. Can you shoot down a plane in this day and age? Are you worried? Do you know anybody flying to New York today? . . . ' and the punchline to his pepper-on-the-hands gag that the studio audience has been watching for comes at last. Chef Bindar finally expels a sneeze so hard that a sponsor's display of teabags flies off his work surface. He smirks at the camera, caught like a naughty boy. 'So is this thing true? Is our flight in danger . . . this PK412?' He wipes his nose on the leaves of a sweetcorn that a studio guest had just husked. 'Find out after the break . . . '

Fifteen minutes later, the first local news agency report is filed. An enterprising journalist

301

watching the *Chef Bindar Show* snags a 'non-denial denial', as it's known, the report quoting an unnamed and lowly official in the PIA Karachi head office as saying, 'We don't know anything about this.'

Not saying for sure that the flight is safe costs the spokesman dearly. His words are duly mangled into the searing headline 'PIA Official Uncertain Whether New York Flight Is Safe'. This is duly picked up and typed into the rolling news-bars that scroll busily at the bottom of the screens of the twenty or so local TV channels — and their eight regional services.

Collectively a nation of almost 180 million people begins to sit up. Pays some serious attention. What the hell is going on?

Suddenly, these damned text messages and tweets are, like a virus, all over everyone's mobiles, people sitting in their cars, buses, trains, trying to get home. Suddenly these messages appear to be right on the money.

America is going to shoot down a civilian airliner . . . a PIA flight? *Our national airline?*

The country starts to hyperventilate . . . rushing to the edge, teetering on the brink of a red-misted madness. This is middle-class Pakistan being turned over now. Sober, reliable men and women getting angry. The electricity grid and telecom system begin to creak and pop along the seams. Heading into peak time everybody is powering up their computers and TVs, fiddling with their radios, churning through broadband. And just for good measure getting on the phone. Two or three phones simultaneously, if they can manage it.

Next step: one of Wikipedia's contributors reports the hijacking of PK412 under sections on 'PIA' and 'List of Notable Aircraft Hijackers'. One of the extremist websites is credited as a source for the information. After an explosion of additional edits, adding more and more inflammatory comments, Wikipedia's editors decide to lock down both sections in protective status.

So high are the emotions, so hungry are people for news, that *#PakistanHijackCrisis* appears for the first time in ninth position on Twitter Trends, an overview of the most popular tweets. Tens of millions of people around the world see the story for the first time.

In such a feverish atmosphere it takes only a short while, outrage feeding on itself, before the first spontaneous events occur: protests outside the US embassy in Islamabad. Throw in the British as well. If none of these is in reach, go for the usual suspects. McDonald's. Pizza Hut. Nike and Levi jeans. Ford. Coca-Cola bottlers. Anything with a Visa or Mastercard sign, anything that reeks of Western imperialism, is going to get burnt or smashed tonight. Or smashed and then burnt . . .

On board PK412

The alarm is raised first by the stewardess partnering Zaafir. Aghast, she wakes Captain Harry Salahuddin from the depths of his first-class recliner, explaining the cockpit door problem. Access impossible. And she's getting a startling response when she dials through to the pilots. 'Please, Captain. You must help.'

Fully awake on the instant, his brain speed-sifting the alternatives within the enormity of the challenge: how, in God's name, do we get inside? Never mind for the moment who is actually in the cockpit.

And the next question: who do I talk this through with?

Pilots troubleshoot engineering queries through dedicated company radio channels. But, of course, from inside the cockpit. His only option is the in-flight phone system, which leads to the third question. What do you dial when you're in the middle of the Atlantic . . . ?

He rabbits through his flight case, the cabin crew manuals, even the in-flight magazine, looking for anything that might have a PIA telephone number, runs his credit card through the system, and dials . . .

. . . but the mania unleashed by Hamza Khan and his acolytes in their Karachi fear factory has jammed up all the numbers he has.

Everybody in Pakistan seems to be on the phone, desperate to speak to the national airline. He works his way down the listed numbers and the respective base stations: Flight Operations. Flight Services. Engineering. Maintenance. Karachi, Lahore, Peshawar and Islamabad. All sounding the engaged *de-de-de-de*. His wife's UAE mobile phone number and his son's home number in Dubai are busy too. He leaves brief messages on both but knows full well they can't ring back. The two lines to the family farm in the Punjab are also permanently engaged. What *is* happening? He has to assume the worst. A huge terrorist outrage . . . perhaps another military coup.

Not good. In his precise, logical way, Salahuddin thinks, this is not good at all.

⋆ ⋆ ⋆

The first-class cabin is dark, and Tristie Merritt doesn't much like the dark. Never has done. Lying awake, trying to sleep leaves her fearful. Who's that drifting beyond those shadows?

Tristie's normal way around this is to work on some trivial mental task until, exhausted, she'll drop straight to sleep. It's what she's been doing for the past twenty minutes, watching the plane's AirShow. There's a sweep of new information every fifteen seconds and she's been playing guess-the-altitude. Evidently 36,000 feet is what the pilots have been told to fly. But they're heading into the wind, you can feel the plane buck and squirm through the seat of the thighs. They get knocked down a bit, then bounce up again. Perhaps 36,014 feet. Then 35,997. That's what she's doing. Guessing the altitude. Tedious for sure, but tiring also ... Tristie's guess 35,954. The AirShow says ... No, 36,077. Out by 123 feet ...

Next to her, Whiffler has nodded off in the middle of a Mr Bean episode. Leaning back against the plush upholstery of the first-class seat, light from the TV screen flashing across his face: Mr Bean zigzagging his Mini around a hospital car park. Button's chair is fully extended, his mouth open, making a high-pitched, whistling snore. She had watched him get comfortable, like a Labrador circling and fussing until things were just right. Finally sorted, pillow and blanket and eye-mask, he arranged the kinks out of his body and was just about to switch off when he reached to the back pocket of his jeans. Touched his wallet. OK. Pause for ten seconds as his brain works through other final items to check. His big hand moved to his crotch. Felt for his balls, little rearrangement. Also OK. And with that he'd gone to sleep. Happy bunny. It made her smile.

At last, an enveloping calm. Her eyes feel so heavy ...

Yet ... her imagination is winding up again. Dammit. Up ahead, is that a muffled scream? A stifled cry? Tristie tries to ignore it. Not her business. The AirShow is about to change so she

306

makes a guess: 36,033 feet. The *thud-thud-thud* of somebody clunking something hard into something solid. Ignore it. And the AirShow says . . . 35,997. Wrong by thirty-six feet.

Thud-thud-thud. A moan. More insistent. Definitely a woman's voice . . . Shit. She can feel her body changing speed, an electrifying charge pass through. Tiredness blown away like a gust. Her brain engaged. Intrigued. Alert. Wanting to know what's going on.

★ ★ ★

Tristie hears herself asking the most stupid question. 'Is there anything wrong?' This to the sobbing, panda-eyed stewardess, heavy mascara streaking her cheeks, clutching the internal phone, desperately trying to dial a number . . .

By the cockpit door a young, muscular steward in a bright blue tailored jacket is hammering at the lock with the bottom of a three-foot-long fire extinguisher. *Thud-thud-thud*. Some way back, watching with detached bemusement, the one passenger she recognises from first class. A Pakistani. He's taken off the grey pullover he had been wearing. Underneath is a crisp white pilot's uniform with four gold braids on each shoulder and an immaculately woven four-in-hand tie-knot. He has a trimmed goatee and pointed moustache.

'My name's Captain Harry Salahuddin. On behalf of the airline . . . ' He answers Tristie's question almost impishly, before extending a hand. 'I can promise you we have perhaps the strictest security protocols in the world ... but ... ', and he opens up his palms in apology, ' ... but we appear to have no pilots and no way to get into the cockpit.'

Pilots' humour ...

The duty producer is playing pencil cricket
with his son via a telephone wedged against
his ear. Pencil cricket gets played in the
newsrooms of major satellite broadcasters only
on public holidays. They are terribly cruel
shifts for rolling news shows. The big-name
presenters are still rostered, everybody works
their usual hours, but why bother? None of
the branches of government works, the courts
and City are closed, the great PR machine is
asleep and almost nothing is moving. And
today's is a public holiday that stretches across
the whole of the UK, most of Europe and the
US and Canada. Instead of hard, vivid stories,
the newsrooms pick their way through pap.
Mindless drivel that they have to expand on
and flesh out. In the background, the producer
can hear one of the station's lady presenters
simpering on air over fresh pictures of a new
polar bear born in Berlin. What is it with polar
bears and Berlin? 'Another three minutes on
this, I'm afraid ... ' he had said into her

earpiece. Major news on a public holiday. Shame of shames.

He rolls the pencil. Each of the six sides has numbers dotted into it with the point of a schoolboy's compass. One through six, except for five, which has W for wicket. On the other end of the phone is his nine-year-old son, keeping score. 'England on ninety-three for no wicket, Dad.'

The duty producer, a New Zealander, rolls the pencil. Six. And his heart bleeds for the little boy his English ex-wife is raising to be an Englishman. 'Six runs, Billy.'

'Yes. Get in there.' And he can hear the sound of his boy scribbling into the scorebook. Giggling to himself about how crap New Zealand are. 'That's over, Dad. Change of end. Pietersen facing . . . '

It's then that the eye of the duty producer is caught by a flashing pulse on his computer screen. Urgent news breaking from one of the wire agencies. The queue of stories jumps, and he clicks his cursor across. Rolls the pencil at the same time as he opens the file . . .

URGENT. PIA Plane in Hijack Scare . . . May 31. Agence France Presse. 'Hold on, son,' he mumbles. Dateline Islamabad. Just three paras, as most flashes tend to be. His eyes skim through the copy. *Blah. Blah. Blah.* Boeing 777. Three hundred sixty-two passengers and crew. *Blah. Blah. Blah.* Ex-Manchester to New York . . . his heart stops. *Ex-Manchester . . . ?*

'Son . . . gotta go.' And he drops the phone. Just like that. Desperate to rush this on air, this thin sliver of something. Break it now, he thinks to himself, live on air . . . Some considered Agence France Presse a bit wild and racy. He glances to feeds from the BBC, CNN and Fox. Nothing. Fucking pussies were nowhere . . . break it now, then tease the story to the top of the hour: a big, sexy package with all the expert talking heads he could lay his hands on, larded with file footage off You Tube and airliners.net. Then it hits him like a hard-on. There will be crying relatives, and where else will they be doing their weeping than Manchester Airport. Magic fucking TV.

'Look at your screens . . . Hijack out of Manchester,' he barks into the microphone, standing like Captain Kirk on the bridge of his ship. In command. And the two presenters touch their earpieces, start fiddling with their keyboards. 'Kill the fucking polar bear now . . . ' and Operation Macchar becomes *the* live world story.

Sky News is first to break the story in the conventional sense, but on the internet the Twitter site CNNbkr is the first to tweet that a PIA Boeing 777 is believed under the control of terrorists. *Over the mid-Atlantic. More to follow*.

More than two million CNNbkr readers feel a horrible sinking feeling, knowing full well what this has to mean.

On board PK412
Eight minutes later

The steward is still hammering away, getting nowhere. Even though Tristie's off to one side, in the forward galley, she can feel the *thud-thud* shaking through the fibreglass panelling.

'I told him it was no use before he even started. It's not even a real door lock he's trying to break.' Stirring sugar into his paper cup of coffee, Salahuddin adds with his voice raised above the racket, 'Don't worry, he'll get bored soon.'

'Captain . . . ' Tristie finds herself lost for words, too shocked to think straight, and ends up talking with anxious hand movements. After everything that has happened today, this last fortnight . . . now this?! She tries to get something going in her head. She manages, 'You seem awfully calm.'

He flicks his hand dismissively towards the crew seat. 'I've got one stewardess out of commission . . . ' Panda-eyes is still dialling through to the cockpit, so tearful she can't see the buttons. ' . . . one steward who's going to pop a shoulder soon. And you want me to add myself to that casualty list? Why? Tell me, why,

312

when I'm the only person who can fly this plane.' From across the tight little galley, his eyes glare. She's half a head taller but he seems a bigger presence. Perhaps it's the reassurance of the uniform. In spite of the rising sense of panic among his fellow crew members, he exudes a strong sense of command, waiting for the idiots to run their panic dry. 'The plane is perfectly safe for the moment. It will take care of itself for another six, possibly seven hours.'

Finally it coughs out of her mouth . . . 'Is this a hijack?' There, she's said it. The word she's tried to avoid. 'Are we being hijacked?'

His face changes. The irritation that had flared moments ago vanishes. Mellow again. 'We'll know shortly. I've asked the crew to do a headcount. If someone's in the cockpit, some passengers . . . then, yes, this probably is a hijacking.' He explains all this as cool as. No drama. Breaks a crumbly biscuit in two and dunks it into his coffee. 'I have to say it feels that way to me.'

'Feels that way? W-why do you say that?'

Salahuddin appraises her for a second, chewing with the right side of his mouth, his arm resting on the high metal work surface. He's trying to work Tristie out. Can she actually help, or will she run away screaming, knock-kneed at the first sign of some trivial scare?

The galley has an internal phone. Salahuddin barks a sharp command in Urdu to the stewardess, who reluctantly couches the handset and slumps down, putting her head between her hands, keening. 'We're . . . all . . . going . . . to

313

. . . die . . . ' A flash of anger towards the hostess whips through Tristie. At least do your mourning in a language I can't understand.

Taking the phone, Salahuddin dials into the cockpit with his thumb. He raises the earpiece to Tristie. Listen . . .

She has no idea what to expect, what she's going to hear. There's a high-pitched yowling. It takes a moment for her brain to click. An Islamic call of some sort mixed in with soft music, heavy instrumentation. And a syrupy voice starts to croon in English.

Salahuddin takes back the phone, listens himself. 'From a CD, it sounds like. The guy singing is Sami Yusuf. Very popular. My granddaughters love him. I think this song is called 'The Day of Eid'.'

'What's the significance?'

Salahuddin touches the point of his goatee. 'The two pilots in there, Hussain and Jamal, are professionals. Or were, anyway. Quality pilots. And good men. But also they wouldn't be fans of Sami Yusuf.' He points past the galley's shiny aluminium inserts and convection ovens towards the cockpit. 'Someone must have taken control of the flight deck. Every time we dial in, this is what we get. 'Day of Eid' or 'Who Is the Loved One?' Or 'Allah o Allah Hasbi Rabbi' . . . '

That's all we need, thinks Tristie. Muslim radicals in a cockpit.

She knows it's time to put her cards on the table. 'Captain. If I can be of any help. I'm ex-British Army. My two colleagues in first class also.'

314

'Not the Dental Corps, I hope.' He laughs at his own joke, putting his coffee cup to his lips, eyeing her carefully.

'No, not the Gob Docs. The Paras.' And just saying that makes her feel good. *The* Paras. Talk to them together or individually and any Para will swear blind they can do *anything*, no scrap or shit-fight they can't bulldoze their way through. The spirit of Market Garden and Goose Green, fighting against overwhelming odds, all those guys tabbing across the top of the Falklands. Just two silly little syllables, Pah Ra, and the whole thing puts some starch in her backbone.

Salahuddin looks intrigued. Slips out of the galley to look at Whiffler and Button snoring. Probably not at their best. Certainly not *Utrinque Paratus*. Ready for Anything.

The captain reappears, brushing aside the curtain. 'But you are not a Para?'

'No,' she replies with a friendly half-laugh, thinking of the only woman she knew who tried for a red beret and broke her leg in two places. 'I started with the Adjutant General's Corps . . . sort of human relations. But . . . ' she adds as enigmatically as possible ' . . . the army taught me all the good stuff.'

Of course, she should have seen what is coming next. The big trap she'd walked into. With a long face, he wants to know just one thing: 'You have killed Muslims, then. In Iraq, perhaps Afghanistan . . . ' Not a question, more like a statement.

'Me?'

'Yes, you . . . ' and he narrows his eyes like a card sharp ' . . . and them?'

Every bone of her body screams for her to lie. It's what all that 14 Coy. training was all about, the deception and spy-craft. She could lie now and he'd never know . . .

'I can't speak for them. We don't really swap scores.' Look him in the eye, Tristie. Make him understand ' . . . But I've killed. I presume they were Muslims, so yes. While I was in Basra. Yes. Afghanistan too. But let me tell you they were killed because of what they were doing. Not because of their religion . . . '

'How many?'

'Does this have anything to do with getting out of this mess?'

More insistent. 'How many?'

'Six. All men.' Tristie shrugs her shoulders. 'I think six.' A couple of the faces flash through her mind. No regrets there. 'It was kill or be killed.'

Perhaps this was only an opening gambit for Salahuddin looks . . . unmoved. Hard to read this pilot. Neither happy or sad. Another steward arrives, saves her further scrunity. A short, portly-looking man with a five-string comb-over who is clutching a passenger manifest.

Distressed. He looks down at the print-off. Up at the captain. Then down again. His mouth opens . . .

'What is it?'

The steward seems to be gulping for air. The only sounds are the despairing *thud-thud-thud* and the pathetic mewling of the stewardess.

'All the passengers accounted for, Captain.

316

Three hundred and forty-five passengers, including . . . ' and he nods towards Tristie '. . . including this lady.'

No passengers missing? Both of them frown. What does that mean?

'But . . . ' and the tubby steward seems to shrink in size, his face cringing, like he's going to get walloped for bringing bad news ' . . . one crew member is absent.'

She makes a mental note of that. Absent . . . great use of vocabulary. Not attending a place or event, especially when expected to. In response, Salahuddin's voice is loud, disbelieving. 'One of the pilots?'

'No,' and the steward wipes at the line of sweat on his top lip. 'Cabin crew.'

'Who?'

The steward cowers, speaks in a soft voice. 'Zaafir . . . '

'*ZAAFIR DID THIS?*' the pilot bellows. He thumps his fist down on the galley work surface, rattling a tray full of clear plastic cups, toothpicks, slices of lemon. 'Zaafir . . . '

Tristie is just about to ask the obvious question, who is this Zaafir, when a mad, possessed skriek starts up. Like an exorcism. Coming from way back to the rear of the plane. Panda-eyes' yowling is nothing to this. A terrible, nail-scratching-blackboard sort of agony. Suddenly the worry becomes about panic. And the officer in Tristie wonders despairingly what it would be like controlling a whole planeload of similarly out-of-control passengers?

Without thinking, she's running behind

Salahuddin. Down the aisle. Her heart thumping. Bewildered faces rub sleep out of their eyes, craning round to find out what's the matter. This awful sound gets louder and louder.

USS Dwight D. Eisenhower . . . *the* Ike
CVN-69
Mid-Atlantic

Thirty-six thousand feet below and a pair of
Navy FA-18E Super Hornets are sitting
patiently, engines running. Cockpit hoods still
high in the air. Two pilots, call-signed Cletus and
Sneaker, go through final pre-flight checks.

Their 1,100-foot long aircraft carrier is racing
to line up into the wind, going full bore to swivel
almost 90,000 metric tonnes of ship as quickly
as possible. The flash had come through from
USNORTHCOM command, a military structure created after 9/11 with responsibility for
securing the air, land and sea approaches to the
continental United States and Alaska. NORTH-
COM and the satellite and air sovereignty
programme NORAD share the same commander, as well as operational headquarters at
Peterson Air Force Base in Colorado Springs.
The signal had come through highest priority.
Operation Noble Eagle. Get two jets up there.
NOW.

In the dark of the ship's Combat Direction
Centre, on the blue-light radar screens, they had
already located PK412 and listened in to the

Shanwick controllers trying repeatedly to raise some kind of answer. Then, by scrolling back through a series of hard drives that download and store all the radio transmissions hereabouts, that one very distinct broadcast from the plane had been identified. ' . . . *If you do not leave our lands your lives will forever be filled with pain. There are so many more like us, thirsting to strike until the law of Allah rules this earth . . .* ' Picked out, and passed on, this scratchy High Frequency recording, to the admiral on the flag bridge, plus the carrier's captain, and to the squadron leader in charge of the Jolly Rogers, the Fighting 103rd, the naval attack unit from which pilots Cletus and Sneaker are assigned.

Things were supposed to move quickly on the order to scramble, but with the ground crew doing their deck-walk, and the USS *Ike* still rolling around the seas, the 103's squadron leader had time to escort the two pilots out to their side-by-side planes. Letting them know that after something like 45,000 regular sorties and 2,200 'scrambles', this Operation Noble Eagle call-out is the one. For real. 'I tell you this because I know it's every pilot's worst nightmare . . . ' and being a basically chummy guy, he'd taken his time with them, lots of sincere eye contact, letting them know he understood any nerves they might feel ' . . . wouldn't be surprised if it were your worst nightmare too.

'But . . . ' the squadron leader had reached out to squeeze the backs of their necks, a gesture he hoped conveyed understanding and compassion

' . . . consider what a different place this world would be if we'd had two pilots like you guys behind each of those planes on 9/11 . . . ' He had pivoted from one to the other, searching for any hint of weakness.

Cletus and Sneaker had gone awfully quiet as they clutched their flight helmets on that windswept deck, pitching this way and that, as the *Ike* tried to turn on a penny. There was no joshing or backslapping about this mission. They hadn't thought to ask, nor had it been volunteered, just how many people are on the flight they are to hunt down.

Perhaps they hadn't enquired because in that final face-to-face conversation, while the world seemed at once complicated and layered, yet it was very simple. After fist-bumping the senior officer, both headed to their planes. Wearing looks that were both fierce and piercingly serious.

The Combat Direction Centre had plotted the plane about 350 miles to the north-east of *Ike*'s position and moving westwards at just under 600 miles an hour. At maximum speed of Mach 1.8, these two birds should be on station, by the hostile, in under twenty-five minutes.

Once in their Super Hornets the two pilots look off to their right. This is the first flight of the day, so a line of colour-coordinated ground crew has been rushed on deck, to check for Foreign Object Debris. Maintenance men in their green roll-neck tops, the guys and girls who handle bombs and armaments wearing red, and the refuellers in purple. Around the two planes are green-shirted crew chiefs doing their final checks and a knot of ground handlers in yellow, waiting for the OK to start directing them by way of hand signals, on to the catapult ramp for the launch sequence.

From the top level of the *Ike*'s island, the above deck area, comes the call from the duty Air Boss, himself a former naval pilot. 'Two minutes to launch . . .'

As the Shooters who run the catapult system prep their equipment, steam leaks out of the long slit-like track in front of the two Hornets. Just as it does for any other day of flying. In fact almost everything about today is the same as on any other day of practice, training and relentless self-improvement. The same, and yet definitely not the same.

The pilots, not men of faith, even in the terrifying circumstances of night landings on a moving deck, find themselves now scrambling to think of something spiritual and prayer-like. As the clock counts down, the tension squeezes the chest. A strange vice-like grip tightening the skull.

On board PK412

The only word to describe the woman standing in front of them is matronly. Big, heavy, in a baggy, light blue, velour tracksuit, bouncing back and forth across two seats in Row 33. Giant projectile breasts. The Pakistani woman is shouting, screaming, bellowing at the top of her considerable voice in a language unknown to Tristie Merritt. Something South Asian. The noise so shrill that the nearby passengers seem to be grinding their teeth against the pain. Their startled heads bob into sight from behind the backs of seats. Up and down the aisles, startled, alarmed looks.

Salahuddin and Tristie are standing in the aisle, a seat's width away. Captain Salahuddin looking alarmed by this Everest of wailing womanhood. The portly steward looking lost. Whiffler is coming down the aisle, yawning and rubbing sleep from his eyes and wearing a What the Hell is Going On? look.

Tristie can't help but notice more and more passengers are grasping whatever it is that the woman's shouting, dominos beginning to fall . . .

It's fairly obvious what has happened. The cord of her inseat telephone is looped over the backrest. She must have been on the phone to someone, and that someone has given her the news. Whatever it is they know down there — the bolted cockpit door, the missing crewman Zaafir — the screams are suddenly in English, and in a different, menacing tone. '*You will never see your children again. NEVER, I TELL YOU . . . NEVER.*' More chilling and infinitely contagious. Tristie puts her hand on Salahuddin's shoulder and when he turns she mouths, 'Hijack,' pantomiming a telephone.

Sharp questions and the first blooms of anger rise in the faces of passengers. An epidemic starting to build.

Salahuddin nods. Yes. Puts up his hands in despair. What are we supposed to do? He glances back at this mammoth female, hopelessness in his face. The realisation she's some three times his weight, and ripped up with the adrenalin of fight or flight that would make her an impossible takedown. Those big untouchable sacks of breast.

Come on, Captain. Be the Man . . .

This creature of Beelzebub, her madness increasingly bewitching the cabin, burning everyone up. Then a shaft of bright light bringing clarity . . .

Before Mad Woman knows a thing, Tristie vaults on to the aisle seat next to her. With the whole cabin watching, she hits her in midscreech, and makes the slap look like nothing. Easy. Like it's a cinch to knock a 300-pound woman to her knees. She falls down to a final scream, the row of seats rocking as she collapses.

Then silence. It hurts like hell, Tristie's hand a giant bee sting. But she makes it look easy . . . and that is what the rest of the plane had needed to see.

Tristie climbs down off the seat. Looks at Salahuddin. 'Talk to these people, your passengers, about what's going on. Give them some confidence. Tell them you're putting together a plan.'

'We are?' Salahuddin blinks, then gives an almost imperceptible shake of his head. Like he's seeing things. 'We are. You are right, of course.' And, back in command, he finger-points this way and that, shouting to his crew how to deal with the Mad Woman in Row 33.

Thankfully Whiffler had read Tristie's mind. He had sensed what was needed, scuttled back to first class and woken Button, who'd raided the in-flight medical supplies. Button, oozing tranquillity, tap-taps on Mad Woman's arm with a syringe of calm-down juice. 'That's better.'

As they make their way back to the front of the plane, past rows of shocked faces, Tristie draws the captain to one side. 'Our biggest problem is panic. The emotion we respond to fastest. And it's the most dangerous by far.

'This is your plane and these are your passengers . . . ' She waves away Whiffler, who's signalling from the galley, making the universal army call for a brew-up. ' . . . we need to be getting them to do things, to distract them from what's going on. I've seen it happen before and it's already building. When people are under stress for long periods, if their minds are given the time and space to roam, there will be madness on our hands. A collective furore. Very few will be unaffected, believe you me. Some will just calcify, go silent, zombie-like. But most will be ready to stampede.'

The captain plays this scenario in his mind, pulls a pained, anxious face while biting on his bottom lip. 'Yes,' he speaks slowly, deliberately, 'all of your points are well made.'

'Excuse me for not knowing enough about Pakistan, but how many major language groups in your country?'

'I would say six or seven: Urdu is our lingua franca but it isn't the mother tongue of many people, less than ten per cent. The big populations are Sindhi. Pashto. Balochi. Punjabi, that's my mother tongue . . . Saraiki. Hindko. These are the main blocs.'

'And how many Pakistanis are there on this flight?'

Salahuddin shrugs his shoulders. 'At a guess, eighty per cent of the flight.'

Tristie always had a head for numbers. Three hundred and forty-five passengers and seventeen crew. 'About two hundred and ninety people.'

'About right.'

'I think we should move people around, try to get them sitting in little groups with their kin, people they feel comfortable with. It's a big task, there could be some anxiety and frustration at times, but it will keep everybody occupied for, hopefully, a couple of hours at least. First, get your people to explain what we are trying to do. Lots of smiles. No stress whatsoever. And bring forward the next meal service so people have something else to focus on. I'll get my big colleague over there, we call him Button, I'll get him to handle the Caucasian passengers if that's any help.'

'Problem.' Salahuddin points a finger heavenwards. 'It feels like we're doing that Hezbollah thing, separating the Israelis, the Jews, from the rest of the passengers. I foresee this causing its own tensions. Big tensions . . . '

'Which we can explain away. With our best *Come Visit Pakistan* smiles. Look. We've got no guns or munitions to threaten people with. We're hardly a bunch of terrorists ourselves.'

'What if people don't want to move?'

'That's fine. No coercion. Remember. There's no real point to this, other than to keep people distracted, get their minds on something different.'

'Like rearranging the deckchairs on the *Titanic*?'

Not helpful.

Tristie looks down and lets out a long sigh, so he knows how irritated she is at this footdragging. It's at this precise moment that she gets distracted. Whiffler is singing in the galley. That tune by the Kaiser Chiefs. Ten feet away, brewing tea for himself and Button . . . he's watching people getting lairy and thinking it's not going to be very pretty. 'I Predict A Riot'. It's unhelpful timing, possibly unintentional, but part of her wants to snicker with laughter.

Eventually Whiffler runs out of lyrics and is left humming.

It helps Tristie focus and she puts her hands up to Salahuddin. Surrender. Self-admonishment. That female instinct: let him think it is his own clever idea. A game that had to be played if she is to get what she needs. A tremolo of anger in her voice. 'You want to talk about deckchairs on the *Titanic* . . . remember, the *Titanic* wouldn't have sunk if the officer in charge of the bridge that night had turned into the iceberg, rammed it, instead of trying to skim around the side. A most natural and intuitive reaction for him, avoiding that iceberg, but it doomed the ship and all her passengers. Let's not try and slide our way around this problem. Let's confront it. Head on. OK?'

Salahuddin examines her, hardly a trace of movement in his solid, drawn features. He's a bastard to read, this pilot. He holds his steady gaze for what feels like a count of ten, then calls over a pair of stewards. No idea what he's saying to them but he's whispering to them, busy, busy, as though it's all top secret.

The only distinct sound is Whiffler, still *tinging* and *twanging* on the aluminium galley insets, drumming, humming happily to himself. 'I Predict A Riot' . . . Waiting for his beloved cup of tea to brew.

Salahuddin swings around from the little knot of cabin crew, and moves towards Tristie. Purposeful at last. 'We can work together, you and me, but whatever happens,' and he flexes his jawbone, 'I mean *whatever* happens, you do not tell my crew that you and those others are ex-army.'

'Is it such a huge problem?'

'Yes, a huge problem.' And he looks her in the eye. 'Your government has helped turn our country into a plaything for incompetent soldiers and corrupt politicians. That is unforgivable. Once . . . ' and with his eyes shining slightly, he jerks a thumb back towards his crew, his people ' . . . once upon a time, I'd like you to remember, before all this madness came from the West, we actually had a pretty decent country. And the best airline in Asia to go with it.'

The Situation Room Complex
Ground Floor, West Wing
The White House
0822 Washington time, 1322 London time,
1822 Islamabad time

The staff officer folds up the tele-message print-out, moves hurriedly from the National Security Council's watch station, twelve short paces up the narrow, carpeted corridor, and eases open the heavy door into the main conference room. The news is that the two Super Hornets are on station, tucked in, as per standing orders, slightly above and five miles behind the Boeing 777. One fighter on either side.

As a relatively junior GS-12, the NSC staffer can't put names to every single face in the modest, hushed room that he has entered, but he's aware it's a pretty stellar crowd. The mood is electric this morning and things are threatening to run amok in the watch station. Foreign leaders, desperate to talk, are being left on hold like this was Papa John's Pizza, not the White House . . . sure, please tell Mr Prime Minister, the president knows you're waiting . . . Yes, please convey to the Madam President that I'm

330

sure he'll join the video conference when he's free . . . Yes, of course, please let His Highness know . . . They'd flicked as many of the calls as possible to the Secretary of State and his people, who are working from a soundproofed cabin next to the situation room, with panels of glass that mist instantly at the touch of a button.

So. Committed to the situation room this frantic morning are the president, Charles Hannah, the Secretary of State, who's half in, half out of all the discussions, and the Attorney General. The Secretary for Homeland Security. The acting head of the CIA. Plus the Transport Secretary paired alongside the top official of the Federal Aviation Administration. All seated round a long, polished table, about the only wood feature left in the whole ultra-modern room. The vice-president and Defence Secretary are hooked in live from two separate air force planes, one heading off to Korea, the other halfway back from Alaska. Somebody is giving a briefing on another video link, the room has six of them, huge, flat screens that dominate their respective wall spaces. One is permanently slaved to a map of the north Atlantic showing a little red dot, PK412, inching from east to west with radial lines plotted outward from New York in increments of 250 miles. It's hard not to see this plane as an intruder, minute by minute getting closer and closer, menacing the US heartland . . .

The staffer wants to be in and out of the room as fast as possible, too many things fizzing through his brain, so he doesn't focus overmuch on the briefing. An East Coast, Massachusetts sort of voice explains from one of the screens the State Department's early take on things: the Arab League in Cairo are denouncing Washington's aggressive posture, getting their condemnations in quickly . . . the Organisation of the Islamic Conference warns that downing the plane will be seen as an act of war on all Muslim nations. Everybody has commented that things are moving so fast . . .

There's buzz about an Iran or a Venezuela-type country calling an emergency special session of the United Nations . . . 'Just loose talk at the moment,' the guy from State notes confidently. 'No chance of getting seven votes off the Security Council . . . and, er, it's our assessment, at this time, that they'll be hard pushed, we feel, to get a majority of the member states . . . ' A point on which he sounds less than totally assured.

A row of seats for the underlings is set back from the main table and everybody there is crouched, eyes concentrated with serious intent as the situation reports continue. The staffer can't help but notice there's a White House staff photographer in the back, quietly clicking away. Consigning this moment to history.

The GS-12 needs to find the chairman of the Joint Chiefs, who, confusingly, is out of uniform. A measure of how quickly things had had to come together this morning. The security detail hadn't quite grabbed the admiral by his arms, legs and belt as they had Vice-President Cheney on 9/11, but it had been near enough. Get Here

Now. The staffer quickly scans the room, craning his neck this way and that, sees his man obscured by the solid shape of Secretary Salazar of Homeland. He holds out a note for the admiral to take and it's snatched greedily. As he waits for any verbal or written response, the staffer follows all the eyes in the room towards the briefing screen . . . he notices first the change in voice. Midwest accent. Kansas perhaps. A different presenter, talking to his audience behind a lectern with a Department of Energy backdrop. Round faced, choleric . . .

'It's a public holiday here and in London, so the really big US and UK investors are not in play . . . but there's already been a significant jump in crude oil futures on the two exchanges in Dubai, the Oman and Fujairah contracts. The Internet oil traders are also spiking this thing through the roof. Up eighteen, nineteen dollars a barrel in one day and still rising sharply . . . Crazy stuff when you consider twenty-five dollars a barrel is the record one-day jump. Tomorrow there's going to be an awful lot of upward pressure. For sure, this will roll through into prices for Brent and West Texas Intermediate . . . ' and the guy from Energy rolls his eyes, tugs at the collar of his too-tight shirt ' . . . because the market clearly anticipates this is going to blow up ugly. Serious ugly. Both short and long term . . . '

The staffer feels a tug on his sleeve and looks down at the admiral, who leans forward to whisper. 'Get the live video from the Super Hornets prepped, and the comms link to the senior pilot. I want it to be the next thing we look at. Let's see what these goddamn people are up to.'

On board PK412

There are three of them in the galley. Whiffler, Tristie and the captain, who's pinched a number of first-class menus and on the blank cover pages is scribbling out diagrams. A sort of catharsis. Schematics of the cockpit door, the plane's fuselage and cockpit in elevation, side elevation and cross-section, and so on. He's got a good eye for detail.

Whiffler, expert in explosives, and their number-one guy on mechanical stuff, is leaning in towards Salahuddin. Peppering him with questions as he draws, questions that an amateur like Tristie would never think of. 'So the power connections are through the L-plates in the door frame . . . what happens when the delta pressure changes? . . . This is DC current, right?'

She leaves the two of them going hard at it, trying to work out a way into the cockpit. The shape of an even bigger idea, the very barest glimmer of an outline, is beginning to form in her mind. A real crapshoot.

A fifth-storey penthouse
Overlooking Regent's Canal
Islington, London
1347 London time, 0847 Washington time,
1847 Islamabad time

The packaging on the steak-and-mince pie with
the nice lattice pastry had said 'Serves Three' but
it was gone in four bites and only one person was
involved. The Weasel. The pie is now warming his
insides nicely, just as the soapy bathwater is
thawing out his exterior. He had woken up
freezing cold in a strange bed.

He sucks on a lit cheroot, sinks into the depth
of bubbles and tries to blow smoke rings. Bring
some character to this antiseptically fancy
bathroom.

Happiness is a cigar . . .

The mobile rings. His Ward 13 phone. A look
of irritation streaks across his face. But he turns
quickly, sloshing the water, in time to see the
damn thing ringing and vibrating all at the same
time, skittling across the black marble washbasin
surround. Moments from tumbling to the floor.

He lunges sideways from the bath, a hand
stretched out, just in time to miss the phone
tipping over the edge. It tumbles. Hits the rim of

336

the toilet bowl and for a shocking second pirouettes on the white porcelain, spinning on its end, before disappearing out of sight.

'Shit,' and with the movement of his lips, the cheroot drops to the wet floor. Sizzling quietly. But the phone is still making a noise. A sort of chirping. Damaged but not destroyed. He levers himself out of the tub with a big slop of bathwater, grabs the handset and presses Answer. Soap and shampoo suds still plugging his ear . . .

Moments later Weasel is standing in front of a TV set, dripping wet, a white towel cinched around his waist.

'Jesus, Tristie . . . ' He points the remote at the satellite box. 'You mean . . . you guys are on *that* plane?'

'*Just tell me what they're saying.*'

'Well, CNN is showing a map of the Atlantic. You're pinpointed on it, about halfway across. Some link to a website called openatc.com.' Weasel pauses to listen to the CNN commentary. 'The correspondent in Islamabad is talking about unconfirmed reports out of Pakistan that the plane has been hijacked by Islamic terrorists. That they're in control. There's talk that probably a list of demands has been sent to the US embassy there and the State Department. That's all uncorroborated. The guy says the country has gone mad with rumour, he's quoting from blogs and Twitter and all sorts of crap, says frankly he doesn't know what to think at the moment. The caption reads . . . 'At This Hour: US Cabinet Reviews Shoot-Down Option'

. . . oh fuck, Tristie . . . '

Her tone is almost wooden. '*Tell me what the other channels have.*'

'Sky News . . . Sky News, where are you?' He fiddles with the remote, his fingers slick with soap.

'*What did you say?*'

'Nothing . . . ' Weasel's phone is wedged into his shoulder as he tries using two hands to dial in number 501. 'I'm in a girl's flat. Somebody I met last night. A city trader.'

Sky's coverage jumps around wildly and to begin with it's impossible to make out what's going on. A white-on-red caption indicates this is LIVE footage from Manchester Airport. Slowly the picture resolves to a shot of the check-in area in Terminal 2. Six counters. Each one is protected by a phalanx of policemen in stab jackets, crash helmets and short-sleeve shirts; every so often one of them chops at the angry crowd with extendable batons. Behind them, serried ranks of firearms officers, looking dead serious, cradle their Heckler & Koch firearms. The protesters are mostly but not all Asian, all hopelessly ill suited to running at lines of tough, well-trained policemen. But they're desperate for news. Pathetic . . . Like any of this is going to make a difference.

After painting a word picture of all this, Weasel's voice is full of dread and a chilling sense of awe. 'The country's going to pull itself to pieces over this.'

'*That bad?*'

'Woeful. Woeful. So bloody woeful . . . and the

tear gas at the airport can't be too far away.'

'*How many involved?*'

'Couple of hundred at the airport, it looks like. Poor sods.' It's sickeningly compelling TV. This isn't just grief, it's raw anger too. 'Wait. There's a news bar scrolling . . . saying . . . ' Weasel reads directly from the screen ' . . . 'Police Confirm Outbreaks of Rioting, Property Damage in' . . . here it comes . . . Leeds. Bradford. Oldham. Manchester. Hell's bells . . . various parts of London: Southall, Newham, Hounslow, Tooting, Balham . . . Bastard . . . Birmingham suburbs: Small Heath, Aston and Moseley. Leicester . . . shit. It doesn't stop.'

'*At least that gives us a chance.*'

'A chance . . . ' Weasel says the words mutely, only half paying attention because back at Manchester Airport, Sky's cameraman has picked out one little scene amid all the chaos. A white kid, perhaps fifteen, has got up around the shoulders of a policeman and is pounding his riot helmet with his fists. The only thing his red, tear-streaked face knows is that a parent or loved one is on the plane, and going to die. The police are losing their rag . . . and the audience is rooting for the child. 'Tristie . . . what do you mean 'that gives us a chance'?'

She explains herself. Quickly and with a minimum of fuss and emotion. First thing is she's travelling without any of her phone numbers and she needs to get hold of someone in Northern Ireland. Urgently. A Mary Sweeney, she says, widow of Dara Sweeney. Probably still living in Newry, County Armagh. If not try

Jonesboro, Forkhill or Killeen. She had sisters there, and would have stayed close by, says Tristie.

'Christ alive, there must be a million Sweeneys in Northern Ireland.'

'*But only one whose husband was killed by a bomb set by someone who went on to win a seat in the Irish parliament.*'

'That does narrow it down . . . Christ, Tristie, what have you been up to?'

'*Just get the number and . . .*' there's a crackle of satellite static on the line ' . . . *you've got to be on your A-game if this has any chance of working.*'

On board PK412

The mad woman in Row 33 may have been silenced but that hasn't stilled the passengers. The ghastly truth about which she had been shouting had rippled from seat to seat right to the back of the plane, mistranslated or garnished with each retelling. Soon everybody has a fragment of what's going on. The Chinese whispers leave no one in doubt of their likely fate. *We are going to die. They shoot down hijacked planes.*

After a brief address from Captain Harry Salahuddin, who tries in three languages to make this emergency sound prosaic, as all pilots do, there is an explosion of calls from passengers who know better. Six dollars a minute. Whack it on the credit card. Nobody thinks for a moment they're going to be alive to pay this off.

Scrambling to listen in to flight PK412 is the Echelon programme, the technological muscle of the National Security Agency, based at Fort Meade, Maryland, and its British equivalent, GCHQ.

Tasking their various listening posts, the Echelon people triangulate the power of vast dishes in Fort Gordon, near Augusta, Georgia, the Canadian base at Leitrim, south of Ottawa, and Morwenstow on the north Cornish coast. It's a slow process trying to get a bead on what's happening on board this plane so that their political masters can make informed decisions.

What they pick up is ninety per cent emotion. Mothers saying goodbye to their children, drawing out each and every word, *Remember what I always told you* . . . husbands trying to reassure wives, *Be brave. I'm fully insured* . . . and so on. The listening posts also suck out of the ether a good amount of what seems like practical detail, which, as eavesdroppers, they can't cross-examine. Little snatches of operational detail: first class seems to be cordoned off. The bad guys are in the cockpit, or perhaps they're in first class. Or both. The cabin crew is moving through the plane asking where people come from, what languages they speak, would they prefer to be seated with their own people . . .

The calls are heart-breaking. Seat 32C, for instance. A young female Pakistani lawyer, attending the Denver symposium on sexual politics and Islamic ideology, is quietly crying into the handset. Imagining the scene in Lahore. Her mother ululating in the background while her father and eldest brother rampage in brutal anger through the family house. Against this, the pleadings of her teenage sister register barely, as a whisper. Wailing how, to keep her memory alive, she will never eat sweet foods again. Nor fried foods . . . From behind her hand, the lady in

32C sobs, 'I don't care about what you eat, Rasheeda. Promise me only that you will study hard. You need to be smart. And be a good girl too . . . ' Just rice and roti and dhal, that will be all that I eat, pledges Rasheeda. And I will only sleep on the floor. So I feel your pain too. So I can be with you. Forever ' . . . I don't want you to sleep on the floor my beautiful sister . . . you will always be with me, and I with you . . . '

In a rambling monologue, a Welshman from Swansea relays to his already grieving son in Sketty something he'd heard and now passes on as fact. 'The terrorists have locked themselves in the cockpit. They're going to fly this thing on to New York, boy. Perhaps have another crack at the Big Apple. So. This is it, lad. I really feel it . . . Don't be cut up about me. Put a couple of pounds behind the bar at the Vivian Arms. Remember me to my mates, even the hopeless bloody twats. I tell you. Bit of Green, Green Grass of Home wouldn't go amiss right now.'

Audio file after audio file paints the same picture, people saying their farewells, knowing they're caught between death and . . . well, death. A scenario that seems all too real and recently lived through, for those NSC and GCHQ analysts who still remain in the shadow cast by 9/11, and who are desperately trying to make sense of this flight for everybody in the situation room.

Bob and Judy Morrow from Sandpoint, Idaho, are the first passengers to achieve a degree of fame. Trying to get hold of their son Trace on his mobile phone, a little bit frantic because who knows when this in-seat phone will get disconnected. Trace is a wayward son, thirty next month and yet to show any interest in leaving home. He was busy chasing the morning line on today's running of the Indy 500 so his parents' call goes to voicemail. Their message, when he finally gets to it, knocks him into a cold sweat. He can hear their fear as they swallow hard on their feelings, trying to stay calm. His mother's reedy voice: 'Little bit of a problem with the flight, Trace. Thought we should speak in case we don't get another chance.'

In the coffee shop, in front of a half-eaten stack of pancakes, Trace is overwhelmed with sadness and guilt, for deeds done and not done. He tries redialling but is told by an anodyne female voice prompt that no such call can be connected. Impotent, embarrassed and angry, he calls through to a cousin who'd just started at KTRV Channel 12 over in Nampa. The local Fox network affiliate. Warns her that he's forwarding a voicemail. Within minutes the Morrows are all over the Fox News Channel, in eighty-five million homes across the country, the first American victims of Operation Macchar to be revealed.

Within the next half-hour, voicemails from at least twenty other passengers are being forwarded to the language-relevant news networks. BBC, CNN, Sky, Fox, the Middle East news channels of Al Jazeera, Al Arabiya and Al Resalah, and Pakistan World TV and Geo TV.

Different languages, same story. Little pleading voices, creased with fear, being broadcast across the world to an audience aghast, unable to turn away from the coming conflagration.

The White House situation room
Five minutes later

It's almost an hour and a quarter since the alarm was first raised, and the room is becoming restless. There've been briefings galore. A few facts, leavened with a lot of analysis and supposition.

Even Bill Lamayette is silenced. On one of the plasma screens there is a live feed of the CIA station chief. The sound is muted for the moment, with Lamayette seen in medium close-up, in a darkened room in a hangar at the Bagram airbase in Afghanistan. Tongue lolling, slipping and slopping in a high-back chair, out of his head with drugs. From off-camera, busy hands fuss over him, trying to revive with cold compresses, cups of coffee and even lit cigarettes. A nudge or two to his bald head, perhaps a slap. *Waaake uuupp, Bill* . . . but the hero of the moment is out for the count.

In an eerie way, Lamayette hangs over the room like a spectre. His warnings about Qissa Khawani and Operation Macchar — this General Ali Mahmood Khan — now seem prescient, even though nobody really knows why. He was trying to tell us something, wasn't he?

But what? If only we'd listened. *Listened to what?* The information is so damned shapeless and muddied.

This sense of time passing and nothing being achieved had already prompted some raised voices. The Secretary of Homeland Security, a bear of a man named Salazar, who had spoken, for added emphasis, with his fists tightly clenched and shaking slightly, ' . . . whatever counsel these foreign leaders might wish to offer, I beseech you, Mr President, remember, your number-one priority is the safety and security of the American people. Preserve. Protect. And Defend.' But it feels too theoretical. So when the chairman of the Joint Chiefs announces they can pick up live pictures of the hijacked plane, there's an intense buzz of excitement. Everybody's dead keen to see this plane, the focus of this nightmare, and a hush quickly settles as the picture jumps on screen.

Silence. Studied, contemplative silence . . .

The shots from the lead navy FA-18H Super Hornet are not as dramatic or helpful as they had hoped. Just another Boeing 777 doing its thing at 36,000 feet. A gigantic aircraft, ploughing across the Atlantic with its wings level, looking like, frankly, any other plane. Two long lines of fluffy white contrails against a stunning deep blue sky.

As pilot Cletus guides his navy plane carefully forward along the length of the Boeing's port side, there's a bump of turbulence that rocks the picture. Everybody in the situation room jumps too, before craning forward to get a closer look.

The livery is white, with huge green PIA letters over the forward section of passenger windows. Most of the window blinds are down, but that quickly changes. The picture is just detailed enough to see them being raised in a rush, suddenly, one after another, and the outline of hands and a few faces pressed tight against the glass.

The live feed is projected up on to a vast screen, as big and wide as a pool table. Despite the size of the image and the extent of interest there's no obvious killer piece of detail. At least at first. You can almost hear people willing there to be an explosion, or a burst of gunfire. Something dramatic and evil. This, however, feels a touch . . . wrong. By comparison, the hijacked planes on 9/11 had slewed all over the skies, obviously flown by amateurs, terrifying those passengers who'd been able to phone out.

President Charles Hannah gets up from the head of the table, walks to the screen and taps the pixels representing the windows of the cockpit with his black HB pencil. 'Why can't we see in there, Jim? Into the cockpit?'

Jim is the admiral, James Badgett, chairman of the Joint Chiefs of Staff. 'Those grey sort of panels . . . well, it looks like the blinds are drawn, Mr President.'

'Is that usual?' The president turns to the room. 'Doesn't that tell us something?'

No soothsayers come forward, but the Federal Aviation Administration watch officer, Todd Packway, raises his voice from the ring of seats to the back of the room. 'The cockpit windows on a

777 are made up of six separate panels of glass. Two main windshields, one in front of each pilot, and to the side of that, each crew has a sliding window. Then there's the fixed aft window, which is . . . fixed in place. It's not unusual to have the blinds drawn on the sliding *and* aft windows during cruise.'

On a separate video link, one of the shift supervisors at the National Security Council's Fort Meade centre interrupts to report tonelessly, like a speaking clock, that the passengers have seen the Super Hornet. There's a huge jump in people using the in-seat phone system. 'Lot of distress . . . we're picking up . . . anxiety . . . ' his voice sounds distracted, he's trying to precis several live transmissions at once ' . . . 'Is this the shoot-down?' Some degree of panic, it sounds like. A few background screams.'

One or two faces swivel instinctively towards yet another giant television, where six live, but mute, TV news networks are squeezed on to the one screen. There's an obvious ripple of excitement among the presenting anchors, perhaps some of those calling from the aircraft are themselves live on air . . .

The feed from the Super Hornet goes pure sky blue for almost a minute, as Cletus climbs then flips his jet on to the starboard side of the Boeing. A similar slow overtaking manoeuvre up the right-hand line. The two blinds drawn down on this side of the cockpit as well.

'Surely you wouldn't draw the shades on both sides of the same cockpit?' asks the president, still standing by the screen. 'I mean, does that make sense?'

No contradiction there. And Packway, uncomfortably cast as cockpit window expert to those gathered, feels obliged to nod his agreement. 'Correct, Mr President. That would not be expected.'

'So, can we get to see inside the cockpit, Jim?' and the president works his hands, as if he is re-enacting a dogfight. 'Our guy flying across his bow, like at ninety degrees?'

'Mr President, we can do that, sir . . . but the equipment, the video equipment is not, well, it's just an ordinary digital video camera operated by the pilot. It doesn't have the sophistication of the combat heads-up display or a surveillance or satellite camera.'

'So he can't fly that manoeuvre?' A hint of disbelief in President Hannah's question.

'No. He can, sir,' and Admiral Mallan, frustrated, shifts his weight in his high-backed chair. 'To see all the way inside, into that gloom, you have to be on the same level, not above or below, like that . . . ' He demonstrates with the image they're watching at the moment. 'There are two ways: the Super Hornet crosses close to the nose, but he'll need either to be fast, like *boom*, and might miss what we need because he's filming and flying at the same time. Or, he can go slower, but the plane'll have to be some distance farther out. Perhaps too far to see anything.'

The atmospherics in the room are getting stilted, embarrassed even. This has become rather small-time. Momentous things are afoot, lives at stake, and they're chasing shadows, literally. Someone who vividly appreciates this is the Attorney General, a razor-sharp Texan called Jenna-Lee Braddock. She's serious no-nonsense, and once succeeded in throwing out a final death-row petition because it was filed twenty minutes after the court's 5 p.m. closing time. She has the dark tanned skin of a snake and glasses like pebbles. She cups her chin in thought, just as she had done when she was a state and then a federal prosecutor. Build the case. Build the case. She raises her hand.

'Perhaps, Mr President, we can review what we have . . . '

From one of the screens an interruption, a lieutenant colonel in uniform from the NORAD headquarters in Colorado Springs. 'Excuse me, ma'am. Mr President, you wanted to know when the plane crossed longitude Thirty West . . . it did so just now. Seconds ago.'

'Just hold that thought, Jenna-Lee, please, will you.' President Hannah moves back towards his seat. 'Still nothing on the radio, Colonel? No call-in?'

'Aside from that first communication, there's been complete radio silence. Nothing. They've missed two scheduled reporting points. And, as you'll see from your screen track, the flight has now passed into the western zone of the relevant flight information region, controlled out of Gander, Newfoundland.' The implication being that the flight is getting closer and closer . . . like a missile.

351

'I see . . . ' The president is sitting down, his eyes somewhat distant and glazed by all of this reality. 'I see . . . ' Bar Charles Hannah, the room's attention swings to the live map plotting the inexorable journey of PK412 across the North Atlantic. There's rising chat among the staffers around the table, those who've worked out the maths. Ninety minutes, two hours tops, and that Boeing will be crossing the Canadian coast. As abstract as a line of longitude is, with the plane now in their half of the ocean, it feels as if the great white has somehow slipped inside the shark net.

The Attorney General is leaning back in her seat and taps her leather-bound folder on the edge of the table, like a judge with a gavel. 'Mr President. Speaking on behalf of law enforcement, I think now's a good time to be clear in our thoughts.' President Hannah waves her on, giving the Texan the floor.

'9/11 was a failure of two things: our intelligence and our systems. Now y'all look at what we've got here and you can see things are working fine. Our functionality is fine, going just great. The CIA . . . ' she tips her head towards the acting director, who bobs appreciatively ' . . . were able to forewarn us of this pending incident. Albeit . . . ' and here Braddock takes a deep breath, for they'd all heard a great deal about the erratic Bill Lamayette, and had listened to his unorthodox calls to the Ulsterwoman called Sheila Davane at British intelligence ' . . . albeit that the call came from an employee under suspension, who'd rigged his

352

own death, destroyed a heap of government property, and then chose to share his information with MI5 instead of through his usual reporting channels.' Breathe. Breathe. Continue. 'So, score one for our intelligence. And score one, too, for our systems.'

She beams. 'NORTHCOM. Operation Noble Eagle. We got us two planes aloft in double-quick time, just like the manual says. Sidewinders, or whatever they've got, are primed. So we remain ahead of the curve, be in no doubt about that. Now that we have some time, let's make sure we get this decision right.'

There's nodding on this point around the table; even President Hannah looks relieved, while the Secretary of State holds up a hand, asking to be excused, to take another call in one of the booths.

'You must excuse me, Mr President, if I crab sideways a little to get to my point . . . ' Unseen, on the video links from the two air force VIP planes, both the vice-president and Defense Secretary roll their eyes. Braddock has a proverb or hee-haw story for every occasion. They call it 'slow-playing' in the South. Makes them think you're dumb.

'Now, my daddy rose to be chief judge on the Fifth Circuit, the pinnacle of a good and proper career in the law. But he never forgot his first client, back when he started out in private practice in Nacogdoches, Texas. It was 1936, and as a token of thanks this Chinaman gave him a piece of bamboo with some itty-bitty carved characters. Said it would bring good luck to my daddy in his chosen vocation. He kept it in his office his whole life. And you know what the writing meant . . . ?' She swivels her little glasses around the room, peering intently, and, of course, nobody knows. ' . . . them little Chinese words said, 'Though The Sword of Justice Is Sharp, It Will Not Slay The Innocent'.'

A few puzzled faces. 'And what's your point?' asks the president, hopefully.

'Mr President, this is a capital case. The highest standards of evidence must apply, because people will die today because of the things you do, or don't do. Yet in all we have listened to this morning, only two things need our utmost attention. Motive . . . I see motive, how hateful America is, how we are disbelievers, *kuffars*, and need to be punished. And I see opportunity. Just like in 9/11, this plane's cockpit has been commandeered. Same modus operandi, we can hear that much from the calls made by the passengers. They're terrified. The flight crew aren't responding to calls from within the plane, or from air traffic controllers. Probably they've been killed. We know that the flight has not maintained radio contact for at least two hours . . . *two hours*. And that's hardly likely to be simple equipment failure. The goddam thing was only delivered by Boeing . . . ' she glances at her notes ' . . . in March of '08.'

President Hannah pulls irritably at the knot of his red-and-white striped tie. 'But where does that leave us in terms of the law? We can't just be making it up as we go along. How would that look to the rest of the world?'

'Mr President, if the plane was twenty miles out and closing, we wouldn't be playing this pretty little game, this moot-court session. Remember, the time we have is a blessing. Let's not turn it into a curse . . . '

'The law, Jenna-Lee . . . please.' This from the video link with the silver-haired, silver-moustachioed Defense Secretary, flying back from Elmendorf Air Force Base, near Anchorage, Alaska. 'No homilies about frogs in downpours, and walking in tall cotton. Just tell us about the law.'

'Anticipatory self-defence.' Braddock smiles grimly, turning to the monitor showing the image of the Defense Secretary juxtaposed with that of the vice-president. 'The law is clear, Mr Secretary . . . and I say this too, not only is the law clear, it is also clearly on our side. I'm surprised at you, Mr Secretary. I would have thought you would know that self-defence is the first law of nature.'

Hannah had been looking towards one of the navy aides standing by the door, making signals like, has it suddenly got hot in here? He senses the friction developing and cuts quickly away from this. 'Perhaps, just so we are all on the same page, you could tell us about this. Your read on anticipatory self-defence.'

'My pleasure . . . ' and to the surprise of those listening, sitting in a state-of-the-art communications centre, all manner of space-age technologies at work, decrypting voices, encoding data and bringing in satellite feeds from the other side of the world, the

Attorney General walks her audience back to 1837. A time of muskets and cutlasses, and a scrap between Britain and the United States over a speck of land in the middle of the Niagara river, just above the famous falls. A thousand rebels, fighting British dominion in Canada, were using Navy Island as a base for their raids, and they were being supplied by Americans crewing an American ship, the *Caroline*. One night, says Braddock, even though Washington was trying to be scrupulously neutral in this matter, the British commandeered the *Caroline* when she was tied up at a landing on the New York state side of the river. The Royal Navy set the ship alight and let her drift downstream, over the falls. Two were killed, including a cabin boy.

'People getting killed. Boats on fire . . . You can imagine the hoo-haa and the outrage,' says Braddock. 'The militias fixin' to give some payback. But in all the talking that followed, it was the British that prevailed. Anticipatory self-defence, it became known as. In common parlance, we might talk about the lesser of two evils, whereby an action is justified if a country can demonstrate, now listen to these words, a 'necessity of self-defence, instant, overwhelming, leaving no choice of means, and no moment for deliberation'.' She is quoting by heart.

It becomes clear how well Braddock has slow-played her audience when she withdraws a small, typed index card from the inside of her bound file. She has gloriously long, ruby-red nails, and she clicks one with her thumbnail repeatedly, as she readies for the hammer blow.

'This is what was agreed on. I'm going to read the actual legal words that have become the bedrock test of that principle. As I read this, Mr President, imagine your predecessor, Martin Van Buren, one hundred and seventy years ago, dealing with the *Caroline* affair, just as you must deal now with your own wayward, rogue craft . . . ' and she clicks her thumbnail one last time, loudly, before starting.

''It must be strewn that admonition or remonstrance to the persons on board the 'Caroline' was impracticable, or would have been unavailing; it must be strewn that daylight could not be waited for; that there could be no attempt at discrimination, between the innocent and the guilty; that it would not have been enough to seize and detain the vessel; but that there was a necessity, present and inevitable, for attacking her, in the darkness of the night, while moored to the shore, and while unarmed men were asleep on board, killing some, and wounding others, and then drawing her into the current, above the cataract, setting her on fire, and, careless to know whether there might not be in her the innocent with the guilty, or the living with the dead, committing her to a fate, which fills the imagination with horror.''

There is a long silence in the room. The timelessness of the incident is eerie, the need for swift action, the commingling of the innocent and guilty, and above all the imperative of doing something that fills the imagination with horror. Eerie, yet also strangely comforting that leaders have travelled this awful path before, faced these terrible choices. And, perhaps most importantly, that significant legal precedents have been constructed to save everybody's blushes.

The floor is still hers. 'Mr President . . . we're not talking here about a ketch tied up for the night. This is a Boeing 777, aimed right towards us at six hundred miles an hour.' The Attorney General lowers her glasses to the table, rubs the bridge of her nose. 'I think if we are being truthful with ourselves, we all know there is only one course of action here.'

On board PK412

The screaming reverberates up and down the length of the plane. The sort of screaming you get on a roller-coaster as they winch you up the ramp. Nothing has happened yet . . . but all your senses shout that the end is nigh.

General rule of thumb, people in a hijacked plane don't like to see the plane that is going to shoot them down scoping out their target from thirty feet above the wing, weapon racks groaning with missiles.

Tristie Merritt shakes Salahuddin, whose face is glued to one of the first-class windows, his face a mask of anguish. 'Captain, captain . . . ' suddenly worried as she touches his shoulder that she is breaking some kind of unspoken taboo, 'he's just filming us. Look at the guy. He's holding a camera.'

Slowly he cocks his finger in the direction of the Super Hornet, speaks very thoughtfully. 'That is the fighter that is going to shoot down my jet. The plane I am in command of.'

'Perhaps, possibly, who knows, Captain.' She has to raise her voice, shout now, against the cries from elsewhere. 'But he's not going to do it *now*. This is just reconnaissance. Get on the horn, please, calm everybody down. We're not in the endgame. Not yet anyway.'

Unfortunately, before Salahuddin can get to the PA system to offer calming words, the navy pilot jumps his fighter from one side of the Boeing to the other, so a second bout of screaming kicks off. Each side of the plane setting off the other, like panicky teenagers.

It takes some time but eventually the worst of the outcry leaches away. Only some isolated whimpering. The curtains that normally separate the two classes are tied back so everybody knows what is, and is not, going on. No secrets. The cabin crew return to plotting where everybody needs to move to.

So. This boils down to Tristie Merritt. Her Airfone. And the telephone number of a caravan permanently parked by a beach in Northern Ireland. Mary Sweeney is the woman's name.

She wills herself: *Let go, Tristie. Slip away . . .*

To get a voice right, you need to let go of whoever you are. Let yourself melt into the shape and feel of the character you want to become, a step through into another personality . . . but she has more than enough chewing at her mind to make that almost impossible to pull off. Tristie can feel the muscles in her throat tightening.

Calm. Stay calm. Shoulders down. Focus. She's sitting in the second row of first class. The blind beside her is open and a shaft of brilliant light cuts across the darkened cabin. Whiffler is sitting on the arm of the next seat, his foot up. Spellbound.

360

'Convinced?'

'Seriously, Tristie, if I closed my eyes and you spoke again, like what you've just been doing, I'd swear you were Kylie Minogue.'

Well. We'll see about that . . .

Cranfield Caravan Park
Kileel
County Down

It's supposed to be summer, the calendar says so, but the weather hasn't turned. The flags and pennants on the south-facing beach flutter like mad and Mary Sweeney can hear the *chink-chink-chink* of the halyards spinning in the wind. Sweeney shivers with the cold. Not a thing left in this life to warm the heart, the old lady would say when asked, and contemplating her present emptiness brings on the usual glance over at the table. The trophies, medals and certificates. The framed photos of smiles, love, affection. Memories of a husband, and an only child. Gone on, into the next life.

She broods in her armchair. Alone, and left behind. A frail pensioner, peering out of the bay windows of her family's forty-foot caravan towards the churning brown of the Irish Sea. Tightly tucked into a quilt, and a tartan rug just for good measure.

'You haven't touched your shepherd's pie.'

A shrug of the shoulders. 'Not feeling so hungry today.' And Sweeney starts to push at the one or two peas that had fallen on her lap, her fingers thin, trembling, purple with age.

'Soon I shall be thinking you don't like my food,' chirps Laura, who's from up the road in Newry and cleans the caravans. Sweeney's nieces and nephews thought that they were doing a big favour by paying Laura a small fortune to look after the old lady. The plate is whisked away, and Laura clatters about in the kitchenette, making it clear she's working hard for her money. 'Bit of a vac coming up, Mrs Sweeney.'

As the small round bottom of the cleaning girl moves this way and that, up and down the caravan, Sweeney resumes her vigil over the Irish Sea. Her face set grim. Every so often a bony hand reaches to part the net curtain for a closer inspection of some unexpected movement, while the vacuum cleaner moans on.

Perhaps she had drifted off to sleep, she doesn't know, but the next thing to happen was a gentle poke in the shoulder. Laura is standing over her, holding a handset. 'A call, Mrs Sweeney,' she whispers dramatically. 'Sorry to wake you, but they said it was urgent. Almost missed it what with the noise, and whatnot.'

Somebody calling me?

Mary Sweeney puts the phone to her ear, full of suspicion and dark thoughts.

The voice she hears is confident, full of bright blue skies, breaking waves and beach parties.

'Mrs *Sweeney . . . it's Mary McCaraher. Calling from sunny Australia. Back on Kangaroo Island.*' The inflection rises dramatically at the end of each sentence, like a surprised question.

'Mary McCaraher . . . ' Sweeney says the

name with a kind of awe, holding the phone now with two hands. 'How long has it been?'

'*Too long, too long,*' says the woman calling herself McCaraher, but even this lament sounds strangely upbeat in an Australian female voice.

The two of them hunker down for a long-overdue catch-up, Sweeney quickly getting into a vivid discussion about her pelvic support problems and McCaraher offering a blow-by-blow report about the men in her life, the reasons why she has not yet married, not yet produced any new little souls for the Kingdom of God. '*Oh, Mrs Sweeney. The number of prayers I said to St Anthony that he would be the one . . .* '

Sweeney tries to console throughout. 'I'll light a candle for you at mass, for you and St Thérèse of the Child Jesus of the Holy Face.' And so the conversation winds on until the Australian makes clear with her pauses and her stuttering tone that she needs more than just talk.

'Now, tell me, Mary McCaraher, you're speaking like you've got yourself in some bother.'

'*You always were too fast for me.*'

'You want your little slip of paper, don't you, pet.'

'*Pleaassee.*'

'Goodness, girl, I'm surprised you lasted this long. I really am. I thought you'd be on the phone just a couple of weeks after you left. You did good holding out this long.' And Mary Sweeney cranes around and bellows for '*LAURA*' in a surprisingly robust voice.

When the cleaner appears, Sweeney waves a

finger at the sideboard full of trophies, the shrine to the memory of her most beloved killed by an IRA bomb at the Killeen border crossing in 1990 as they took one of the family greyhounds south, to the Dundalk races. Pride of place goes to the Queen's Gallantry Medal awarded to both father and son posthumously. 'That picture. The framed one. Of Mr Sweeney and Luke, with their dog Toto. Pass it here, will you.'

Laura, a bit spooked to be touching anything on a table she'd been forbidden from dusting, gingerly passes over the heavy silver frame. Father and son in close-up, smiling their big gap-toothed smiles. Panting happily between them is Toto, a brindle-and-white Group 1 greyhound champion.

Sweeney reaches to the back, unplugs the backboard, and digs out a tightly folded wedge of paper. 'Here it is,' she says into the phone, looking first at the corporate logo.

In blue, the letters ANZ, and at the foot, 13 Grenfell Street, Adelaide, South Australia. Mary Sweeney carefully articulates the eleven digits.

Way back, she had read the scribbled note that McCaraher sent, thanking her for the memorably happy five-week stay as a lodger when the old lady had still been living on the outskirts of Newry. At the same time, there was a favour. The younger woman was entrusting to Sweeney the only copy of an access code, so as not to be tempted to waste the little windfall she'd just banked, £20,000, locked up tight in a safety deposit box. Rainy-day money.

Thirty-six thousand feet up — and a thousand

miles west of the caravan park — Mary McCaraher, aka Tristie Merritt, quickly works on a sheet of paper to rearrange the random numbers, as she winds up the call to Mrs Sweeney.

The 0800 freephone number represents a time in her past that was . . . past, finished. A number that she hasn't had to call upon since her days with 14 Intelligence Coy, at the fag end of the 'Troubles'. Several tours of duty back, before Iraq and Afghanistan.

It chills Tristie to realise the huge gamble she's about to take. With her men's lives, with Ward 13 and those detailed plans for the Trident missile programme. Everything they've worked for in fact, she's about to put on the line. *Faîtes vos jeux.* Red or black. *Mesdames et messieurs* . . . place your bets, please.

The 0800 number is a connection right into the operational heart of MI5. *Rien ne va plus . . .*

On board PK412

Five minutes later the call is answered by a male voice, somebody who sounds like he's been coughing up his lungs for the past week. '*Hello.*' Hoarse and breathy. '*How can I help you?*'

'This is Casablanca.' Tristie speaks carefully, knowing some world-class hardware will be scrutinising all the stresses and strains in her voice.

'*Casablanca, how are you? Just give me a second, will you.*' The sound of keys being struck furiously and another long wet cough. There will be various voice prompts to clarify her status. With each question there are alarm-answers as well, in case she's being held under duress. The unique micro-tremors that represent a person as individually as their fingerprints are then rendered via an algorithm into a scored voicegram. Given three or four sentences, the computer is expected to be able to answer, Is this the real Tristie Merrit on the phone? Yes or no? with a degree of probability. Is she under duress? Yes or no? . . . and so on.

She looks around the first class cabin. Now dim with the blinds down except for the one window open next to her. In the rest of the plane, people are chewing their way through lunch service. Occupied and for the moment becalmed. Lovely word that. Becalm. To render motionless for lack of wind. Giving them something to eat had definitely taken the edge off the hysteria. And after lunch, they'll begin the big move-around of the passengers.

Once she'd said her goodbyes to Mary Sweeney she'd felt the need to lay out all of her plans, firstly for the benefit of Button and Whiffler. What she'd done for MI5, the pull it should still give her, and how she wanted to use that in these circumstances. They had to understand that this would be an all-in bet. 'You tell me not to, that you're not comfortable with this, and I'll not call . . . ' Tristie had offered. But they saw the logic of what was being proposed. Button had glanced at Whiffler. It took less than a second, then he turned back, speaking for the both of them. 'No regrets, Tristie. Let's fucking well be 'aving 'em,' Button confirmed.

Tristie had also given an abridged version of her MI5 connections to Captain Harry Salahuddin. Something that won't turn him too queasy. To her surprise, he had seemed genuinely relieved that she would be talking directly with somebody in authority. 'At last some chance to stop this madness,' and the pilot had clapped her on the shoulder.

Next comes the first MI5 voice prompt. '*So what was the weather like in Casablanca?*'

The answer comes from the song 'Casablanca', track two of the 1982 album by Bertie Higgins. She tries to keep the beat in her mind.

It was a ghastly tune. Island rock, they call it. She recites the lyrics as tunelessly as possible to aid the voicegram. Something about popcorn and Coke, and champagne and caviar. Button and Whiffler's eyebrows rocket up as she talks about making love one summer night. Tap, tap, tap in the background. No alarms so far. She's over the first hurdle.

'*What airline did you say you flew out there on?*'

'Joshua.'

'*Are they any good?*'

Next answer lies in the opening line of the Dolly Parton song 'Joshua', the singer's first American country-music number one. A song about a girl orphan and the hard life she lived, no doubt picked especially for her by some spook with too much time on his hands and his nose in the Merritt personnel file. Again Tristie enunciates the lyrics slowly — the tale of the black dog who growled at the fearful girl.

More action on the computer, algorithms crunching away. There is a third lyric relating to a song called 'Harder Better Faster Stronger', but she doesn't get the voice prompt. No question for her to feed into. What is the significance of that?

A stray piece of music trivia pops into her head. Something learned in a bar in Aldershot, one of those pub quiz nights, that Bertie Higgins is the great-great-great-grandson of the German poet Goethe.

But it makes her think of Goethe's Faust, and Doing a Deal with the Devil.

'*Ms Merritt. Long time no hear.*' And that's when Rumbly Throat on the keyboard hacks and coughs one last time, then says, '*Who can I put you through to?*'

MI5 Headquarters
Thames House

Now that the intelligence has blossomed into confirmation of a full-blown hijacking over the Atlantic, PK412 moves out of MI5's jurisdiction and becomes a straightforward police/diplomatic matter.

Sheila 'Noppy' Davane's people are therefore folding up their tent on this one, going through the laborious process of funnelling everything they have: the unconventional brilliance of Lamayette and his firebrand holy man, condensed into what is known as the national intelligence machinery, organised through the Joint Intelligence Committee. This aggregation by the JIC will see solid leads churned in with random trivia and thoughts-for-the-day from agencies as diverse as M16, the Serious Organised Crime Agency and even HM Customs and Revenue. Rather like watching the most unpalatable cuts of meat being processed into wholesome sausages, the whole Joint Intelligence Committee business is something that gives Davane the willies.

Severely ticked off with herself that she had, in some fashion, failed, Davane had called up

Professor Grigor Rothko, to try to understand the significance of Qissa Khawani, and the background to radical theological doctrine in the wilder parts of Pakistan.

The security services keep on their books a number of dons from Oxford, Cambridge and other universities. In good times and bad you need people with the intellectual faculties to buzz-saw through all the guff and see a thing for what it is. A peculiar human skill no computer or microfilm archivist has yet been programmed to achieve. But the downside is they also are prone to the twin evils of preciousness and longwindedness. Two things Davane can barely stomach on an average day, let alone one as dramatic as today. That is why MI5 picks people like their deputy director-general Bill Grainger for their most senior and visible positions; to suffer these people gladly. Thoroughly respectable yet complete shameless strokers of politicians, lawyers, civil libertarians and academics alike. Mata Hari in a pinstripe suit.

After ten minutes of probing, she's more or less got what she wants from Professor Rothko, and now wants to be done with the man.

Rothko, on the other hand, feels he has more to contribute. Insight and analysis from a finely tuned brain. 'I mean, who are we to insist these people change their ways, to follow a Western norm . . . ' Stroking the stem of a tiny glass of sherry, he has been hypothesising on Pakistan into a small lens atop his computer, which is linked through to MI5 and a monitor to the side of Davane's desk. In the background, through the windows in his study, she can see the ancient masonry and sloping turrets of Trinity College, Cambridge. He finishes the sherry in one satisfied gulp and momentarily disappears from the lens' view to refill from the bottle at his feet. He pops back into vision, looking alarmingly florid. Pulling on his dark blue cravat as if he'd come close to blacking out.

' . . . We blithely commend Islamabad for upholding what we call democratic principles, but who are we kidding? Bullshit, I say to you. There's hardly a democratic red blood cell in a single vein of a single limb in any typical Pakistani politician . . . '

Rothko's ire had been pricked by the latest news from Pakistan, an urgent resolution, adopted within the last ten minutes by their lower house of parliament. The Pakistan National Assembly had been in session when news broke of the hijacking and the reaction had been sensational. The chamber almost never spoke with one voice, but it seemed to today, the only dispute being which politician hated America the more intensely. Of course, moderates tried to make themselves heard, cautiously expressing hope that the plane and her passengers might be spared, reminding the chamber not to rush to judgement, that a cool head made the wisest choice. But such a febrile atmosphere played into the hands of the extremists — these were elected representatives after all, with one eye on the voter and the other on the excruciating drama carried on live TV. There was no appetite for reason, or the logic of wait and see. So, with the assembly sitting much later than usual, and flagged excitedly as Breaking News by the international networks, the vote had instructed the government to treat any downing of flight PK412 as an act of war against the people of Pakistan; to immediately seize US assets within the country, including any and all military hardware; and to effect an immediate default on all outstanding loans to American financial institutions, including, possibly, probably (the angry MPs hadn't quite thought this through yet), the World Bank and the International Monetary Fund.

Rothko sniffs dismissively. He has a rich, plummy voice like that of a well-fed barrister. ' . . . The trouble with democracy is that the ratbags are a lot better at it than we ever give them credit for . . . and in a place like Pakistan that's a recipe for disaster . . . '

In Davane's mind Rothko's subsequent thoughts on the role of the executive, legislative and judicial branches fade into a drone of chatter. She still has the thick bundle of passenger lists in front of her and she's gone back to examining the names, their passport information and financial records. Trying to find the loose thread, the slight dissonance that all these conspiracies eventually offer up. Soon she's lost in the maze of printed detail.

' . . . to give them credit, this plot is a rather elegant contrivance . . . ' Rothko is examining the colour of his sherry. The pause is deliberate, demanding the question *How so, Professor?*

But Davane doesn't look up from her papers,

374

and her tone is as flat as possible. 'How so, Professor?'

'It's quite simple really. Washington finds itself in an impossible position. They're damned if they do and damned if they don't. Checkmate. They can't shoot down the plane without outraging the rest of the world, and they can't leave the plane be, without showing themselves to be pitifully weak to a home audience. Clever to set that up.'

Davane manages a 'hmmmmm' in response.

'Checkmate indeed. From the Persian *Shaah Maat*.' Rothko says the words with exaggerated fluency. '*Shaah Maat*. The king is made powerless. Paralysed without being hit by anybody. The king is astonished, amazed, perplexed. Humbled.'

Go away. She can feel her irritation with the professor's musings sharpen, his intellectual calm become unbearable, almost toxic.

'The US have been itching to shoot something out of the sky since 9/11 and now they get their chance. Only it hasn't quite worked out the way they thought. They're so much more vulnerable now than they ever were. So many broken relationships, so little trust, so much indebtedness around the world. Hardly the triumphal beacon.'

Davane frowns, her attention caught. She looks up at his image. Rothko is again rolling the stem of his glass between his finger and thumb. The cat who caught the cream. 'What do you mean by that?' she snaps at him.

'I suppose from a conventional point of view it

would be considered a failure to have to take control of the plane so far away from land, from any possible target. You'd want surprise if you were planning to ram the thing into a structure. But you only get surprise on take-off and climb, or descent and landing, when, by definition, the plane is flying low and fast within the area of a major city. Not in the middle of the Atlantic. Yes?'

In truth, this is a question that had nagged at Davane, irritated her even. What *is* the plan here? Why initiate the hijacking in the middle of the Atlantic? Had something gone wrong on board that pushed the time frame forward?

'Do you have a particular insight, Professor?'

The professor's answer to a simple question annoys Davane. 'How many people in Washington have the authority to shoot down a plane?'

Typical academic, answering one question with another question. She lets out her breath in a long waft of frustration because she knows the answer to Rothko's question, but needs to pull it from the back of her mind, from the briefing document she'd read a while back. Entitled *Delegated Authority to Interdict*.

It had once been so simple: only the president had the power.

She closes her eyes as she conjures up the documentation in her mind. 'Now the president is assumed to have delegated authority to the Secretary of Defense, who delegates to the combatant commander at NORAD, which is to say the United States Northern Command, the authority to declare a hostile target. Ideally confirmation will come from the highest level possible within that chain. But ... ' and Davane's eyes open again as if she's reading from the actual brief 'but in an emergency situation, as lowly a figure as the designated representative of the air component commander of NORAD/Northern Command has interdiction power in the very rare occasion where a telephone fails, or they cannot get higher consent.'

Rothko peers forward until his face consumes the whole camera lens. 'Don't you think that's strange, rather obvious in fact. Surely this would be known or guessed at beforehand by a hijacker? So, what's he expecting to do? Outrun a fighter jet?'

What are *you talking about?* Davane shakes her head. More damned questions. 'Professor. Just tell me what you're thinking. Please.'

'I don't know ... ' and he shrugs his shoulders, as if it was a throwaway thought, pulls back from the camera. 'There was a certain comfortable orthodoxy about things before 9/11 which the terrorists were able to exploit. In consequence, after the excitements of that memorable day, we ripped everything up and rewrote the rules. But that was eight, nine years ago. Now there's a different but just as settled orthodoxy ... the people who plan the really shocking incidents don't butt at you head to head where you're strongest, they come at things obliquely. Which is why your current problem seems too inept to be true ... '

Davane's reaction is fierce. 'Might seem inept

to you, Professor, but there are still three-hundred-plus people up there, with frankly little chance of reaching America . . . '

And the silver-haired woman from County Antrim is about to flay the Cambridge intellectual when Pyjama-girl, one of her designated assistants for the day, bursts through her office door. Panting.

'Ms D-D-Davane . . . Somebody calling for you. Urgent.'

'Who?'

'Cassandra . . . no . . . ' And she looks down at her pad. 'Casablanca. Merritt. Captain Merritt . . . Lately of 14 Company and the Army Joint Support Group. Tristie Merritt. We used her in Northern Ireland . . . Casablanca. But I can't access the file. She's on hold now.'

Merritt. *Where have I come across that name before?* Merritt. 'What's the fuss all about?'

'PK412. She's calling from up there,' and she thumbs towards the ceiling, 'the hijacked plane.'

'We've got somebody on board?' And Davane shuffles urgently through the wedge of passenger-list paperwork as Pyjama-girl keeps reading. 'Tristie Merritt. British citizen. Confirmed as sitting in first class. Seat One Delta.'

'Professor. Been great as usual . . . '

Rothko speeds up, sensing he's about to be cut off. 'Just hope you know what you're doing . . . '

'Yes. Much thanks . . . ' Davane talks over his final words.

' . . . circular firing squad . . . '

'Yes. Got to go . . . ' And with a shake of her

head — *circular firing squad?* — Davane punches out of the video connection to grab her telephone. But before she clicks on to the flashing line, she signals to Pyjama-girl. *Recording?* The assistant nods vigorously. *Downing Street?* queries Davane. Yes. Online, Pyjama-girl mouths. Listening in.

Davane nibbles at the tip of her tongue, her eyes distant. Thinking, thinking. Finally she speaks, breathing her words slowly, quietly. 'I want everything on this woman. From the MoD in London, our archives, Belfast, the Joint Support Group. Every last jot.' *Who knows what I might have to hold over this Merritt woman's head . . .*

And then in a blink she's sweetness and light. 'Hello, hello. So good of you to ring through . . . ' and the forced smile shows her teeth, a grim sight, like grey chips. Thirty years of sucking Fox's Glacier Mints. 'Now. Before we start things off, do you mind if I call you Tristie?'

She listens. Pause. Her forced attempt at civility falters. The skin around her eyes tightens as if she is looking down the length of a gun barrel. 'Yes . . . of course you can call me Noppy . . . '

★   ★   ★

Tristie Merritt worked in Northern Ireland, but it was a long time after the worst of the Troubles was over. That meant she never dealt with Noppy directly. But her name was still legendary. Spoken of in hushed tones, like some cup-winning hero from another age, when the tackles

379

were for real and the referee always turned a blind eye.

In 14 Coy., the received wisdom on the Troubles had been that peace came only because those promulgating the war were finally made to collapse. The paramilitaries on both sides were exhausted and broken by all the betrayals and the double and triple-dealing initiated by MI5 and the local Special Branch. There were very few people who survived all of this intact, who could stand over the wreckage of that whole wretched business. Sheila 'Noppy' Davane was one of them. Like the Terminator in a tweed skirt. Last man standing.

So it's quite something for Tristie to be talking to her . . . knowing what she's about to try to pull off.

' . . . that's how come we are where we are.' She hears herself speaking as brightly and positively as possible. In ten minutes of close questioning, she'd given Noppy as much of a sense of what is happening on the flight as possible. It boils down to this: they have no idea what is going on in the cockpit and no obvious way to breach the door. A steward called Zaafir is inside. There's been no announcement on the PA system, but when you ring through on the internal phone there's a never-ending loop of a Muslim singer giving it the full throat-warble.

'Tristie, can I speak with the captain please, the one who's dead-legging?'

She hands the phone over to Salahuddin, who's feeling confident in the part he's going to play. Angry pilot.

He puffs his chest out. 'This is Captain Saeed Salahuddin of Pakistan International Airlines, and I demand that you cease harassing my plane with your Hornet fighter jets.'

For the moment, Tristie can't hear Noppy's side of the conversation. But she imagines what she's telling him, with her practised, droll Irish accent, that MI5 don't have any fighter jets, not yet anyway, chuckle, chuckle, but that definitely his message will get to the appropriate people, like the decision-makers in Washington. Soft and soothing.

' . . . Of course I am,' says Salahuddin emphatically. He lids his eyes. 'Jeddah? . . . Three. Three runways . . . ' He covers the phone, shakes his head. 'This woman is testing me, my knowledge of airports, to make sure I'm who I say I am.'

He puts a finger in his ear. 'Jeddah is unusual because it has three runways and they're all parallel to one another . . . Sixteen Right, Sixteen Centre and Sixteen Left . . . Why, miss, do you want to fly there? . . . Good. Pleased to meet you too . . . Here is Merritt again.' He gives Tristie something like a wink, says he'll be walking through the cabin, making himself visible to the passengers, taking questions. She nods, gives a thumbs-up and takes back the phone.

'*He's a prickly little sod, that pilot . . .* '

'Perhaps if you met under different circumstances. He's a bit touchy about the plane being shot down.'

'*I guess I'll have to give him the benefit of the doubt . . .* ' Davane is working hard to get onside, the us-versus-them tactic.

'*I suppose you're surprised I know so much about Jeddah Airport?*'

'It did sound like you were an expert.'

'*Just making it up.*' She can hear Davane grinning. '*Going on my first haj this year. Got my bags packed. Can't wait . . .*'

Us versus them. And Tristie's just about to blow that right out of the water.

'Tell me, who's online with this call at the moment?'

Davane has an ever-so chummy approximation of a best-girlfriend voice. '*I'm really not certain, Tristie . . . the communications people have patched this through to Downing Street or Chequers, wherever the prime minister is, but who is listening right now, I couldn't say.*'

'Is anybody on this call Stateside?'

'*No. Wouldn't have thought so. Not yet. But it'll get passed over almost as soon as we're finished.*' She can almost hear Davane's brain clicking: you go ahead, tell me all the little secrets, and we'll parse them, and drip-feed them to Washington . . .

'Good. Because this is what I want.'

'*I'm sorry, did you just . . .*'

'This is what I want, and I don't have much time.'

'*For a second there . . .*' and Davane chuckles ' *. . . I thought I heard you say, This is what I want.*'

For the first time she raises her voice. Serious. 'Noppy . . . shut up and pay attention, we don't have much time.' Button and Whiffler both

382

wince. There's a singular fierceness in her eyes that both men have seen before. Not to be trifled with.

She gives Davane the backstory. Everything about Ward 13 and the long journey here. Starting with Sir Dale Malham, his missing £1.2 million, the Money for Old Rope access code he uses to control his fortune built up on the back of the armed forces. Dougal MacIntyre's computer. The DRAM chip containing enough classified information to make redundant the Trident missile programme, and with it the four Vanguard submarines. The threat to the Ministry of Defence, the broken Military Covenant, the deadline which runs out tomorrow and the adverts in *The Times* . . . Everything. She also offers up the names of Button and Whiffler. They would have connected them to her by now anyway, from the passenger list, but at least it shows good faith.

'*Sure you haven't forgotten anything?*' is Davane's laconic reply. '*Bullion heist perhaps?*'

'I think that's about it.'

'*And so, apart from being able now to bring an end to a half-dozen police investigations, explain, if you will, what any of your crusading has to do with me or Her Majesty's Government?*'

'Because, whatever happens on this plane . . . that DRAM chip and all the information on it survives. I'm not carrying it with me. And, without me to safeguard it, who knows where it might end up?'

On her end, Davane makes a low soughing

noise. Not quite reaching a moan, but stronger than a sigh. '*If you know what's good for you, you won't . . .* '

Tristie cuts across her. ' . . . I've seen reports that Trident is going to cost fifteen billion. But you know how these things work, long lunch here, couple of consultants there, and it's suddenly twenty-five billion. You factor in maintenance costs over the next thirty years, and you're looking at perhaps seventy-five or eighty billion . . . Jeez.'

'*Have you thought what would happen to this country if every Tom, Dick and Harry with a wee grudge did what you are doing?*'

You want to play philosophy? . . . 'Noppy, if everybody was doing it then I'd be a fool to do any different.'

'*I was always taught that the path of Duty is the way to Glory. If you aren't happy with something you keep it to yourself. Work through the problem. Or keep buggering on, to use Churchill's words.*'

'Well, to paraphrase somebody cleverer than me, if everybody is thinking the same way then nobody's actually doing any thinking.'

Button's knuckles are white, clutching tight on the seat, as he listens in. The other side of him, Whiffler is pacing nervously up and down the aisle. This is as much their future as it is hers. Tristie tries to ignore them. ' . . . Now wouldn't it be a hell of a thing to have all that money wasted, flushed down the toilet, because of a little DRAM chip that got lost and ended up, I don't know, in unfriendly hands.'

Noppy's voice goes deathly cold. A whisper. *'Girl. I don't know you, but I think you must have heard of me. So let's dispense with the air kisses. Take this piece of advice from someone with a ton of experience in these matters. Don't. Focking. Well. Do. This.'*

That Antrim accent is ugly as all hell. But it's the world's greatest brogue for making threats. Good enough that Tristie bites her bottom lip, trying to work out whether she really is tough enough to make this all-in bet. *Rien ne va plus . . .*

She's saved from this indecision by a bubble of anger that just about overwhelms her. 'Listen, Noppy. There's a strong chance I'm going to die in the next couple of hours. What that means for you is this . . . I don't care to be threatened. When you get hold of my files, you'll see the life I've lived. For reasons of self-preservation my life is a small circle of just what I need. Just enough room for the very few things that matter to me. Now that I can see how this hijack is likely to play out, that circle is tightening. Getting real small. All the shit gets pushed outside. Your threats and indignation, for instance. And all I've got inside my little circle are the people who fought with me, my bloody soldiers, and protecting them from their government, our government, from what it was we thought we were fighting for.'

Noppy clicks her tongue over her teeth. *'That's a nice little speech. So nice in fact that I'm sensing some wool being pulled over my eyes.'* Click, click with the teeth. *'You see . . . I* hear the shrillness and histrionics, and I guess I have to take what you say at face value. But then, something doesn't make sense. If I were you, and I'd got myself so unhinged by injustices perpetrated against me . . . ' Click, click. ' . . . then my one little bargaining chip, well, I'd have kept that little DRAM chip as close as I could. No matter what I was up to.'

Big grin. Trapdoor shuts. 'Then you'd be making the same mistake everybody else does. Women like us. You and me. Nobody takes us seriously, do they? What can a *female* know? And that's how we beat 'em. Don't we, Noppy? Because they don't take us seriously until it's way too late.'

Them and us.

The hiss and whine of satellite static hides a lengthy stillness. Impasse. Dead air. Stand-off. The Ulsterwoman draws a breath to speak, not to succumb, but with a weary sense of resignation in her voice. '*So tell me what you want* . . . '

Tristie tries to keep the relief out of her voice. 'Thank you, Noppy. I promise, you'll have no regrets . . . ' Button reaches across to muss with her hair, a big shit-eating grin on his broad, smiling face.

'*I'm just the water carrier here, remember. No promises.*'

And she spends the next couple of minutes going through what the Attorney General has to write in his letter. The names, Tristesse Merritt, Barry Ackwith, etc. The list of their 'crimes', and the AG's irrevocable undertaking that, following a detailed Shawcross exercise, he had determined it would be against the national interests to prosecute the aforementioned for the incidents described. Both now and in the future. Please instruct cessation of any outstanding investigations, etc. Cc'd to the Director of Public Prosecutions, the Minister of Justice and the prime minister.

'*Shawcross?*' Noppy exclaims. '*That's legal textbook stuff. They don't teach that at grenade-throwing school or wherever you went.*'

'No point picking a fight unless you've worked out how to finish the guy off.'

Tristie looks at her watch. It's still on London time. 1437. 'By fifteen thirty hours I would like my people in the UK to tell me that the news about the three hundred and fifteen million is on the *Sun*, the *Daily Mail* and the BBC websites. The sort of splash you can't walk back. Dress it up how you like, but that three-fifteen-over-three-years goes out.'

'*What about the DRAM chip?*'

'Three forty-five p.m. Just under seventy-five minutes from now. We exchange the computer and the chip for the AG's letter. Put the letter in a sealed, clear plastic file. And be waiting for my call on the steps of Thames House. Right on the junction of Horseferry Road and Millbank . . . ' She pictures the spot in her mind. A four-way roundabout with a tiny traffic island dwarfed by the eleven storeys of Thames House and its sister building, Imperial Chemical House. Two massive neoclassical structures of white Portland stone, looking imperiously across the north end of

387

Lambeth Bridge towards the South Bank.

'*Listen. I don't do drop-offs and walkabouts.*'

'Yes you do. Today, you have to. For good or for bad, Noppy, I'm trusting you.'

'*Well then, you should be trying harder to make me like you. Maybe I'm thinking in seventy-five minutes this might be over already . . . Ms Merritt go swim-swim with the fishes.*'

'If you think life's hard now, dealing with your hook-handed preachers and bedsit terrorists, you just wait till a plane full of innocent Muslims has been shot out of the skies. Try to wrap your security services around that little problem.' And Tristie finds herself thinking about Salahuddin. Not a radical by any stretch of the imagination, but a man with genuine indignation over Iraq. Presumably Afghanistan too. 'There are at least twenty local authorities in Britain under whose jurisdiction the Muslim population is over ten per cent. MI5 got enough CCTV cameras to cover that? Enough of your spooks and snitches, and law courts and prisons?

'Think about it, Noppy . . . think about what the world's going to look like if this plane goes down.' And on that cheery note, she hangs up. Let the old girl think a bit about the hell-storm everybody is flying towards.

Then she turns to Whiffler. 'Let's sit down with the captain, go through in detail why we can't get into that cockpit. We must be missing a trick. Somewhere.'

But where? Where?

MI5 Headquarters
Thames House

Noppy's office is deathly quiet, has been for almost a minute, until the arrival of Pyjama-girl, who advances nervously across the carpeted room. Clutched to her chest, the files she's been able to dig up on Captain Tristesse Merritt. From what she'd been able to casually glance over, the woman is pretty, stunning even. Determined. And deadly, if all the redacted and access-sensitive protocols are anything to go by.

Sheila 'Noppy' Davane doesn't use the office-standard fluorescent lighting. The only illumination of her brooding form is from a green-hooded brass lamp on the desk. Thus lit, she looks decidedly malevolent, her face lined with dark crevices. She's still holding the phone in her hand.

'Ms Davane?' And Pyjama-girl inches forward. 'The call was forwarded. Everybody's in a COBRA meeting. They want you to join them in Downing Street . . . '

COBRA stands for Cabinet Office Briefing Room A, the name for an emergency gathering of ministers and senior civil servants to chew over any breaking crisis. It meets perhaps four or

389

five times a year. Fuel disruptions, flooding, whatever. Now a hijacking that is unleashing a wave of civil and racial disturbance in Britain that could make the Brixton and Toxteth riots look like a pre-school food fight.

The Ulsterwoman snaps out of her trance and blinks at her assistant. 'That woman is talking to someone, she has eyes and ears on the ground. Someone in London. Using a mobile. Must be. I want them found. Tell GCHQ they must be traced.'

And as Davane takes the files from Pyjama-girl and then waves her off, the young woman is sure she hears her boss muttering, 'Nobody *focking* well speaks to me like that.'

The White House situation room
Fifteen minutes after Merritt's call
0952 Washington time, 1452 London time,
1952 Islamabad time

All presidents hide things from their electorate — wheelchairs, mistresses, drinking — but Charles Hannah has only one, rather pathetic, little secret. When nervous, really troubled, he picks his nose. Digs in. Not something the official photographer ever commits to posterity. It's a nervous tic that cries out, *I really wish I didn't have to do this*.

Everybody in the room has their battle face switched on and the mood is grim because the basic decision has been taken. This plane has to be shot down. Not now, but soon, and by those two US Navy jets if need be, though preferably by forces from within the NORAD command structure. So the rest of the world can see the USA and Canada standing together. Mutual protection. Joint airspace sovereignty, and so on. But to get to *soon* — and when exactly *is* soon? — they need the Canadians. And everybody's waiting for the Canadians to call back . . .

According to the filed flight plan, PK412 will enter NORAD airspace in Canada, making land near the Inuit settlement of Nain in Newfoundland. That a flight to New York crosses into Canada first has injected an extra set of decision-makers, who have to be assembled and briefed, and then cajoled into confirming or at least acquiescing in the shoot-down.

To ensure no time is lost, the NORTHCOM/ NORAD commander, an American general, had scrambled four Canadian CF-18 Hornets from 5 Wing, based at the RCAF base at Goose Bay, only 250 miles from Nain. That action hadn't needed Ottawa's agreement. Each Hornet is carrying two wingtip-mounted AMRAAM air-to-air missiles, as well as internal Gatling guns that fire 6,000 20mm shells a minute. The CF-18s will link up with the two US Navy Super Hornets, which are at this moment in the process of being refuelled in midair.

Washington had presented its case to its Canadian counterparts by live video link from the situation room. Included in this had been excerpts from the rambling radio transmission from the 777's cockpit . . .

‘ . . . *To enjoy the blessings of our Lord, Allah requires us to die and kill in his name. Read the Koran and you will find this truth, this absolute truth and never again can you deny this because the Koran says so . . .* ’

. . . and lots of windy talk from a nervous President Charles Hannah about the time-tested structure and integrity of NORAD, the single military theatre concept, You Need Us And We Need You.

But the tone has been set by Kent Jemison,

the craggy country lawyer turned Canadian prime minister who had noted, rather suspiciously, that this was not a typical NORAD incursion. He said his own minister of national defence was telling him this was something neither his military nor politicians past or present had hypothesised. Moreover the premise of NORAD's recent war-gaming, Jemison pointed out, had been to deal with sneak attacks, cruise missiles fired from offshore vessels being a favourite scenario. Not a lumbering jet that's clearly signalled its intentions from out in the middle of the Atlantic.

The distress of the passengers trapped on board, being broadcast round the world, had also given Jemison reason to pause. 'It pains me. I tell you it pains me,' and he had shaken his head with great sorrow, perhaps a little too theatrically. Already, he said, there had been reports from Ontario that the country's modest Pakistani population were showing their feelings. Riot police deployed in the cities of Pickering and Guelph, and the districts of East York and Rexdale in Toronto. And his country's shrill, America-phobic liberal left would be outraged once they worked out Canada's role in the decision-making. Acting on this, as only a politician would, Jemison was as circumspect as possible in everything he said and did: *Let the record show I never . . .*

Just before signing off from Ottawa, to huddle and come up with a decision, the prime minister had stroked his lumberjack beard, looking straight into the lens, and noted, in his homespun rural way, that, darn it, the simplest technical decisions can carry the most grievous political and strategic consequences. 'I hope our friends in Washington understand what we're going through here. Few people in my country appreciate NORAD and why we keep signing up to being your junior partner . . . ' Grim shake of the head. ' . . . For all our sakes, I gotta make sure we take the right decision here. Mr President, we're aware of the time constraints so I'll get back to you on this presently . . . '

Presently? That had been twenty minutes ago . . . One of the aides in the communications room scuttles in to say they're having technical difficulties re-establishing a secure and encrypted live link with Ottawa. As if confirming this, the plasma screen jumps from black to a picture filled with white noise . . . ominous.

Inside a black Jaguar XJ 2.7
En route to Downing Street

Sheila 'Noppy' Davane, stuck in traffic behind a temporary police cordon, fumes. 'Who the hell is protesting today?' Pyjama-girl is by her side, on a call to one of the assistants coordinating the COBRA meeting.

Davane's driver cranes forward, slowly reads off a couple of the signs. 'Hands Off Our Fishing Grounds . . . Hooked. Gutted. Fried By This Government.'

The Ulsterwoman shakes her head irritably, puts the carphone that she'd been using over the top of her shoulder, telling the man to whom she'd been talking to hold. Gets back to reading through what she'd been able to access of the personnel file of Tristesse Merritt. One item of particular interest, a news story from the *Observer* dated less than four years ago.

PIG SLURRY MYSTERY OF IRA MAN'S DEATH

Carrickmacross, Ireland — The badly decomposed remains of Albert 'Click' Norris, former IRA crime boss turned Sinn

Fein parliamentarian, are being examined today by specialist Garda forensic officers, after a skeleton was discovered earlier this week under more than a tonne of rotting pig slurry near remote farm buildings, about fifteen miles west of the market town of Dundalk.

Mr Norris, a *Teachta Dala* for less than a year, went missing in January 2006. He was last seen leaving a traditional ceilidh in Castleblaney with a mystery blonde, subsequently dubbed the Icepick Chick by local media.

'That's definitely 'Click' in there,' said a plainclothes member of the Garda's Special Detectives Unit who was working the site and requested anonymity. 'But who did it for 'Click', how and why . . . only the pigs know and they ain't talking so much.'

Exactly a year after his disappearance, Norris — divorced with no children — was officially declared dead by the Monaghan coroner, after the minister of justice in Dublin waived the normal seven-year rule to facilitate a parliamentary by-election. Probate papers revealed Norris controlled a multimillion-pound empire of property, transport and farm holdings on both sides of the border.

Despite one of the largest investigations ever mounted in the Republic, the identity of the woman dubbed the Icepick Chick, after the Sharon Stone character in the movie Basic Instinct, has remained a mystery. The search was scaled back at the start of the year and, for their part, both the London and Dublin governments have denied any involvement in or knowledge of Norris's disappearance.

'It gives me a thrill, a real jolt in my old bones to know that bastard is definitely dead,' said Mary Sweeney, a 68-year-old widow, whose husband and son, both Catholics, were killed in 1990 at Killeen, on the Belfast-Dublin border crossing. They had gone to help a Protestant businessman from Belfast strapped to a so-called proxy bomb in his car, when it was detonated by remote control.

Norris was widely reported to be the de facto commander of the South Armagh Brigade, the IRA's most effective unit, from the mid-1980s until just before the Republican Army's military council announced its decision to end active combat in 2005. He then reinvented himself as a parliamentarian, winning election to the Dail Eireann to represent the Cavan-Monaghan district immediately to the south of County Armagh.

The judicial ruling that he had died allowed Irish media to fully report on Norris's murderous and criminal exploits and in the subsequent by-election a candidate from the rival Fianna Fail party was returned with a comfortable majority.

'He let it be known he was to be called Click, because, if you crossed him, it would be the last thing you ever heard,' said Sweeney, who said she has no doubt Norris was responsible for the blasts that killed her family . . .

Davane takes the phone off her shoulder and talks to the man who's been waiting. 'Max, are you telling me that Tristie Merritt is this . . . this Icepick Chick?'

'I'm telling you no such thing,' booms the voice down the telephone. Colonel Max Molloy's initials are in the margin of the photocopied newspaper clipping, assigning it into Merritt's file, which has a conspicuous number of UK EYES and SECRET stamps. Davane had reached Molloy at home. He was one of Merritt's last commanding officers and an old Northern Ireland hand himself. She can picture him now: standing military-straight in front of a roaring fire, solid oak beams, blond corduroy trousers, golden retrievers flopping around his feet. Molloy's next response is more nuanced. 'Do I know it was Tristie who did that . . . officially, no. If you're looking for a paper trail on this, forget it. Am I happy that Norris is dead . . . absolutely bloody delighted.'

'B-b-but . . . ' Davane can't fathom it. Those IRA volunteers and sympathisers, the ones who shape-shifted into grey-suited politicians, men like Norris, and Gerry Adams and Martin McGuinness, the security services had been trying to set up these people for years. And Merritt had done it *on her own?* . . . Davane, who had ended any involvement in Northern

Ireland in early 2001, always assumed that some criminal connection had caught up with Norris. This completely blind-sides her.

'Sheila, I love you to death, but since you moved to London, you've become such an old softie. Rejoice. The guy's dead. A-hundred-and-sixty-plus dead soldiers and policemen avenged. A big result for those of us keeping score.'

'But how did she get inside his . . . ?' These guys had a hundred goons watching over them. They were even known to use food tasters. She is genuinely bewildered, until an obvious puritanical thought slaps her in the face. 'Was she sleeping with him?'

'I can't answer that.'

'You can't, or won't?'

Police and fire brigade sirens roar past Davane, heading in the opposite direction. Molloy has paused. 'Do you know her background?'

'Kind of . . . ' With her thick fingers, Davane quickly reorders some of the pages in the file. Finds something that intrigues, from a consultant, based at the Duchess of Kent's Psychiatric Hospital at the Catterick army garrison in North Yorkshire. She skim-reads aloud. 'Merritt brought up in care homes, allegations of abuse and suchlike . . . '

Molloy's voice softens, suddenly confidential. 'Hundreds of boys and girls in care homes in North Wales were forced into a paedophile ring run by senior members of the local social services. It's all fact, out there in the public domain, went on for more than thirty years.

Before she could join us at 14 Company, Merritt had a thorough mental health check. I insisted. She made no bones about what had happened to her. She had the guts to square up to everything because she didn't want it to defeat her. The psychiatrist did his thing, whatever it is they do, and came away saying she showed no obvious signs of impairment. None of the self-loathing or guilt or anger that can bedevil these poor people . . . '

'She could've fooled you all . . . '

'Then that would be a plus mark in her favour. Remember. Deception is the game we were playing and we needed the best to be any good at what we do. Anyway. I'm not saying she was unaffected. The psychiatrist pointed out two things. One, that abuse victims sometimes suffer from an underdevelopment of the — have I got this right? — the hippocampus, something like that, part of the brain anyway. In moments of extreme stress, she can be surprisingly calm, logical, effective even, whereas of course you and I might be jumping up and down, losing our rag.

'Second, and this was of particular interest to us, Tristie dissociates. Probably a defence mechanism that she learnt when she was very young. She creates different characters within herself, alternates to her own personality. I feel an absolute cur telling you this, but she can think herself into separating what happens to her body from what happens to her as a person. Like an actress, doing a love scene. The physical contact happens but it means nothing. In practical terms, she could be humping logs in a mud pit one minute, and the next looking stunning in an evening gown, drawing attention away from her surveillance partner. That's what she does. She dissociates. As much as I know about this is that to get close to Click Norris, it was her idea to get a work attachment with a primary school in Dundalk. She turned herself into this blonde Aussie surf chick, with long-lost Irish connections. Watched a heap of episodes of *Hi-5* to get the character and the bouncy voice right, and off she went. Wearing these God-awful rainbow-coloured overknee socks and her hair in pigtail bunches. Crazy really . . . ' And there's a sound of a hard-as-nails army man sighing gently. Perhaps a little bit in love.

And you're calling me soft . . . Davane looks at her watch. 1503. Less than half an hour to the first of Merritt's demands. The Jaguar is still boxed in by the traffic and she feels the tension coiling in her stomach. The COBRA meeting, come on, come on.

' . . . but it was her way of keeping her head together. So, to answer your question, was she sleeping with him? I don't know, but would she, if it would serve the mission, save lives, whatever . . . I suspect, yes.'

Davane turns over an A4 sheet with a printed picture of Merritt. A snatched shot, telephoto lens, taken outdoors, perhaps on the sidelines of something like a regimental football match. She's almost hidden by the arms and shoulders of her fellow soldiers. A small, pensive smile on her face. She's wearing a beret, her camouflage-print combat jacket and trousers. Her stable belt (red-blue-red) and beret (green) in the colours of the Adjutant General's Corp. Nothing in the picture to suggest she is so out of the ordinary . . . in fact, in uniform and away from the demands of 14 Coy., she looks diminutive, sparrow-like. 'You miss her, don't you?'

The regret is clear in Molloy's voice. 'I never came across an operative like Tristie. Before or since. Definitely one of the best females we've ever had. When challenged, there was an aggression there. Cunning. Resourceful. A hunger for survival, and a capacity for ruthlessness that, well, it made me glad that she was on our side.'

'Exceptionally rude as well.' The Jaguar puts on a spurt of speed to cut across traffic moving around St James's Park.

'Coming from the queen of courtesy herself, I find that a bit rich. Look, Sheila. She had issues. She was something of a loner, not one of the boys in that sense. And there was an underlying mistrust of, and hostility towards, authority. We all have a little bit of that, but she had an extra plateful, believe you me. To be fair, once she believed, in you, or the mission, she'd follow through. So, if Tristie's on that plane, up there, she's your ace in the hole. I can't say more than that.'

The rear entrance to Downing Street is to the east of the park. Davane can see it zip by, lined up alongside the massive structures of the Treasury and Foreign Office. Taking the roundabout at speed, the Jaguar screeches and Davane jams up against the door, Pyjama-girl

402

squishing into her. She speaks with great effort. 'I don't understand how she ended up serving in Iraq and Afghanistan? I didn't think 14 Company deployed there. Too many dark faces.'

'There were some issues with getting army females to do the pat-down checks on Iraqi women. The militants suddenly started using women, grandmothers, little girls, strapped up with explosives. Multi-National Division South-East command in Basra asked us for our best female soldiers. Tristie was top of the list. Same cultural problems in Helmand too.'

'Well, if she's really *that* good, how come you let her go?'

'You've read about the injury . . . shredded her insides. Meant that she wouldn't be able to have children. She attended a Ministry of Defence tribunal to discuss compensation. One of the MoD lawyers, a civilian, a complete shit of a man who we've had problems with before, well, he thought he was out of earshot, so he made a joke about how expensive it is raising children these days, how Tristie should be thanking the MoD for saving her all that money. Ha bloody ha. He didn't know that Tristie reads lips. She picked up a thick glass ashtray, threw it across the room. Crowned him. Knocked the silly arse on his bum. Unfortunately, by the time I could go into bat for her, she'd quit. Typical in a way that she didn't reach out, try to cash in a favour or two. Just left, dropped out of sight.'

'Bollocks to that, Max, she sounds like a crazy to me.'

'Sheila, my love, my sweet, nobody who has

any sanity would be doing the work we do.' This from the soldier who, inevitably within army circles, is known as Mad Max. Followed by a warm, rich laugh of contentment. 'Dammit all, you were the first person who made me understand that.'

The White House situation room
1009 Washington time, 1509 London time,
2009 Islamabad time

The equanimity shown by the Canadians has been galling. Frustrating. Ottawa is so far behind the decision-making curve. It adds to the disquiet in the room. More than thirty minutes since Prime Minister Jemison had said he would get back to them 'presently'.

With PK412, they have been blessed in having an abundance of time on their hands, a luxury compared to the Operation Noble Eagle storylines that had been acted out. The assembled participants can check and cross-check every order and memo, scribble the perfect aide-memoires and make the paperwork clear and accurate for the inevitable inquiry to follow.

Yet having more than enough time has strangely undermined the simple decision to shoot the plane down. Too many people are in on the process, too many ums and ahs. The phone calls from on board the 777 are weighing on minds. And in the rioting shown on the newscasts from across the world they can clearly see the consequences of what they're about to

405

do. Anti-American sentiment on a massive scale ('not anti-damn-Canadian sentiment, of course,' the Homeland Security boss Salazar had grouched). Simple decisions are becoming harder and harder to make, as if time itself has become the enemy.

The most pressing logistical issue for Washington is to get Ottawa's agreement on where exactly to shoot down the Boeing 777. This must happen sooner rather than later, within Canadian airspace and over her territorial waters. Both parties had received from NORTHCOM/NORAD headquarters in Colorado a brief but powerful presentation about the AMRAAM's kill probability, the missiles that both sets of Hornet fighters are carrying. The speed of the missiles (very fast), that of the target (modest), and how hard the target would be able to turn (probably hardly at all). Kill probability, excellent. Which is why AMRAAMs go by the nickname Slammer, the briefer had added. No need to elaborate on that point.

Then comes the proverbial devil in the details. Jemison, the Canadian PM, is back now, the satellite glitches sorted, glowering into the camera. He prefaces his remarks by saying they've not reached consensus and there's an impolitic groan among the planners working in the background of the room. But Jemison, working his jaw from side to side, has one bit of meat to hold out: 'Without prejudicing my cabinet's final decision, and for the purposes of planning only, if this shoot-down is to take place, under no circumstance can the craft or any substantive piece of it land on Canadian soil.' He is at pains to point out that his position is grounded in practical considerations. Look at Lockerbie, Scotland, he says, when Pan Am 103 exploded at 31,000 feet. Eleven people had died on the ground. Burning, fuel-soaked wreckage had fallen in a line over one nautical mile long, slammed to earth so hard, and left such gigantic craters, that the impact had registered as an actual seismic event.

The Canadian prime minister signs off again, says he must get back to try to force through some sort of cabinet agreement. So the situation room is left to consider how far a Boeing 777 would fly, having been hit, but possibly not destroyed, by an air-to-air missile.

Nobody in the room could be certain. The FAA administrator had tried to explain some likely parameters: the best case, assuming quick and total destruction, would be a freefall from a height of 36,000 feet, taking as long as two minutes or as little as forty-five seconds, depending on the drag coefficient of the various plane pieces. The latter had been the Lockerbie scenario. One voice raised the 1983 example of Korean Air KAL007. That 747 had been attacked with cannon fire plus two air-to-air Soviet-era missiles, but had managed to stay airborne for twelve minutes before finally spiralling into the sea.

Worst case, said the administrator . . . under zero power most planes can glide horizontally ten times their vertical altitude. Thirty-six thousand feet is PK412's altitude. Just over seven miles. Multiply by ten. So, let's call it seventy miles of potential glide, Add another ten miles for margin of error . . . the American and Canadian senior military officers working at NORAD headquarters in Colorado and watching live agree they can take this as the outer limit of possibility. Far enough that the plane couldn't make land, but close enough that the Canadian government could be ready with a mass of helicopters and search craft.

So. At least part of a decision had been made. Eighty miles off the Newfoundland coast will be the point of engagement. On the plasma screen showing the dotted-line projected track of the 777 somebody has made a computerised slash mark at the POE. Less than an hour's time. More like forty-five minutes.

* * *

Around the situation room conference table, attention is now fixed on the six news channels, each showing a different version of the same thing. The Middle East and Islamic world in uproar. Jerky pictures of ambulance and fire crews wading into burning rubble. Soldiers sprinting for cover, cowering behind upturned cars, firing head height at unseen insurgents. Dateline Tel Aviv. Jerusalem. Cairo. Beirut. Damascus. Amman. Istanbul. Jeddah. Kuwait City. Dubai. Bahrain. Doha. Then comes Iraq . . . Baghdad. Basra. Mosul. Karbala. Najaf. Ramadi. Kirkuk . . . the Iraqi cities all blur into one after a while. Another trillion US dollars to put back together again. Just as disturbing are the reports coming out of Afghanistan . . . more fuel on the fire.

For the most part these are suicide bombings, but some are mortar attacks, a few straightforward machine-gun assaults. All aimed at US embassies and consulates, or businesses with American-sounding names. Banks. Hotel chains. Car showrooms. Anything Yankee.

Hence the continuing violence of the president's nose-picking. *Please make this nightmare stop . . .*

Hannah's chief of staff, Frank File, wears his perpetual harassed look, terribly put upon, and has asked a CIA briefer whether this explosive violence might have been coordinated. A conspiracy . . . why not? Some mysterious guiding hand would make the room feel more together, more resolute. 'We're looking pretty closely at these communications to see whether there's any coordination to this,' the briefer says by video from the CIA's Counter Terrorism Center in Langley, 'but it looks too random. Too careless and stupid, dare I say. This is being driven by the Internet. People blogging and tweeting their outrage back and forth, whipping themselves into a frenzy. The TV have no pictures to show so they run the tweets as a newscrawl under their main feed, put up their correspondents to talk about what's being blogged and how hot it is out there in cyberland. It's really one lot of Muslim zealots trying to outdo another, but stretched out all round the world wherever there are Muslims . . . like a perfect storm really.'

From the background of advisers somebody mumbles a little too loudly, 'Citizen journalism.'

At which the president snaps, 'Today I have come to hate citizen journalism. Absolutely hate.'

The room solemnly turns to a different screen, of which the Secretary of State asks, 'And what is the status of Pakistan?'

'Burn, baby, burn,' a hopelessly inappropriate, very Marine Corps response from the shaven-headed boss of the unit guarding the US embassy in Islamabad.

There is no Lamayette, and the rest of the CIA staffers are furiously shredding documents and demagnetising hard drives. Ambassador Nancy Zoh and the rest of the top staff have been helicoptered off to a US base in Afghanistan (The Defense Secretary whispers to an aide on board his US Air Force VIP flight, 'It's quite a day when you make people safer by evacuating them *into* Afghanistan'). But the embassy flag still flies proudly, and the huge diplomatic enclave is in the hands of a core of battle-hardened veterans. Both the defence and army attachés are back to being real soldiers again, hollering along the embassy roofs, marshalling the defences.

The 'Burn, baby, burn' Marine Corps master sergeant is the only person available on the ground for a live briefing with the White House on a shaky video phone. The sergeant, his shiny face smudged with crud and soot, clearly relishes his role. He speaks in a lazy California drawl. 'There are some guys popping grenades at us

410

from a way back, beyond our field of fire . . . couple of mortar rounds every two or three minutes. Hopeless aiming . . . some dude in a pick-up truck tried to ram his way inside, quarter of an hour ago, but the bomb went off when he hit a pothole. We watched the whole thing on night vision. Made a big splash, what with all those gasoline drums in the back. Stupid douchebag . . . excuse me, Mr President.' A little high with the adrenalin.

The sight of the Marine Corps soldier prompts the Secretary of State to share a reminiscence. He'd been serving as a political officer in the Islamabad embassy in November 1979 when it was overrun by a Pakistani mob. In the subsequent pitched battles a Marine corporal died and the embassy was wrecked, everybody scarpering into the fortified vault-like communications room on the third floor.

The Secretary of State's voice is barely above a whisper. 'Rumours had gone around that we'd captured the Grand Mosque in Mecca. Or bombed it, or some nonsense like that. Just a rumour, for God's sake, and suddenly there were people arriving in buses, climbing over the fence, wrestling bare handed with the Marines. Like the end of the damned world.'

The Secretary of State immediately realises his choice of nostalgia could have been better. If Pakistan's wildly volatile crowds would destroy an embassy based solely on rumour, what would they do for something based on fact, played out live on television?

The president attacks his nose. The others can

411

barely watch, anxious he might hit a blood vessel.

But those worries are swept aside when the man with the speaking-clock drone from the eavesdropping National Security Agency flashes on to one of the screens. He sounds agitated and looks decidedly nauseous. 'We've . . . we've just had a chance to listen to a heck of an interesting call from the PIA flight . . . I'll play it through for you presently . . . '

Gone is the monotone, replaced by a gasping quaver. ' . . . but the synopsis is that British intelligence appears to have an asset actually on board the flight. A woman by the name of Merritt . . . and she's blackmailing MI5 with secrets concerning our Trident missile programme. Communication protocols . . . '

It takes a second for the cogs to click and whirr into place. ' . . . she's demanding something like five hundred million dollars.' Pandemonium follows. The whole room shrieks with one voice . . .

WWHHHHHAAAAAATTTT!

The president rises from his chair like a ghost, his hand trembling with rage, and points at one of the communications minions. 'Get that Limey bastard prime minister on the phone, right now.'

On board PK412

The three members of Ward 13 have been getting an unasked-for crash course in Urdu and Punjabi swear words. *Choot* and *kuthi* and *bhenchoud*. Logic says these are the nasty words, because things are not going well.

This cockpit door is getting to be a pain in the arse . . .

On the flight there's a team of wrestlers from Gujranwala City. Remarkable physical specimens. Small men, bulging with layers of muscle, like Oddjob. Totally hairless. They're travelling to the US to compete in a collegiate series, and hopeful of snagging a scholarship or two.

According to Captain Salahuddin, their group leader had been delighted to find out that all the problems could be solved by simply busting down a door. He had twirled his fine sergeant-major moustache, very confident. *One door only, you sure? . . . Is no problem for me.* He'd clapped his hands like a maître d', and his sturdiest guy had trotted forward. Shaped like a human brick. Bracing himself at one end of the twelve-foot-long tight corridor leading to the cockpit entrance. The captain, Tristie, Button and Whiffler squeezed into the little recessed

413

area in front of the forward left passenger door to watch. She couldn't see any good coming of this . . .

There was a sharp military command from the wrestling leader, and the first guy, grinning madly, hurled himself forward. No doubt thinking this was a great honour, to be first . . . she couldn't watch as he thundered towards the door. Three paces only. *Thud-thud-thud.*

The *yeeeooowwll* that followed told its own story. Button the medic went to help. The wrestler's arm was weirdly lengthened and there was an awful elongation to his shoulder that looked all wrong. 'Popped it,' muttered Button, as he walked the guy off to give him some painkiller shots.

Like robots, another nine wrestlers tried. And failed. No doubt their willingness was partly old-fashioned pride. But she can see fear in their eyes, a little bit of panic too. *I have to do this, or our plane will be shot down.* They went at the door with their shoulders, their knees, kicking with their feet. Even with the serving trolleys. The results were the same.

Salahuddin waves Tristie forward to the cockpit door and, as she passes him, she commiserates with the crestfallen boss of the wrestlers. He looks deeply ashamed. This was not the first attempt by the plane's passengers to bust through the cockpit door . . . everybody on the flight knows (or has been told today) about the story of United 93, how passengers thwarted the 9/11 hijackers by storming the cockpit. Others aboard PK412 had tried in ones and twos. Young and old, fiercely determined and braced by a terrible fear. Not the danger they would face once inside the cockpit, but what lay slung underneath the wings of those Super Hornets. No way is Ward 13 discouraging any of this. The more the merrier. So now the wrestlers understand the reality, like everybody else who had tried and failed, and they stumble back to their seats very frightened.

Whiffler pushes open the forward left toilet, stands in the doorway, so there's enough room for the three of them to look closely at this undefeatable cockpit entrance.

Salahuddin places his palms against the fascia, pushes slightly, before shaking his head and turning to look at them both. He appears to be biting his lip to hide a reproachful nod. 'As we are the national airline of Pakistan, the country which is well-known as the Home of the Terrorist, it was in fact the Americans who made us accept these tough specifications for all our security fittings. Very much framed by what they'd suffered with al-Qaeda. If PIA want to get permission to fly to New York or Chicago, this is what you must fit . . . '

He goes on . . . 'Problem one. The access panel has been depowered. I don't know by whom, or how, but you see when I try to enter the codes, nothing happens. No numbers appear on the LED screen. Unfortunately for us, post-9/11, all these doors are required to have locking assemblies that include a component, in this case a latch and four different bolt-action claws, that remains locked whether or not the door is energised.

'Problem Two. The door's centre, hinges and latch have to withstand repeated jolts of two hundred joules of energy, roughly the same as a three-hundred-pound man travelling at ten feet a second, running straight at it. As you saw . . . ' he waves airily towards the wreckage of ailing wrestlers being treated in the first-class cabin ' . . . this door has passed with flying colours.'

From the side, a grim-faced Whiffler adds his twopence worth. 'And the captain's already told me there's thirty-five pounds of armour layered into the door structure to stop a bullet or a grenade . . . a skin of metallic mesh to stop an axe attack or anybody puncturing or sawing through . . . and fibre-glass face-sheets made of a material with even more stopping power than Kevlar . . . '

Salahuddin butts back in. '*And* the door frame is machined out of aluminium so you can't cut it out . . . the whole structure is anchored with steel bolts. You can't pound it down . . . the design specs called for no more than ten millimetres' deformation in any hinge, latch or lock under three thousand Newtons of force. That's equivalent to six hundred and seventy-five pounds travelling at twenty-four miles an hour. There's no way to punch through.'

Salahuddin, strangely, smiles an enigmatic smile.

Tristie ducks inside the toilet. 'Is there no way here?' She taps the waist-high mirror fastened to the shared wall with the cockpit. Both of them shake their heads. Whiffler speaks. 'Basically the same strength as the doorway, but without any of the supposed weak points, like hinges. And in a toilet, you can't even take a run at the thing.'

He points across the small corridor. 'On the other flank of the plane, you have the cockpit shielded by the fittings of the first-class galley, all fixed fittings, like the ovens and heating elements. They take up most of the width. What's left is enough for one small crew wardrobe and a slightly bigger closet, just behind you, where they hang the coats. But still that big thick bastard of a reinforced wall. You can't get through.'

Tristie feels, at least, an obligation to go through the obvious. 'Down below?'

Salahuddin tugs at the point of his beard, that damned twinkle in his eye. 'Despite what you see in the movies, there's no access from up here to down there, inside. Beneath us is the forward cargo compartment and the only way in is through the forward cargo door. It opens outwards, about fourteen feet aft of the front passenger door and below us.' He holds up an index finger. 'There is a room immediately underneath the cockpit, where the main hardware for the avionics is housed and maintained, but access for that is through an exterior panel door immediately behind the nose-wheel housing. You have to go outside, to get inside.'

'Hang on a second ... ' A piece of some stupid movie rings a bell in her mind. 'Are we missing something here? Acid or something ... isn't there something on this plane we can degrade that lock with, or the hinges?'

Whiffler throws up his arms in mock desperation. 'Tristie, are you mad? Acid? You can't even get toothpaste on to a flight now. Somebody's going to bring a jug of acid on board?'

Fair point.

Keep going, Tristie. Never let a problem beat you down. Time to think aloud. 'How about mercury? That's a corrosive. Somebody got a thermometer on board, a bunch of thermometers. We could pool the mercury.'

'Not allowed to bring those kind of thermometers on board for that same reason.' Salahuddin's turn to shake his head. 'Anyway, not fast enough, too slow. And you couldn't hold it in place. It would slide off the joints.'

She can feel a giant-sized pain needling into her head. Think, Tristie. Think. You must be missing something. 'I don't suppose any of your countrymen on this flight, Captain, look like the type who might have sneaked some weapons on board? Something useful.'

'Sorry not to be able to play to the national stereotype. But no, they look blissful and peace-loving. Like all Pakistanis.'

Tristie can't tell whether he sees the humour. They're on a plane that's been hijacked by one of his people. 'I know it's late in the day to be asking, but are there any air marshals on board, off duty maybe, anybody licensed to carry a gun?'

Salahuddin leans back against the cockpit door. His eyes piercing now and angry. 'Do you think the Americans would allow us to bring armed men on a plane to New York carrying one hundred thousand pounds of aviation fuel?'

'I see your point.'

Salahuddin sizes her up carefully. 'All our flights have an axe on board, an air-crash axe, as part of an emergency pack, with flares and shovels, that sort of thing. In case we crash somewhere remote.'

Whiffler's eyes light up. 'Where?'

'Safest place on the plane.' He jerks his thumb behind him. 'Stored in the cockpit . . . ' Another flash of amusement.

'Fuck me . . . ' Whiffler bangs hard on the toilet wall. Frustrated. 'I sure would like to meet the guy who thought up these damned stupid rules. Stick a ruddy axe up his cockpit door. Sideways.'

Tristie feels Salahuddin's been playing them like a fish. 'Truth time, Captain . . . ' He's certainly got well under Whiffler's young skin. 'You're enjoying this a little too much. Why the impish smile?'

Salahuddin takes a pace or two away from them, turns and braces a shoulder against the cockpit corridor. His eyes are smiling gently.

'Can I just say, Ms Merritt, you look at me now just how my beloved wife does. Such a pretty face you have, don't spoil it with angry thoughts. Please.' And Salahuddin uncrosses his arms, opening himself up. 'When she and I have arguments it is always the same thing. I tell her that wisdom consists of fully understanding the consequences of one's action . . . all the consequences, not just the obvious ones. I love

419

her very much, but she will not think things through. Perhaps this is a female condition. Certainly she finds what I have to say on matters very tedious. Carping, I think you call it.'

Tristie's immediate reaction is that this discussion is heading towards danger. She doesn't want the captain getting maudlin. 'As a female, I can say that Mrs Salahuddin has my commiserations . . . ' Let's not be thinking about loved ones. Not now. 'Please focus, Captain, we're trying to get into this cockpit . . . '

The pilot looks down at his highly polished shoes, wistfully searching the floor for the right words. When he's finally ready to speak, he looks between the pair of them and Tristie is startled to see him fall to pieces in front of her, shoulders heaving, his eyes full of tears. 'I wrote an internal memo five, maybe six, years ago, to the chief pilot 777 fleet. Copied all across the airline, to my brother officers as well, outlining the consequences we now face, building this wall of steel between the flight crew and the rest of the aircraft.' He sobs softly for a moment or two, before wiping his eyes gently. Pulling himself back from the edge. 'OK, so we're fighting terrorism and that is a good thing, but has anybody thought about the unintended consequences of how we chose to protect ourselves?'

Whiffler sounds a bit brusque. 'And?'

The pilot looks at him squarely, voice still unsteady. 'And nothing . . . ' His fists clench by his side. ' . . . nobody listened. I sent the same memo again in 2005 after a Cypriot 737 crashed in Greece. There was a problem with the settings

420

for the air conditioning, and the pilots and passengers were overcome with hypoxia. Oxygen starvation. One steward managed to claw his way towards the cockpit with an oxygen bottle, but must have wasted too much time trying to get the access code off the chief purser, who was probably delirious. As he got into the flight deck, the plane ran out of fuel. Crashed. One hundred and twenty-one dead.

'Less than a third of the number on this flight . . . ' For Salahuddin and Whiffler, the finger is almost out of the dyke, the emotions between the two men suddenly running very strong. On the edge of full-blown despair. Having totally immersed themselves in technical detail, they're ready to quit, convinced there is no logical solution.

'Fuck . . . these stupid, stupid, idiot people.' Whiffler spits out his words. Not good. His face is reddening and tension comes off him in waves. Tristie puts her hand on his shoulder, squeezes hard. 'Tristie . . . so help me God, if we get out of this, I will never go anywhere without a couple of charges of high explosive. Bit of CL-20 maybe, and some detonator cord. Never ever. Not happening again . . . '

Salahuddin is leaning against the door, now clutching his head. 'It's funny that you should say that.'

'Why?' she asks, still kneading Whiffler's neck. Trying to keep him upright and productive. She can feel his shoulders tremble, starting to shake.

'In my memo, I hypothesised that the only way to get into the cockpit would be to trigger a

421

massive decompression event from within the cabin. Deliberately. Like blowing open a window. How you would do that, I don't know, but the cockpit and cabin are fitted with a range of pressure sensors. Who would be able to get into the cockpit . . . I have no idea; anything not fastened down would be sucked straight to the pressure breach. But the theory stands. If the differential in pressure rises too high, the door is designed to pop open, to equalise, like a relief valve. Perhaps we could . . . ' But Salahuddin groans, slaps his forehead a stinging blow with the heel of his hand. ' . . . but, of course, *you idiot . . .* '

'*What?*' Whiffler and Tristie speak as one.

Never did a man look so completely miserable before. 'The actuation system to pop the door latch is electronically controlled. The door locks open and close through the action of steel armatures. They're moved backwards and forwards by solenoids. Electromechanical solenoids, which need current to magnetise. But *there is no* current in the door. The whole door system has been depowered. See . . . ' and he turns back to the LED access pad. Blank. Dead.

'Could we at least think about trying, Captain? Something along those lines . . . '

Whiffler grabs a paper towel, blows his nose. 'Wouldn't work. Wouldn't put current back into the door, Tristie. Even if we could somehow explode a window . . . damned if I know how to do that with, what, spoons, paper cups, plastic forks. Like a frigging *Blue Peter* project . . . '

Button hollers at them from the first-class cabin. Sharp and urgent. 'Tristie. Better come and have a look. Port side.'

They move quickly to join him, taking up position next to the windows. Salahuddin presses his nose against the clear plastic fascia and grumbles something that sounds like 'Bastards'.

The CF-18 Hornet that's parked about a hundred yards off their port wing is painted in what professionals call gunmetal grey. But, given too its menacing shape, it reminds Tristie more of the colouring of a mako shark. About the deadliest hunter known to mankind.

Just the tiniest maple leaf, red on a white background, is stencilled below the bulky ejection seat. The word *Canada* is reversed out and almost invisible, above the engine intake to the rear of the cockpit. The tail is painted in celebration of fifty years of NORAD. And that's when this plane's intent hits. NORAD. The US Navy Super Hornet that buzzed them before might have been, perhaps, nothing more than a spotter. She unfolds one of the TV sets, and thumbs her way through to the flight show channel to find out where the hell they are . . .

She uses the length of her thumbnail to measure the distance on the screen against the scale. Her heart sinks. Crap. They must be very near Canadian airspace already . . .

Just the one crewman, or woman possibly, with a battle-green flight suit and a hint of orange for the life jacket. Scanning them through a super-shiny black visor. No hint of humanity, like skin or hair, or a bob of the head. More like

423

an android, process driven, no doubt. Obey order . . . select target . . . arm missile . . .

Salahuddin leans over the plush first-class chair. 'What is the significance of *this* plane, please?'

No point bullshitting themselves any more. 'Probably, this is the plane that's going to shoot us down . . . '

COBRA meeting
Downing Street, London, SW1A

Sheila 'Noppy' Davane thinks this has to be a historic diplomatic low point. She listens to the US president raging at the shrinking British prime minister, a handful of senior cabinet members cosseted around him. Shell-shocked civil servants behind them line the long expanse of this panelled room.

' . . . and you were going to share with us the fact you lost this critical software feature, the essence of the whole goddamn Trident programme, *exactly when?*'

There's a lot of mumbling and looking down at notes. A ghastly lie is about to be told.

'I'm afraid, Mr President, I'm guilty as charged. Guilty of taking my eye off the ball on this one. If you feel that I've let you down . . . ' An understatement, but the British prime minister oozes reasonableness, in a classically trained public-school-to-Oxford-to-merchant-bank sort of way. '*Mea culpa*, Charles, my dear friend,' and he proceeds to castigate his own people, mocks their intelligence, says he never thought for a second . . .

The prattle of politicians lying to each other

and lying to themselves always sounds the same to Davane after a while. She doesn't much care for the politicians she serves and they don't like her. An uncomfortably needlesome and irritating reminder of the limitations of democracy, an affront to their cosy sensibilities.

Davane is standing deliberately out of sight, at an angle to both the screen and the wide-angle lens that is beaming reciprocal vision back to Washington. Leaning against a column.

Just minutes before, Davane had been waved into the COBRA meeting by a grim-faced Home Secretary, and limped stiffly towards a distant place at the baize-coloured table. The discussions were mostly about the escalating riots, what to do, but she noted that a synopsis of Merritt's file was lying open in front of both the Home Secretary and the prime minister. That was when all hell had broken loose.

It started with one of the female assistants, trying to run through the heavy oak door faster than the door was willing to open. The room winced as she ran into the door's sharp edge, trying to relay news that President Charles Hannah was on the warpath. Clutching her head, looking like she might faint, she managed to get out, 'He knows about Merritt and the Trident.'

A wide shot of the situation room had flashed on to their screen. Big brother, muted for the moment. The president was leaning over a long table, glowering into the camera with an almost unhinged look of deep malevolence.

The prime minister had quickly leaned

forward to eyeball each of his COBRA room conspirators. 'We're all clear what it is we're saying to the Americans?' One part statement of fact, one part question. A last chance for the naysayers to speak, and it took a minute for the PM to iron out the few remaining malfeasants.

It was then that Hannah had been switched through. And he'd been going at them ever since, sounding — to Davane — like an overpowered, under-oiled machine. 'If you *think* the American government will *stand by*, and not put *every* resource into tracking *down* those treacherous thieves *you're* about to pay off . . . '

A long time ago, early seventies, part of Davane's M15 training had been entrusted to a portly former grammar schoolteacher, no longer considered safe around teenage boys, but evidently OK to instruct future generations of the security service. He had taught Russian and Latin, and over the months drummed into Davane the necessity of embracing chess. 'Use the game, Sheila, to order your thoughts,' the teacher would exhort, 'to give you an organising principle. Otherwise all this chaos and skirmish that we see from one day to the next means nothing. Search for the deeper and more patterned purpose, then you will have isolated your enemy's strategy.' All secrets flowed from two simple questions. *Cui bono?* Who benefits? And *Cui malo?* Who is harmed?

As the Ulsterwoman listens to President Hannah venting his frustrations, reduced now in her mind to the faint sound of an insect drone, she works through the permutations. Racking her brain. *Cui bono? Cui malo?* Her mind goes over and over the same point . . . what am I missing here?

And she keeps coming back to Cambridge professor Grigor Rothko . . . Britain, the US, Canada, Pakistan, the Middle East, the Islamic world, each staring down respective gun barrels. And the first shot is about to be fired . . . in a perfect circular firing squad.

In chess terms, Davane is quick to recognise that America (Britain and Canada too) faces zugzwang, German for 'a compulsion to move'. An insidious, strategically awful place to be. Doing nothing is not an option. It is *your* turn. You *must* move, even if it's like being in a burning dinghy in shark-infested waters . . . you don't want to. Washington must act even though movement in any direction will significantly weaken her position.

What else had Rothko said, when she was so quick to hang up on him? Her palms feel sweaty, genuine alarm ringing through her, as the president's hectoring rumbles on.

'*Just hope you know what you're doing?*'

She grits her teeth, squeezes her eyes tight shut. The sheer physical force of her complete focus elicits a mouse-like squeal of concentration. She can't see the querying expressions of the rest of the room, is beyond caring anyway. A number of the civil servants throw her looks of complete contempt . . .

In the dark space of her mind, there's a sliver of something edging in and out of her reach, a flash of colour in the shadowy depths. Through sheer willpower she will get to it ... I *will* ... that message from the cockpit. From 'Zaafir'. Moving into reach, her hope rises, then, like quicksilver, it fades to black ... A scratchy high-frequency radio message because they were in the middle of the Atlantic, beyond the range of normal VHF. No radar coverage ...

Her corpulent grammar school instructor bellowing, *Cui bono? Cui malo?* And Professor Rothko peering into the lens ... *Just hope you know what you're doing.*

OK, Sheila, she's demanding of herself, in the wide-open spaces of your imagineering, answer me a question. If this is bad — the certainty that this Pakistan Airlines plane is going to be shot down — what about this situation could be even worse?

Her eyes flick open. A look of complete horror. Her mouth agape. *Oh my God* ... A knife-edge of ice-cold fear cuts down her spine.

Davane bolts forward, jarring the long table and several chairs. What were once querying looks in the COBRA room turn to abject bewilderment, as this silver-haired, roly-poly auntie from the darkest of M15 shadows barges in front of the video camera, waves her arms, turns to face the two sets of audience that she MUST connect with and SWAY ... *Oh my God* keeps running through her mind. I've heard that voice before ...

'Mr President, you've had your turn ... please, will you now shut the *fock* up ... '

On board PK412
1028 Washington time, 1528 London time,
2028 Islamabad time

There's a scene in *Schindler's List* when Ben Kingsley's character, the key Jewish fixer for Oskar Schindler, finds himself swept up and herded on to a train headed for one of the death camps. As the train slides away from the platform, Schindler, actor Liam Neeson, runs from one boxcar to another, desperate to find Kingsley. In each carriage, as Schindler scans the faces, he doesn't find anger, or pleading, or a murmur of protest, even movement. Just beaten-down blank faces. Empty of hope, and squeezed of all feeling.

It was Jews then; mostly Muslim now. Tristie's looking at those same faces, row after row of them. Empty of all hope.

The Ward 13 trio walk through this nightmare of death-pale, soon-to-be-dead faces, in an awkward convoy, guiding the injured, young Gujranwala wrestlers and their team leader towards the back of the plane. No more hysteria. No display of anger, despite the new fighter jet that's buzzing them. A few tears, a little sobbing, and time for hushed farewells on Airfones. From

430

various quarters, the sound of different prayers being intoned, eyes closed or turned to heaven. Quiet fearfulness. Waiting on the inevitable.

Every so often, the bleakest irony, the babble of a toddler. Happy to be alive.

As they edge towards the rear, the cadre of travelling parents and well-wishers accompanying the wrestlers spring to their feet. There's a welcome and relieving hubbub of noise and activity. Hand luggage comes thumping down from the overhead lockers high above, and soon the air is full of the smell of muscle balms, exotic, potent stuff, and the squeal of bruised men being manipulated and massaged.

Button and Whiffler are standing just fore of the rear toilets, next to a particularly miserable-looking lad with a droopy left arm, helping him get something from one of the lockers over the central tier of seats. Button's a huge man, with a giant wingspan, and even he has to stand on tiptoe to reach inside.

Watching, Tristie finds herself doing some dead-reckoning. It seems strange not to have taken it in before, but this aircraft cabin is huge. As in a seriously high ceiling. Certainly compared to the Lockheed Tristars that the Royal Air Force use to trundle around the world.

She stops Salahuddin as he walks up the aisle. 'This cabin is very high, Captain.'

His mood is on automatic pilot as well. 'What of it?'

'I don't suppose there's any space up there, between the internal overhead cabin lining and the skin of the plane?'

431

'Why do you ask?' *Come on, Salahuddin . . . pull your finger out.*

She chooses her words carefully, says them slowly. 'Because I haven't given up yet.'

He rocks his head this way and that. Unsure. Unwilling — who knows. He rubs slowly around the shape of his lower lip, considering his options. He seems to have pulled himself back from proud-but-defeated. Finally he dredges up a response with a weary shrug. 'The Boeing 777 is the first modern airliner with a truly circular fuselage . . . '

Tristie scans from one side to another. 'But . . . isn't the width of the cabin a lot more than the height?'

'We are standing on an inserted floor surface, Ms Merritt. The fuselage is basically a long circular tube. Twenty foot and four inches wide in all directions, rivet to rivet.'

She jabs her index finger upwards. 'Again, how much space between the cabin fittings and the actual plane fuselage?'

'Down the length of the fuselage? At its midpoint, the highest value? About forty inches.'

She frogmarches him into the nearest galley, a little to the rear of the trailing edge of the plane's wing, and shutters the curtains. Two stewardesses and a purser look up, mute and indifferent. Waiting. For infinity.

'*Forty inches?*' She measures up to her hipbone. 'That's more than three feet of crawl space.'

'Some airlines use this fact to create a dedicated crew rest area. Build in some cots, a little private stairway. Very nice. But you want to go into the cockpit, yes?'

'Of course.' She feels a need to stir up a spark of urgency here.

He reaches up to one of the plastic storage trays and rummages around for a letter-writing set. Clicks on a colourful ballpoint pen, *Madame Tussauds — Amsterdam*, and gets sketching. Basic side shot of a plane. Tail. Undercarriage. Fuselage.

'This is my Boeing 777 with its nice straight body. Look. Perfect . . . ' Then he draws a series of dotted lines bisecting the plane just to the rear of the cockpit window. ' . . . until you get to the nose section. Section Forty-one, we call it. The nose is actually the same shape and design as the Boeing 767, a significantly smaller plane. They do this for interoperability. To make it easier for the airlines.'

She looks over his shoulder. 'OK.'

'The 777 fuselage has to shrink dramatically to fit into that smaller 767 cone, the barrel-shaped Section Forty-one nose. Like squeezing a litre into a pint pot. It's the crawl space, your three feet, that is sacrificed. The three feet is there from the back of the plane to the bulkhead at the front of first class, that's your basic tube shape, but it's not there by the time you get to the cockpit. The crawl space has tapered down to nothing.'

'It can't be *nothing*.'

'Nothing.'

'I don't know what you mean.'

'I mean *nothing*. English. As in no thing there.'

'Do you know this, it's on a plan you've actually seen? Or is this an educated guess?'

Salahuddin looks stern, his jaw rigid. He chooses not to answer the question directly.

Instead the pilot holds up the ballpoint. Shows it clearly, thumb and middle finger stretched over either end. 'This pen is just perhaps six inches long. I would be astonished, absolutely amazed, if there was more than the length of this pen in crawl space by the time you reached the over-cockpit area.'

'*You are kidding me* . . . ' Tristie can feel the adrenalin beginning to kick in. 'We've been playing with zero *this*, and calamity *that*. And you've just given me a glimmer of hope, you beautiful, wonderful man . . . ' He puts his hands up to ward off the cheek-kiss he correctly senses is her next move.

Rushing out of the galley, almost straight into Whiffler and Button, she gives them the quickest brief on what she plans to do. With her left hand shaped into a letter C, she mimics the size of the pen, Salahuddin's guess at the possible crawl space.

Whiffler snorts his approval. 'That's a good 12 inches. We're well sorted.'

'Whoa. Stop now.' Tristie rolls her eyes. 'Back up, you're saying that's a foot long? Christ Almighty, Whiffler, *that* . . . ' she looks at the arc between her thumb and middle finger, ' . . . *that* is not 12 inches.'

Wounded now. Whiffler bristles. 'How come you're the expert on what a foot is?'

Pause.

Standing in the aisle, with passengers now focussing expectantly on them, Button and Tristie look at each other. Not quite believing. It doesn't seem the right moment to be having *this* dicussion. Then the huge medic, perhaps not the smartest guy in the team, barks his reply.

'Because she's got a bloody foot, you idiot.'

To which Whiffler pulls a dismissive face, like they're both clearly out of their minds, before mumbling, 'ten, maybe eight inches then.'

'Halve that and you're getting close . . . ' Tristie shakes her head in disbelief, on the edge of laughing out loud. Any other time she'd rip him full of holes. A good soldier could tell the difference, *hear* the difference, between a 7.62 and a 5.56 round. But if that same soldier was male, and you asked him about inches . . . well, don't hold your breath.

She carries on, a new confidence whipping through her. Part of this was optimism, part amusement at Whiffler. He is *her* soldier, *her* responsibility, and she is damn well not going to lose any of them. 'Button, round up some more willing wrestlers, anybody else in the cabin who looks stout. We're going to need to build a human tower of sorts. Whiffler, stop worrying about your tadger and follow me . . . '

Salahuddin is padding quickly behind them as they run up the aisle. He extemporises all sorts of questions and worries. Fretting about the avionics and cabling ducts. Forty per cent of the avionics and flight control systems are in Section 41, many of them engineered into the overhead panelling. Drama. Drama. Most of all he wants to know how they're going to penetrate the fibreglass fascia of the cabin linings. 'This is a very specialist job. I don't even know how to begin getting through all the decorative panels and support structure. Very complicated.'

'Captain, that's why we have Whiffler here. He and Button are Paras. And the Paras are the world's experts at breaking things. So you and I get to stand back and watch.'

Whiffler is already balanced on the headrest of the first class seats, bobbing around between the front of the first-class cabin, the bulkhead and the narrow corridors that link the galley to the cockpit. Looking upwards. Pushing and probing. Testing for weak points. Energised again.

'Whiffler. I need a decent-sized hole up there. Soon as.'

'Sure thing.' He bounces like a monkey from a first-class seat, levers one foot across the aisle, on to the fixed shelf of one of the lockers so he can feel the ceiling panel for the first time. Legs akimbo, almost at full stretch.

Tristie turns away . . . some make-or-break phone calls to make.

The White House situation room
1035 Washington time, 1535 London time,
2035 Islamabad time

All eyes are on the naval steward who strides importantly to Charles Hannah carrying an embossed silver platter, with a nice lace doily and, on it, the presidential headache tablets.

Hannah snaps back three pills and the water, freezes for a moment, dabs a handkerchief against his reddening nose, then swirls back into the present. Hawkishly poised over the long table, fingers splayed, staring across the Atlantic at this house-of-mirrors-plump M15 woman, clad in a buttoned-up Harris tweed suit and skirt, like some ghastly matron out of a Harry Potter movie. Moreover, her excitable Antrim accent, which seems to compress all her words into the roof of her mouth, leaves some in the room wishing the video feed had subtitles.

He tries a bit of controlled breathing before returning to the subject at hand. ' . . . so you're saying that this recording from the plane is not Zaafir, the steward we had been led to believe . . . '

In his vision, the woman identified as Sheila Davane looks first to the president, then at her prime minister and immediate boss, the Home Secretary. Insofar as one can tell, they seem to be encouraging her, egging her on. Plainly she is not someone used to the limelight, but she is someone for whom the words prickly and irritable seem to have been invented.

Davane reaches out of shot for a plain manila file. Takes from it a photo, holds it towards the lens, obscuring her face. 'The voice you heard belongs to this man . . . ' a young, Manchester-born trainee chef, with a pencil-thin moustache and wispy chin-beard, standing in front of a black flag with white Arabic lettering, wearing an Arafat-style keffiyeh ' . . . his name is Hassan Imani, formerly Glen Lynch. Age around thirty. Converted to Islam in prison where he was serving time for handling stolen goods. He was one of eight men convicted of conspiracy to murder others and endanger aircraft. The so-called Heathrow Airliners Plot . . . '

In the room in Washington, several aides move quickly around the table, fanning out a series of copied reports that originated seconds earlier from MI5 headquarters in London. Written corroboration of what Davane is saying . . .

'Most of the accused filmed martyrdom videos, including Hassan Imani. The normal *bogshite* about going to paradise, killing *Kuffars* and so on. The media rebroadcast a lot of the video material in the news, transcribed it and put the audio online, MP3 files, normal court reporting.'

Davane looks back at the prime minister one last time. 'What we heard this afternoon from

PK412 is an audio recording of Hassan Imani's suicide video. Word for word — voice analysis, everything, confirmed. Some guy with a tape recorder is in that cockpit, playing games with us . . .'

'Games?' The Secretary of State leans forward. 'Can't this be Imani himself?'

'He's in jail.' And Davane leans back against a thick table, wincing slightly, to let that fact sink in. 'We just double-checked with his prison governor.'

The permutations of this, that's what's killing everybody. What does it mean? Finally Attorney General Braddock turns to the acting director of the CIA, a haunted-looking man, with dark, staring eyes, much taken to wearing black. 'Does this make any sense to you, John?'

All eyes turn to John Romen, career hatchet man. Romen, for his part, is startled, needs some time to think. He was actually miles away in another thought process altogether. *The directorship of the CIA is within my reach, should be mine by rights.* But this unwelcome intrusion of events from the real world means things are not going well, not at all.

In the waiting-around for Ottawa to make their decision, the Defense Secretary had queried from his VIP plane whether the CIA could share some of the more recent cables from Bill Lamayette on the subject of this General Ali Mahmood Khan character. 'Least we can do is see what Lamayette has been warning us about these past weeks, this Operation Macchar thing.' Acting CIA director Romen had instinctively looked to his partner in the dark arts of Washington subterfuge, the National Security Advisor, and the NSA had suddenly remembered needing a toilet break. With no blocking plan, and no obvious allies around the table, the cables had come tumbling out, each one prophetic in its detail . . .

From two months ago: *I CANNOT STRESS ENOUGH THE INADVISABILITY OF UNILATERAL ACTION AGAINST GENERAL KHAN . . . HE PLAYS A LONG GAME . . . AND SOMETIMES THE BEST COURSE OF ACTION IS TO WAIT.*

His last message before 'dying' in a Peshawar bomb blast . . . *GET IT INTO YOUR HEADS: PAKISTAN IS LIKE CHICAGO WARD POLITICS IN THE 1920S. EVERYBODY IN THE GAME IS UGLY. IT IS WHAT IT IS. DEMOCRACY AT WORK. THERE ARE NO GOOD GUYS AND THEY ALL WANT TO THINK THEY HAVE THEIR FINGER ON THE SELF-DESTRUCT BUTTON. GENERAL KHAN ACTUALLY DOES . . .*

Everybody in the room had groaned, and groaned again, as they read through the sheaf of cables, glancing up every so often at the screen showing Lamayette still flopping around in a drugged fugue in an interrogation suite at Bagram airbase. Lawyers have a term for this sort of evidence. Exculpatory. Gee, he was trying to tell us we'd have a problem on our hands . . . and you know what, we do.

So, Romen is a man under a serious cloud. Everybody in the room is worried, but only he is worried for his job, being the person who most clearly dropped the ball. Moreover, he is a man who likes his subject matter to be rational and orderly, nicely laid out in briefing papers for him to peck at. But now he is exposed: no briefing papers, nobody's opinion to hide behind, and no instinctive ability to function in such a mad-minute scenario. His skills lie elsewhere. So he deftly paddles the ball back as hard as he can. 'I've got a lot of respect for Ms Davane's work; I'd go with her analysis soon as anything we could come up with. Perhaps — Sheila, is it? — perhaps Sheila could talk to their strategic motivation . . . '

Davane crosses her arms, irritated. Her face scrunches inward, very pugnacious. '*Strategic motivation?* Are you guys asleep over there? The US shoots down a plane with three hundred people on board, and the first thing you do is release the hijacker's mad ramble from the cockpit to make the point this was self-defence. Case closed: some riots around the world, lots of broken glass, unhappy people, but basically, manageable in the scheme of things. Then comes news that the mad ramble was actually somebody else's mad ramble, somebody we know is locked up in jail. Ah, you say, but the radio transmission . . . ' and she punches one hand into another in admiration ' . . . that's why the hijacking *had* to happen in the middle of the Atlantic. No VHF radio. Not enough range. And anyway, we could have triangulated that signal to the Boeing's position. High-frequency radio is the key to this. But HF signals bounce around the upper atmosphere like a skimming stone. Meaning in effect we think that high-frequency ramble came from the plane but it could just as easily have been transmitted from, I don't know, France, or the Caribbean . . . you just need to know the Shanwick frequencies, which are all a matter of public record.'

Davane leans closer still. 'Just to be clear. I'm not saying the plane has *not* been hijacked. Clearly there's been some kind of loss of control. But it's been orchestrated to ensure that when the dust settles and the wreckage and bodies come up from the bottom of the sea, there will not be sufficient compelling proof . . . no balance of probability, or whatever legal matrix you guys are using to . . .'

Romen senses his opening, his chance to shine. His voice bristles with indignation. 'You must think our countrymen and women extremely incurious and unintelligent . . .'

The Ulsterwoman stalks so close to the lens that the whole screen in the situation room is taken up by her jowly face, crevassed with lines. Her pale grey eyes leer into the camera . . . a pantomime monster. 'Don't you worry what *I* think. Worry about what *they* think . . . Do the words IRAQ, GATHERING THREAT and WEAPONS OF MASS DESTRUCTION not mean anything to you? How much mistrust of one superpower can the global order endure before the same thing has to happen? One third, *one third*, of your citizens still believe 9/11 was an active federal conspiracy! . . . what are these people going to make of PK412? Will they give

442

you the benefit of the doubt on whether those three hundred people had to die? When all of this evidence is fed through the prism of the Internet, you've got . . . ' Davane waves a hand, to summon up the right expression. ' . . . you've got a doomsday scenario. Checkmate, which I learnt today is from the Persian, *Shaah Maat*. It means the king is made powerless. Paralysed without being hit by anybody. Likewise America. We see her today astonished. Amazed, Perplexed. Humbled. That is what these constant references to Qissa Khawani are about. A massacre of innocents in the 1930s by British forces that should have become a rallying cry across the whole world. This is Qissa Khawani twenty-first-century style. So, my commiserations . . . '

'*COMMISERATIONS* . . . ' The president startles the room with the anger in his voice. There's a prickle of sweat over his top lip, a blush of red colouring his neck, and a slight juddering through his right hand. 'What the hell are you talking about commiserations for?'

Clearly Davane hasn't got the hang of the video lens, for she steps even closer, looking, in Washington, as if she's pressed up against a porthole. 'I say commiserations, Mr President, because I presume you will still be shooting down this plane . . . '

The smooth, silver-haired vice-president coughs his surprise from his airborne office. 'Did you say we'll *still* be shooting down this plane?'

Various cabinet figures from Transportation and the FAA, plus their senior staffers, start to huddle, whispering louder and louder. Nodding their understanding, shaking their heads, for the penny has finally dropped.

'We haven't solved the problem . . . just got ourselves a different one.'

And the Ulsterwoman stares gimlet-eyed at her audience, the rest of the COBRA room totally obscured. 'Unless I'm mistaken that plane is going to fly itself to New York, come what may. The flight plan I saw indicated all the waypoints had been entered up to and including John F. Kennedy International. The flight management system will do what it's told. Fly around and around its final waypoint until it runs out of fuel, at which point the automatic pilot disengages and . . . ' her pause is dramatic, timed to perfection, just a hint of a little twinkle in her eye ' . . . and over a city of nine million, Flight 412 becomes a hundred-and-fifty-tonne coffin with no place to land . . . '

Moments later the video conference is over, and there's a nervous scurrying in the room. One of the few still seated, in a cloud of wonderment, Admiral Jim Badgett, Chairman of the Joint Chiefs of Staff, whistles softly through his teeth. He speaks for the whole room. 'We sure are in a real pile of doggy doo-doo.'

444

On board PK412

They're by the doorway of the first galley, in economy, forward of the wing. Button and Tristie. Button holding an Airfone and a pre-paid credit card from a stack Tristie has. Whiffler's wobbling atop a small pyramid of wrestlers and passengers, trying to whack through the underside of the roof's cabin lining, hefting an aluminium galley inset that's deliberately bulked up with soft drink cans.

Button, as ever, looks untroubled though keen to help. 'With all this crap going on, do you really think they're listening in, GCHQ?' he asks.

'That'd be my bet . . . they know my voice and their computers would match me up in a heartbeat. We might be trying to do good work here, but we're no less expendable for that.'

'Why can't we get Weasel or someone to put the DRAM chip in an envelope, just post it to them?'

She flicks away an irritating bounce of hair from her eyeline. 'Because, Button, we need to trade it for the immunity document. They know now who we are and what we've done. I've fixed up the handover to be in London someplace, which is why they'd be especially alert to any calls to the London area. Three hundred passengers on the plane, perhaps only ten, twenty per cent using the phones now, how many of them would be calling London? Not many . . . ' Forward and aft, the same vacant faces watch them, waiting for the horror, that explosive *craaack* of the airframe giving way. What a way to go. Please God, if it comes, make it quick. ' . . . Weasel already knows to ditch the phone I called him on. But we've got to get word to him. Just confirm things. *And find out if we got the MoD's dough . . .* '

Button bites his lip, nods his great shaggy head and gets dialling.

'*Helloooo*, Piglet . . . and how the hell are you today?' Button chuckles quietly at whatever the response is. 'Good one.' Some mordant soldier gag probably, about how far up shit creek the three of them on the plane are. ' . . . Do you happen to be near the Internet, young friend? Try the Sun's website.'

Button turns his back and unfurls his long frame against the doorway of the galley, the phone cord stretched to the maximum.

'Be careful what you say now, laddie . . . ' He rubs his bristly chin with the back of his hand. ' . . . Is it now?'

Button is suddenly interested in the eyelets and hooks that hold up the galley curtains, counting them off with his sausagelike fingers. But listening all the time.

'I'm sure Weasel would appreciate a call . . . you know the number? . . . I thought not . . . ' and he reads it out from a piece of paper Tristie hands him. Eleven digits. They'd all agreed on a basic encryption system when Ward 13 first came together, to transmit any set of important numbers to one another over open lines. Subtract four from the value of the fourth digit, six from the value of the sixth and so on. 'Why does it start with four and then change every second number?' Tristie had asked them, knowing the key to any code is simplicity. Answer, *'Because* England beat Germany four-two to win the World Cup.' They'd teased her about the code. So what, the code is simple, but effective enough to keep Noppy's computers gummed up for a while . . .

Tristie scrutinises the back of his nodding head, thinking she might just tear Button's hair out if he doesn't let on soon. Twelve months of planning, Ward 13 . . . and all she can do is listen second-hand to the news arriving. Her mind fills with images of flag-draped coffins at RAF Lyneham being escorted down ramps of C-17 transporters, of Wootton Bassett, the nearby Wiltshire town where so many have taken to standing in silence as the hearses pass through, and of the quiet rage and terrible impotence of those who made it home, alive . . . but shattered.

Will all this be worth it?

Button's face doesn't give anything away. 'Yeah . . . he might appreciate the help . . . good enough, mate . . . cheers.'

He clicks the button to end the call, houses the phone, thanking the nervous mother whose seat the phone belongs to, and happily *coochie-coos* the little dark-haired girl on the woman's lap.

Button stretches out the aches and stresses in his body, like a lion after a long snooze, turns to Tristie. 'Well . . . ' big-bastard smile on his face 'we got the money.'

The next thing, she has hopped up into Button's arms, squeezing the life out of his neck. Fizzing with relief. His voice is inches away yet his words seems so small and remote, as if he's whispering to her from the far end of a hangar. ' . . . Piglet read me the story, the actual yarn from the Sun and the Daily Mail website just to make sure . . . three hundred and fifteen million bloody quid, girl . . . Defence Secretary saying he's going to make a formal statement to the House tomorrow . . . Exchequer to make it official . . . you fucking did it, Tristie.'

The White House situation room

Nothing anyone can say will change Ottawa's mind. Not now that they too know the key element in the prosecution case, that the angry, rambling voice from the cockpit is actually a recording, and may not even represent a genuine threat . . .

Which is why the Canadians say, No.

Prime Minister Kent Jemison reaches out to the edges of his table, braces himself, and makes his final pronouncement. 'So, Mr President, my friend, as provided for under the terms of our agreement, we must decline. If you wish to pursue this as a legitimate NORAD engagement, that is your prerogative, but my government will be standing down our forces effective immediately.' Everybody in the room has tried, worked all the angles they could think of, but there hasn't been a threat or inducement that's made a blind bit of difference. The truth of it lies in Jemison's barely concealed look of blessed relief, as he signs off. Happy to take his politician's head out of the noose.

One small concession. Ottawa will not object to a US aircraft engaging the Boeing 777 in Canadian airspace. 'Makes good common sense,'

Jemison had offered, in a conciliatory tone.

And everyone looks at their watches like automatons. Point of engagement. Twenty-one minutes . . .

There's a surge of movement out of the room, into the corridor outside, mingling with a steady flow of others streaming back and forth.

In this flux, the president has his face in his hands for a moment, and flops back into the executive chair, feeling the pinch. Those closest to him clearly hear his exasperation. 'After half a century, who would have thought some nobody in Pakistan would be the guy to drive a wrecking ball through NORAD?'

Admiral Jim Badgett, Chairman of the Joint Chiefs of Staff, speaks soothingly. 'Mr President, NORAD is ninety per cent US forces anyway, so let's worry about the symbols later. We need to agree on the mission profile as it stands now, for those two navy Super Hornets.'

President Charles Hannah looks up, and his eyes scan the room. A couple of key figures have excused themselves. 'Of course we do, Jim. I'd like to hear everybody's thoughts, the principals, of course, when they're back in the room. Then I'll make that call.'

Badgett again. 'Shall we institute a first-stage alert to the New York and Jersey authorities . . . ' he finishes the question weakly ' . . . if we let the plane run out of fuel?'

A quick, decisive presidential shake of the head. 'No. I don't think that's an acceptable option.' Then an intriguing idea curls its way into Hannah's thought process. He ponders it, tap-tapping his fingers on the magnificent sheen of the conference table. 'Yes . . . but before we get to that stage, of making that call, I want to look into the eyes of this General Ali Mahmood Khan. Get a sense of the man. See if there might not be an off button to this whole thing. A way of drawing back from the edge. Even at this late stage.'

'You mean a negotiation?' Badgett blinks his incomprehension. 'This is seriously late in the day . . .'

'No, Jim. Not a negotiation . . . but a dialogue. Let's hear what the man has to say.' And the president's voice is calm, and assured, authority restored. At last he can see his way through this, a little doorway of light opening in the distance. 'It takes just one person to have the courage to ask the first question.'

★ ★ ★

Immediately outside the situation room, from along the tight thread of carpeted corridors and tucked-away meeting rooms, come mutterings of concern about the spineless Canadians and the future of NORAD.

But the National Security Advisor and the acting CIA director have more base motives in play. James Romen has pulled his erstwhile confidant to one side, prevented him re-entering the room. Giving the man a sharp taste of the misery he's suffering. He hisses his words with venom. 'Do you understand . . . those freaking cables from Lamayette . . . to think I trusted you, and to think frigging Lamayette was basically right all along . . . they're going to clean my clock, when this is over . . . whatever big plan you and the president have of reforming the CIA in his master's image, forget it . . . because you need me and I'm fucking dying in there, man.'

The National Security Advisor, seriously buck-toothed, is rock steady, shameless, and tough as old boots. Goat's eyes, no sign of shock or tension. Chosen to put a bit of bite into the president's security priorities, he'd had almost four decades of gun-slinging and knife-wielding in the dark alleys of the global oil game, and finds Washington politics by comparison, and people like this Romen, too soft, too damned obvious.

So he takes the bull by the horns, steps well inside Romen's personal space and, with a finger, taps out his message on the other man's chest. Strong, rich, east Tennessee accent. 'Listen. Quit your pissy whining and get your game-head on for today. Understand this. For you, the key play here is that Trident DRAM chip.'

Romen frowns. His face saying, *You mean we can forget Pakistan?*

The National Security Advisor clamps his hands on Romen's shoulders. 'You make sure your people in London get at least one of those pukes involved in stealing the damned thing. All the better if there is some kind of British Army tie-up 'cos then we can rub their stuck-up noses in it big-time, hold the mother of all swords to their necks and then drip-drip the story at this

452

end. Remember, kiddo, all we need is for fifty per cent of them folks out there to think we know what we're doing. We can't be Superman all the time, but we can be halfway competent. That's why we need to get an arrest on this DRAM thing. We'll show 'em there's nothing we won't do to protect the United States of America.

'Understand this and you may get the key to the big boy's toilet, James . . . ' Slap, slap on Romen's cheek, with a gunslinger's cool smile. 'The administration of Charles Hannah does not compromise when it needs a huge distraction to stop them grubby little media types from pissing all over the president.'

The Green Bean Coffee Shop
Camp Lemonier
US Combined Joint Task Force Djibouti, Horn of Africa
1741 local time, 1541 London time, 1041 Washington time . . . Nineteen minutes to estimated point of engagement

The ensign trots towards the coffee shop, a hand shielding his eyes from the blaze of the setting sun and the little zephyrs of sand that cut across this 500-acre desert-blast camp.

In air-conditioned comfort, Lieutenant Commander Nancy Breen watches the young man as he moves from being framed in the windows to the translucent, sealed door panels designed to keep out the unforgiving Djibouti summer heat. Instinct tells her he brings bad news. More bad news; for the coffee shop's chocolate shot machine is kaput.

'What is it, Ensign?'

'MacDill. On the phone. Urgent, ma'am. The White House on the hoof about something.' MacDill Air Force Base in Tampa, Florida, where Central Command, USCENTCOM, is based. Camp Lemonier used to fall under USCENTCOM, as did every US military asset from the Horn of Africa, through the Gulf and into Central Asia. Then it was transposed into the newly created AFRICOM, based out of Stuttgart, Germany.

Which is why Breen is a little put out, discomposed, as she strides quickly into the broiling heat towards the camp's intelligence HQ, threading her way past the sand-painted hard billets used to accommodate the 1,800 military and civilian staffers.

Anxious calls from Stateside are not usual. Camp Lemonier is a political hot potato, a base for Predator strikes into wild and woolly places like Somalia to the south, and Yemen to the north; a staging point for naval anti-piracy efforts in the busy, strategic straits of Bab el-Mandab, and an out-of-sight holding area for select, high-value detainees.

The latter is Breen's particular area of expertise. She is the camp's military liaison with a twelve-strong team of Behavioural Science Consultation operatives, known as Biscuits. A mix of CIA staffers and deniable freelancers. The interrogators.

When she grasps the handset, it's still clammy to the touch. Disconcerting. 'This is Lieutenant Commander Breen . . . ' Instinctively straightening. She recognises the voice on the other end. An army lieutenant general, based originally at Fort Bragg, but now working out of MacDill. One of the military's top psychologists.

'Breen. A heads-up for you on General Ali Mahmood Khan.'

'What exactly, sir?'

'In about one hundred and twenty seconds' time you're going to get a call asking you to present the general for a live video link-up with the White House. It appears he was high value, after all. So he needs to look . . . decent. You understand?'

Breen puts a hand to her mouth, anxious, not wanting to say the wrong thing. Not yet. 'Can you just hold for a moment, sir.' And she quicksteps behind her desk, starts roaming through her computer files. Lists of detainees and the day-to-day sequencing of their interrogations. Sleep deprivation, the old Yoko Ono albums and Star of Israel flag treatment. Here we are . . . General Ali Mahmood Khan. She opens the file with a double click. Scans the latest paperwork. Rechecks it, because the guy is a general after all. *I thought so* . . . and she picks up the handset again.

'Sir. That detainee is deceased.'

No small measure of panic in the voice. '*Whaaaat?*'

'Sir, we sent through a notification to AFRICOM almost forty-eight hours ago. I believe the Biscuits did the same, to Langley. Asking for direction on the corpse.'

'How is that possible? Don't tell me bedsheets, please?'

'No, sir. Not at all.' Breen smarts a little at that. *What kind of operation do you think we're running here?* 'We haven't done a full autopsy, but this is what it looks like. The detainee pulled all of his hair out, sir. He had a good head of hair. Must have timed it to perfection between

456

the hourly inspections. Balled it up with a lot of spit and faeces, and packed it, like a wedge, into his airway. Drifted into unconsciousness, at which point his tongue muscle would have loosened, closed things off for good. Died from lack of oxygen.'

Breen feels a little peppy to have got that right. She *had* known it was Khan. The paperwork to AFRICOM *was* correct, all properly time-stamped. So, with confidence restored, she offers a small observation of her own. 'I got a sense, talking with the Biscuits, that the deceased knew something was coming . . . something ominous.' And now, feeling positively on top of her game, Breen pushes the point. 'Sir, so what should we do with the body?'

But there's nothing on the other end of the line.

On board PK412

Meanwhile, at last, there's a hole in the ceiling of the cabin. It had started off as a series of cracks, forced by Whiffler and his swinging aluminium galley inset. He and the wrestlers had then taken turns forcing their fingers through, trying to break off or peel back as much of the fibreglass composite as possible. Nasty work, evidenced by the vivid smears of blood at the workface.

But, at least, there's an opening. Sort of a modest, star-shaped rip. And as a consequence there'd been no suggestion that anybody but Tristie be the one to try to worm up into the roof cavity.

Captain Salahuddin is kneeling on seat 1D, dismally looking up at the hole. 'I do wish you the best of luck, Ms Merritt.' He doesn't quite shake his head in hopelessness, but near enough.

'When I get up there, what should I expect?'

'Up there?' Salahuddin blanches. 'To be truthful I don't really know. It'll be pitch black first of all . . . ' And suddenly helpful, he *clap-claps* his hands, rabbits off an Urdu instruction for, presumably, a torch. 'You will find a series of cross-ways spars, like ribs, designed to reinforce the shape of the fuselage. If

458

there is room, you must cross these, to keep going forward. Of course, the roof will be tapering downwards all the time. Less and less space the farther forward you get. Other than that, a lot of foil-wrapped cladding will separate you from the actual skin of the fuselage.

'Can I rip that off, if I need to, to get more space?'

He makes a who-knows face, palms upward. 'I don't think that would make any difference. But maybe. Why not? What have we got to lose?' And he moves on, quickly. 'Just don't pull any of the wiring. Running underneath you, from the back of the plane forward, will be a lot of cables. Bundles this thick,' he makes an O with his thumb and index finger, 'coming over the cabin and into the cockpit. Bundles and bundles sleeved together with tie-backs and cushion clamps.' And, putting aside the 'no-touch' rule, he rests a worried hand on Tristie's arm. 'I imagine there'll be many sharp edges. Exposed metal beams and brackets, hex nuts. That sort of thing. So painful.'

'I'm OK with that, Captain. If the cause is good enough,' and she starts to disrobe. Talk of hex nuts and clamp brackets means she can't afford to snag on anything. The pinstripe ivory twill skirt suit has to go. She lays the jacket on the seat-back next to Salahuddin.

He sizes her up closely. *You're really going to do this?* Searching her eyes for any sign of weakness and, evidently satisfied, offering a smile of encouragement. 'The way the beams and spars are laid out you might find you need to go

sideways, even backwards, just to keep going
forward, if you know what I mean.'

She nods her understanding. It's a horrendous
proposition. Slide, slither, get there how you will.
She unzips the side panel of her skirt. Steps out
of it, and lays it flat on the seat-back, flicking a
little piece of dirt off the lace hem. 'And when I
get into the cockpit?'

Mouths open, their eyes on little stalks, about
a dozen men are staring at her. Salahuddin.
Whiffler. Button, and the eight or nine
goggle-eyed Pakistani wrestlers . . . quite a sight.

'What is it?'

Oh.

Now Tristie understands. The woman wears
undergarments . . . shock horror. A garter-belt
pantyhose. *Quick, make the sign of the cross.*
White lace thong with polka dots and matching
bra . . . *She is the Devil . . .*

'What did you guys think I had under my suit.
Army fatigues?'

A touch of irony, as Sheila 'Noppy' Davane waits by the vast, neoclassical structure that houses Britain's domestic security service. Her protection team consists of two of Tristie Merritt's former comrades. Current, serving members of 14 Coy., who do a lot of M15's muscle work.

All three scan the approaches to the junction where Horseferry Road comes in from their left, heading straight over the roundabout to the north end of Lambeth Bridge, as Millbank runs up the side of the building and continues parallel with the river.

Just the lightest traffic. Except, of course, for the two vans parked as inconspicuously as possible. A bespoke laundry service and a flower delivery agency, complete with Interflora logo. Nice touch. The laundry service is M15's. The other, Davane presumes, with a wry grin, must be somebody scrambled on behalf of the CIA. All told, probably about twenty different sets of people are waiting to listen in live to her cell phone . . .

Boy. She'd enjoyed giving it both barrels on the link-up with Washington. Real catharsis. There's something ornery and obtuse hard-wired into her Protestant, Carrickfergus-farming DNA that loves drawing America's attention to the perils of terrorism. Such johnny-come-latelys they are. This, after monitoring the cash flood coming across the Atlantic all those years, for Sinn Fein and the Provos, from church groups, social clubs and bars. Dippy Irish idiots, most of them were, with their mawkish, romantic sense of patriotism.

See how it feels, friend?

Her phone rings, and she's quick to answer.

'*Noppy. I've got to make this speedy.*'

'I'll bet you do.' Davane looks left and right. 'How close are you to the Canadian coast?'

There's a long pause. Wasn't expecting that, were you? She can hear a quiet discussion in the background. '*Salahuddin guesses about a hundred and fifty miles.*'

'Well, you've got seventy miles to go, then.'

'*That's when it's going to happen?*'

Davane doesn't offer anything. Just sniffs rather loudly, before continuing, all business. 'So let's get this over with. I've got your letter from the Attorney General. Just as well he was in London . . . ' She tightens her grip on the slim brown attaché case.

'*You don't sound particularly cut up.*'

'Tristie, I had a look at your file. You do good stuff. You did choose a worthy cause with those injured soldiers. And well done, by the way, from Colonel Molloy. He likes you very much, and I

462

do trust his judgement. So between the three of us, things could have worked out . . . but for today's unfortunate circumstances, of course. If I could have helped, well, I would have tried. Belie that reputation I have.' One of the 14 Coy. squaddies moves away from Davane's shoulder . . . points across the bridge facing them, to a pale grey Bentley. Moving very slowly, about halfway across, travelling at kerb-crawl speed towards them. They can't get a read on the plates. Not yet.

'*A car is approaching you, Noppy. Nice car. You need to get into it. Just you. Not Pinky and Perky by your side.*'

It doesn't surprise Davane in the slightest that Merritt's got a pair of eyes on the ground. Good eyes evidently because the body they're attached to is not visible to her and her protectors.

Merritt, you're actually OK, Davane acknowledges. Better than OK. 'The Bentley?' The silver-haired Ulsterwoman has to squint a little, even with her thick bifocals. 'I'm not getting in.'

'*When you see who's in the car, you'll get in . . . I promise it's safe.*'

One of the army guys is reading the plate number into a cuff-microphone. Delta Three. Juliet. Uniform. Romeo. Three.

'*Pinky and Perky can trot along beside the car, you're not going far.*'

'We'll see about that.'

'*Noppy. I've got to run. It's getting a bit sporty at this end . . .*'

'Tristie . . . ' But the line is dead.

The Bentley pulls to a halt at the roundabout

at the north end of the bridge, maybe thirty yards away, giving way to a trail of cyclists passing down Millbank. That's when the realisation hits Davane. Her instant reaction is to choke and splutter, and — dammit all — appreciate. Another plus-mark for this girl Merritt.

She nudges the cuff-mike soldier. 'Stop the plate check. Look . . . ' And she points to the front of the car. Delta Three Juliet . . . stupid way to check vanity plates. It spells out D3 JUR3. Or, from a distance, DE JURE, a Latin legal expression, meaning 'by right'.

Davane and her protectors can't help but be entranced as the car eases towards them, and its cream-coloured, retractable canvas roof starts to fold away mechanically. One layer into another, until all is safely tucked out of sight. Twenty-five seconds, and by that time the Bentley has eased up on to the kerb in front of them. There's a heavy bass, reggae beat.

The liveried chauffeur quietens the music. And beckoning to Sheila 'Noppy' Davane, from the back seat, with his gold-encrusted fingers and a Caribbean smile of purest white teeth, is the most irritating, vexatious barrister in Britain. Defender of villains, upholder of human rights, perpetual scourge of the police, and M15 in particular. Thick dreadlocked hair spilling over his shoulders. Basking in the fact that the car, his taste in European women, the music and the Rastafarian dreadlocks drive most people, certainly every last *Sun* and *Express* reader, to absolute distraction.

In the most polished of upmarket accents, the barrister belly-laughs his welcome. 'Do come and join me, Ms Davane.' So speaketh Beveridge Clairmonte, native son of Hagley Gap in the Blue Mountains of Jamaica, LLB, qualified 1984, Queen's Counsel 2007.

With the shiniest of white teeth, he radiates bonhomie. 'Let's put past hostilities to one side. I believe my client might have something of value for you, and vice versa. Shall we proceed without further ado?'

The White House

In a small communication suite off the main situation room an urgent conference is taking place. Leading it is the Secretary of State. Although the president is also present, he's been asked to say nothing and stay out of vision of the various phone cameras. 'Keep yourself in the background, Mr President . . . but you need to listen to all of this . . . so you know what's happening out there.'

The past five minutes have been a roll-call of disaster. From the US embassies throughout the world the first diplomatic reactions are being filtered, passed up to the State Department's various bureaus and on to the White House.

By phone, from the State Department complex on C Street, comes a trembly voice, wired with too much coffee. 'So far we've heard word formally from . . . ' The undersecretary of political affairs, reading through a long list of countries ' . . . Tajikistan. Afghanistan. Brunei. Malaysia. Maldives. Niger. Jordan. Oman. Indonesia. Kyrgyzstan. Nigeria . . . ' There's a pause, paper is shuffled, and the roll-call continues. ' . . . Bahrain. Bangladesh. Chad. Morocco. Tunisia. Algeria. The UAE. Pakistan, obviously.' The undersecretary takes a long, despairing breath. 'The footprint is the Middle East, South, South-East and Central Asia, and basically the whole of sub-Saharan Africa.'

The Secretary of State shakes his head, as an aide silently shorthands all of this for the record. 'And this has come through in the past two hours?'

'Pretty much,' replies the disembodied voice. 'But mostly in the past hour. That's when it really took off.' Something like awe in his voice because this, this . . . wildfire has never occurred on anybody's watch before.

The Secretary of State turns to the president. 'I know you've made the decision to interdict this flight in the best interests of protecting the American people. I understand. But this is what the rest of the world thinks: those names are the countries that have already signalled — remember, the plane is still in the air, the passengers alive — that there will be definitive and forceful diplomatic repercussions. And these are our *allies*. Where there are parliaments they either have voted or will soon; where there are absolute rulers, they have ruled. Most likely it will fall like this: if these countries host US military bases, they will move to have these closed, or make the functioning of the bases deliberately unworkable. Where there are Status of Forces Agreements allowing our troops to operate, they will sue to have these cancelled. Mostly these SOFAs operate with at least a year's notice period . . . but so many countries suing us, all at the same time, and for the same reason, will give this an irresistible force. I am sorry you have to be here, but there's no gloss to put on this, this . . . ' and his face blanks for a moment; the situation doesn't compute with normal vocabulary ' . . . this collapse.'

From his side seat, President Hannah looks truly aghast, the chief executive watching his Fortune 500 company unravelling into a penny stock in a matter of hours. 'I can't believe this is happening. Happening to me . . . '

On board PK412

Tristie tells herself, I am not giving up, *I am not*, but I have to go back. She's about ten feet forward of the entry hole Whiffler made, perhaps over the galley on the right side, but has to go back. It's not going to work . . .

Jesus. The pain, you wouldn't believe. Dragging her hips across saw-edged wing-nuts gouging her flesh, inching along, snagging every damned thing . . . All her clothes are long gone. Discarded. She's naked.

She shoves back against one of the aluminium cross-spars, to retreat in the direction of the hole. It's hard to push against the friction of your own dead weight. Shoulders strained, neck muscles weary. She has to cant her head, like a miner working a thin seam. It's cold. In the torchlight, her breath clouding. Her heart thumping. Her skin frozen numb.

As she works her way back, Tristie's feet feel the jagged edges of the opening. 'Whiffler . . . Whiffler.' A note of panic in her voice. 'I need you.'

She lets herself sink on to the icy floor of the cavity.

Whiffler puts a hand on her foot as he pokes

469

his head up through the gap. 'What is it, Tristie?' He can see her in the torch beam, looking back at him over her shoulder. He boggles a bit when the first thing he sees is her clenched backside, before looking up the line of her leg, repeating, 'Tristie, what is it?'

Whiffler still has the most ridiculous pudding-bowl haircut.

She realises why she feels so short of breath. There's no oxygen supply up there, other than what percolates up from the hole. It explains the tightness in her chest, and the sudden panting. 'You've got to . . . get me . . . some oil. Cooking oil . . . Olive oil . . . anything . . . I saw some . . . in first class . . . the focaccia bread . . . Go.'

But he doesn't move. He looks around the roof space, testing struts, pulling on brackets. When he speaks, his voice is apologetic. 'Just wondering what you need the oil for?'

She gives a long sigh of exasperation. Her lungs feeling curiously deadened. 'Because there's a slot . . . I need to get through . . . over there,' and she points to her ten o'clock, ' . . . little bigger than . . . the size . . . of a letterbox . . . and I need . . . to be . . . oiled up . . . to have a chance.'

She can almost hear his smile. 'You're kidding?' Tristie Merritt, naked oil wrestler. *Woo, woo.*

'No, Whiffler . . . and I'm going to need . . . your help . . . can't reach . . . my back . . . and legs.'

He disappears like a mouse down a hole. No doubt the only person on the plane smiling.

Off the main White House situation room

President Charles Hannah breaks the dismal silence in the small communications suite. 'There must be some way we can work this out?'

'Work this out how?' The Secretary of State looks up from a series of mindless jottings. Cubes. Lots of cubes.

'You know, *work* . . . Christ, we can't be the first administration that needed to buy a friendly face . . . Cajole. Fudge. Encourage. Incentivise these countries, to make this thing go away.'

The Secretary of State's expression is tired and blank. He dabs a button on the telecom console. 'Is the prince still on the line?' Somebody within the snug suite nods and moments later there's a burst of white noise and then a live picture on a wall-mounted screen, satellited from a French chateau in horse-racing country. One of Washington's trusted back channels to the Middle East. 'Mr President . . . out of sight, please.'

Prince Abdullah of Saudi Arabia sits at a wide desk, in front of an expensive bookcase full of leather-bound tomes. Looking extremely well fed in a dark polo-neck fleece. The foreground is cluttered with a forest of gold-plated pens, sticking up from their holders. The Yale-educated prince has no formal role within the US-Saudi structure but has served several US presidents as an honest, astute sounding-board of information and opinion, both within the kingdom and the Gulf states, as well as the wider Muslim world.

'Good afternoon, Abdullah. I want to thank you for your patience.'

The prince waves his hand. It is nothing. 'We are old friends. If I can be of any assistance, God willing, I want to be.'

Grave tone. 'Events are forcing us towards a decision . . . '

'I can assume what that decision will be . . . ' and from his ornate study, the prince wags his finger at the camera ' . . . in a world of change, this will have consequences.' Rubs his hand back and forth across his silvery moustache. 'Perhaps consequences that you and I, with our fixed world view, cannot begin to imagine.'

Pause. The only sound is the quiet hush of the air-conditioning.

The Secretary of State says: 'We believe that we have no option, at this point. It is our hope that at least if the world does not support us, they will at least understand the terrible choice we had to make.'

'What terrible choice, my friend?' The prince holds up a meaty hand and counts off slowly. 'One. You now believe the recording played out from the plane to be false, maybe there is not even a terrorist on board. Two, perhaps there is not even any weapon involved. Three, Canada does not stand with you. Four, the Islamic world

472

is in uproar. Five, you have mid-term elections in four months and fund-raising for the presidential primary cycle starts in earnest in nine months. No doubt the president's people are telling him how this will be political suicide: how it won't play in Peoria, to have the president appear to be . . . ' and the prince makes inverted commas with his fingers ' . . . to be 'weak' in the face of a bunch of Muslim crazies. Did I miss anything out?'

The Secretary of State shuffles uneasily in his chair. 'I'm still here.'

'Your problem, Mr Secretary, is that nobody is listening. You're either the fully fledged super-power you claim to be, in which case nobody will believe that the country that builds the plane, teaches the airlines how to fly the plane, even sets the rules of how the cockpit doors should and should not work . . . that this country with the most powerful armed forces and the smartest universities does not have a way to solve this problem. Or you're not that superpower, in which case your problems run deeper.'

The Secretary of State tap-taps the end of his pen on a presidential jotting pad. 'As crazy as it seems, Abdullah . . . that is the very truth of the situation.'

'What do the Pakistanis say?'

A hopeless shrug of the shoulders. 'Next question . . . ' The previous Musharraf adminis-tration had reworked the constitution so significantly it was no longer clear whether it was the president or the prime minister who controlled the real levers of power, or therefore

473

whom Washington should be entreating. The Secretary of State had been on video link with Islamabad only fifteen minutes before, trying to convey the latest news, that the cockpit door was disabled, how sorry they were, etc. All the prime minister had wanted was to have his cabinet watch him shriek about appropriating US assets in the country, and demand a scheme of reparation payments. Domestic political posturing.

The prince looks to one side, and a bare, elegant female hand places a cup of steaming coffee in front of him. He smiles his thanks before turning back to the camera. 'Understand this and you will understand the problem you face: in our hearts we are a nomadic people. The whole of our history and culture tell us we are always journeying across deserts, looking to protect our flock, searching for that next waterhole, or oasis. Which is why we say, *It is good to know the truth, but it is better to speak of palm trees* . . . That is why, my friend, these people are not interested in the truth, *your* truth. Every politician in the Arab and Islamic world will take from this tragic story what they know their peoples want to hear.

'And that can only be bad for you. Very bad.'

By Lambeth Bridge
A hundred yards from M15's headquarters

The barrister Beveridge Clairmonte leans forward to tap his chauffeur on the shoulder. Pull off the road here. They're on the London Eye side of Lambeth Bridge and the Bentley convertible eases like a hovercraft, up and on to the pavement, at this point a generous twelve feet wide. Clairmonte has a deep voice, Paul Robeson-like. 'I am sure Ms Davane can waive normal parking rules on this occasion.'

'Hhhhmph' is all that Davane can manage.

They'd not done more than twenty miles per hour or covered five hundred yards since leaving M15's headquarters. So, as Davane looks around, she sees her two protectors from 14 Coy. easing out of a jog. Looking alert yet relaxed, scanning this way and that. Behind them the two vans, laundry and floral services, are jockeying for position, doing their best to be inconspicuous.

And as in a bad movie, Davane is aware of five or six young crew-cut males, granite jaws, thousand-yard stares, suddenly finding Lambeth Bridge an excellent place for playing musical statues. Pretty ordinary tradecraft from her colleagues in the Metropolitan Police. Public holidays mean no street vendors; she makes a mental note to pass that on too.

Clairmonte opens the door for Davane and offers her his hand. She declines. With a bow, he motions her towards the bridge's balustrade, the railings, an intricate latticework of wrought iron, painted the same deep red as the leather benches of the House of Lords. The downstream side of Lambeth Bridge.

Davane leans against the railing, flips up the lapels of her tweed jacket against the sudden chill coming off the river and tries to organise her hair, which, after a ride in an open-top car, is no longer as composed as she likes. She sees the tide coming in fast, and the Thames looking as mucky-brown as ever.

Clairmonte joins her, gazing way downriver at a distant object. A plane coming into land at City Airport. He is six-one, six-two, that sort of height. Strong shoulders, pale skin. Perhaps a bit of Botox around the mouth and eyes, because his skin is a touch too tight for his smile to look comfortable.

Between the two of them, there's a well-worn groove of effortless animosity, such that they don't have to rush into conversation. Small talk would be an insult to either party, and both of them understand the rules . . .

Davane and Clairmonte are standing beside a lamp standard that rises thirty feet above the railings. There are pairs of these lamps either side of the apex of each of the bridge's arches. Five arches in total. Because she can't see under the structure, Davane guesses they're over the second arch. Not quite midpoint.

Having finished with her hair, she wants to get on. 'How is this going to work, then, learned counsel?'

'We wait for a call.' And taking a Nokia phone from his coat pocket, a rather fine camel-hair number, he looks at it carefully. 'Pre-paid, of course. Brand new. When the call comes I pass it to you.' And the barrister's own displacement activity is to part his dreadlocks from the back, so they fall equally down both shoulders.

Behind Davane, watching closely, are the two men from 14 Coy, one of them already on the cuff-mike, passing on the news that a call is expected, incoming. Unknown number. Confirmed. The M15 surveillance camera and tracking audio had picked up the same information from their vantage point in the laundry service van.

In the flower delivery van, amid the hastily assembled CIA field team, also privy to M15's radio traffic, there's a serious outbreak of swearing.

'I don't suppose the gentlemen on foot who've formed a discreet semicircle around us are your employees, contractors and/or agents thereof.' Clairmonte doesn't even bother to look, so obvious are the guys hiding behind their newspapers.

Davane juts out her jaw, in the vague direction of Parliament. 'Most certainly, they are not.'

'Whose, then?'

'That would be only guesswork on my part.'

Clairmonte's questioning eyebrows are flecked with grey. 'You do have the amnesty document with you?'

Davane holds up the brown briefcase. 'Everything the girl Merritt asked for.'

Reassured, his voice softens. 'So why the big snatch squad?'

It's the Ulsterwoman's turn to brood over the skyline, some of the most recognisable landmarks in the world. She picks out the desolate flagpole atop the magnificent Gothic Victoria Tower, indicating that Parliament is not in session. Yes, of course, the Whitsun break. My, these parliamentarians work hard.

Another piece of local history that this blow-in from the colonies would not understand . . .

Georgie Porgie pudding and pie
Kissed the girls and made them cry.

George Villiers, first Duke of Buckingham. Murdered, 1628, on an earlier version of Lambeth Bridge. Just yards from where they now stand. King James was so enraptured by George's boyish good looks, it made the business of marriage and royal offspring almost impossible. Hence the rhyme.

Davane is musing on the history and culture of this country. She herself has taken a faithful oath to defend her monarch's realm. The most important commitment in Davane's life, and something to which she has given her entire being. *This* monarch. Queen Elizabeth II. Descended by blood from the very same James I

478

. . . She is convinced of one thing. In real and unforgiving situations, if the state is to survive, it must act, must be prepared to do anything that is 'necessary' to ensure its durability, irrespective of the cost of 'freedom' . . . good people may have to suffer. Like the rise and fall of the Thames, statecraft has its own unstoppable rhythm. And Davane is about to cast a stone in that dark tideway.

The immediate question for Davane is whether or not to tell the truth. It boils down to this: Merritt is clearly the brains of the operation, and there's no earthly way the barrister can contact her now.

Less than a quarter of an hour to go . . .

In words that are strangely difficult for her to form in her throat, Davane finally answers. 'Your client will receive everything she asked for. But nothing more. She forgot extradition, to face appropriate charges in another jurisdiction . . . perhaps America. Maybe the excitement of the moment convinced her she knew what she was doing. But the law can be so treacherous . . . ' and she glares at Clairmonte before leaning once again on the balustrade ' . . . so treacherous, once you're out of your depth. Don't you think, counsel?'

With great relish, Davane anticipates the look on the face of this elegant prick of a barrister. Merritt's mistakes were undoubtedly based on *his* errors of advice. So she half-turns, expecting something delicious to savour.

Instead, Clairmonte rocks back on his heels, roaring with delight, Father Christmas and

Falstaff rolled into one. 'My. She surely read you like a book, Davane.'

It's all a little disconcerting for Davane, at the centre of this encircling mantrap of police, M15 and CIA officers. She thought she'd played her hand to perfection . . .

White House situation room
1048 Washington time, 1548 London time,
2048 Islamabad time . . . Twelve minutes to
scheduled point of engagement

The round-table discussion is almost ended, the room dead quiet but for the single voice. A lot of lives at stake . . . either way. On the ground, or in the air.

The consensus is leaning heavily towards taking down Flight 412 in the next dozen minutes. President Hannah has required each of the National Security Council to keep their remarks to thirty seconds. This is no time for oratorical windiness.

In the ugly but brutal analysis, it boils down to this: off the Canadian coast, take down a few hundred foreigners (plus fifty-four US citizens at last count, including a former Peace Corps contingent), or condemn to death perhaps several thousand Americans somewhere in the Tri-State area when this behemoth of a plane and its passengers crash out of the sky. The Chairman of the Joint Chiefs of Staff, Admiral Jim Badgett, delivered grim news, backed up by the team in attendance from the Federal Aviation Administration. The query had been whether you could nudge the thing out to sea, like flipping the wings of the V1 Doodlebug rockets in the Second World War. Badgett shakes his head emphatically. No. There is no plane, civilian or military, that could safely tip the wing of a 777, such that it would change course permanently. Moreover, the flight management system would compensate and simply fly a slightly different bearing to its next programmed waypoint.

Only the Secretary of State had voiced a serious objection, and when prodded, confirmed this could be taken as a 'no' vote. He predicted an avalanche of diplomatic nightmares, a tidal wave of disaster completely paralysing US interests around the world.

Last to speak, before the president, is the National Security Advisor, who's in the middle of a history lesson.

' . . . I know that a number of you are troubled by the fact that Canada is not by our side on this, that they've opted out. Perhaps you're thinking somehow we should do the same, follow their lead.' The NSA rolls his tongue over his buck teeth, which catch the light from the overhead spots. He savours the silence, the dramatic moment.

'Nineteen sixty-two, same thing. Canada walked away from us, in the midst of the Cuban missile crisis, two gut-wrenching days in October, *the* pre-eminent crisis of the last sixty-plus years. Nuclear annihilation on the line. And the Canadians wouldn't follow our lead, refused to upgrade their force status to

DEFCON3. Why do I mention this? Because we've been here before, because in the end, Canadian shilly-shallying didn't count for diddly-squat, and it won't count today.'

The NSA frames his next words with a deliberate quaver of emotion. 'The Evil Empire folded, we prevailed, and a young president by the name of Kennedy, striving to advance the same agenda of hope, outreach and tolerance as this administration, showed the world that more important even than this . . . is the security and peace of mind of the American people.'

No vote is called. Not needed. The Secretary of State's concerns are noted, and he accepts this, along with the directive that his staff urgently work up some big 'blue sky ideas' that might knock the worst edges off global reaction.

'Right, Jim . . . ' The president turns to the Chief of the Defense Staff. His face studded with steely grit. The hardest decisions take the most courage, he keeps reminding himself. 'Tell those two boys up there. Let's do what we have to do. Pass the word.'

Inside the Volkswagen van at the south end of Lambeth Bridge

There are three M15 operatives seated in the rear of the van, flicking fingers across keyboards, talking into headsets, scrutinising a bank of monitors. Behind them, stooped as ever, the shift supervisor has his eyes on four different video feeds and can feel his blood pressure rising. All this information pulsing at him. 'I don't care what Vodafone says . . . we're sweeping this bridge.' The supervisor slams the phone down. The default screen shows a two-shot of his boss Sheila Davane, Noppy, and that arrogant prick Beveridge Clairmonte, QC.

The video camera and a directional mike for audio are housed within the overhead structure of the Volkswagen. Both work by remote control, with an operator adjusting the focus and zoom with a keyboard toggle.

The barrister's sonorous voice is distinctive. '*Aren't you interested to know how I came to meet Ms Merritt?*'

'*Why do you think I care?*' Davane absolutely does not like this man. '*Probably rescuing blind puppies from a glue factory.*'

The supervisor feels he needs to put a rocket

under proceedings at his end. 'I say this again . . . we don't know the incoming number, OK . . . but how many mobile phones are powered up on this bridge? Come on, we are better than this, people.'

The very fact that the bridge is currently deserted offers a crucial advantage to M15. In the area that their scanner is locked on to, there are so few mobile phones emitting signals that it should be relatively straightforward to isolate any radio transmissions. The process of phone mast triangulation, but worked backwards. They had already eliminated Noppy's number, and the two guys from 14 Coy. A little bit of fishing in various databases had produced the number for Clairmonte's carphone and post-pay office mobile.

Now, they just need one more number . . . this new phone that the barrister holds in his hand.

The Nokia rings and Clairmonte's reaction is clear on the video . . . 'OK, people, where is that call coming from, give me the number?' The supervisor leans over his three keyboard whizzes.

Five, ten seconds pass.

'Almost . . . hang on . . . ' As one hammers on the keys like Jerry Lee Lewis, the others turn to watch the electronic net closing. ' . . . coming up . . . now . . . and . . . got it!' And the SIM card details and pre-assigned number flash on the screen in red. Clairmonte has the phone to his ear, out there, on Lambeth Bridge, just as the supervisor slams his fist into the Volkswagen panelling. 'Lock it in, please. Let's listen and learn. And tell me where the caller is . . . '

On the monitor, the barrister passes the handset to Noppy. The van now hears her voice twice over, from the intercepted call and from the directional mike.

Davane: '*Can we get this over with, please?*'

Unknown male voice. Trace of a Geordie, possibly Wearside, accent. '*I just want to hear you say sorry.*'

'*Sorry?*'

'*No. Sorry, as in 'I'm sorry for betraying the trust that Captain Tristie Merritt placed in me.''*

Davane: '*What're you talking about?*'

The supervisor starts to shake with frustration. 'Please, a location ... how much longer do I have to wait?'

Geordie: '*These muppets on the bridge pretending to read newspapers ... you think we've just fallen out of a tree or something? What is it with you people, why is it that nobody we've been fighting for can do one damn decent, honourable thing and stick with it?*'

The youngest of the communication officers, to the supervisor's left, is shaking his head. Index finger pointing at the screen. 'This isn't making sense ...'

The supervisor clasps him by the shoulder, looks over at his display and the myriad of intersecting lines overlaid on a map of London. 'What isn't?'

Davane: '*I'm saying this under duress and it's all shite to me ... I'm sorry for betraying the trust that Captain Tristie Merritt placed in me.*'

'I've checked this twice now ... that call is coming from Lambeth Bridge. Right where

486

they're standing . . . I've trigged the air cells on Abingdon Street and Millbank on the north side of the river, and the roundabout on Lambeth Palace Road to the south. Same thing. They all intersect *there*,' and he stubs his fingers on the soft plasma screen. 'Somehow he's with them right now, *on the bridge.*'

'That's impossible . . . ' The supervisor rechecks the data entries, then the live picture on the video monitor. A mistake now and he'd be counting penguins in the Falklands until retirement . . . The chauffeur had been given his taxi fare, told to get home. That left four people. Davane. Clairmonte. Two from 14 Coy. On another monitor, he checks that neither of the soldiers is talking. They're just watching, looking all about.

Geordie: '*Thank you . . . now pass the attache case to Clairmonte.*'

Davane snaps, '*Where's the computer?*'

'*About twenty feet from where you're standing.*'

The supervisor sees a shape in this mass of bewildering information and tries to join up all the dots, with one simple explanation. 'Bloody hell, is the caller in the boot of the Bentley?'

'*Give the case and the phone to Clairmonte . . .*'

The supervisor folds his arms, smiles, happy either way, that the triangulation is correct, and about how this is playing out. 'Well, if he's in the boot of the car, that'll be the easiest arrest of the week.'

Watching the monitor, they see the barrister

take the case, flick open the locks with one hand and take the phone with the other. He removes a clear plastic file, holding the attaché between his knees, then pulls out a document.

Everybody waits as Clairmonte reads and re-reads. Slowly.

He nods his dreadlocked head. '*This is good. Exactly what Ms Merritt would have wished. I'll hand you back to Davane.*'

Davane's harsh Ulster voice: '*Now my computer, the Trident stuff . . .* '

'*Take five paces back, Noppy.*'

'*Noppy . . . ?*' Davane bites off the rest of the question.

'*Tell Clairmonte, too.*'

Everyone in the Volkswagen laundry van is riveted to the main feed. The barrister on one side, and Davane and the two soldiers on the other, shuffle backwards. Glaring at each other, expecting the worst.

A flash of movement whips across the monitor, too sudden and unexpected to register in anybody's mind. 'What the crap was that?' the supervisor screams, scanning all his feeds. Nothing, except that Davane has backed into one of her protectors and both have tumbled to the floor.

The second guy from 14 Coy. is barking into his cuff-mike. '*He's under the bridge. Repeat. Contact under the bridge.*' And he holds up high the grappling hook that had shot across the screen, hauling a thick mountaineering rope behind it. The reaction inside the Volkswagen is a very perplexed *Huh?*

Davane struggles to her feet, barely supported by her bodyguard . . . Off screen, the directional mike picks up an altogether new sound, the roar of an engine, over which Davane's voice can just be heard. '*Pull it up, come on,*' and within seconds a thick padded case is hoisted over the railings and clunks on to the pavement. Nicely framed on camera, as Cuff-mike screeches, '*Jesus . . . look at him go.*'

The supervisor shouts back: 'Look at who go? Where's my bloody vision. I want pictures now.'

And, as he watches the wake streaking into the distance, Cuff-mike files a police-standard report. '*White coupé cruiser. Sunroof. Approximately twenty-five feet long. Heading to sea, ex-Lambeth Bridge. Making perhaps thirty knots.*'

'Have you got that, India Ninety-nine?' snaps the supervisor, and serenely, two thousand feet above, comes the response from the day crew flying one of the Metropolitan Police's three Eurocopter EC145s.

'*Affirmative. Have craft in sight. Will liaise with MPU . . . Thank you.*'

The supervisor grinds his jaw, conceding to himself the best he can hope for now is a share, a tiny slice, of the glory. The penguins are still a possibility . . .

'*Marine Police Unit, this is airborne India Ninety-nine. Please intercept white coupé cruiser, travelling downstream, thirty knots, approaching Westminster Bridge . . .*'

The supervisor punches open the rear doors of the Volkswagen Crafter, getting a cigarette ready, and stalks around the rear of the truck, stewing. On the other side of the road, Davane is being protectively manhandled into a Metropolitan Police Volvo that has screeched to a halt, bathed in flashing emergency lights. Her two minders seem to be fighting off a posse that can only be from the CIA, trying to force their way to Dougal MacIntyre's missing laptop.

Barrister Beveridge Clairmonte calmly watches the roof of his Bentley Azure T slowly unfurl, the briefcase and amnesty note safely locked in the boot. Mission very much accomplished. He has already given the small huddle of Metropolitan Police surveillance officers a warning shot about the absolute nature of legal privilege for barristers such as himself. '*Getty* v. *Getty* 1985 . . . in case you care for some bedtime reading,' and the wary policemen had duly backed off.

The supervisor flicks a match, lights up and sucks in a lungful of Lambert and Butler. They *would* catch this Geordie guy, the man in the white powerboat. Nothing on the Thames could outrun one of those Targa fast response units, and he laughs out loud: a ninja grapple hook! . . . his father, an old-time beat copper, would say, you live long enough, you see everything.

★ ★ ★

The Weasel looks at his watch, decides ten minutes is enough. Half a thermos flask of creamy, sweet tea and a nice pork pie sit nicely in his tum.

Indeed, the sun is a touch lower in the west,

hopefully right in the eyes of anybody looking upstream from Lambeth Bridge. He's pretty certain there are no more coppers on the bridge — they'd gone after that white Sealine cruiser as though it were a one-man crime wave. He pities the driver. But not too much. Funny how easy it is to pull a bet with a bored rich kid. Must be that attention deficit disorder, or something. *Five thousand pounds says you can't get your dad's cruiser from Lambeth Bridge to the QE2 Bridge in* . . . You're on, soldier boy, the rich kid had jeered, making the vilest imaginable upper-class snort of contentment.

Weasel looks up at the huge span of the second arch under which he's been hiding. Designed for four lanes of traffic, and pavements on either side the width of two men lying head to head. All told, more than enough space for his little nine-foot inflatable Zodiac to make itself invisible while all hell was breaking loose upstairs.

He stands up carefully. Balances, and edges forward. Wouldn't want to tip up into the Thames now. He uncouples the mooring hook from a steel piling extruding from one of the bridge's granite supports and lets go. Balances again, shuffles back, and the modest eight-horsepower outboard bubbles into action with the push of a small black button.

Feeling like one of the waterborne warriors known as the Cockleshell Heroes, Weasel spins the boat in a tight circle and *put-puts* upstream, in the direction of Kew Bridge.

No big plans, except a few jars with Piglet

. . . Piglet had been watching things go down with a spotter scope, and keeping the Weasel clued up by small marine walkie-talkie . . .

They'll raise a glass to Tristie, and Button, and Whiffler. On the one hand, £315 million locked away, banked, and an amnesty to boot. On the other, three good people dead . . . he feels the dread hollowness in his gut . . . more names for a list already way too long.

On board PK412

The torch lights up what's left of the cavity ahead . . . Tristie's wedged sideways against the roof, frozen, naked and greased-up, and she's made it beyond the first-class galley on the right side of the aircraft. The olive oil worked a treat. But now the fuselage cladding sucks at the clamminess of her skin, like tentacles . . . frosted breath is all she can see for a moment . . . wait, girl, and it will clear. Wait . . . she thinks of Captain Salahuddin and his Tussauds biro, the span from his thumb to the middle finger . . .

I would be astonished, absolutely amazed, if there was more than the length of this pen in crawl space . . .

Well, Captain, no need to be astonished. The dimensions of the Mount Everest that lies ahead is the height of a foam mattress and the width of a coffin. And pinching in tight from all sides.

She's on her front, trying to worm *over* a cross-spar, while at the same time sliding *around* a stainless-steel box, an electrical bus of some sort. Body arched both backwards and to the side, a mermaid in mid-kick trying to squeeze around an S-bend. The smallest matter in all this is what's beneath her. A half-dozen broken-ended shafts of cotter pins, which are piercing her skin, snagging her stomach in place.

Just don't pull any of the wiring . . .

Four bundles of multicoloured wires snake ahead of her . . . her body feels spent, but in her brain there's enough gas in the lighter to keep a low flame flickering. You've done it before, Tristie, rappelling, climbing walls, this is a piece of cake . . . The wiring feeds into an access panel within the floor, a grey metal surround. Only a tennis racket's length from her fingertip. Might as well be on the other side of the world. If only she could move . . . just that little bit . . . *Just don't pull any of the wiring.*

Yes, and so what, Captain, if I do break your bloody plane . . .

A surge of helplessness, her pulse hammering in her neck, and a sudden blood-rush darkness of mind. Her fingers coil and tighten around the wiring cables, as if she's about to wring the life out of them . . .

The virus leaks past her every defence, insidiously, without fanfare. The great unravelling. Her sanity. All its carefully contrived normality creaks, splinters, falls away. Wedged tight, no way forward or back, for the first time it enters her mind that she will die . . . *watch and learn, this is how people go to pieces* . . . and the most intriguing headline will be 'Naked Female Found In Pocket of Aircraft Fuselage'. Someone with an itch to write is bound to scratch *that* curious wrinkle, spouting endless theories.

. . . *Terrible forces fuse in her mind* . . . *the*

black holes of childhood engulf her . . .

. . . Social Services-docketed, tagged, abandoned and abused . . . a soul rotting from the inside out . . .

And yet. And yet. Where does determination come from? The torchlight of determination sparks, explodes, takes over every fibre and particle of her existence . . .

Sympathetic detonation, they call it in the army . . . one anger detonating another . . . fast cook-off time, in terms of explosives . . .

Grappling. Hauling now on the electric cables, nudging forward, inch . . . by inch. Pain, the pain is nothing.

The first crack as a wire bundle shorts, and sparks arc and dance in front of her almost visionless eyes. She keeps pulling, mechanically, one hand over another amid a kaleidoscope of flashes, bright, skittering around like snowflakes . . . fingertips reaching . . . slowly, her life squeezing out of her in this aluminium vice . . .

'Echo Whisky'
FA-18E Super Hornet
The Fighting 103rd, Jolly Rogers
Eight minutes to point of engagement . . .

On one level the pilot, call-signed Cletus, understands the momentous nature of what is happening, what he and his wingman are being asked to do. Not a witness to history, but history itself. No doubt, in time, he will dwell on the gravity of his orders.

'Echo Whisky, you are weapons free when combatant aircraft reaches . . . ' and a long list of coordinates spells out a point of engagement just a short distance away. After this, it's in his discretion when to initiate contact.

. . . But on another level, he's glad this thing is coming to a climax. The tension. The exhaustion. Make it difficult to feel 'removed'. Or alert even . . . Holding position five miles astern of the Boeing 777, checking, rechecking his systems and armaments, then re-rechecking. Listening to the same call go out from air traffic controllers on the international distress channel and their standard Gander frequency . . . *'Pakistan 412, request you acknowledge immediately . . . Pakistan 412, request . . . '* That slow, measured

Canadian accent. On and on, and on. Like the sleep-inducing midnight chimes of a grandfather clock.

Dammit. He's feeling another crimp of that tension in the old bladder. Cletus has had to use the relief bag twice on this flight; threading your wanger twice through long underwear, a liner suit, an exposure suit, then a G-suit . . . too much.

The two naval pilots had experienced a supercharged dose of adrenalin when this thing kicked off, and they'd taken to the skies, afterburners engaged. But nothing bleeds away adrenalin more quickly than plugging into tedious routine, leaving the body chewed out, like stale gum, and the mind sagging. The longer this pattern of nothingness drags on, the more operational degradation will occur. Mental fatigue. And Cletus knows, pilots can make a terrible hash of the most simple decisions, even telling left from right, if they suddenly have to rush into action after a long period of watching displays, twiddling fingers.

Which is why Cletus's first reaction is delight, on hearing the Gander controller's final sign-off.

'*Pakistan 412. You have not acknowledged Gander's repeated request for clarification of your intent. You will shortly be entering Canadian territorial airspace. The next transmission will be from a defensive unit of the North American Aerospace Defense Command . . .* '
The controller holds his mike open. A last thought. Now and in the future, there would be pilots across the Atlantic, radio hams, colleagues,

supervisors, journalists, union reps, lawyers, academics, scrutinising this valedictory fare. It'd be up on YouTube in a flash.

'*Pakistan 412 . . . This is Gander, wishing you . . . Godspeed.*'

No response.

Enough already. Cletus takes one last sweep of the cockpit array of flight systems, all liquid crystal, colour displays. Lingers for a moment over the display status of his Advanced Medium Range Air to Air Missiles, especially the diagnostics for the on-board radar system. The heart of the AMRAAM's capability. All showing green. This is a genuine fire-and-forget weapon . . .

He looks along both wings to the white-tipped, sleek, grey spears that hang there. Straining to be unleashed, top speed Mach 4.

. . . so smart, that they don't ram themselves into the target and take the risk that some microcircuit gets whacked out of kilter and doesn't detonate. Instead, an AMRAAM has a 22-kilo hollow-charge, blast-effect warhead, which detonates above, behind or to the side of the target, whenever the missile's proximity system judges it in lethal range. The warhead's nickname, Slammer, comes from the almost two hundred rod-shaped projectiles that blast outwards, many times supersonic speed, slamming into, instantly shredding, anything in their path. Engines, control surfaces, wing roots, fuselage skin, personnel.

With his gloved finger, Cletus lightly *tap-taps* the shiny, glass-faced system one last time.

Willing it not to flicker red . . . the AMRAAM is so smart the computer reads which side of the target the missile is approaching, and focuses the projectile blast in a giant plume, left or right, up or down, depending on target position. Optimising the destructive power.

He keys his radio mike. Time to take over.

'Pakistan 412, course 210. Speed 490. Altitude 360 . . . this is call sign Echo Whisky, US Navy Super Hornet.' He looks forward and to his left. Beyond the heads-up display is the Boeing 777. Cruising, wings level. About five hundred feet below. His wingman, Sneaker, is starboard-side, gives a clear thumbs-up, showing the white of the palm of his Nomex flight glove.

'Your intentions are not clear at this time . . . You may be subject to joint US-Canada defensive measures for violation of NORAD airspace . . . request you reply, confirm your intentions immediately.'

Silence.

In the cockpit of PK412

The thirty-milligram capsules of temazepam, brand name Restoril, should have been enough for a medium-sized horse. Six of them, maroon-and-blue capsules. Knocked back with a bottle of water, *glug, glug,* immediately after he'd shuttered the cockpit door. But Zaafir has come to, lying on his back. Scratching like mad, every inch of his skin, dipped in hellfire. A not uncommon allergic reaction.

As he stares up at the roof of the cockpit, his mind is all over the place, hallucinating, disoriented, never clear or lucid. The familiar cries of Sami Yusuf. *Allah o Allah Hasbi Rabbi.* Mainly wondering whether — and this is the magical spell of benzodiazepines — this is heaven, or some staging post?

Confusing things even more is this mechanical voice, nibbling at his consciousness. *'Your intentions are not clear at this time . . . '*

Yes. Think clearly, he says to himself, trying to swim up through the mist of sedatives. *Is this heaven?* Well, what had been promised . . . ?

The Martyr . . . He does not feel the pain of his wounds and He is forgiven for all his sins; He sees his seat in Paradise; He is saved from the torment of the grave; He is saved from the great horror of Judgement Day; He marries 'the black-eyed'; He vouches for seventy of his family members; He gains the crown of honour, the precious stone of which is better than this entire world and everything in it.

Resigned gloom descends upon the young Pakistani. Scratching furiously, arms, legs, knuckles, back of knees, Zaafir takes a deep breath. Resigned. Not heaven. But maybe a ledge on the pathway to Paradise . . . ?

In his drugged, confused state, casting around for positive omens, he's intrigued by a tapping sound from above. *Kertink-kertink-kertink*. Metal on metal. Insistent. From above. *Perhaps* . . . and his mood lifts . . . *an angel calling for me?*

He tries to focus his wandering vision on the ceiling, but it slides alarmingly this way and that. He places his fingers either side of his eyes, tightens the skin. Be still, he pleads, and finally earns a semblance of stability.

The roof slopes at an angle towards the flight deck. Above him rows and rows of black dots, wandering in geometric patterns like ants. From a far corner of his mind, the word circuit-breaker comes. Circuit-breaker, yes. But that effort alone makes him nauseous, ready to swoon again . . .

' . . . *confirm your intentions immediately.*'

. . . until he remembers Mohamed Atta, ringleader of the 9/11 hijackings, his final words of encouragement, 'The virgins are calling you.'

Kertink-kertink-kertink.

How reassuring. Those virgins are calling

501

. . . *kertink-kertink-kertink*. Zaafir notices the D-ring handle in the ceiling, the edges of the access panel barely noticeable in the upholstered roof of the cockpit. A blind door.

D-ring . . . Opening . . . Paradise . . . Virgins. Sweet. A perfect row of dominoes waiting to tumble.

It takes Zaafir a minute to stand, for the walls to stop bending away from him. There's a black, box-like pilot's case in the corner, perfect to stand on. *Stop your swaying, hold it*, and then he is ready. His time has come.

Paradise awaits.

★ ★ ★

In Echo Whisky Cletus feels a tightness in his scalp, and that stinging in his bladder. After this it gets serious . . . one last sweep of the system displays. AMRAAMs looking perfect.

'Pakistan 412, course 210. Speed 490. Altitude 360 . . . Echo Whisky, US Navy Super Hornet. You have now entered territorial airspace of the North American Aerospace Defense Command. This is your final warning. You will be subject to joint US-Canada defensive interdiction . . . request you reply, confirm your intentions immediately. Repeat. This is your final warning.'

★ ★ ★

This little squeak of light from PK412's cockpit opens in front of Tristie. Like a baby trapdoor,

502

hinged on the far side, it makes a *whuup* sound as it pops up. Then two black, beady eyes glare up. At her. Through her. Right past her.

A big frown breaks over the staring face.

Whuup. The panel closes. Not so fast. She's jammed the tips of her fingers under the rim, and the lid snaps shut on top of them. His strength against her fingers.

From deep inside, from the very marrow of her existence, comes a surge of rage, hatred and pure madness. 'No chance. Not today. Don't mess with me now.' Not a scream, but a roar. 'I AM NOT READY TO DIE.' Say it again . . . Full throated, straining lungs, bursting throat. A noise that shakes and kicks and never lets go . . .

Next thing she knows, the panel is open, abandoned . . . fingers numb, sensory system far past registering such mundane things.

She tumbles through the tiny aperture. Freefalling from seven feet. Naked, straight down. Catching the top of her shoulder as she crashes on the jump seat, snapping her collarbone, just tucking her head in, before impact with the floor. Upside down, wiped out. Don't try this at home.

★ ★ ★

Zaafir's brain has shut down, leaving him just . . . shocked. Catatonic. Only one mental cue card is left. *What is happening here?*

He backs towards the cockpit door. Unsure of his facts, unstable in his wooziness. Scratching

503

furiously at the webs of skin between his fingers. His hopes still clutching to the faint possibility this creature is some sort of herald . . .

The temazepam speaks: but a naked woman cannot be a chaste woman. And she did not look at you with downcast eyes . . .

The woman staggers to her feet. Wild eyed. Clutching her useless right arm. Open flesh wounds. Blood streaking down her body. Naked. Her breasts . . . oh my, those breasts. Zaafir, even without a head galloping with sedatives, struggles with breasts in general . . . those breasts in particular.

Oh my . . . he could almost reach out and touch.

The woman advances, stalks towards him, a look of pure hatred engulfing her features. Her functioning arm cups her left breast, bounces it towards the hijacker . . . taunting him. You want some?

Oh my, those lovely, full, bouncing breasts . . . *Allah Akhbar*.

This, the final significant thought that passes through his head. He dies, knowing a little of what Paradise might look like. The woman named Tristesse, sad product of a meaningless one-night stand, puts every last atom of effort into a kick between Zaafir's legs that drops him to his knees like a wretched supplicant.

Oooooooh. Zaafir's voice box gets a final workout, up several octaves.

His body teeters forward as she slams her knee up into his nose; a coming together of hard matter travelling fast, and soft mush doing not a great deal. It produces an ejaculation of blood and trauma to the brain from which he never recovers. The cerebral cortex loose inside his skull, like dice in a cup.

She stands over him . . . waits. Tries to bring the various pieces of herself back together.

The door . . . open the door. The voice comes from the other side. *Tristie . . . Open the door.*

The shock . . . shock is setting in. Pale and shaking. Cold and confused. Tristie looks around. Her mind blanking, some kind of memory lapse . . .

From the far side of the door, Salahuddin screeches. *Two point five amps. Find the circuit-breaker.* Pounding on the door.

The Sami Yusuf recording wailing . . . *Allah o Allah Hasbi Rabbi.*

Tristie, lost in dissociative amnesia. Glass cockpit, a thousand shades of colour, dials and buttons, flashing lights, shimmering in mesmerising, paralysing detail.

Two point five amps . . .

★　★　★

'Control, Echo Whisky.'

'*Echo Whisky, go ahead.*'

'Control, can you confirm . . . ' Cletus pauses. He looks to his eleven o'clock at the PIA jet, cruising along like any other jetliner. He thinks, my question should be, *You really sure you want me to do this?* 'Control, can you confirm this mission is weapons free at this time.'

'*Echo Whisky stand by.*'

505

Someone rings to check with someone else, who's probably got to buzz through to someone a level higher. Possibly the president himself. Perhaps because he needs more time himself, perhaps because he knows the form-filling involved in something simple like a fender-bender, Cletus hopes this final confirmation will take a while.

In fact, it takes less than ten seconds.

'*Echo Whisky, Control. Confirm, you are weapons free. Interdiction now required.*'

★　★　★

Tristie's feeling particularly fragile and put upon, her body sliding down the wrong side of a huge high. 'Don't shout at me . . . ' she hears herself mumble, her fingers not quite under control, but enough to pull the suction cup off the cockpit phone. She throws down the MP3 player with *Sami Yusuf Sings the Classics*, whatever that racket is.

She's seriously running on remote control now. With her functioning left arm, she feels for a pulse, but the two captains are stone dead. A spray of orange phlegm across the windscreen.

Banging on the door. Everybody shouting. Circuit-breaker. Two point five amps.

OK. Here we go. She looks up at the two overhead maintenance panels. Feels a tremble of dizziness as her neck straightens . . . all those circuit-breakers. Twenty-fives. Sevens, fives, a fifteen, a ten, even a half-amp. Here we go . . . two and a half amps. She chooses the one badged WARN SPKR, right next to STICK SHAKER, pokes it in and, obligingly, the capsule pops out. Like a Pez dispenser.

'It will be a line above . . . ' Salahuddin positively squeaking with anxiety.

'Got it . . . ' And she feeds it into the slot. DOOR.

Whiffler's voice. 'OK, OK. Power's back on.'

She imagines Salahuddin flagging him to shut up. 'Quickly now. Go to the door.'

Easy for you to say. She tugs on Zaafir's body with one arm, flopping it away from the door. A small thought worries at her. About the radio, about telling someone . . . but in the pain and fuzziness of her brain, it doesn't happen.

Too much urgency on the other side of the Door. Heavy hands pounding. The Door.

'You must reset the door . . . ' The Captain's muffled voice. *Quiet, damn you, quiet,* she can hear him shouting.

'How do I do that?'

'Get a biro. Anything with a sharp tip.' Pause. 'Check the pilots.' Pilots. Oh yeah. Corpse in the left-hand seat . . . she rolls him back enough to snake her left hand into his breast pocket, pickpocketing a dead man. ID card. Name card holder. She can feel his matted chest hair. Creepy . . . Ooop. Yes. Got it.

And back to the door. Stabbing the white reset button, blanking the previous code from its memory.

'Punch in a code, any code . . . one — one — one — one.'

When the LED screen is full of ones, she

507

pauses for a moment, her weight slumped against the door. Bit of housekeeping to be done . . .

'Listen, Salahuddin, I need you to stand back from the door. Get behind my men.'

'*Stand back?* Are you mad?'

'Trust me, with three dead bodies it's like a morgue in here. One of them's sitting in the chair you need, looking very heavy and permanent . . . Button, Whiffler. Listen. I don't care who does what, but you two go in first. Think it through between yourselves. Head straight for the chair on the left. I've unhooked the pilot's straps. Straight body lift, tug him up and back, drop him to the rear . . . then let Salahuddin through.'

Button's voice. 'He's stood behind us, Tristie, nodding his head. Let's get it on.'

'One other thing, boys, I don't want you to fall over yourselves here . . . ' She holds down the reset and entry buttons. Five seconds. The new code flashes. Flashes. Flashes. Then blank. New door code ' . . . I've got no clothes on. This is not for your benefit. Remember. Or there will be consequences.'

Moments later the door bangs open. Button and Whiffler burst through. Like Formula One mechanics working a pit stop — there's a blur of movement, sharp grunts, explosive power, and the whole thing is over. One empty left-hand seat. No distraction.

Salahuddin's turn. He hesitates for a moment, framed in the doorway, struggling to take in the sacrilege. Eyes widening. Bodies, vomit on the windscreen, wisps of burning smoke curl downwards from the access panel.

Button has moved in front of Tristie, shielding her nakedness. 'Captain ... ' She reaches her arm out, touches Salahuddin's shoulder, the pain almost taking her breath away. 'Captain, we really need a hero, round about now ... '

But already, they've taken too long.

★   ★   ★

On board Cletus's Super Hornet, a series of green check lights mean the AMRAAM has a lock on the Boeing 777, drawing its guidance from the Hornet's own radar image. Location, direction and speed. From this, the missile plots an interception track until its own radar takes over and achieves autonomous self-guidance.

So. This is it.

Cletus pushes lightly against the tension. Feels the resistance. Holds. Pause. Then pushes through. There's the barest tremble through the wing frame as the missile's actuation system fires up, a great gout of flame shooting from the rear. Then the 350-pound warhead streaks away ... making a perfect track towards, *Lord have mercy on their souls*, a civilian airliner.

Cletus keys his mike, heart heavy. 'Fox Three.' His controllers would understand the brevity code. The AMRAAM is on its way.

He has to drag his gaze back to his display systems. Concentrate. Wait for the computer hand-off. One panel goes from green to black, another from red to green. Target acquired. The missile is now self-homing. Touching the dizzy pulse of Mach 4.

Cletus calls in again, suddenly weary. 'Pitbull.' They'd all be holding their breath now . . . various control and situation rooms, waiting for his visual confirmation of the kill. Coming soon . . .

Crackle of static, then a shrill voice. '*Pakistan 412 declaring an emergency . . . hijack attempt has been ended.*'

Pause.

What?

'Say again 412?' But Cletus's fingers are already working the touch-screens. Self-destruct . . . how do I initiate this fucking SD function?!

★ ★ ★

The command is roared over the radio, the Super Hornet pilot shouting through the loudspeakers in the cockpit.

'*BREAK LEFT . . .*'

Salahuddin's features are pinched, ready. From the captain's seat, he swings the Boeing 777 over. Full rudder. Maximum wheel. Suddenly, like a circus ride, with G-forces against her, the plane's rolling over past the horizon and falling. Whiffler, in the co-pilot's seat, the outside of the roll, is screaming madly. Anything not locked down, like the three corpses in the cockpit, takes to the air . . . and comes crashing down. *Thud — thud — thud.*

KRRRAAAAAAACCKKKK.

510

There's a mighty kick astern, and a lot of acoustic power, like a depth charge, shunts the plane forward. Tristie's strapped into the jump seat, her head through the neck of one of Button's jumpers, something long enough to cover most of her up. But her broken collarbone means her right arm is still flapping around inside. Trapped.

Salahuddin has a bullfighter's smile on his face as he barrels along sideways and down. 'This is real flying.' Clutching the wheel, jammed hard left. 'Better not . . . push this . . . old girl . . . too far,' he says through clenched teeth. 'She's either going . . . to come to pieces . . . now . . . or take us home.'

They hold on, waiting for the sign, things coming to pieces.

And wait.

Ne-ne-ne-ne. Couple of klaxon things start up. *Whopp-whopp-whopp* warning sounds.

As he begins to right the plane again, Salahuddin looks at Tristie mock-sternly. 'Did you pull the wiring up there?' He's flying with one hand, on the internal phone with the other. Trying to get damage reports from the various cabin crew stations.

Nodding his head to whoever he's speaking to. 'OK . . . Good . . . Thank you . . . No damage? Excellent.'

Ne-ne-ne, still blaring. Lots of *whopp, whopp, whopp.*

When he's finished, Tristie glances back at the tiny panel door she had squeezed through. 'How do you think I got this far?'

Salahuddin looks a little po-faced. *You hurt my plane.* Then turns to an array of switches above his head, adjusts a knob, then to his side, checks something important. Dials and buttons. Working through his systems, occasionally a question to Whiffler. Methodical, reasserting control, and at one with his aircraft.

The *ne-ne-ne* alarms are first to be cancelled, or ignored and switched off. One shrill track, after the other. Then the *whopp-whopp-whopps*.

Finally, all is quiet. Alarms, radio calls silent, the horizon where it should be, like the cadavers, flopped on the floor.

Tristie thinks a question is in order. Salahuddin has got clearance for an emergency landing at a nearby Canadian Forces Air Command Base. Goose Bay. 'Instead of keeping us on tenterhooks . . . tell us whether this *old girl*, as you so inelegantly call her, is going to get us on the ground or will she come apart at the seams?'

Whiffler turns too, equally keen to know. Through the broad cockpit windows, there's some vast inhospitable terrain below. Razor-sharp mountain ranges, for one thing.

No answer. Just a quick knowing glance, from the captain to Tristie, on to Whiffler, and back to her again. But the bastard is definitely smiling.

Epilogue

Less than three hundred miles from the planned point of engagement, Captain Saeed Harry Salahuddin lands his Boeing 777, *City of Risalpur*, at the Labrador airbase of Goose Bay. It helps considerably that Goose Bay is one of the Shuttle's alternative landing sites . . . Runway 08/26 is so long Salahuddin doesn't need to touch his brakes or reverse-thrust the engines. In the cockpit, he'd done his best to disguise his fears, playfully mocking Tristie Merritt. In fact, he has had to nurse the plane all the way in, jockeying the two engine throttles for turn and descent. Gingerly trying his best to put the least strain through the tailfin rudder and tailplane elevators, and without vital flight management systems because of Merritt's casual attitude to on-board wiring. He suspects grave damage has been done by the exploding AMRAAM, and he is proved right.

On the ground, the engineers are shocked. The plane's massive tail assembly stretches sixty foot into the air. The skin on the vertical plane looks like a colander, dapples of sunlight clearly visible through it. A few of the old-boy engineers take photos, later get their books out and lay pictures of their Boeing 777 against those of Flying Fortress B17s returning from daylight raids over Nazi Germany. Same sort of damage.

The plane had rolled to a halt at a slight angle

across the centreline, emergency slide rafts deployed, everybody scampering to waiting trucks and ambulances. The passengers, of all ages and cultures, embracing, holding hands with strangers. Even kissing.

The airbase hasn't seen anything like it since 9/11, when the 7,000-strong community of Happy Valley-Goose Bay did their best to accommodate thousands of passengers from diverted transatlantic flights.

It had complicated things that among several on-board functions, Tristie Merritt disabled the entire Airfone system. The Boeing 777 went *click*, off air. To the obvious consternation of relatives, politicians and anybody with a stake in keeping that thing flying. The talking heads on live television strike a duly sombre note . . . running apocalyptic captions like AIRFONE CLUE TO SHOOT-DOWN CONFIRMED?

Goose Bay is a tiny town and Labrador a virtually nonexistent media market. So there is no way immediately to generate live pictures of the Pakistan International Airlines flight landing . . . nor of the passengers walking from the plane. A media staple.

The venerable Canadian Broadcasting Corporation scrambles into action with an extended version of *Labrador Morning*, hosted live from the airport car park, with the Boeing in the distance, looking as though her guts had turned inside out, chutes deployed and doors open.

When they finally come through, the CBC television pictures are hard to deny and suck the worst of the tension out of the flashpoints and

514

rumours that had ignited around the world. Some, of course, achieved a momentum of their own and would take longer to burn out. But most prove a one-day wonder.

Salahuddin stays in the cockpit, quietly closing down his plane. Checking off his systems, one by one. Detail-oriented to the very last. Even as firefighters bustle around, putting out the smouldering debris above the cockpit, and Canadian military and police details start poking around the three corpses, asking questions. When there is nothing more to be done, he quietly excuses himself from the cockpit, locks the toilet door behind him, and sobs his heart out.

Much later, he collects a hatful of gongs and citations for his outstanding airmanship and courageous leadership during a time of terrible crisis. These include, unusually, a Super Airmanship Award from the joint US — Canada Airline Pilots Association, and the first ever nomination of a foreigner for the National Aeronautic Association's Wright Brothers' Award, 'for significant public service of enduring value to aviation in the United States'.

Despite always dedicating his prizes to the 'real heroes' of PK412 and detailing their exploits wherever he can, Captain Salahuddin never again sees Merritt. Nor Whiffler or Button.

But very often he will think of them, especially her. And being a logical man, his mind will turn over and over that same question — the physics, or mechanics, of how a woman *this* size with *those* curves managed to fit through a panel *that* size.

Captain Saluhuddin knows it happened, but never resolves it satisfactorily. His wife sharply encourages him to move on . . . stop thinking about this other woman in your life.

★　★　★

The flame sputters and dies. Even in Pakistan, where the government rushes to laud itself for the resolve, steely-eyed courage, level-headedness, etc., with which it had handled matters. Though little, if any, of this was ever in evidence.

From his new roving posting, based in Kabul, former CIA head of station Bill Lamayette continues to cable statements at variance with the more dreamy-eyed assumptions of his homebased masters. Initially these generate polite enthusiasm, but as time passes, old habits re-establish themselves. Big organisations simply can't unlearn this stuff, and the number of people who read his missives falls to less than five, two of whom are archivists.

James Romen is confirmed as the new CIA director, in place of Lamayette's mentor, General Jerry Stangel, who, in turn, disconnected from the adrenalin and drama of Langley, dies within weeks. It never emerges that Romen had been one of the wunderkinds responsible for conceiving the General Khan rendition, and even watched the live feed from the Karachi golf course that fateful early morning.

One of Romen's first initiatives, palling around

with senior department heads in a break-the-ice sort of way, is to run a weekly sweepstake. Each week they select a different swear word, and bet on the number of times it appears in Lamayette's cables. Subtext — the guy is a joke.

President Charles Hannah is delighted, in due course, to increase US aid to Pakistan in all forms, but especially military. Meaningful oversight of this remains negligible.

The last time that Lamayette, the US government and CIA policy converges to everybody's satisfaction is in the pursuit of Washington's money, embezzled and salted away by General Ali Mahmood Khan. This happens within days of Operation Macchar being foiled, Lamayette having been given carte blanche.

Having promised so much death and destruction, and delivered so little, the two sons of General Khan have found boltholes hard to come by.

Hamza, his elder son and confidant of Pir Durbar, and Shafiq, the younger, the porcine eunuch type, are picked up and helicoptered off to distant parts. Neither of them has an ounce of their father's wit and cunning. They argue and fight between themselves, devoting their energies to selling each other out. In this mean and cold game, the children of the Tiger of Baluchistan are like helpless newborn kittens, and only Lamayette can be the winner.

Anticipating an almost regal enthronement after the downing of PK412, the Khan brothers had transferred all of their father's ill-gotten wealth into Pakistani banks. But like a sponge,

517

what the banks sucked up, they could — with just a little local political pressure, a twist of the arm here, a Federal Investigation Agency raid there — give back.

Islamabad uses all its influence to return Washington's money. The Government Accountability Office's comptroller-general is delighted to accept a personal invitation from the president of Pakistan himself, to receive a cheque for the aggregate amount of General Khan's embezzled funds ... $219 million plus change. Lots of photos and big toothy smiles, warm endorsements and glowing reports filed back to Congress, where there's a genuine aura of wonderment, *I think we can really do business with these people ...*

It finishes for Lamayette where it all started. The same eighty-two-foot-long Monte Fino Sky Lounge cruiser, on to which General Khan had been delivered like a rolled-up length of carpet.

Bobbing in the choppy early morning seas about ten miles south-east of the sugar-loaf-shaped Churma Island, just beyond the urban sprawl of Karachi.

He is standing on the dive platform at the stern of the cruiser, one leg inside the Zodiac inflatable, tying his final knots, checking the tension of the lines. This, the very same Zodiac that was used to exfiltrate General Khan from French Beach. *It's the only way to wash my hands of this whole fucking sorry business,* he had blurted out to Kirsten Ackerman in the middle of the night. She was asleep at the time, her leg curled over him, her pretty face rising and falling on his chest.

Shafiq Khan has his whiny, seven-year-old girl's voice on. 'You said you'd give us a chance.'

When he looks up, Lamayette's face is purple, sweat beading across his bald, mighty skull. 'This *is* a chance, you idiot. More of a chance than you were ever willing to give.'

Hamza tries a different tack. 'What if I said there is more money . . . we could share it? You and me, Mr Bill.' Immediately there's tugging and jostling between the two brothers.

Shafiq and Hamza Khan are sitting back to back, trussed up by tape at the neck, shoulder and hip. The lightweight thwart, or seat bench, has been removed, and the two of them sit low in the dinghy, the rigid collar of inflatable tubes rising to their shoulders.

'Now listen . . . ' And Lamayette holds up a standard Swiss Army penknife. 'I am taping this here . . . ' and he leans over the transom, the rigid rear panel of the dinghy ' . . . on to the outside edge, near the outboard.'

Shafiq faces astern, his pudgy eyes glaring. Hamza's angular body is pointed forward, so he coils around, watches over his shoulder.

'All you have to do is work together, stop fighting like a bunch of fucking pansies. Get the knife, solve the problem.' Lamayette looks the picture of reasonableness, a teacher who's just set the class a problem to work on.

Last job . . . he hand-tightens a series of finger — bolts on the outboard, locking it in place, creating an autosteer that will drive the dinghy straight and true . . . tugs the bow rope so the

519

stubby nose follows him around the dive platform to the edge of the stern . . . starts the fifteen-horsepower engine, selects a medium power setting that roars in his ears.

There's a babble of excited anxiety from the two brothers . . . they have to shout over the noise of the outboard.

'What . . . what are you doing with us?'

'Mr Bill. You can stop your threats now. We give in.'

'Shut . . . the fuck . . . up.' Lamayette looks at the two of them one last time, holds the rope tight; the dinghy, already under power, slews this way and that. He points over the horizon, due south. 'About ten thousand miles that way you'll see your first icebergs.'

He gives the rope one last pull, to get the nose pointed in the right direction. Then, off, off they go. Shafiq and Hamza . . . on a Big Adventure in the wide-open, shimmering blue sea.

Although bound up together, the brothers are free to move, get up, walk about, with the proviso that their wrists are linked. Tied with fifteen-weight fly-fishing line, sturdy as you can get. The lines are taut, and threaded through the various eyeholes and closed oarlocks on the dinghy. If Hamza moves his right arm, this has an equal and opposite effect on Shafiq's left, and vice versa.

All they have to do, for the first time ever, is think, be nice to one another, work together. If they can, then one of them will get to the penknife.

Faithful Jahanghir shakes his head, sickened

by Lamayette's charity. He had watched all of this from the stern of the cruiser, with considerable disdain. 'You should have shot them in the stomach, left them in the mountains.'

'Maybe . . . ' Lamayette hauls himself up the ladder. 'Probably it comes to the same thing . . . '

'It's that woman, she is doing strange things to you, Mr Bill.'

My friend, you don't know the half of it . . .

Hamza and Shafiq Khan are never seen again.

★ ★ ★

The air force base at Goose Bay, where the Boeing 777 lands, has seen better times. It used to host a permanent training facility for the Royal Air Force, as well as air forces from Germany, Italy and the Netherlands.

By the time the PIA flight touches down, the personnel on the ground is nothing like it was. The physical structures remain, the hangars, taxiways, bunkers, but the human capability has long since shrunk, transferred away.

From Thames House in London, a stream of messages are sent by M15, pestering in their intensity. Direct to the Goose Bay AFB; to M15's liaison officer at the Royal Canadian Mounted Police headquarters; to their sister domestic spook agency, the Canadian Security Intelligence Service, and to the British embassy in Ottawa.

Isolate Tristie Merritt . . . I need to speak to

her. The messages are in the name of the director-general of M15 but are authored by the one person. Sheila No Oil Painting Davane.

Even Britain's honorary consul to Newfoundland and Labrador gets a call on his mobile phone, in the middle of a family lunch, and is startled by the almost unintelligible torrent of Ulster-speak. *I focking want her . . .*

Reinforcements do arrive, but in the first couple of hours the skeleton workforce at Goose Bay struggles to cope. The passports (very few have got Canadian visas, of course), the medical checks, treating the injured, finding counsellors, meals, organising phone calls, hotel rooms, bus, transport vouchers. It's hard enough just fighting off the media.

Goose Bay's arrangements are improvised, and soon the system is creaking. Passengers are taken to empty accommodation blocks or given washing facilities that were once security-proofed, but are no longer. They never stand a chance against the three members of Ward 13. Not with people who want to drop out, who want to lose themselves, and are trained in such arts by the best armed forces in the world.

Thames House eventually gets the news. A few of the passengers appear . . . to have disappeared. And Davane doesn't even bother asking for names. *That Merritt girl is good . . .*

Money is the key to their escape. Tristie, Button and Whiffler have plenty, and they find a no-questions-asked friend in a rundown bar for too-drunk-to-fight fishermen. The skipper of a

Portuguese trawler, the *Santa Maria*, has had to dock in St John's, Newfoundland, for emergency repairs to the winch system. *No weench, no feesh*, he explains in a heavy accent. The *Santa Maria* is supposed to be hauling up cod and plaice from the depths of the Grand Banks.

The captain eyes them carefully, keen to make sure they know what they're letting themselves in for. Waving his arms dramatically. 'Maybee we go 'ome to 'urope . . . maybee nixt munth,' he says. 'You passenger, no talk . . . ' He zips his lips with a wild hand movement. ' 'Til then, high seas feeshing. Big wave. Up, down . . . feeshing always. Cod, plaice, shrimp. Out there.' He waves off towards the east, beyond the poster of a pouting Jenna Jameson. 'Nobody see us, 'til nixt munth. Seeeks week even.'

Sounds absolutely perfect.

Acknowledgements

This is a debut novel and one of the things the self-help books and writers' groups say is, Be Very Careful About Using Family Members As Critics. Thankfully that does not apply in my case. For the person who contributed most to the book that is *Bolt Action* is my Mother, an extraordinary woman who also does not care one bit for the thriller genre that I aspire to. Nonetheless, through endless hours of jotting and read-throughs she hacked at, sandpapered down and generally purged my writing of all the stuff my daughters would describe as, Icky. If you've got this far in the book and generally had an acceptable time, my Mum is the reason.

The process of getting a book printed has never been easier thanks to self-publishing and the encouragement, hand-holding and advice available everywhere from college courses to the internet. Yet it also has never been harder. Harder still if, when you started, you were truly awful, as I was. One agent who saw my first completed manuscript said, You Write Like You Have Never Read a Book in Your Life. Then *click*, no advice, nothing, just conversation over.

From rejection after rejection to, lo and behold, publication is a grinding study in loneliness, and putting one foot in front of the other again and again, until you get somewhere. That this book was published is because of three crucial people who sustained me.

Jo Frank was the person who saw my writing at its very worst and, yet, was able to carrot-and-stick me in such a skilful way that I wanted nothing more than to write and write some more, and prove everybody wrong. She has no equal like that. Patrick Janson-Smith was an enormous and reassuring ally, somebody who left the High Court after testifying in the Dan Brown/Da Vinci Code case to call me, *me!*, to say he loved my work and was 100 percent convinced I had what it took. Crikey. *Me?* And finally, the irrepressible Charlie Viney, who never stopped believing. He took a manuscript completed just as the world was tipping into global financial chaos and emerged triumphant with a deal from a publishing industry that otherwise was cutting, trimming, axing and sacking right across the board. He laughs at impossible odds.

At Hodder, this book has been the subject of the most excellent care and nurturing encouragement from Nick Sayers and Anne Clarke. They pointed out a lot of obvious ways to make the book better, which I should have thought of, but didn't, and several that weren't obvious at all, but had just the same effect. And it has been Kerry Hood, the best in her business, who has taken on the hardest job of all for an unpublished author: Getting Out The Good Word.

There were many people who contributed to *Bolt Action* but the most constant source of advice and comment was Jimmy Hurley, for whom Ward 13 was an actual stopping off point, at one time. For the avoidance of doubt, he is not Tristie Merritt, but he could be any one of the other members of her team, except that he gets hay fever, doesn't like jungles, isn't very happy with heights etc. etc.

Several people have also happily offered answers to gormless technical queries of mine but asked that I not reveal their names. Others who were of the greatest possible assistance include, in Fiji, Jimmy Samson, Jamie O'Donnell and Sharon Ferrier-Watson of Air Pacific, Dick and Kelera Watling, Dominic Sansom of Samba and, of course, Mere Samisoni, John, Selina, Philip, Ili and Alisi; in the UK and elsewhere, Ben B., Dr Chris Jones, Chris Roberts, John Wright and Ben Herter. I would love to pretend that any mistakes were their fault, but that would not be true and I alone carry the can.

Spare a thought too for Jules Bromley who has read all of my scripts (or at least pretended to) for the last five years, and to my fellow Arvon Foundation students from that one-week course in 2006, and Cath Staincliffe and David Armstrong too, plus Andrew and Sarah Clark, George Manners, Mark Fenhalls, Jon Higton, James Evans and Charlie Ponsonby — who have been great allies along the road.

Finally, there is no way on earth that this incredible journey could have started — let alone concluded — without the support, love and encouragement of my wife Vanessa who has backed me to the hilt and more, having seen something in me that, Lord only knows, remains a mystery even to this day. As to my wonderful children, (tip of the hat to PGW) without the never-failing sympathy and encouragement of Jack, Coco, Leila and Lucky, this book would have been finished in half the time. But it is for them that I write, and it is their dreams that make me want to go to work each morning.

Malton
North Yorkshire
March 2010

We do hope that you have enjoyed reading this large print book.

Did you know that all of our titles are available for purchase?

We publish a wide range of high quality large print books including:
Romances, Mysteries, Classics
General Fiction
Non Fiction and Westerns

Special interest titles available in large print are:
The Little Oxford Dictionary
Music Book
Song Book
Hymn Book
Service Book

Also available from us courtesy of Oxford University Press:
Young Readers' Dictionary
(large print edition)
Young Readers' Thesaurus
(large print edition)

For further information or a free brochure, please contact us at:
Ulverscroft Large Print Books Ltd.,
The Green, Bradgate Road, Anstey,
Leicester, LE7 7FU, England.
Tel: (00 44) **0116 236 4325**
Fax: (00 44) **0116 234 0205**

Other titles published by
The House of Ulverscroft:

THE PERFECT LIE

Emily Barr

The pretty picture of Venice pinned to her mother's kitchen wall has always inspired Lucy Riddick: for her it's a dream destination — an ideal place to lose herself. And now she needs to do just that. The secret she's been keeping from her boyfriend and her friends has finally caught up with her. Now Lucy needs to disappear — and fast. There's no better time to pack her bags and head for Italy. But what if, when she sets foot in Venice, Lucy finds that the thing she has been running from, the one thing she has been trying to escape, is already there, lying in wait for her? Time to run away again? Or time to end the chase, once and for all?

DO NO HARM

Carol Topolski

Everyone knows about Virginia: her stellar reputation as a gynaecologist; her commitment to her women patients. But does anyone know about the knives? Everyone knows about Faisal too: about his gentle charm; his brilliance in the operating theatre. But does anyone know he's a traitor? And Gilda — everyone knows about Gilda: she never poops a party; she struts about town with her cackling posse and she's a loyal friend. But does anyone know about the rubber? However there's someone who really does know Virginia, who knows all about her because they've been this close from birth. Someone who knows what she does when they're alone together. What they do with the rosewood box. With the belts. Who knows that good doctors can go bad.

CHOSEN TO DIE

Lisa Jackson

Detectives Regan Pescoli and Selena Alvarez have been searching for the Star-Crossed Killer for months, never imagining that Regan will be captured by the very madman she's been hunting. Regan knows exactly what he's capable of — and avoiding the same fate will take every drop of her courage and cunning. As Selena joins forces with Regan's lover, Nate, to dig deeper into the case and the body count rises, the truth about Regan's disappearance becomes chillingly clear. Something evil is lurking in the snow-covered mountains. With time running out, the only way they can save Regan will be to get inside a killer's twisted mind and unravel a shocking message that he is revealing.

FOREIGN INFLUENCE

Brad Thor

Scot Harvath, a former Navy SEAL, is now a field operative in a secret and uncompromising new spy agency. He is summoned when a bombing in Rome kills a group of American college students. Evidence points to a dangerous colleague from Harvath's past and a plan for further attacks on an unimaginable scale. Harvath must re-establish contact with the man, lure him out of hiding and kill him on the spot. But what if it is the wrong man? Simultaneously, a young woman is struck by a taxi in a hit-and-run incident in Chicago. But eventually the police give up on their investigation. Then the family's attorney uncovers a shocking connection to the bombing in Rome and the perpetrators' plans for America and Europe . . .

NO TURNING BACK

Marcus Sakey

Four friends: Alex is failing as a father; Ian keeps dangerous secrets; Jenn wants adventure, and Mitch wants Jenn. They are all just scraping by, finding comfort in each other and the hope that things will get better. But as their twenties fade in the rear-view mirror, none of them are turning out to be who — or where — they hoped. In a time when CEOs steal millions while their employees watch savings dwindle, these four are tired of the honest approach. They're going to stop waiting and start taking. They have a failsafe, victimless plan that will change their lives for ever. What could possibly go wrong . . .

THE ANATOMY OF GHOSTS

Andrew Taylor

1786, Jerusalem College, Cambridge. A disturbed fellow commoner, Frank Oldershaw, claims he's seen the ghost of murdered Sylvia Whichcote haunting Jerusalem. To salvage her son's reputation, Lady Anne Oldershaw employs John Holdsworth, author of *The Anatomy of Ghosts* — a stinging account of why ghosts are mere delusion — to investigate. But Holdsworth's presence in Cambridge disrupts an uneasy status quo in a world of privilege and abuse. And as for Holdsworth himself, haunted by the ghost of Maria, his dead wife — and Elinor, the very-much-alive Master's wife — his fate is sealed. He must find Sylvia's murderer or the hauntings will continue. And no one will leave Jerusalem's claustrophobic confines unchanged.